*Dragons
in Amber*

Also by Willy Ley

THE CONQUEST OF SPACE (*with Chesley Bonestell*)

THE LUNGFISH, THE DODO, AND THE UNICORN

ROCKETS AND SPACE TRAVEL

Dragons
in
Amber

Further Adventures

of a Romantic Naturalist • *by* WILLY LEY

New York • *The Viking Press*

Parts of Chapters 6 and 12 appeared
in *Natural History Magazine*

PRINTED IN U. S. A. BY VAIL-BALLOU PRESS, INC.

Contents

List of Illustrations . DRAWINGS BY OLGA LEY

vi

Foreword

AMONG the letters I received after publication of my earlier book, *The Lungfish, the Dodo, and the Unicorn,* there was one in which my correspondent said that he had been looking for such a book for a long time, that he had always wanted to read a book of that kind. And then he asked me why I wrote it. I replied, "For the same reason." That goes for the present book too; I wrote it because nobody else had.

In looking over the table of contents I am surprised by one thing. Natural history is generally regarded as a rather static science which had its heyday and its revolutions during the nineteenth century. For a static science, a lot has happened to it during the two and a half decades since I sat in college lecture halls hearing about these same subjects. What I have written about amber now could have been written then, minus a few historical facts and a few examples. But as for the footprints of *Chirotherium* (Chapter 3), I was authoritatively informed that they would remain mysterious forever. Chapters 4 and 5 could have been written then, but as for the milu (Chapter 6), I was told that "by now it is probably extinct." The giant panda (Chapter 7) had "been seen alive by only one or two white men." The bird takahe (Chapter 8) was "extinct." The ginkgo (Chapter 9) was considered "a very rare tree"; this particular judgment was influenced by the fact that this was in Europe where the ginkgo *is* a rare tree.

Two of the chapters of this book, "The Story of the Milu" and "The Story of the Fish *Anguilla,*" originally appeared in condensed form in *Natural History Magazine,* published by the American Museum of Natural History in New York City; the editor kindly permitted the use of these articles in this book.

The illustrations this time are all—with one exception—either drawn or redrawn by the same artist, my wife. The one exception is the drawing on page 123. That is a contemporary cave painting and there is no way of giving the artist credit by name. For all I know, he may have been my (or Olga's) ancestor.

Willy Ley

Montvale, N.J.
August 1950

Part One

RECORDS IN STONE

1: The Tears of the Heliades

WHEN I open my desk drawer I always see a number of things which shouldn't be there, but which have by long usage established a kind of right to rattle around where they don't really belong. There is a small screwdriver, the shell of a marine snail from the Mediterranean, a lump of Wood's metal which will melt in hot water, and a bead of amber.

The last is, as one should expect of a piece of jewelry, a very pretty bead. Its color is a nice full-bodied yellow clouded with white. It has a smooth and pleasant feel, and I know that it is hard enough to resist successfully any attempt to scratch it with a fingernail but that a knife would produce a deep scratch easily. I also know that its specific gravity is such that it would sink in quiet water but be tossed around by agitated water, most especially by agitated salt water. I know that it would turn a darker color if left for a month or so in a box with a radioactive substance. I know that it would radiate with a deeply beautiful blue luminescence if placed under an ultraviolet lamp—a test for genuineness. I know that chemical analysis would show it to contain at least 3 per cent —more likely 5 to 8 per cent—of something called succinic acid—a test for its place of origin. I know that it could be ignited with a match and that it would burn with a smoky flame and a pleasant smell, just like a piece of pine wood that is not pale in color but reddish-brown because of the rosin it contains. My amber bead would do that for the simple reason that it is itself rosin, the fossil rosin of an extinct relative of our pine trees of today.

The piece of amber from which this bead was turned—it owes its solitary existence to the fact that it was overlooked when a necklace of amber beads was restrung—could have come from one of a number of places. It might have been found on the shore of southeastern England, say Kent, or Essex, or Suffolk. It might have come from the Danish shores, most likely the western shore of Denmark, or from any of the Frisian Islands which protect that coastline. It might have come from any place along the German shore of the Baltic Sea. But the chances are overwhelming that it came from a specific place in East Prussia, the rectangular promontory called the Samland. The mathematical probability is somewhat better than 99 to 1, because for the last 75 years the Samland has produced roughly 99½ per cent of all amber. As it happens, I don't have to bother with probabilities at all, however, because I brought that necklace with me from the Samland.

If you look at the map you will see that the German coastline runs almost due east until it forms the Bay of Danzig, where the Vistula empties into the Baltic. Then the coastline begins to turn north, forming two shallow estuaries of brackish water. The one to the south, its water sweetened by one arm of the Vistula and by the river Pregel, is called the Frisches Haff; while the one to the north, replenished by the river which is called either Memel or Niemen depending on your native tongue, bears the name of Kurisches Haff. The curious thing about these two estuaries is that they are not open bays but are separated from the sea by long and narrow tongues of sand which leave only narrow and shallow passageways for ships, in each case at the northeastern end of the Haff. Each entrance is guarded by a city, originally fortified, Pillau at the Frisches Haff and Memel at the Kurisches Haff. Memel is also known by its Lithuanian name of Klaipéda, and again it depends on your own nationality whether you wish to call it the last German or the first Lithuanian city on that coast which from there on runs due north.

Between these two Haffs is the Samland, an almost square promontory, measuring some 25 miles from west to east and around 20 miles from north to south. Its northern coast differs from most of the remainder of the Baltic coast by its formation. Most of the Baltic coastline is what one would expect to find—sandy beach that slopes gradually into the tideless basin of the Baltic Sea. The Samland coast consists of sand and marl, too, but it does not slope; it rises vertically from the sea like the walls of a fortress. Much of it is forested on top, and the beach at the foot of that strange vertical sandy coast is narrow, so narrow in places that it cannot be walked but has to be waded. If there were mountain goats in the Samland (which is decidedly not the case), they might negotiate these stretches with dry feet by jumping from rock to rock, because for hundreds of yards out from the coast the sea is dotted with

The Samland district and vicinity

countless 20-ton boulders, brought there originally from the Scandinavian countries by the glaciers of the Pleistocene period and left over when the receding coastline was washed out.

It was almost precisely 2000 years ago that the civilized world became acquainted with the amber of the Samland. Two works, both written during the latter half of the first century of the Christian era, constitute our main sources on amber for that time: the *Natural History* of Gaius

Plinius Secundus—Pliny the Elder—and the *Germania* of Cornelius Tacitus.

But amber was known earlier. Traded down to Italy through Germany, or through France, and possibly around Spain, it had reached the Mediterranean Sea in early historical times, even in times which are not strictly historical. It was Thales of Miletus who, in about 600 B.C., discovered that amber, after having been rubbed with a piece of cloth, attracted small and light objects, dry blades of grass, and other vegetable matter and lint. And because Thales was a Greek whose word for amber was *elektron,* the natural force manifested in this attraction was later called electricity. Amber is mentioned under the same name in the *Odyssey.* In book xv you can find the story of the "cunning trader" who enters a house

> bringing a necklace of gold that with droplets of amber was beaded.
> *Odyssey,* xv, 460

This sentence bothered many translators for a long time, because the word *elektron* was also used for an alloy of gold and silver and nobody felt quite sure which was meant. But then Heinrich Schliemann discovered the tombs of those old and almost mythical kings of Mycenae on Greek soil, and the tombs yielded several hundred amber beads; chemical analysis for succinic acid proved that they were true amber from the north.

Direct and tangible evidence of the use of amber also survives from the bookless period which preceded the early civilizations of the Mediterranean. Amber beads have frequently been found in graves from the Bronze Age of Great Britain. On the European continent such direct evidence goes back even further. Near Woldenberg in the province of Brandenburg (that is, in the general vicinity of Berlin) a carving made of amber has been found, a representation of a young wild horse, which has been dated as Late Stone Age—Neolithic, if you insist on the technical term. And near Schwarzort, a township at the Kurisches Haff, directly in the amber country, small and strange manlike idols fashioned of amber have been found, also dating from the Late Stone Age. They were carved in some way from flat pieces of amber and several small holes were drilled through them, no doubt for the purpose of stringing a gut through the holes so that they could be worn. I have seen those idols at the Amber Collection of the Albertus Universität in Königsberg in East Prussia; they were obviously amulets.

At Schwarzort in East Prussia amber was indubitably a very common material; in the Mediterranean it must have been fairly rare up to about 50 B.C. In value it certainly ranked with other gems—but now we can turn for direct information to Pliny's *Natural History*. The passages about amber (book XXXVII, *The Natural History of Precious Stones*, chapters 11 and 12) are close to the end of the enormous work; maybe Pliny was tired by then and raced toward the end of his almost incredible labor. At any event his notes do not seem very well ordered in sequence. They are poorly balanced. And the whole is cast in choleric temper. For some reason Pliny felt strongly about the subject of amber and at least chapter 11 appears to have been written with the point of his old cavalry sword rather than with a stylus. The chapter even begins like a charge of the heavy horse:

> Next in rank among the objects of luxury we have amber; an article which, for the present, however, is in request among women only. All these three last-mentioned substances hold the same rank, no doubt, as precious stones; the two former for certain fair reasons. Crystal, because it is good for taking cool drinks, and murrhine vessels, for taking drinks that are either hot or cold. But as for amber, luxury has not been able, as yet, to devise any justification for the use of it. This is a subject which affords us an excellent opportunity of exposing some of the frivolities and falsehoods of the Greeks; and I beg that my readers will only have patience with me while I do so. . . .

Now we don't have to bear with Pliny all the way; we need only to mention some of the highlights. The first "frivolity" has to do with a legend that amber comes from the river Eridanus, and the fact that many had identified that river with one which Pliny knew as Padus, the Po of our maps. "The falsity of this is abundantly proved by the testimony of Italy itself," meaning that one does not find amber either on the banks of the Po or elsewhere in Italy. Other Greeks had spoken about the islands called Elektrides (amber islands) to which amber was carried by the Padus. "Fact is, however, that there never were there any islands called by that name, nor, indeed, any islands so situated as to let the Padus carry anything to their shores."

Then he mentions scornfully that one "Demostratus calls amber *lyncurion* and says that it originates in the urine of the wild beast known as the lynx; that voided by the male producing a red and fiery substance, and that by the female an amber of a white and less pronounced color." This really was a silly story and probably the result of several mistakes. On the one hand, it seems that tourmaline and the often yellowish and semitransparent belemnites (actually the fossil remains of an extinct group of squidlike marine creatures) were confused with amber. On the other hand, the word itself is likely to be a miswriting of *lygurion* —"Ligurian wares"; the Ligurians played a role as traders in the ancient amber business world.

But the one that has surpassed them all is Sophocles, the tragic poet; a thing that indeed surprises me, when I only consider the surpassing gravity of his lofty style, the high repute that he enjoyed in life, his elevated position by birth at Athens, his various exploits and his high military command. According to him, amber is produced in the countries beyond India, from the tears that are shed for Meleager, by the birds called *meleagrides*. Who can be otherwise than surprised that he should have believed such a thing as this, or have hoped to persuade others to believe it? What child, even, could possibly be found in such a state of ignorance as to believe that birds weep once a year, that their tears are so prolific as this, or that they go all the way from Greece, where Meleager died, to India to weep? "But," it will be said, "do not poets tell many other stories that are quite as fabulous?" Such is the fact, no doubt, but for a person seriously to advance such an absurdity with reference to a thing as common as amber, which is imported every day and so easily proves the mendacity of his assertion, is neither more nor less than to evince a supreme contempt for the opinions of mankind, and to assert with impunity an intolerable falsehood.

Between this sentence and the next there must have been the equivalent of a deep breath. Abruptly attitude, language, and style change; choleric thunder is replaced by the collected reasonableness of straight instruction. "There can be no doubt that amber is a product of the islands of the northern ocean and that it is the substance called *glaesum* by the Germans." The form *glaesum* is somewhat Latinized; what the Germans said themselves must have been something like *glaes,* the word which later changed its meaning and became "glass." The Romans, Pliny continues, had a fleet in those parts of the northern ocean, commanded by Caesar Germanicus, and they called one of the islands in that sea Glaesaria.

As to its nature, there can be no doubt either: amber is produced by the discharge of a pinelike tree, "like gum from the cherry and rosin from the ordinary pine. It is a liquid at first, which issues forth in considerable quantities and is gradually hardened by heat or cold or else by the action of the sea." Nor is this a new idea: "our forefathers believed it to be the sap of a tree and called it *succinum*." This word, used by Pliny throughout to designate amber, is quite clear in its meaning; *succus* is the juice or sap of a plant, *succinum,* therefore, is sap stone. As for proof that it is hardened pine rosin: "it emits a pinelike smell when rubbed and burns, when ignited, with the odor and appearance of torch-pine wood." In addition, there is proof that it must have been liquid originally, because you may find small objects, like gnats and ants, imbedded in it.

About the place of origin, Pliny goes on to say, something more has been learned recently. Under the reign of the emperor Nero, one Julianus, the manager of the gladiatorial spectacles, sent a Roman knight to Germany to procure amber. That knight was still alive as of the time of writing; Pliny does not actually say that he talked to him but it is a logical assumption that he did. Anyway, the knight first crossed the Alps on one of the good Roman roads and then went down the Danube, presumably by ship, to Carnuntum.

Carnuntum was a famous city then, main base of the Roman Danube fleet. It was finally destroyed during the Middle Ages by the Hungarians; its extensive ruins are close to the present city of Hainburg. At Carnuntum, Pliny's knight, traveling for Julianus and Nero in quest of amber, was still on Roman soil and safe, but he was also at the border. He had to go north from Carnuntum. Pliny tells us that it is about 600 miles from Carnuntum to the German amber coast. Unfortunately he neglects to say along what route and in what manner the knight negotiated these 600 miles. But with modern maps at our disposal, we can easily conceive what would be the most likely route. Near Carnuntum the river Marsch, coming from the north, empties into the Danube. Presumably the Roman traveled up river as far as he could go, then made a short trip across country until he reached another and much larger river, the

Vistula. And the Vistula brought him either into the Bay of Danzig or into the Frisches Haff, in any event to the immediate neighborhood of the amber country.

. . . visiting the various markets there he brought back amber in such vast quantities that the nets used to protect the *podium* [the parapet for the emperor and the nobles which jutted out into the arena] were studded with amber [probably meaning that amber studs were inserted into the knots]. The arms too, the litters, and all the other apparatus were decorated with amber, a different kind of display being made each day of the spectacles. The largest piece . . . brought to Rome weighed 13 pounds. [Roman weight, slightly less than 10 pounds U.S.]

Cornelius Tacitus, of the next generation of Roman writers, knew a little more about the German amber coast, but before I can turn to Tacitus I have to deal with some poetical matters. By doing so, I can confirm one of Pliny's assertions: that the Eridanus is not the Padus.

The legend referred to as one of the Greek "vanities" was the story of Phaëton and of his sisters, the Heliades, which was told by several classical authors, the version which is best known now being that of the Roman Publius Ovidius Naso.

Phaëton, the son of the sun god Helios and of the beautiful Klymene, had no greater wish than to be permitted to drive the sun chariot across the sky. His father at first refused permission but consented in the end, warning his son with strong words not to whip the fiery horses. Storming across the sky, Phaëton forgot the warning and whipped the horses, urging them to greater speed. Bolting, the horses lost their way and came too close to earth; a drought resulted. Even mighty rivers dried up: *"siccat Hesperiosque amnes, Rhenum, Rhodanumque, Padumque"* (Rhine, Rhone, and Po). Earth complained to Zeus, who launched a thunderbolt at the sun chariot. Phaëton was killed and fell into the Eridanus. The naiads of the river found the body, carried it ashore, and buried it. Phaëton's sisters, the Heliades, and his mother Klymene found the body and wept over it. Because they had helped Phaëton to climb into the sun chariot, punishment was extended to them too: their feet changed into roots, their clothing to bark, and their bodies to tall poplar trees. They continued to weep, but now their tears no longer mingled with the waters of the Eridanus, they hardened and turned into amber, which comes only from the Eridanus.

The first part of this is clear—when the summer is very hot and the earth is about to be burned it must be because the sun is nearer than usual, presumably because unskilled hands drive the sun chariot. Then one day a thunderbolt flashes across the sky and the hot spell ends with lightning and rain—Mother Earth has successfully appealed to the highest authorities. The latter part is clear too: amber is the product of trees and it comes from a river called Eridanus.

Which river is the Eridanus? Ovid made it clear that it was not Rhine, or Rhone, or Po, each of which had been taken by somebody to be the Eridanus. Herodotus, "the Father of History," had stated that the Eridanus was a river flowing into the northern ocean. He had some doubts, though, because he added that he had not been able to find any-body who had actually seen the ocean which was supposed to be to the north of Europe. Strabo carried the skepticism to its logical (or illogical) conclusion: "The Eridanus is the river that flows in Neverland."

If Strabo had known where amber could actually be found, he would have been less skeptical. He was about two generations earlier than Pliny and in his day the Baltic amber had not yet been "discovered" by Rome; the amber which reached the Mediterranean then came from the North Sea. In the North Sea amber is found in quantities which make it an article of trade in only one area: the west coast of Denmark and the adjacent German territory, in general, to the north of the present Hamburg. There was even a report around which pointed to that area, made by Pytheas of Massilia (Marseilles). For some reason Strabo de-tested Pytheas and called him flatly a *pseudéstatos* (liar); but Pliny gave a clear version: "Pytheas says that the Gutones, a people in Germany, inhabit the shores of an estuary . . . at one day's sail from this territory is the Isle of Abalus upon the shores of which amber is thrown by the waves in the Spring . . . the inhabitants use it for fuel and sell it to their neighbors, the Teutons."

The only island in the whole North Sea which is one day's sail from a German coast is Helgoland. At present it is just 1 mile long and slightly less than half a mile wide. But in 1075 A.D. Adam von Bremen stated that Helgoland was "8 miles long and 4 miles wide" (his mile

was about 400 feet less than our statute mile). Most likely Helgoland
was still larger a thousand years earlier.

If amber came from that area it must have been brought south along
a river which in those days was never mentioned by name, *unless it was
called Eridanus*. And that was the Elbe. Somebody who had only heard
about the geographical conditions might well "reconstruct" the facts by
assuming that the amber was somehow formed in the river and carried
by it to the shores of the islands where it was found—actually the Frisian
Islands and Helgoland—calling them Elektrides or amber islands. The
amber trade route ended at the Po, and confusion of the river of "origin"
with the river of trade would easily bring about the result which made
Pliny bellow about the *vanitatis Graecae*.

At present the quantities of North Sea amber that are found are
utterly insignificant, but even a century ago this was not so. Around
1800 some 3000 pounds of amber were collected every year on the west
coast of Jutland; finds of pieces weighing several pounds each were reported from the islands of Sylt, Römö, and Fanö. During the years
1822–25 (stormy years, which means rich amber years), a Danish
merchant of Ringkjöbing collected 686 pounds on the shore near his
hometown. And it is significant that there is a township on the west
coast of Denmark which is called Glesborg.

It was probably the expedition of the Roman knight whose name
Pliny failed to mention that helped to shift the amber trade route from
the Elbe to the Vistula. And it is quite important that Tacitus wrote
en passant (especially *because* he wrote it *en passant*): "Here . . . are
the sources of the Elbe [in Latin *Albis*], formerly a famous and oft-
mentioned river, now known mostly by hearsay." The meaning is, of
course, that the Albis was famous when it still was the Eridanus; now
that it is just the Albis it is no longer important.

When we come to Tacitus, it is already the Samland, and only the
Samland, which was the amber country. We know that he never saw it
himself, but people who have lived in the Samland (as I have) can see
clearly that he had eye-witness accounts to go by. He wrote that beyond
Sweden, in an easterly direction, "there is another sea, sluggish and
almost without movement [there are no tides in the Baltic], which
seems to surround the whole of earth because the last rays of the setting

sun, until sunrise of the next day, keep the sky so bright that it darkens the stars." Tacitus tried hard to describe something he did not know himself, the improbable "white nights" of the eastern Baltic in mid-summer. "Imagination adds that the gods and the flaming coronets on their heads become visible." This is a splendidly chosen phrase for a description of the aurora borealis, which can be seen on the Samland coast on not too rare occasions.

Proceeding to the inhabitants, Tacitus wrote that "they only, of all the peoples on the earth, find *succinum* on the beach and in shallow parts of the sea, which they themselves call *glaesum*. But they don't know, and in their low state of culture do not even ask about, its nature and origin; in fact for a long time it lay unused among the jetsam and flotsam of the shore until our craving for luxury gave it fame. They don't make any use of it themselves, but pass it on as they find it; *in astonishment they accept the pay offered*." After repeating what Pliny said about the nature of amber and the proofs for it, Tacitus arrived at an interesting conjecture. One has to assume, he wrote, that there are countries and islands in that sea where dense forests grow, which, stimulated by the sun, produce amber rosin in profusion, which falls into the sea and is then washed up on the German shore.

This splendid guess, which contained only the one mistake that Tacitus believed these amber forests to exist in his own time, brought to a close the first period of the cultural history of amber. Tacitus died during the early part of the second century, probably in 120 A.D.

When amber is mentioned next, enough time has passed to have wrought profound changes in the political scene. The geographical scene has changed too; it has moved directly into the amber country. The next document is dated 1264 A.D., and while the language is still Latin the parties concerned no longer are. It is a document of the Grand Marshal of the Order of the Teutonic Knights, conferring upon the Bishop of the Samland the right to the amber in a certain place, near the present Lochstädt. Amber is no longer a subject of barter for the far-distant games of a heathen emperor. Now profoundly Christian knights deal in a businesslike way with their Church, but one does wonder what *they* bartered in that deal.

The Order of the Teutonic Knights originated as a kind of by-product of the Crusades, beginning as a hospital for Germanic knights in the Holy Land. But at one point the knights got tired of crusades against agile Saracen fighters and of adventures beyond the sea. They decided, instead, to extend their own domain into the nearby east. They have since been pictured as "robber barons," not quite correctly. They considered themselves mainly colonizers, armored and on horseback, but followed by whole columns of retainers, masons, artisans, and peasants on foot. They traded, but they were by no means above weighing the scales in their favor with a long sword—as who in their day was? In Russia they finally ran up against Alexander Nevski and had to retreat in disorder (those that were still alive), but the area that later became East Prussia and some neighboring territories were firmly in their hands. Those in their territories who were not Christians were baptized. Or else. In addition to being warriors and short-range crusaders they were businessmen.

Amber was valuable and had acquired a very special use, both laudable and profitable: it was the raw material for rosaries. But the trade had to be organized properly so that it would yield a maximum of profit. The Grand Marshal issued an order which was enforced brutally. Nobody, but absolutely nobody, was permitted to possess raw amber. Only the Grand Marshal himself could make an exception, such as the treaty with the Bishop of the Samland. All the amber found at the shore had to be turned over to the Grand Marshal without delay. Whether there were any organized attempts at collecting amber in those early days is uncertain. Later, it seems, the local population had to provide manpower for this purpose, or else it was the labor of convicted criminals, because an order was issued prohibiting the collecting of amber except under supervision of the Beach Master, whose duty it was to hang from the nearest tree anybody who was observed picking up amber. The large number of local legends about cruel Beach Masters, and their ghosts haunting the scene of their multiple hangings, proves that these orders were enforced relentlessly, day after day, night after night, to the very letter.

But seeing to it that every bit of amber found was turned over to the Grand Marshal was only the first half of the job. The amber had to be

made into the article of trade—rosaries. If that were done in the amber
country, however, the workmen might acquire amber illicitly. Hence
it was forbidden to process amber, not only in the Samland, but anywhere on German territory. The Order shipped its amber to Bruges, ·
where a special guild of amber turners had come into existence. They
called themselves "makers of rosaries"—paternostermakers. There is
documentary mention of this guild as early as 1302, and by 1420 we find
that it numbered 70 "masters" and over 300 "helpers and apprentices."

Apparently the principle of permitting the processing of amber only
at a long distance from the place of origin—thus making the man with
a chunk of raw amber in his pocket automatically a criminal and the
one with a rosary automatically honest—could be violated by the
Order itself, or at least by the Grand Marshal. At the castle of Marien-
burg on the Vistula there has been preserved a book known as the
Tresslerbook, in which the treasurer of the Order recorded disburse-
ments. The first entry hinting at an exception to the rule is under the
date of 2. March 1399, stating that "7 marc silver" were paid to the regional head of the Order in Königsberg "for food and lodging for Johan
the *bornsteynsnyczer* [amber cutter] for half a year." Further entries,
running through October 1402, record payments to Master Johan for
rosaries and "pictures" made of amber.

It was only logical that the Order should employ an artisan for its
own needs at the source. What "Master Johan" produced was obviously
not for sale. But the principle was definitely shattered in 1480 when the
King of Poland suddenly granted to the city of Danzig the right to
found and to maintain its own guild of paternostermakers. There was
an old rivalry between the Teutonic Knights and the Polish nobility
which contributed largely to the Order's decision to turn Lutheran after
the Reformation, when the Poles decided to keep their Roman Catholic
faith.

The Order countered by establishing an amber turner in Königsberg.
The name of the man is on record; it was Hilger, and he is mentioned
regularly from 1499 to 1510. He, like Master Johan, must have worked
almost exclusively for the Order, because a later source, one Andreas
Aurifaber, stated as late as 1551 that "all amber was shipped to Danzig

to be worked and sold." Aurifaber also stated the average yield. Of course "one year brings more than another," but "if one year helps the other" the amount is 110 kegs.

After 1510 came a number of years of utter confusion. Because of the Reformation Grand Marshal Albrecht became Duke Albrecht. The guild of amber turners in Danzig, and apparently several other guilds as well, complained about him to the German Emperor. His amber policy was attacked right and left. Simultaneously the market also collapsed. The Order had turned Lutheran; Lutherans do not use rosaries, and the Catholic countries did not want to buy from the Lutherans. The Order decided to hand this suddenly worrisome business to somebody else. In 1533 Paul Koehn von Jaski, head of a wealthy family of merchants in Danzig, signed an agreement which simply transferred the amber monopoly to his house. Only white amber was exempt because it was believed to have outstanding medical properties.

Trade with France, Italy, and Spain had collapsed for religious reasons, but trade with the Near East was brisk, resulting in yearly payments of around 15,000 gold dollars to Duke Albrecht. The Germans discovered that there is a Mohammedan counterpart of the rosary, and "Mohammedan rosaries" were the biggest single item in the trade for centuries, clear up to the Second World War. Armenian traders came to Königsberg, bringing silken carpets ornamented with gold threads; in one transaction of which the details have been preserved, nine kegs of raw amber were exchanged for four carpets. Another item was reported by a French traveler,[1] who, in 1640, met four Armenian merchants in Patna in India. They had just returned from Danzig where a number of statues had been carved for the temples of an Indian king. They had had another very profitable order: a statue of a demon with six horns, four ears, four arms, and six fingers on each hand, but unfortunately they had not been able to find a piece of amber big enough for this carving.

The house of Koehn von Jaski had the monopoly until 1642, when Frederick William, the Great Elector, bought it back for 40,000 thalers. From that moment on amber was State Property, with capital letters.

To protect said State Property all kinds of laws were issued. Posses-

---

[1] J. B. Tavernier, *Les six voyages, etc.* 1676, vol. II, p. 417.

sion of raw amber was of course forbidden. To walk the beach where such amber might be found was forbidden too. One needed a special permit to approach the seashore. Those living at the seashore, like fishermen, had to swear the Amber Oath every third year. With that oath they promised to denounce any smuggler, even if he should be the closest blood relative. There was a special Amber Oath for priests. To administer the oath and to deal with culprits there was the Amber Court. "Beach riders" patrolled the shore, especially after storms. And while only smugglers caught in the act were still punished by hanging, life was not easy. The local inhabitants not only had to turn in all the amber they might find accidentally, they had to go out and look for it. To provide incentive they were promised pay, and even were paid: weight for weight, salt for amber.

But all this did not do what it was designed to do. Though the government paid so little for the raw material—salt was no longer a very precious substance—it did have enormous expenses. It had to maintain the huge control apparatus of beach riders, supervisors, paymasters, amber judges and their helpers, all of whom had to be paid in good silver thalers. And the government was underpaid in turn by the still existing guilds. It was a rare year in which the amber monopoly did not produce a net loss. Wars did not improve matters, interfering with collection on the one end of the business and with sales at the other end. In 1811, during the Napoleonic wars, the Prussian government gave up.

Before I turn back to 1600 or so in order to tell the scientific history of amber for that period, it might be amusing to look at the names under which this material was traded.

Amber has two obvious and outstanding characteristics: it is a "stone" that will burn, and when rubbed it will attract small particles of matter. The Germans seized upon the first characteristic for the name. *Burnsteyn, Börnstein,* are old forms; the modern word is *Bernstein,* which simply means burning (or, rather, combustible) stone. The Swedish *bärnsten* and the Dutch *Barnsteen* are of course the same word, as is the Polish *bursztyn.* The old Germanic *glaes* has not survived anywhere in its original meaning. The Latin *succinum* (sap stone) has survived only as an alternate word in Spanish as *succino.* The more common Spanish word is *electro,* and the Italian is *elettro,* both of course derived from the classical

Greek *elektron,* which in turn seems to have been derived originally from *elektor,* meaning sun glare. But in modern Greek the name is *berónike.*

The Arabic name is based on the second characteristic. It is *kāhrabā* (literally, straw robber), also existing in the form of *kāhrubā.* The first form is also the Persian name. Modern Turkish *kehruba* (in vulgar Turkish, *kehribar*) is obviously the same. The English word *amber* was taken over from the French and the French got it from the late Latin *ambrum,* which derived from an Arabic word *anbar.* But that word also means "whale." The result was confusion between two products of the sea, which the French solved to some extent by speaking about *ambre jaune* (yellow amber) and *ambre gris,* the latter getting into English with only a slight change of spelling.

Interestingly enough, the words used by the peoples living near the amber country differ radically. In Finnish amber is *merrikiwi,* meaning sea stone. In Estonian there are two words, *meriwaik* (sea wax) and *meripihkaa* (sea rosin). The Russian word is *yantar* and the Hungarian, quite similar, is *yanta.* While the connection has not been proved to the full satisfaction of philologists, this is probably the same word as *dzinters* in Latvian and *gentars* or *genitar* in Old Prussian, a non-Germanic language. The clue to all these words is furnished by the Lithuanian name *gintaras.* In Lithuanian *ginti* means "to defend"; *gintaras* logically has the meaning of "protector" or "defender"—in short, amulet. In fact, amber is worn as a protection against disease in Lithuania and western Russia, just as it was by Roman girls in Pliny's time [2] and later by warriors of all nations and races.

One might expect that the learned men of, say, 1600, would have been at least as advanced in scientific knowledge of amber as Pliny and Tacitus, whose works they knew virtually by heart. Strangely enough they professed a different belief, partly to prove that they had advanced beyond Tacitus. The famous Athanasius Kircher, S.J., pointed out that

---

[2] Roman ladies are known to have carried balls of amber, up to the size of tennis balls, but no reason or purpose is furnished by any classical writer. It may have been just a luxury item; it may have been a somewhat unserious amulet. But I have occasionally thought that there may have been a practical reason: such amber balls could have been used to remove lint and similar things from ornate dresses while the dress was being worn in public.

there were no islands to the north of the amber coast, as Tacitus had thought. There was Sweden. If the amber trees grew in Sweden, why didn't the Swedes harvest amber at the source? They didn't, he concluded, because amber was not a product of trees, Swedish or otherwise, but a mineral. In that he agreed with two others who had preceded him, the famous Georg Bauer who called himself Agricola and who reworked the German word "burn stone" back into Latin as *lapis ardens,* and the equally famous Philippus Aureolus Bombastus Theophrastus von Hohenheim, who called himself Paracelsus.

Amber, they said, was a mineral, a product of the soil like asphaltum or petroleum. In fact, petroleum was probably just liquid amber or amber solid petroleum. There was proof for this assertion. Amber often contained liquid-filled bubbles—petroleum which had not yet hardened. Presumably there was an oil well at the bottom of the Baltic and the petroleum rose to the surface, at least some of it still liquid, which explained why gnats and flies could be found imbedded in it. Father Kircher put special emphasis on some small fishes imbedded in amber which he had seen in collections. Unfortunately these fish were fakes, put into hollowed-out pieces of amber which were then filled with turnip-seed oil and resealed. Such faking has been going on since about 1500 and a large number of these pieces have been preserved, many of them "done" so clumsily that one wonders whether they ever deceived anyone. On the other hand, no fish or frog has ever been found naturally imbedded in amber, nor any other vertebrate animal or part of one, with the sole exception of a small and probably young lizard.

After two centuries of belief in a unique oil well at the bottom of the Baltic, there came a multipronged attack against these ideas. The opening salvo came from France, originating in the study of Georges Louis Leclerc, Comte de Buffon, in about 1750. The industrious and incredibly intelligent Buffon did not say very much about amber directly, but he devoted beautiful quarto volumes to proving that some "minerals," especially coal, were of organic and specifically vegetable origin. They were, Buffon asserted, the remains of old forests. Petroleum too was organic material. Anybody who knew what Agricola and Paracelsus and Sebastian Münster and Athanasius Kircher and many others had thought about amber now had to conclude that amber was of organic origin, whether you took it to be a "petroleum product" or whether you still sided with Pliny and Tacitus.

At about the same time the great Swede Karl von Linné (Carolus Linnaeus), outstanding naturalist and founder of modern systematic botany, was busily collecting facts about amber. He was convinced that it was of vegetable origin and was trying to assemble proof for his belief.

And a Russian scientist, Mikhail Vassilievitch Lomonosov, officially a chemist and first Russian professor of chemistry at the newly founded Russian Academy of Sciences, incidentally creator of the Russian literary language, author of the first Russian textbook on chemistry, also discoverer of the atmosphere of the planet Venus,[3] and neglected prophet in various fields, came out in 1757 with a long and loud denunciation of the whole petroleum theory. In a speech delivered to the Academy in St. Petersburg he stated that amber had to be accepted as the rosin of some tree and that any other explanation was nonsense.

Ten years after that speech there appeared in Königsberg itself a small but important book on amber, just about 150 pages, with the title: *Attempt at a Short Natural History of the Prussian Amber*. The author's name, Friedrich Samuel Bock, is really not important; what is important is that he was a native of the Samland and a resident of Königsberg, that he had lived all his life at the source of amber and in the center of the activities connected with it.

The great savants who had philosophized about the nature of amber had lived in southwestern Germany, in Switzerland, and even in Italy. They might have crossed the Elbe; they certainly had never crossed the Vistula. They told of oil slicks on the Baltic—no skipper or fisherman had ever encountered them. They told how amber was washed up on the shore still in a tarlike condition—no collector had ever found it like that. They even thought that oil might be dripping out of the sands of the Samland's vertical coast. All this was ridiculous to anybody who knew the locality. On the other hand the similarities with rosin were such that anybody who had *not* read the learned discussions noticed

---

[3] See *Ostwald's Klassiker*, vol. 178 (1911), entitled *Physikalisch-Chemische Abhandlungen M. W. Lomonossow's;* translated from Latin and Russian manuscripts by Professor B. N. Menschutkin.

them at once. And everything that was found imbedded in amber without having been put there by some nature-faker pointed at one thing—forest. There were flies and gnats and ants in large numbers, the insects which would crawl along the trunks of pine trees. And something none of these faraway savants knew was known to Bock and other East Prussians. Sometimes amber was found in the soil, quite far down. But it was associated not with oil or anything like it, but with a special kind of soil, a "blue loam."

True, continued Bock, the trees of the Samland did not produce amber. Nor did the trees of the Swedish provinces across the Baltic. Nor were there any islands in between. But since the amber pointed so clearly at forests, why not think of forests that grew at the time of Pytheas and Pliny, maybe in Sweden, maybe on islands which did not exist any more? This would mean that those islands had sunk in the intervening centuries, but so had some villages which were now off shore. And as storms washed pieces of wood and potsherds from those villages ashore, so they brought amber from those sunken forests of the past.

The old islands that once bore the amber-producing trees must have been situated much closer to the present East Prussian coast than to Sweden. Amber was thrown ashore in Sweden, but rarely and in insignificant amounts. Amber was also found in Pomerania (farther west on the German shore of the Baltic) and in larger quantities, but still nothing to compare to the golden harvest at the Samland shore after a heavy storm. Logically, therefore, one had to assume that the old islands had been due north of the Samland and quite near; they may have been visible from the shore on clear days. It was with this thought that Herr Friedrich Samuel Bock left his readers.

Some fifty years later an East Prussian scientist, Wrede, pushed this thought further in the logical, and, as it turned out later, the correct direction: into the further past. Wrede had followed what was then brand-new geological reasoning, coming mostly from France. There had been long periods in the history of the earth which preceded historical times. Count Buffon had tentatively spoken of more than 80,000 years; others found even that too short. Even more important for the problem at hand, there had been animals and plants in places where these animals and plants did not exist now. And there had been species of animals, and presumably of plants too, which did not exist at all any more. Amber was the product of a pinelike tree, there was no longer any doubt about that. But no living pine tree produced amber, hence it had to be the rosin of prehistoric pine trees of a type that had become extinct a long time ago.

Thus said Wrede in 1811, the year when the amber monopoly of the Prussian state, in the form which had been handed down from the time of the Great Elector, collapsed completely.

Its collapse was a good thing for all concerned. It cleared the way for the combination of new management on the commercial end and new science on the explanatory end which was finally able to solve the amber problem.

2: *The Secret of the Blue Earth*

IT MUST not be imagined that the Prussian state—by then the Kingdom of Prussia—relinquished the amber monopoly easily. Groups of people, whether they are tied together as commercial firms, societies, churches, or as political units, from townships to empires, are even more reluctant to part with property than any single individual is. People knew enough about practical economics even during the eighteenth century to realize that an operation which results in a loss may become profitable if production can be increased. Those 110 kegs of yearly yield which Andreas Aurifaber had put on record in 1551 were not enough. The problem was to obtain more amber from the sea. Some progress in that direction had been made in the past; more seemed at least possible.

Originally it had been simply a matter of collecting what the waves threw ashore. Single pieces of amber, often entangled in strands of sea kelp, could be found at the shore at almost any time, but the time to *look* for amber was after a storm.

What the Baltic can do if the wind and other conditions are just right has been demonstrated on several fairly recent occasions of which we have reliable records. In 1862 the harvest of a single morning near Palmnicken amounted to 4400 pounds of amber. And after a wind-driven flood of January 1914 the people of Rauschen collected 1910 pounds, officially certificated. In the late 1920s old fishermen still told visitors about that flood; after the waters had receded they saw amber piled up on the shore in a long line of little hillocks, some of them 2 feet high.

Such lavishness is and always was exceptional, but the fishermen had

23

learned how they could improve their luck a little on stormy mornings.
The breakers which rolled up the shore carried amber, sometimes loose,
more often entangled in the sea kelp. But much of the possible harvest
went back into the sea. To prevent that the men constructed special
"amber catchers," nets built along the general lines of a butterfly net but
much larger, with handles 20 or 30 feet long. Standing hip-deep in water,
they thrust these nets into the advancing waves. When a net was full
they shook the contents out, and the waiting women and children
eagerly tore the masses of kelp apart and stuffed their collecting bags
with the "Baltic gold."

Records dealing with such particulars are too scarce to enable us to
date the introduction of "catching" with precision. A picture of an
"amber fisherman" with long-handled net and collecting bag tied to his
chest like a misplaced rucksack appears in a book published in 1677.
Such "catching" was practiced occasionally only 30 years ago and even
now some families may still get out their gear on stormy mornings.

While "catching" was designed to increase the harvest after a storm,
another method, first mentioned by Andreas Aurifaber, helped to get
amber from the sea on days when the Baltic was as smooth as plate glass
and the sky a cloudless expanse of blue. Several men would row out in
a broad-beamed boat. One of them had a tool that looked like a heavy
spading fork on a long handle, the prongs bent in a sharp curve. The
others were equipped with nets on long handles, similar to those used
for "catching" from the shore, but smaller. The man with the fork
would rake the bottom of the sea or else work his tool under a likely-
looking boulder and dislodge it. Simultaneously the others would pass
their nets through the area of disturbed floating bottom mud and—it
was hoped—floating amber. This was called *Bernsteinstechen* or "amber
poking." It was tedious work, but while the harvest was small it was
fairly reliable.

Both "catching" and "poking" seem to have come into use at the time
when the Jaskis of Danzig were lessees of the amber monopoly. This
may account, to some extent, for the fact that the House of Jaski could
pay a revenue to the former Grand Marshal of the Teutonic Knights,
while the Order itself had found the going difficult.

One wonders why diving, like pearl diving in the South Seas, was not tried. It never became customary, although teen-age boys may have tried it on occasion. The government hired two professional divers in the city of Halle in 1725, sent them to East Prussia, and put them to work. But the experiment ended in financial failure.

One more approach remained: to try to get amber from the *land*. Sometimes, if you were lucky, you could find amber by digging. The old treaty between the Grand Marshal of the Teutonic Knights and the Bishop of the Samland referred to that possibility; it would have been meaningless otherwise, because Lochstädt, the place mentioned, is on the shore of the Frisches Haff where sea amber could not occur (see map, page 5). And one of those old ordinances of the Great Elector cautioned the Beach Riders to be on the lookout for suspicious digging. An attempt at actual mining was also made. A retired general persuaded a number of professional miners from Thuringia and neighboring provinces to go to the Samland with him. Unfortunately the details are meager. They may have tried to drive horizontal galleries into the coast from a place near sea level. That the locality was the west coast of the Samland can be deduced from the fact that three places on the west coast (Palmnicken, Great Hubnicken, and Great Dirschkeim) are mentioned as having yielded amber. But the attempt was given up soon, because the loose sand could not be held back, filled the galleries, and even caused the death of a few of the miners.

Another and more successful attempt was made during the reign of Frederick the Great in 1782. Again professional mining experts supervised the work, but they had learned from the earlier failure. A vertical shaft was dug to a depth of about 80 feet from the crown of the high coast. Then horizontal tunnels were dug into the sands, a few of them breaking through the vertical coast some 30 feet above sea level in order to get some fresh air and a little light to the place of operations. The miners did find a good deal of amber, sometimes single pieces, but usually accumulations which they called "nests," with long barren stretches in between.

However, it was not enough to warrant expansion or even continuation of the mining operations. And when, at another spot near Kraxtepellen, such mining attempts caused a long stretch of coast to collapse suddenly, the whole scheme was abandoned. This failure may have contributed to the decision to rid the state of the monopoly. If mining had been lucrative, or at least promising, one could have hoped to accomplish something by systematic work and efficient organization. But since the amber supply seemed to depend on the accident of storms blowing in the right direction, the whole operation was simply not reliable enough to be pursued energetically. The privy councilors just had to look at the long list of years that had ended with a deficit to see how unreliable it was.

In 1811 the amber monopoly was for sale or lease. At first there was a repetition of the Koehn von Jaski episode. A merchant by the name of Douglas organized a number of other businessmen and the Douglas Konsortium became the lessee. But the changed times could be detected even in a legal document. When the Teutonic Knights had handed the rights over to the Jaski family the document had said "for all time." The new document said 25 years, from 1811 to 1836. The business group did badly and lost interest even before that period had run its full course.

And then, at long last, the local inhabitants got into the picture as free men. The right to collect amber by any method, including mining, was leased to individuals in theory, in practice usually to communities. For the first time the fishermen worked with real enthusiasm. Travelers who visited East Prussia in that period from 1837 to about 1860 remarked on the very large number of small craft engaged in amber poking; especially off Brüsterort, the "cape" of the Samland, hundreds of vessels could be seen on clear days. For the first time in history, there was no forced labor and no smuggling. And since the beach was now accessible to anybody, the fishing villages could start another type of business: they became seashore resorts. And for the first time in history the Department of Internal Revenue experienced a succession of years of profit from amber. It was almost incredible.

Then interest shifted for a while from the Samland to the Kurisches Haff, the lagoon to the north of the peninsula (see map, page 5). The long sandy peninsulas, like enormous artificial breakwaters, which transform the bays on either side of the Samland into lagoons, are of relatively recent origin. A third one which might have enclosed the whole Bay of Danzig did not develop fully. Local geologists who investigated these unique formations with both professional zeal and regional patriotic fervor came to the conclusion that they could not be more than 7000 years old at most. The Frische Nehrung, the one closer to Danzig, certainly must have been a chain of sandbanks and low sandy islands for most of the time. The Samland itself was solid land even 7000 years ago. In fact, it must have been much larger in area, though it probably was no higher than it is now—a maximum of a little over 200 feet. But we know from a century of recorded observation that the coastline recedes between 1 and 2 feet per year, an unusually fast rate. When that Roman knight went to the Samland for Emperor Nero, it must have been about a mile larger in both the westerly and northerly directions. Even then the coast became lower the farther east one went. At the seashore resort of Cranz, there is no longer a bold high coast, but only sandy hills. Just east of Cranz begins the Kurische Nehrung, the "breakwater" that makes the Kurisches Haff into a lagoon. This one is famous for its tall wandering sand dunes which have destroyed at least half a dozen small settlements in historic times, yielding weird sand-dried and sand-devastated remains after a lapse of centuries. The dunes, blown by the wind, generally move in the direction of the lagoon, making it shallower and shallower as time goes on. It is the opinion of the experts that this long peninsula, unlike the one near Danzig, formed as a whole, and that there were no outlets to the sea except the one at Memel. Only one other spot, at the extreme southern end not far from Cranz, is under suspicion. It is still a peat bog and may have been open water when Nero's knight "visited the various markets there."

Let us finish this short geographical survey with the names of the three main settlements on the Kurische Nehrung. The one you reach first coming from Cranz is well known to every naturalist. It is Rossitten, for many years the seat of a famous ornithological station which established the traveling routes of most European migratory birds by catching large numbers of specimens, ringing them, and then letting them proceed on their way. Rossitten, incidentally, is also the place where motorless aircraft stayed aloft for the first time for more than six hours; apparently the numerous seagulls had taught the pilot well. Somewhat higher up on the Nehrung is the town of Nidden, which has somehow managed to escape any important connection with the story of amber.

Still higher up is Schwarzort, where the amber idols from the later stone age were found.

This originally tiny hamlet of Schwarzort was to figure prominently in the new chapter in the story of amber. The activities off Schwarzort at first had nothing to do with amber at all. Goods shipped from Königsberg to Memel traveled most cheaply by water. They were brought first from Königsberg to Cranzbeek, a township at the Haff, and there loaded on barges and conveyed to Memel along the "inside" of the Nehrung. Since the winds continued to blow sand from the dunes into the Haff it became necessary to dredge the channel occasionally. In the course of this work not less than 1000 pounds of amber were brought up from the Haff near Schwarzort in 1855. When dredging had to be repeated two years later, amber was again found in substantial quantities.

Then a man by the name of Wilhelm Stantien, a well-to-do innkeeper in Memel, had the idea of changing the pattern. Why not dredge for amber, incidentally keeping the channel open? He leased the right of producing amber by dredging and equipped a fishing boat for this purpose. That was in 1854. The venture proved successful. In 1860 Wilhelm Stantien joined hands with the merchant Moritz Becker, forming the firm of Stantien & Becker, which at first restricted its activities to the Haff. They began with three small dredges operated by manpower, then bought their first steam-powered dredge. Only half a dozen years later they had in operation 22 large steam dredges which scooped the sand from the bottom of the Haff to a depth of 35 feet. The sand was dumped on the Nehrung and searched for amber. During the summer months, a thousand people found employment with Stantien & Becker.

Unfortunately the winters are severe in East Prussia. The Haff freezes every year, and most years the Baltic also freezes for 100 yards or more from the shore. The total working time per year was 30 weeks as a rule, but these 30 weeks produced an average of 165,000 pounds of amber (185,000 pounds in 1868). In addition to the dredging operations, divers were employed, partly for direct recovery, partly to point out good spots for the dredges. But after a while the harvest from the bottom of the Haff began to dwindle. The year 1886 was decidedly disappointing; the following year proved that it had not been just bad luck. The deposits in the Haff were exhausted, as far as industrial exploitation was concerned. In 1890 Stantien & Becker discontinued operations in the Haff.

They were doing something far more useful elsewhere. Twenty years earlier, in 1870, they had leased the right to obtain amber by open-pit mining at Kraxtepellen. Remember that all the earlier attempts at mining amber had taken place in the vicinity of that village. Stantien & Becker, however, did not pick the place for that reason, but based their judgment on a new factor, one which gave them a virtual certainty of success.

That new factor was the scientist, more specifically the geologist. During the time of the state monopoly he had been banned from the shore as a possible smuggler. Even the short-lived Douglas Konsortium had still looked at him with a faint distrust. But when all restrictions fell in 1837 the scientist could no longer be restrained. He was now at liberty to walk the beach, to look at geological formations, to collect samples, and to dig a little if he felt so inclined. He could try to fit what he saw into his general knowledge of the earth's past, a knowledge which had increased formidably since 1811 when Wrede said that the amber forest had to be considered a prehistoric forest and that the original amber-producing pine must be an extinct tree. By about 1850 geologists had a reasonably clear picture of the various geological periods.

To the geologist who walked the amber coast it was quite clear that everything he could see—everything above sea level, that is—was Tertiary. In some places one could see the more detailed structure of that coast without any time-consuming and expensive digging. At the very top there was, of course, "alluvial material," the soil in which the present-day forest grew or in which the local inhabitants planted their turnips and seeded their rye. After a few feet of that there came a layer of considerable thickness—about 12 feet at Kraxtepellen—of Pleistocene marl and sands. This material was still ascribed by the geologist of 1850 to a shallow inland sea.

Underneath the marl there was a thick layer—55 feet at Kraxtepellen —of something that came to be known as "striped sands." One has to see it to realize how descriptive that name is. Imagine a fairly tall building, built of light yellowish brick as the main material. Now imagine that the supply of yellow brick failed to arrive from time to time, but that the workmen had bricks of various darker colors on hand and would not wait for the arrival of more yellow brick. The result would be a dozen courses or so of yellow brick, then a single course of brown brick, two more courses of yellow brick followed by a course of dark gray brick, followed again by yellow brick, and then suddenly by a course of reddish-brown brick. The interesting and, to the geologist, highly significant feature is that some of these dark "brick courses" are coal, soft lignite from the Tertiary.

They were quite thin, at most a few inches thick in some places. But they were coal, and local fishermen had hacked away at them in accessible places for fuel for their stoves. In fact, every once in a while some enterprising merchant hired a mining expert to give an opinion whether open-pit mining would pay. Luckily for the landscape, no mining expert was ever convinced enough to talk his employer into such a venture. But the geologists, digging for samples in the coal seams, found some fossilized parts of plants; a few very nice fossil leaf prints were recovered near Rauschen. It was quite obvious to anybody with some knowledge of plants that the fossils found were trees, or rather parts of trees. Classification was left to Professor Oswald Heer of Switzerland, who was then the ranking expert on Tertiary fossils, especially plants and insects.

Professor Heer is said to have mumbled that it did not need him to see what they had dug up there in East Prussia. The remains were indubitably swamp cypress and sequoia (Heer himself still used the term *Washingtonia;* for the reason see Chapter 10), both types still alive in North America. Both were also typical of the Tertiary forests in Europe —why did these people in East Prussia think that their particular bit of lignite had a different origin from any other in Europe?

Of course the East Prussians had a reason for wondering, and that reason was amber. Both in commercial operations and in scientific digging amber had been found in single pieces and in so-called "nests" in the Pleistocene marl and sand, as well as almost at any point in the striped sands. Now the striped sands proved to contain coal, too. Coal seams were former swampy forests. Amber was a product of trees. The connection was not hard to guess. The one thing that did not quite fit in was the fact that no amber had ever been found in the coal seams themselves. It was above and below them, in what a mathematician would have called "random distribution," but with the one gap in the "randomness" that there was no amber in the coal. Of course, none might have happened to be found yet—the investigation was just beginning; or, more likely, the transformation of forest wood into coal might have transformed amber too, and what outside the coal seam was obvious and sought-for amber was changed beyond possibility of recognition, ground up in the coal.

Well, anyway, below those striped sands there was a layer of dark brown clay, hard as stone most of the time and from 3 to 10 feet thick. A local term for it was "Bock," which really means billygoat; the geologists adopted it without inquiring into its original meaning. And then there came something interesting. It was still Tertiary, naturally older than either the striped sands or the Bock. It was a layer of tiny granules of a well-known mineral, most of the time imbedded in a matrix of clay. This mineral is decidedly green in color and its technical name, from the Greek word *glaukos* for green, is glauconite. That layer from the early Tertiary was so definitely green and so sharply separated from the other layers that it was called locally the "green wall." Below the green wall there was a "gray wall," a very fine sand, still with much glauconite, but no longer enough to give it color.

Because of the fact, in itself purely accidental, that the level of the Baltic is close to the gray wall some of the early surveys stopped at that point. But in a few places the land was high enough so that the sea revealed still another layer under the gray wall. Its name, while not strictly correct, reveals its nature: quicksand. It is a grayish sand with rather sharp granules, used locally for scrubbing pots and pans. It was this layer of loose and water-logged sand which made the first attempts at mining so dangerous, so that the later miners of the time of Frederick the Great carefully stayed above the gray wall.

In the meantime, however, persevering, strong, and lucky fishermen had dug through the quicksand, too. And then they had found, some 15 feet below water level and dangerously close to the shoreline, a layer which they called the "blue earth." It was that blue loam which had been mentioned by Friedrich Samuel Bock. Digging into the usually hard blue earth, they found amber, not in large quantities but far more regularly than in the layers above the green wall. By doing this they had proved that there was actually an amber-bearing blue-earth layer quite deep in the ground (if you dug down from the crown of the coast). Mineralogically it is about the same as the green wall, glauconite sands with clay. In spite of its name, the blue earth is not blue. When wet it is simply black. When thoroughly dry, as for example a museum specimen, it is dark gray with a kind of greenish sheen. Only rarely has it been reported to look bluish-green, and I suspect that those reporters remembered the name very hard when they looked at it.

Later test diggings established the fact that the fishermen had not been thorough enough. They had entered only the top of the blue earth, which is comparatively poor in amber. This upper layer is 6 to 10 feet thick. Then follows a layer much richer in amber, 3 to 6 feet thick, and then comes the "true" blue earth, or "stone earth," never more than 3 feet in thickness, but incredibly rich in amber. It later became possible to estimate the quantitative relation between the mass of the blue earth and the amount of amber imbedded in it. Calculated for all the blue earth, the figure is about 1 pound of amber in every 1000 pounds of blue earth; it is not hard to imagine how rich that 3-foot layer has to be to give this over-all result for the total thickness of 15 to 20 feet.

Below the blue earth, as we know now, there is a layer of quartzite sands, then another rather thick layer of "lower quicksand," and a considerable thickness of glauconite sands and gray clay. If exposed this would look very much like the striped sands higher up. Interestingly enough, this layer carries in its upper strata a thin seam of blue earth, between 1 and 2 feet thick, complete with amber. And all that rests on rock which was definitely formed during the Cretaceous period.

All the layers, from the buried "old" striped sands to the more recent striped sands near the top, are of Tertiary origin, but *not* from the same subdivision of the Tertiary. The striped sands near the top, with their occasional seams of lignite and the underlying Bock, belong to one subdivision, while all the glauconite sands, including the fabulous blue earth itself, belong to another subdivision, an earlier one. That there is a fundamental difference between them was first realized in 1860. Beginning in about 1850 a local society consisting of scientists, public officials, and businessmen sponsored a geological survey of their province. The society bore the name of Society for Physical Economy and at that time functioned rather like a local chamber of commerce. "Their" geologist, G. Zaddach, not only contributed heavily to the scientific understanding of the factors involved in the amber problem, but could also explain why the amber "business" had had all its ups and downs.

All amber, Zaddach stated, came originally from that blue-earth layer. The coal seams up in the "striped sands" did not contain any. Nor had the forests which had formed the coal anything to do with the origin of amber. They were much younger. Amber had been fossilized a long time before even the first tree of the lignite forest took root.

As for the blue-earth layer, a large number of test borings had definitely established that it was below sea level everywhere and for an unknown but probably large extent even below the sea. It touched the present-day shoreline at only two points: on the west coast from Palmnicken northward not quite to Brüsterort and on the north coast, beginning just east of Brüsterort to about Neukuhren. All the amber which had been collected at the seashore, or "caught" or "poked" just off shore, had been washed out from the blue earth at the bottom of the sea—some thousand pounds every year since the time of Pliny. And, as a recent example had shown (Zaddach referred to the 4400-pound harvest near Palmnicken in 1862), the sea occasionally piled amber up on the shore during a storm. That had happened during the geological past too, and accounted for all those "nests" which miners had found above the "gray wall." Even the deposits in the Haff off Schwarzort, which Stantien & Becker were just beginning to exploit by dredging, were not "blue earth" but also nests which must have accumulated there before the Nehrung existed. Amber findings elsewhere along the Baltic coast, in Pomerania and on the island of Usedom in the Bay of Stettin, were also such nests, secondary deposits.[1] The original deposit, the blue earth, touched land only at the points mentioned. Logically any systematic exploitation was bound to be a hit-or-miss proposition, unless the blue-earth layer could be mined directly.

---

[1] Some of these occasional inland deposits were no longer even nests; they had been scooped up by the slowly moving glaciers of the Pleistocene period from the nests near the seashore and carried inland. This accounts for such otherwise inexplicable finds as the 7-pound piece of amber dredged up from the Oder River near the city of Breslau. Zaddach, when he was engaged in this work, was still unaware of the former existence of these glaciers.

Reassured by the information contained in Zaddach's monograph (printed at the expense of the Society for Physical Economy), the firm of Stantien & Becker did not hesitate to sign another contract with the Prussian government. Dated January 19, 1870, it obligated the firm to pay the Collector of Internal Revenue the equivalent of $1500 per year per acre of land utilized for the mining of amber. It was a rather high price, but Stantien & Becker had done well in the Haff, and as an additional incentive the government promised that nobody else would have the right to obtain amber by mining. The latter promise could be made because the contracts with the various communities had mostly expired in 1867 and had been renewed only for "shore collecting," "catching," and "poking"; the communities in their clumsy and underfinanced efforts at mining had ruined the shoreline, destroyed arable land, incurred debts, and generally displayed their lack of experience. That Stantien & Becker had done well to sign the contract became apparent soon: during the following five years they produced by mining some 10,000 pounds per year, worth then between 450,000 and 600,000 German marks, with a yearly expense of about 300,000 marks. In fact, after some years the Prussian state took advantage of a small paragraph in the contract and raised its rate by 20 per cent.

In 1875 Stantien & Becker started a larger and deeper mine near Palmnicken, going all the way down through the blue earth until sterile ground was reached again. This mine, which now really tapped the source of all the amber the sea had washed out in previous centuries, made even the geologists feel slightly dizzy. The very first year of operation, 1875, ended up with 450,000 pounds of fossil rosin. The next year did the same; the following year tallied 600,000 pounds. By 1885 production had climbed to slightly over 900,000 pounds per year. It went on like that for the next ten years, with yields varying between 600,000 and 850,000 pounds. Actually these figures include amber found at the shore and "caught" with nets, but since the yield from these sources amounted to "only" 10,000 to 12,000 pounds per year they do not change the picture much.

In 1895 the mine produced for the first time more than 1,000,000 pounds, almost 1,200,000 pounds, to be precise. Consequently, one is tempted to write, the Prussian state decided that amber, after all, should be direct state property once more and did not renew the contracts. The firm of Stantien & Becker disappeared from the scene as such, having been bought out by a payment of 9,700,000 German marks (not quite $2,500,000), and a special organization was founded, the Royal Amber Works Königsberg. It engaged in numerous activities. It operated the existing mine—near exhaustion at that time—and opened a new one nearby. It maintained collecting agencies which bought amber from the fishermen who brought it in; since amber was again state property it had to be turned in, but this time for cash. It operated a factory where amber was made into jewelry and cigar holders; it operated a chemical plant where inferior amber was processed into chemical materials, so-called amber oil and amber varnish. And by sacrificing the necessary amount of money it absorbed a threatening invention.

It must be explained here that amber does not have a true melting point. Being a fossil rosin, it is not uniform chemically. At a temperature of about 370 degrees centigrade (say 700 degrees Fahrenheit) it seems to melt but actually is decomposing; what is left after hardening is no longer amber. Since it could not be melted, tons of otherwise pretty but very small pieces had to be put into the distilling vats every month.

But in 1880 somebody outside the amber industry found out that such small pieces could be made into big pieces by heating them to about 160 degrees centigrade (320 degrees Fahrenheit) under high pressure. The results were hard to tell from naturally large pieces, except by the regular cylindrical shape. Stantien & Becker had tried to fight this "ambroid" as an "imitation," but their efforts only resulted in raising the price which the new monopoly had to pay to absorb the invention. Afterward most cigarette holders and cigar holders were "ambroid."

The production level of about 1,000,000 pounds of amber per year was maintained until 1914, when the First World War broke out in Europe. Even then the stoppage was not complete; the lowest year, 1915, still produced a little over 200,000 pounds. The record year after the first war (and probably for all time) was 1925, when, after modernization of machinery, the figure of 1,250,000 pounds was reached. After 1930 production dropped; in 1932 it was only 75,000 pounds, and for the year after that, the year in which Hitler became Chancellor of Germany, the figure actually reads zero. In 1934 it climbed back to 230,000 pounds, in 1935 it was 220,000 pounds, and after that no figures were handed out.[2]

A figure like "1,000,000 pounds per year" must not evoke the mental picture of endless rows of shipping crates, all filled with beautiful yellow amber, suitable for jewelry. That kind of amber is what the fishermen had collected or "caught" or "poked." The digging machinery of the amber mine brought to light *all* the amber in the blue earth, over 80 per cent of it suitable only for chemical processing. The type of earth-moving machinery used there was what is technically known as a "digging ladder," the type which has buckets on an endless chain moving around a boom. First all the sand and soil above the blue earth was moved out of the way. Then the blue earth itself was scooped up and brought in lorries to the "washroom" where high-pressure water jets transformed the heaps of black soil into an incredible mud-soup which was agitated and stirred and sieved and resieved in various ways until all amber of all kinds rested dripping in hoppers. There was some mechanical presorting, but most sorting had to be done by hand. All along the line a sharp lookout was kept for pieces of scientific interest.

The "sorting list" comprised more than eighty different types, but since many of the classifications referred to grain size only, the complete list is of no interest. There were three general classifications: amber which for one reason or another was good for chemical processing only; amber which was clean but of too small a grain size to be used for anything but making ambroid; and finally amber which was suitable for jewelry and related uses, the uses my readers are apt to know.

There are five main varieties used in the jewelry trade. The first is called "Clear," because it looks like clear yellow glass. A large piece of

---

[2] Of the later fate of the amber mine only a few scattered facts have become known. Early in the war a report came that "mining has been discontinued temporarily." This could mean anything and did not even have to be true. I recently learned by direct correspondence from an East Prussian who had paid a short visit to Palmnicken in January 1945 that the mine was active then and that the Russians made sporadic air attacks on it. A newspaper article published in March 1949 in the American Zone of Germany stated that most of the professional amber workers and enough raw amber to last for 20 years were brought to western Germany in 1944 and that the Königsberg Amber Works are now split into two: one in Hamburg (British Zone) and one in Tübingen (American Zone), where amber rosaries (including Mohammedan rosaries) and amber jewelry are being made to satisfy orders from the Benelux nations and from Great Britain. East Prussian amber workers, hearing about this, fled through the Iron Curtain and reported after arrival that the amber mine drowned in 1945 and was under water for several years. In 1948 the Russians drained it and reported for the summer of 1948 a daily production of 200 pounds.

Clear is a rarity, while very small pieces, say about the size of a 1-karat diamond, are quite common. The rarest kind, which for some reason was in special demand in France, is called "Ice-clear," an almost colorless version of the Clear. The second type is called "Flom," a local term for goose grease. If you are well acquainted with goose grease, this is a rather good descriptive term. The amber is essentially clear, but looks as if it were "misted" with fine dust. The third variety, unlovingly called "Bastard," is the most common. It is the typical cloudy amber, which looks as if some milk had been spilled into the clear mass. There are several degrees of cloudiness and there are color variations too: the whole may look whitish or yellow or brownish-yellow; even reddish-brown tinges may occur. The fourth variety is "Bone"; a piece of this, lying on a table, may be taken for ivory or even meerschaum. The fifth variety, finally, is "Foamy," completely opaque, very soft, and not polishable.

Close examination of the "Foamy" with slight magnification, or even without, revealed that the appearance was caused by countless small bubbles. From this one might infer that the other varieties also owed their distinctive characteristics to bubbles, and microscopic examination proved that to be true. In fact it was even possible to draw up a table, stating the approximate number of bubbles and their average size. In Flom there are about 600 bubbles per square millimeter, each bubble measuring 0.02 millimeter in diameter. In Bastard the bubbles are much smaller, from 0.0025 to 0.012 in diameter, but there are 2500 of them per square millimeter. In Bone the bubbles are still smaller, between 0.0008 and 0.004 millimeter in diameter, and there are 900,000 of them per square millimeter. Foamy is a kind of exaggerated Bone, with bubbles large enough to be visible to the naked eye. Naturally their numbers are smaller, because each bubble is so much larger, and even Nature can get only a certain number of bubbles of a given size into a given space.

There is one more item to be added to the discussion of jewelry aspects before we proceed to the scientific story with its still unexplained "mystery." In Pliny's *Natural History* one can read that Archelaos of Cappadocia "cleared" amber by boiling it in the fat of a suckling pig. Pliny was not handed a tall tale by somebody; it can be done. If amber with only a few bubbles, like Flom or mildly cloudy pieces of Bastard, is boiled in oil for a long time, the oil will fill the fine bubbles and a clear piece will result. Andreas Aurifaber watched "clearing" in 1572, as did one Johannes Wigand in 1590, and both added that the fat did not have to be that of a suckling pig, as Pliny had reported. A hundred years later, "clearing" was quite common and experimentation had shown that turnip-seed oil produced the best results. After 1900 it was learned that it was possible to change the color of the stone at the same time by addition of suitable substances, which, for obvious reasons, were never mentioned in print. If you should own a necklace of amber beads, clear but of a rich brown color, the probability is overwhelming that they are really Flom that was cleared with coloring ingredients.

It is reported that Immanuel Kant, whilom professor of philosophy in his native Königsberg, master of abstract thought and originator of the first theory about the origin of the solar system, kept a piece of amber for some time. It was what today is called an amber inclusion, with a fly imbedded in it. It conformed perfectly with the spirit of the times that visitors would quote the poem of Marcus Valerius Martialis (Martial), a friend of the younger Pliny:

> While an ant was walking about in Phaëton's shadow,
> Resinous drops quietly enshrouded the fragile creature,
> Look at it now, unnoticed it was while still living,
> But through entombment transformed into a gem.[3]

And Kant, on one occasion, remarked, "If thou couldst but speak, little fly, how much more would we know about the past."

What even Kant could not imagine was that a later science would be able to make the fly speak. In fact, all that we know about the amber forest is based on inclusions like Kant's fly, because the forest disappeared so completely that no trace of it is left, save the hundred thousand inclusions known to science. But we first must touch up the geological information presented by Zaddach with some modern knowledge.

In Zaddach's time the Tertiary period was subdivided into three sections: Eocene, Miocene, and Pliocene, the last-named being the young-

---

[3] Of course they didn't quote it that way. They quoted:
> *Dum Phaëthontea formica vagatur in umbra,*
> *Implicuit tenuem succina gutta feram.*
> *Sic modo quae fuerat vita contempta manente,*
> *Funeribus facta est nunc pretiosa suis.*

est. Zaddach had assumed that everything above the Bock, in particular the striped sands, had formed during the Miocene subperiod. Of the deeper layers he knew only that they were older, since an important subperiod had not then been recognized. We now count as follows, with the most recent period on top:

NAME	MEANING OF NAME	DURATION (MILLIONS OF YEARS)
Pleistocene (or Ice Age) ended 30,000 years ago, *not* a part of the Tertiary	most new	1
Pliocene	more new	6
Miocene	less new	12
Oligocene	a little newer	16
Eocene	dawn of the new	20
Paleocene	oldest of the new	5

Total time elapsed from the end of the preceding Cretaceous period to the end of the Pleistocene—60 million years.

In this scheme the striped sands and the Bock are Miocene, but everything from the green wall down to the lower quicksand belongs to the early portion of the Oligocene. The layer of striped sands below the blue earth is still older and must have formed during the Eocene. Since this Eocene deposit carries a thin layer of blue earth in its upper strata, the whole problem seemed simple. The amber forest had begun to grow near the end of the Eocene subperiod, reached its full extent during the Oligocene, and then disappeared, just as did the Miocene lignite forests which grew on the same spot much later.

But the theorists who reasoned this way were due for a disappointment. As persistently as the lignite seams higher up gave every indication of swampy forest, something like the Everglades today, the blue earth equally persistently displayed all the earmarks of a marine deposit. The mixture of clay particles and sand grains alone is enough to cause visions of a quiet sea, probably shallow and most likely tideless, where particles which had been suspended in moving water currents quietly settled to the bottom. In addition, the blue earth contains a number of fossils. Sharks' teeth, picked out of the mud-soup by sharp-eyed sorters, are in our museums now, carefully classified and labeled

Carcharodon obliquus, a relative of the great white shark of our own seas. There are oyster shells, first mentioned by Friedrich Samuel Bock, which are even more significant than the sharks' teeth. To begin with, the specific variety, *Ostrea ventilabrum,* is a typical fossil of the lower Oligocene of northern Europe. Its presence alone indicates the time. And then oyster shells tell something about the sea in which they grew. Sharks' teeth just indicate water; oyster shells prove that the water was not deep, that presumably a shore of some kind was at the horizon, and that the water was at least not very cold. Another blue-earth fossil is a sea urchin, also indicative of fairly shallow water. Then there is a crab, labeled *Coeloma balticum,* which would surprise nobody except an expert if it were seen crawling around alive at the shore now.

All of this makes for a consistent picture of a shallow sea, much like the Baltic of today, except that a somewhat warmer climate is indicated. But the most frequent fossil of the blue earth is amber, and the inclusions in that amber give an equally consistent picture of a different landscape. To begin with, there are pieces which show clearly that they are rosin which dripped from a wounded tree branch directly on the soil underneath. It did not drip into water, but onto dry soil. Inside the amber you find gnats, ants, flies, mayflies, and beetles, occasional tufts of hair, pine needles, the blossoms of various trees—everything spells "forest."

The conclusion (which was reached first by Zaddach) was inevitable: even the blue earth was not the primary amber deposit. It was a secondary deposit. The amber had either been brought by rivers into the sea where the blue earth was being formed or else the sea had gradually washed its way into the original deposits. A repetition of this process is going on right now and we know that it has been going on for a long time. Now the sea, the Baltic in this case, is washing away the Samland and with it the blue earth, forming tertiary deposits ("tertiary" is used here purely numerically, without any reference to the Tertiary period) like the one it formed in the Haff off Schwarzort in almost historical times.

It follows from this conclusion that even the thin blue-earth layer of the late Eocene is also a secondary deposit, and the original amber forest must have flourished still earlier, presumably during the early Eocene or even during the Paleocene. Moreover, no primary amber deposit is known, which means that we not only don't know precisely *when* the amber forest grew, we also don't know *where*. We can only say that it cannot have been in any area which is now land. If, say, the amber forest had grown in what is now Poland and rivers had brought the amber to the sea where the blue earth formed, we should have found traces of this old route of transportation. The present concept is, therefore, that another land reached down into the vicinity of the present amber coast from the north—say, for simplicity's sake, that Sweden extended southward almost to the southern Baltic shore of today, while the sea was displaced southward correspondingly. Then the sites of the original amber forests washed out by the sea in late Eocene and early Oligocene days, the courses of ancient rivers which may have transported the amber, and any primary deposits that might be left would all be at the bottom of the Baltic, the only place where they could escape investigation.

Unfortunately a lot of nonsense has been written about amber in trade journals and on some occasions even in professional scientific publications, because for a while the jewelry trade was in the habit of calling any fossil rosin or even tree gum by the name amber, which should be reserved for the substance labeled "succinite" by mineralogists and geologists.

The main "offender" in that respect is the so-called "Sicilian amber" or simetite. This is a fossil rosin, or, since it does not contain any succinic acid, more probably a tree gum, which formed during the middle Miocene, many millions of years later than true amber. It is being washed into the Mediterranean by the rivers Salso and Simeto (hence the name) and washed up again by the sea, much as true amber is by the Baltic. In color, simetite can be chrysolite green or brownish black, but usually it is bright red, or blood red, or yellowish red, or purplish red; in short, red. It does contain inclusions, as does another pseudo-amber, copal. Copal is a tree gum from trees still in existence. The kind that is encountered in the trade, however, is usually fossil. Much of it comes from the small island of Zanzibar, while "copal" from kauri trees comes from New Zealand. Even the fossil copal is much more recent than simetite and may be only a few thousand years old. It can be easily recognized, by the fact that if you hold it in your hand for a while, it begins to feel sticky. It softens when touched by alcohol, which will almost dissolve small pieces.[4]

"Canadian amber" is even more recent than copal, and no real "succinite" has yet been found in the Western Hemisphere. But true amber does occur in a few places other than the Baltic. North Sea amber is, of course, the same; most likely there was a blue-earth deposit in the sea in the vicinity of Helgoland. True amber also occurs in small quantities near Kiev in Russia and in Rumania near the Carpathian mountains. This "rumanite," of which about 1000 pounds per year were sold for a time, seems to come directly from a weathered blue earth deposit. Its age, at any event, is early Oligocene. The fossil rosin called "burmite" seems to be real amber too; the phrase "seems to be" being used chiefly because of the lack of adequate and reliable information.

Burmite is found in northern Burma, especially near a hill locally known as Nango-tai-maw, situated in the Hukawang Valley not far from the city of Maingkwan. It is found in Tertiary (probably Oligocene) bluish-gray clays, distributed in typical "nests," obviously a secondary or tertiary deposit. If it is not the same as Baltic amber, it certainly is a closely related fossil rosin of about equal age.

The fact that even rumanite and burmite come from secondary or tertiary sites is disappointing because as a rule a paleontologist learns as much (and more) from the surroundings of a fossil as from the fossil itself. Things being as they are, the reconstruction of the amber forest rested entirely with the "little fly" and the other inclusions. Fortunately they were numerous. The Amber Collection of the Albertus Universität, which had absorbed the collection of Stantien & Becker, numbered 70,000 specimens in 1914. All in all, some 120,000 inclusions must have been seen by scientists at one time or another before this collection was destroyed by fire during World War II.

While the amber itself is the product of a pinelike tree, called *Pinites succinifera,* the most numerous inclusion of a vegetable nature is not

---

[4] Linseed oil, oil of turpentine, alcohol, ethyl ether, benzene, chloroform, and acetone dissolve between 15 and 23 per cent (by weight) of true amber. Best solvent is aniline, which will dissolve between 30 and 31 per cent. Results vary with the specimen under investigation.

from the tree which exuded the amber rosin. Most numerous are oak tree blossoms or parts of them. Not less than fifteen varieties of oak have been distinguished from such parts. In addition to the oak trees, there are remains of many beech trees, chestnuts, and maples, as well as of *Ilex,* the well-known Christmas holly. One tree which seems to have been reasonably common was *Juniperites,* a relative of our present-day juniper. Mistletoe has been identified too, and about a dozen pine trees. Botanists are not too certain about the number of varieties of pine, because while other trees are represented by inclusions of flowers and of leaves, or by leaf prints of now decayed leaves on which a flow of amber hardened, the pine trees are represented (in addition to pollen in the amber) mostly by fragments of wood, and it is hard to distinguish pine varieties clearly from wood fragments only.

The list so far reads like a list of trees one would expect to find in a forest growing in southern Sweden, which was located in the latitude of today's East Prussia. But a plant inclusion that was identified rather early—in 1858—was two blossoms of a cinnamon tree. This find was later corroborated by one with the leaf of a cinnamon tree. Then there were very fine leaf prints of palmetto, and as soon as a botanist—the then very famous Heinrich Robert Goeppert of Breslau—went to work on the material, remains of four different kinds of palm trees turned up. One of them was a very fine specimen of a date palm blossom. One set of inclusions proved that at least one variety of the age-old cycad trees had grown in the amber forest. Right next to it grew olive trees and sandalwood. Laurels were represented, as were geraniums.

None of this sounds like the Baltic of today. The shores of the Mediterranean are the nearest place that some of the plants on this list can be found now. But some point to areas still farther from the amber coast. The palmetto alone suggests Florida and the low southern parts of the state of Georgia. The most beautiful and biggest flower found in amber —1¼ inch across—is one of the *Stuartias,* also called "silky camellias," three varieties of which now grow in the United States and one in Japan. There were magnolias, which now grow in the United States and in Japan. Even one of the pines (*Pinus baltica*) resembles most closely the present *Pinus cembrifolia,* or red pine, of Japan, while another reminds experts of the larch of today.

There is no forest anywhere on earth today that is a precise counterpart of the amber forest. But if such a forest grew anywhere, it would probably be in northern Florida, not in Europe. The reason for this can be found in the change in today's forests made by the glaciers of the Ice Age. Coming down from the north, these ice masses pushed the existing forests, then apparently very much alike in northern Europe, North America, and extreme eastern Asia, ahead of them. In America and in the extreme Asiatic east there were no east-west mountain chains, and the forests could recoil in what our war-trained generation is likely to call "elastic defense." America, therefore, kept its *Liriodendron* (tulip tree), its catalpas and palmettos. They could go far enough south to escape the ice and come back north afterward, as far as climatic conditions pleased them. But in Europe the Alps formed a southern rampart beyond which no vegetation could go, especially since that rampart sent out glaciers of its own. Such forms which could not literally weather the climate simply died out there. Naturally, this does not mean that the plants of the amber forest, or the living relatives of those plants, could grow in East Prussia now or even that they would have come back if the absence of the Alps had permitted them to escape in the first place.

There is no doubt that Eocene East Prussia (or whatever land there was in that general area) was warmer than the area is today. But it did not need a truly tropical climate to support such a forest. Experts are satisfied that a general rise in temperature of about 10 degrees Fahrenheit all the year round would be sufficient to account for everything that has been found.

Although the amber forest must have had many pines—how else would we know about it?—it was a very mixed forest, and some of the "other" trees have even left something like amber themselves. Four different types of "other" rosins and/or tree gums have been found in the blue earth. One must be a pine rosin, but not from the amber pine. Utilizing the Latin name for Danzig (Gedanum), geologists named it "gedanite"; it looks like the transparent yellow form of amber, of strangely pale color, say like yellowish wine. As distinct from succinite, this gedanite is completely soluble in linseed oil. It is also much softer than true amber and far more brittle.

Next in line of the near-ambers we have glessite; the name, of course, is a resurrected version of the old Germanic name for amber. Glessite is the rarest of all. Like gedanite, it is much softer than true amber. Its color is an opaque brownish yellow. No inclusions have ever been found in glessite, or at least none was ever recorded. If some were to show up they might furnish a clue to the type of tree which produced glessite. If we go by general similarities it is still possible that glessite, like amber and gedanite, is, loosely speaking, a pine rosin; that is, it probably was produced by one of the conifers, if not by a true pine or fir.

That is almost certainly not the case for the two others which still have to be mentioned. Their names are stantienite and beckerite, in honor of that firm which did so much to bring amber not only to the "marts of commerce" but also into the study of the scientist. Stantienite, the *Schwarzharz* of the workers in the amber mine, is a dull black in color, completely opaque without a hint of transparency even in thin slivers. It is excessively brittle, and does not contain even a trace of succinic acid. Nor is it soluble in any of the substances which will dissolve at least a portion of true amber. Beckerite, the *Braunharz* of the miners, is in many respects similar to stantienite. It does not contain any succinic acid either and is noticeably heavier than amber. In color it is usually brown, sometimes a grayish-brown, and it is also opaque. Although the *Harz* in the German names means pine rosin, both these substances are obviously fossilized tree gums from trees far removed from pines and firs. Which trees are responsible for their existence is not known; if their relatives still flourish somewhere it is most probably in tropical countries. Remember, northern Europe was warmer then.

The animal life of the amber forest, as far as we know it from inclusions, also points to a warmer climate, though the evidence requires a little more expert knowledge to be visible. One ant is apt to look like another ant, even to a general zoologist, and it needs an expert to recognize the inclusions as tropical forms. Among those found is one which now occurs especially in Ceylon and which has the curious habit of living in the trees and making nests by "weaving" leaves together with fine threads. The ant itself does not have any organs which can produce such threads, but its larvae do. The adults, therefore, produce their nests of living leaves in the following manner: one "gang" holds the leaves together with its mandibles, while another "gang" holds its own larvae in its mandibles. A gentle squeeze sets the larva to spinning, and once the threads have dried and hardened the others can let go, to proceed to the next leaf. Such ants occur in amber; one has been found holding a larva. There are also lots of "spider webs" in the amber. Some of them may have been spun by ants; others are decidedly spider webs.

There is one beautiful piece showing the net of a spider where you can still see even the fine drops of sticky substance which holds the insects. This particular piece of net is indistinguishable from that of the present European form *Epeira diademata,* also known in Europe as the "cross" spider, because of the markings on its back. In another case a spider was found with an uncompleted meal, a lot of insect legs sticking out from a small cocoon of spider web.

In addition to ants and spiders, there are numerous termites, again indicative of a warmer climate, since northern Europe has no termites now. Then there are earwigs, numerous cockroaches (some closely allied to present tropical forms), and equally numerous moths, some of them prettily colored. There are cicadas, praying mantises, "stick insects," and beetles. Some of the larger ones still show their furious attempts to free themselves from the sticky substance. Among the beetles there are some types which now live a parasitic life in ant hills; presumably they did the same then. Several of the forms would be pronounced American by an entomologist if he were handed living or freshly killed specimens. Surprising is the large number of caddis-flies—no less than 152 varieties of them have been classified by patient researchers. Mayflies and ant-lion flies are also common. A very pretty specimen of a fairly large cicada shows its wings turned upside down, obviously from trying to pull away from the liquid rosin. That such attempts sometimes succeeded is proved by a few pieces showing the legs of mosquitoes, the owners of which apparently escaped by sacrificing a limb. Several pieces show honey bees, in a few cases complete with pollen-stuffed yellow "pants."

It was the late Father E. Wasmann, S.J., who emphasized that researchers should pay attention to the types of insects found together in the same piece of amber. He pointed to a bug as an example—"bug" used in the strict entomological sense of an insect of the suborder *Heteroptera* of the order *Hemiptera* of the insects. The bedbug is a typical if unpleasant representative of the true bugs, but most of the very many varieties known are plant-juice feeders which are of concern only if they attack fruit trees. All of them have a strong smell and most of the time that smell is horrid, but there is one variety in tropical Asia which smells overpoweringly of reseda blossoms. Father Wasmann knew of the bug *Ptilocerus ochraceus* of Java, which has feathery tufts of hair, exuding a substance which attracts ants of the type *Dolichoderus*. Whatever it is that *Ptilocerus* produces, the ants are intoxicated and possibly even anesthetized by it; they offer no resistance when the bug picks one after another as victims and sucks their body liquids from them. In one piece of amber Father Wasmann found a specimen of such a bug, somewhat smaller than *Ptilocerus*. He called it *Pro-ptilocerus* and could point out that less than half an inch away there were two heaps of ants of the variety common in amber, *Dolichoderus tertiarius*. Their heads and antennae looked normal, but their abdomens had shriveled to empty bags. *Pro-ptilocerus* had done in the amber forests what *Ptilocerus* is still doing in Javanese jungles.

A more amusing example of the age of certain insect habits is provided by an inclusion of *Chelifer*. This is a tiny insectlike creature which looks like a scorpion without a tail. The group is called pseudo-scorpions or, because they are sometimes encountered in old books, book scorpions. Because of their tiny size they are not very mobile, but time and again somebody has claimed to have found one clinging to a mosquito or similar insect. At first this was disbelieved completely. Then it was thought to be an accident. Then it seemed as if it might not be accidental, after all. And then Dr. Adolf von Bachofen-Echt published a photograph of an amber inclusion from his own collection, showing a pseudo-scorpion (family *Chernetidae*) clinging to a mosquitolike insect (family *Braconidae*)—indubitably the first aerial passenger on record.

Animals which are not insects are comparatively rare in amber, mostly, one should think, because they were bigger and had strength enough to extricate themselves even if they happened to be caught. Some small scolopenders are known and a few small earthworms, also about a dozen land snails, two each belonging to the types *Hyalina* and *Vertigo,* now living in North America and East Asia, respectively. Only one vertebrate animal has ever been found in amber. In 1875, a young lizard,

minus the tip of its tail, was discovered. The total length of the lizard
and its tail, as far as preserved, is 1⅝ inches. Because the gases that had
developed during decomposition of the body made it hard to see, Richard
Klebs, who was in charge of the collections of the firm of Stantien &
Becker, broke the piece open for more detailed examination. (It was later

Amber inclusions

(Top left) Beetle (*Diopsidae*), now occurring only in tropical countries; (top right)
Schindalmonotus hystrix, a very small member of a class of the *Myriapoda* (millipeds)—
the identical species is now living in South Africa; (bottom left) *Cheiridium,* one of the
"pseudo-scorpions"; (bottom right) another "pseudo-scorpion" riding a mosquito-like
insect.

glued together again.) This action can be regretted now because modern
methods of investigation could have learned much from the "few
charred remains" which were found inside the hollow space. But Klebs'
work showed that the lizard is almost identical with a young specimen,
the same size, of *Nucras tesselata,* a lizard now living in tropical and
southern Africa.

All other "inclusions" of vertebrate animals are fakes. Among them, frogs are especially common. Because of their crudeness and because they are so frequently found, Professor Karl Andrée of the Königsberg Amber Collection once suggested that they may have been made as charms rather than as deliberate nature fakes. A "viper in amber," mentioned by Roman authors, has not been preserved. It may actually have been a young snake but might as easily have been an earthworm, since earthworms do occur in amber.

But while there are no other actual inclusions of vertebrate animals, larger animals have left traces of their presence in the amber forest. There are several specimens of cast-off reptile skin—probably lizard, because lizards shed their old skins in pieces, while snakes usually crawl out of their old skins so that it is left behind more or less as a whole.

One especially nice piece shows the footprint of a small mammal. The rosin must have been on the forest floor and quite soft when the mammal stepped on it, leaving a deep and very clear imprint of a narrow sole and four toes. In spite of the depth of the print there are no claw marks, possibly indicating that it was a small carnivorous mammal with retractible claws like those of our cats. A much more definite "trace" of a mammal is a flea, more precisely two fleas. The first amber flea was a specimen in Richard Klebs' collection which was investigated by Alfons Dampf and named *Palaeopsylla klebsiana*. Although one flea may look very much like another flea to a layman, experts can tell them apart. Fleas, in fact, are almost as good as labels. They are usually so well adapted to a host's hair and skin that they either can't or won't accept a different host. Among the fleas of today there is none which is a precise counterpart of the amber flea. The ones which most closely resemble it are parasitic on insectivores, like shrews. Large—which means about squirrel-sized—shrews are now all tropical and the majority of large present-day shrews are tree shrews.

Whether the rather frequent tufts of hair which can be found in amber are those of tree shrews, as one would expect from the geological period as well as from the strong hint provided by the flea, is an unanswerable question. The classification of small tufts of hairs of animals—extinct animals, to make it worse—is an almost impossible job, especially since these hairs are imbedded in amber so that no serological tests can be made. But Dr. Adolf von Bachofen-Echt of Vienna, one of the most patient explorers of the amber fauna, feels that he has succeeded in one case. That particular specimen of hair is tentatively classified as having come from a dormouse. Incidentally, if even single hairs of present-day bats were found in amber, their identity could be established. One could not always identify the species, but one could be positive in saying "bat." Of course scientists have looked for bat hairs, and Dr. von Bachofen-Echt has a few specimens which he believes to be bat hairs. They are not identical with any present-day type, but their structure is such that they faintly suggest bats and fail to suggest anything else.

Birds also have left traces—mostly feathers. Most of these are torn and twisted and wrenched out of shape, indicating that they were still attached to the bird when they touched a fresh amber flow. Only rarely does one find an undamaged feather, presumably blown to a spot of fresh rosin by the wind. Single small bird feathers are also hard to identify, but at least three cases can be taken as established. One feather indubitably belonged to a woodpecker. Another one came from a titmouse. The third case is especially interesting, because the feathers have been identified with a bird which no longer occurs in Europe. Woodpeckers and titmice are now European as well as American forms, but the motmot (*Momotus*) is now restricted to Central and South America. These motmots form a family of their own, but are allied to the bee-eaters of the Old World, which they also resemble in external appearance.

As has been mentioned, many bird feathers look as if they were torn off the birds' bodies. Doctor von Bachofen-Echt has his own ideas. He has found quite a number of pieces of amber showing half insects of various kinds. One can see that some of them were slightly dislocated after they were imbedded. The conclusion is that these were partially caught insects and that birds tore off what was still accessible. Naturally some feathers were lost during this procedure on occasion.

In spite of what some books state, the great majority of the inclusions are the actual insects and parts of plants and not just "hollow casts which give the illusion of being life-like in spite of their total lack of substance." This idea was once advanced by a scientist named A. Tornquist, and seems to have appealed to some writers because of its strangeness. What Tornquist described does sometimes happen. Sometimes the insect originally imbedded has decayed completely without leaving any palpable substance. But that is the rare exception, not the rule, as Tornquist wanted to make out. That he was mistaken was proved almost immediately, especially by one Nikolai Kornilovitch who published papers with such titles as "On the structure of the leg muscles of Tertiary amber diptera." To the regret of experts most of Kornilovitch's papers have been published only in their original Russian. Later Hanns von Lengerken succeeded in actually freeing tough beetles from the enveloping amber.

A final point which must be mentioned is a concept evolved by Professor Hugo Conwentz, who continued the work on the trees of the amber forest after Professor Goeppert died. Conwentz, like everybody else who stopped to think about it, was appalled by the amount of amber. Goeppert's calculations showed that the blue earth contains (or contained originally) some 10,000 million pounds of amber. Later calculations, depending on their assumptions, halved or doubled that figure. No matter which figure you are willing to accept, it is enormous, since we are dealing not with the weight of the whole forest (as in coal seams) but with the weight of a product of only a certain kind of tree in that forest, and with that product only in secondary deposits.

Conwentz felt that a special explanation was needed. Normally the flow of rosin from a pine tree is a protective measure. The rosin seals a wound against moisture and bacteria or fungi. Sometimes a piece of broken branch is completely soaked with rosin, now as well as then. But Conwentz could display enormous pieces of amber which had formed in the trees themselves, dissolving the tissue around them like a gigantic abscess. This too happens nowadays, but it is not normal. Conwentz came to the conclusion that the amber trees were not normal, that the rosin production which had started as a protective reaction became pathological in itself, that the trees were weakened by a disease-like overproduction of rosin, that they suffered from "succinosis."

Whether the concept of "succinosis" is needed or not is a matter of opinion. In Conwentz' time radioactivity was not known, hence there was no way of measuring the duration of geological periods as accurately as we can do it now. In fact, the measurements (embodied in the table that appears earlier in this chapter) give figures about ten times as large as those Conwentz used. The answer to the concept of "succinosis" is probably "a million years of accumulation." Spread over a million years, the yearly amber flow from the trees is around 10,000 pounds, which is a rather reasonable figure. If we collected all the naturally flowing pine rosin in a large forest now, we would probably get a similar amount. The only thing against the idea of a million years' accumulation is that one should expect to see changes, so to speak to see evolution at work, over such a time interval. Since we apparently don't, the amber forest "must" have lasted a far shorter time—this has nothing to do with the duration of the period itself—and the 10,000 million pounds, or whatever, need succinosis for an explanation. But that counterargument is probably wrong for another reason. The Tertiary period was, as we know for certain, the period in which the mammals evolved and diversified into all the kinds we have now, plus many that are no longer with us. But the plants we now have existed more or less at the beginning of the Tertiary. And so did the insects. The groups in which changes are to be expected happen not to be preserved, their individual members having been too large to be trapped by amber rosin.

3: Footprints in Red Sandstone

ONE OF the stories a professor of mine liked to tell had as its central character a minor Russian nobleman who owned an estate at the seashore in the vicinity of Riga. Said nobleman, the report ran, was in the habit of inviting artists, writers, composers, and scientists to his estate for the summer months. One summer one of the guests asked why Professor so-and-so, an astronomer, had not yet arrived. "Because," replied his host, "I did not invite him this year." The guest, feeling that something was amiss, merely said "Oh," but he did not have to wait long for an explanation. "That man," the host continued, "is an outrageous liar. Last time he was here he tried to tell me that he could measure the height of the mountains on the moon."

Measuring the height of the mountains on the moon (from the length of their shadows) is a rather elementary problem in trigonometry, but let's not go into that here. I recount this story merely because the one I am going to tell may sound equally incredible. It has to do with footprints, fossil footprints of an unknown animal, nicely preserved in red sandstone from the Triassic period, but without any bone to go with them. And the problem was to determine not only the size but also the shape and the type of the animal which caused them, without any clue other than the footprints themselves. Just to make things a little more baffling, these footprints happened to have a highly misleading shape.

The first specimens of such prints were found a little more than a hundred years ago and the case made its entry into scientific literature in the then customary form of a printed "Open Letter." Its author was a Professor F. K. L. Sickler and the letter was addressed to the very

famous anatomist Johann Friedrich Blumenbach, professor of medicine
at the University of Göttingen. It was published in 1834 and the title
deserves to be quoted in full, not because it is a very good title but because it contained virtually all the information then available. It read:
"Open Letter to Professor Blumenbach about the very strange reliefs of
tracks of prehistoric, large, and unknown animals, discovered only a
few months ago in the sandstone quarries of the Hess Mountain near
the City of Hildburghausen." [1]

Hildburghausen is an old and small city, situated some 40 miles south
of the better-known Erfurt in Thuringia. The sandstone quarried there
is a rich deep red color; the castle of Heidelberg and the cathedral of
Strasbourg are built of stone of that type. Quite often it splits naturally
into thick slabs, as if there had never been a natural fusion between
layers, but only a kind of superficial hanging together because of the
weight of the layers piled on top. It was in such places, where the stone
split naturally, that the prints were found, usually the lower slab with
the original imprint and the upper slab with a precisely fitting raised
cast of the print.

I have not seen the originals which caused Professor Sickler to write
his Open Letter, but I have seen the specimens that were in the collection
of the Natural History Museum in Berlin. They made the sense of
surprise and wonder which is apparent even in Sickler's deliberately
stiff wording quite understandable. The dark red stone is flat, sometimes
with a faint "wavy" contour which is more apparent to the touch of the
hand than to the eye. And in the middle of such a flat stone there is suddenly the perfectly clear and rather deep print of a hand. Usually that
handprint is somewhat too large for a human hand to fit well and when
you try it you also find that the proportions are not quite the same. The
fingers are much thicker and heavier, and so is the thumb, while the
palm is too wide near the fingers and too narrow at the other end.

Still, the similarity, at first glance, is almost breathtaking. The differences do not show until one proceeds from general "looking" to detailed
examination. In many of the better specimens, there appears a tiny hand-

---

[1] *Sendschreiben an Prof. Blumenbach über die höchst merkwürdigen, vor einigen Mona-
ten erst entdeckten Reliefs der Fährten urweltlicher, grosser und unbekannter Tiere in
den Hessberger Sandsteinbrüchen bei der Stadt Hildburghausen.* (Kesselringsche Hofbuch-
handlung, 1834.)

print, like that of a child, immediately in front of the large handprint. And a good number of such slabs are overlaid with an irregular network of criss-crossing ridges—"ridges" because this is usually clearer on the "casts" on the upper slabs—which do not puzzle a trained observer for a minute. They can be seen almost anywhere now after a succession of hot days when puddles have dried out and the left-over mud has cracked. With enough material it was easy to find specimens where a print had

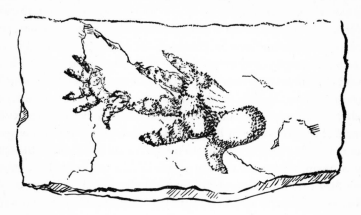

Prints of *Chirotherium barthi*

been ripped apart by such a crack and other specimens where the print had been made over an already existing crack.

The general picture was clear almost from the outset. The area where workmen now quarried red sandstone from the flanks of the Hess Mountain had once been desert, wind-blown sandy desert. Either it rained occasionally, or else a river flooded the area periodically, as the Nile has done all through human history, and then there were places where a footprint could be preserved, at first temporarily, in hardening mud. And if wind-blown sand covered these prints deep enough so that the next moistening, whether a river flood or a rainfall, did not soften the old hardened mud again, the prints lasted to our time, the sand becoming sandstone under the pressure of other deposits piled on top of it.

Considering the shape of these tracks it is not surprising that discussion began at once, *furioso e fortissimo*. To Friedrich S. Voigt the whole case was perfectly simple. These were the tracks of a giant ape—let's call him *Palaeopithecus*. Others shook their heads, especially Alexander von Humboldt. Apes are rare and tropical and Hildburghausen was not in the tropics. More likely the tracks belonged to a large marsupial, something like the kangaroo of today. One Professor Link, who wrote in French, preferred to believe that it might have been a large toad—quite large since a large track is about 9 inches long. Then Voigt revised his opinion in part. He had a large track, presumably one where the imprint of the thumb had either broken off or happened not to show, and he declared that this must have been a bear, "possibly the famous cave bear itself." But he also had much smaller tracks of somewhat different shape; these must have been made by a monkey, "probably" a mandrill.

Nine different papers on the "Hess mountain quarry tracks" appeared in 1835, the year after the publication of Sickler's Open Letter. One of these nine, written by a Dr. Kaup, made the one lasting contribution of that year: he named the tracks, or rather the animal that had caused them. Of course nothing was really known about them except their shape. But that was enough for a name—after all, by order of the school commission one had spent six years learning Greek; now apply what had been learned. The tracks looked like hands; the Greek word for hand is *cheiros*. Unfortunately all safety stopped at that point. Did the animal that had made the tracks belong to the reptiles? If so, since *sauros* is Greek for "lizard," the name would be *Chirosaurus*. But if it was a mammal the name would have to be *Chirotherium*. Dr. Kaup believed with von Humboldt that it had probably been a marsupial and hence a mammal, but he still was careful. The title of his paper read: "Animal tracks of Hildburghausen, Chirotherium or Chirosaurus."

Later usage dropped the "chirosaurus" so that the tracks came to be called "chirotherium tracks" in all books in any language. It is unfortunate that it was the wrong term which was retained. We now know that the animal was a reptile, but the name still is chirotherium.

For a few years it seemed as if the mystery surrounding these tracks would remain centered on Hildburghausen. But in 1839 there appeared in the *London and Edinburgh Philosophical Magazine* a report by P. G. Egerton, with the title: "On Two Casts in Sandstone of the Impressions of the Hindfoot of a Gigantic Chirotherium, from the New

Red Sandstone of Cheshire." Egerton's article dealt in the main with the tracks to which the title refers and which had been discovered near Storeton in 1838. But he could point out that chirotherium tracks had actually been discovered first in England. Some had been found in 1824 in the sandstone of Tarporley (near Chester, also in Cheshire) but had been neglected until the Storeton tracks came to light. Of course the Storeton find, two "handprints," each about 15 inches long, was impressive because of its size. The Tarporley tracks were smaller and apparently not very clear.

France was brought in when Daubée, in 1857, published a contribution in the *Comptes rendus* of the French Academy of Science, dealing with the *découverte de traces de pattes de quadrupèdes* in Triassic sandstones of Saint-Valbert, near Luxeuil (Haute Saône). Between these two dates, the second English and the first French, more had been found in Germany, in Hildburghausen as well as in other places. That the mysterious hand-animal had also lived in what is now Spain was reported for the first time in 1898 by Calderón in the *Actas de la Sociedad española de Historia natural*. Several years later chirotherium tracks were found in America; the reason they were discovered so late is clear from the place names occurring in the following short quotation, taken from a recent authoritative publication: [2]

> Well represented in North America in Lower and Upper Moenkopi of Little Colorado River region by total of eight species. Chirotherium occurs as far east as Snowflake, Arizona, and as far west as Rockville, Utah, a lateral distribution of 250 miles. . . .

The main problem all through the history of the chirotherium tracks was, of course, "What kind of animal made those tracks? How did it look?" But before we go into that we should gain a better idea about the age of the tracks. You remember the discussion about the age of amber and the names of the major geological periods mentioned there. Before our planet entered the Present and Recent periods, there was the Pleistocene period, also known as the Ice Age, lasting about one million years. Before that we had the Tertiary period; before that the Cretaceous

---

[2] Frank E. Peabody, "Reptile and Amphibian Trackways from the Lower Triassic Moenkopi Formation of Arizona and Utah," *Bulletin of the Department of Geological Sciences,* vol. 27, n . 8 (University of California Press, Berkeley and Los Angeles, 1948).

(it lasted about 65 million years), and before the Cretaceous the Jurassic —of about 35 million years. And before the Jurassic there was the Triassic period, also estimated to have lasted 35 million years.

The word "Triassic" itself hints that it has three clearly distinguishable subdivisions, usually called Lower, Middle, and Upper Triassic, the last, of course, being the most recent. It so happened that German geologists went to work on this period first and they naturally used German names. They called the Lower Triassic *Buntsandstein,* which is simply a contraction of the two words *bunter Sandstein,* meaning "colorful sandstone." Part of this has been adopted into geological English so that an English or American geologist will calmly say—to stick to our theme—"chirotherium tracks occur mainly in the middle Bunter." The Middle Triassic was called *Muschelkalk* by the German geologists. *Muschel* means any clam, while *Kalk* does *not* mean chalk, but limestone. That particular word is used in full if there is need to refer to this specific formation in Central Europe. The Upper Triassic was called *Keuper* by the Germans (a miner's term), and this, too, is used in English when the European formation is under discussion.

All finds of chirotherium tracks in continental Europe can be dated as Bunter, or Lower Triassic, which makes their average age about 190 million years. Only in England have chirotherium tracks been found in the Keuper—25 to 30 million years later than those in continental Europe. Nobody can tell whether tracks may still be found in continental Keuper too, or whether chirotherium actually lasted 25 million years longer on English soil. I have the feeling that Englishmen would be the first to subscribe to the latter hypothesis.

Naturally there were several species in Europe too. If the number of tracks is an indication of the abundance of a species, and not just an indication of some special habits which produced more tracks in places where they might be preserved, the most common variety was *Chirotherium barthi,* so named by Dr. Kaup. Sickler himself established a smaller form which he called *Chirotherium minus.* Later his own name was attached to still another species, *Ch. sickleri,* which is the smallest yet known. Its prints are only 3 inches long, as compared to the 9 inches of *Ch. barthi* and the 15 inches of Egerton's *Ch. herculis.*

All this, however, would have been prettier by far if the red sandstone had been kind enough to yield some fossil bones too. Scientists hovering around the quarries of Hess Mountain were quite certain that it would, sooner or later. After all, a chirotherium must have died somewhere, sometime, in the area where it had lived. Even if one assumed that it could defend itself most effectively against attackers, there was still old age. And there was thirst—remember it was a desert area.

Whether the corpse of an animal in a desert area will fossilize depends entirely on circumstances, which most of the time are against it. The likely thing to happen is that the body will be torn apart by hungry carrion eaters and all the soft parts gulped down as fast as possible. The bones will be gnawed; some of the smaller ones swallowed, the larger ones carried about. What is left will be dried by the sun and eroded away by wind-blown sand. But just in the desert the precise opposite is also possible. If an animal is not killed by a predator or does not die "on the surface" from natural causes, but is killed by a sandstorm and left dead and deeply buried, the chances for preservation are excellent. The body will desiccate rather than decompose and will fossilize as a "mummy."

True desert animals do not succumb to sandstorms as often as one might think, simply because they are adapted to a life where sandstorms form a part of the environment. While they may be buried alive by a sandstorm they usually manage to stay buried *and* alive until the danger has passed. Occasionally they do die. That this did happen in the past as it happens now is demonstrated by a unique find which brings us back to the neighborhood of chirotherium, both in time and space. This is a sandstone slab, measuring about 3 by 6 feet, found about half a century ago at Hesslach near Stuttgart. Its geological age is Keuper, the youngest of the three subdivisions of the Triassic, and very young Keuper at that.

On that slab you can see the remains of twenty-four small reptiles of crocodile shape. The largest of them is, as well as it can be measured, 34 inches long. They must all have perished together in the same sandstorm. This little *Aëtosaurus,* as it has been named, belonged to a group of reptiles now completely extinct, the suborder of the *Pseudosuchia.*

Like the equally extinct *Parasuchia,* they were related to the crocodiles, but of a different branch of the family. One may translate the technical terms as pseudo-crocodiles and para-crocodiles without being too far off. It is worth noting that the little pseudo-crocodile aëtosaurus was completely encased in armor, each plate with a neat little decoration. An armor-encased body should fossilize easily, but in spite of this feature only this one slab of Keuper sandstone with aëtosaurus on it has ever been found. Obviously their customary mode of death was accompanied

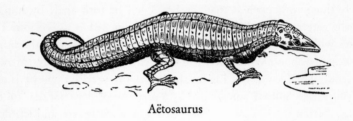

Aëtosaurus

by destruction of the body—say some other reptile's longer teeth and stronger jaws—and death in a sandstorm was a rare exception.

The scientists who were patiently waiting for chirotherium bones from the Hess Mountain quarries did not then know about this particular instance, but they knew quite well what desert conditions would or would not do and their hopes were not too farfetched. But unfortunately the hopes are still unrealized.

In addition to hoping one could guess a little more. It became clear just at that time that large mammals had not existed in Triassic days. That ruled out all guesses about apes, bears, and monkeys. But there was still a choice left. Chirotherium could have been a reptile, or it could have been a large amphibian. In the periods preceding the Triassic there had been large amphibians, grotesque, heavy, and large-headed salamanderlike monsters of crocodile size. And in 1841 the then very famous English Professor Richard Owen thought that he could point his finger at a specific group. Because of the strange labyrinthine structure of their usually enormous teeth one group of these ancient giant amphibians had been named labyrinthodonts. Remains of them had been found in England. Chirotherium tracks had been found in England too. They did not occur together, nor was it certain that tracks and bones belonged to the same reasonably short time interval. But Owen thought that it might be so and he announced that the originator of the chirotherium tracks was in all probability a labyrinthodont.

Some other paleontologists shook their heads and decided that they would not believe anything for a while. But the word of Owen happened to be the word of authority and many patiently tried to fit the known bones and the known tracks together. The whole episode cul-

Richard Owen's labyrinthodont walking cross-legged

minated in a drawing published by Charles Lyell, and reproduced above, showing a 6-foot toadlike labyrinthodont walking cross-legged. Some consecutive tracks which had been found indicated that the "thumb" was on the outside. Lyell therefore had to postulate that the right foot was put down to the left of the left foot in walking.

It was a bit strong for most informed observers, but the best they could do was to keep quiet. They had to admit that 6-foot labyrinthodonts had existed. They had to admit that some of them were generally toad-shaped. All they could really say against Lyell's picture was "We don't like it." They could not show how the originator of the handlike tracks had really looked. Nor could they produce tracks of labyrinthodonts to show that they had been different from those of chirotherium. The result was that between 1855, the date of publication of that drawing, and 1915, the choice consisted of either acceptance or resignation. Bones had still not been found, and a fact which D. M. S. Watson had pointed out in the *Geological Magazine* (December 1914) was in itself not conclusive. Watson had noted that whenever there were consecutive tracks the trackway proved to be quite narrow. This pointed to an animal of narrow build, probably tall. Probably a reptile. But those that were not yet tired of the discussion could say with at least equal justification that a trackway resulting from a cross-legged walk would of necessity be quite narrow.

In 1917 a graduate student, K. Willruth, who devoted the thesis for his doctorate to chirotherium, came up with another idea. Part of his thesis was a paper which had been written in 1889 by a geologist named J. G. Bornemann but which, for some reason, had never been published. Bornemann had emphasized that a single spoor might teach something but that a trackway would teach much more, like length of stride, etc., etc., and that study should, therefore, be concentrated on trackways.

The advice was good, but you then could not avoid running into the difficulty of having the "thumbs" on the outside. Willruth tried to find a way out of this problem; it may have been due to the fact that he had *not* read Owen's paper that he evolved a novel idea.

There is no law that says that there have to be five toes on a reptile's foot. Very many reptiles do have five toes but geological history is full of three-toed forms. And since the mammals can have anything from five toes (monkey) to a single toe (donkey), and since there are even some forms where the number of toes on the hind feet does not agree with the number of toes on the front feet (tapir), there was nothing to prevent one from assuming that chirotherium was four-toed. The four "fingers" were its true toes. But the "thumb" was no toe, it was a fleshy appendage of some sort, possibly the lower end of a heavy skin fold, which made the impression on the ground. Willruth's teacher, Professor J. Walther, not only accepted his student's thesis, he also agreed enthusiastically with the conclusions. Everybody had been fooled; we had here an animal of narrow build, progressing normally in a natural manner on hind feet which were several times the size of its forefeet. If it had not been for that accidental appendage which produced a false thumbprint on the ground all this would have been clear from the outset.

As regards the restoration of normal walk to chirotherium, Willruth's thesis was a long step forward. As for the fleshy appendage, one can only say that many a pretty hypothesis has been ruined by an evil fact. The fact in this case consisted of the great clarity of many chirotherium prints. It is not only possible to count the fingers, it is sometimes even possible to count the joints. And on such specimens one can see that the "thumb" has joints too, just what it should not have if it were a fleshy appendage. It also spoke against this idea that the "thumb" was always as deeply impressed as its two neighboring "fingers." That, in itself, indicated an internal bony stiffening.

In short, Willruth's brave guess miscarried. But it took only a few more years to bring the case of the unknown fossil to a conclusion. In 1925 there appeared a small book, only 92 pages, devoted to chirotherium tracks.[3] Its author was Professor Wolfgang Soergel, then professor of geology and paleontology at the University of Tübingen, near Stuttgart. Professor Soergel, as became evident from his book, had spent years in a concentrated study of all the tracks he could find in museums and collections in southwest Germany. While he did not neglect other types he worked especially on tracks of *Chirotherium barthi,* the most common form and a rather large one.

The "thumb," Soergel saw soon, was on the outside of the foot and was a toe. Anatomists number fingers and toes in the same manner in which musicians mark piano scores, from the inside out, beginning with the thumb and ending with the little finger. The only difference between an anatomical picture and a piano score is that the piano score counts 1, 2, 3, 4, and 5, while the anatomical picture uses i, ii, iii, iv, and v. The "thumb" of chirotherium, therefore, was not i, it was v. This is not so surprising as it may sound. If you look at the foot of any lizard—well, almost any lizard; it does not apply to some—you'll see that the outside toe v is spread apart from the remainder of the foot to a fair degree, while i on the inside is usually more or less parallel to the others. Once you realize this the whole picture becomes clear; the long confusion had been due solely to the fact that everybody who saw such a track succumbed to the impulse of putting his own hand into it for comparison, putting the right hand into the left footprint.

Looking around among fossils for a skeleton of a reptilian foot which looked about the way the foot of chirotherium must have looked, Soergel found that there was one which "fitted" closely, except for size. In Triassic layers of South Africa the fossil foot of a small pseudo-crocodile (*Euparkeria capensis*) had been found. It was definitely, as one could tell from the bones, a right foot. Digits i to iv are roughly parallel, but digit v on the outside is spread away from the remainder of the foot.

---

[3] W. Soergel, *Die Fährten der Chirotheria* (Jena: Gustav Fischer, 1925).

Soergel drew a picture of the probable footprint of an euparkeria; it resembles that of a chirotherium but not quite closely enough to be confused with one. And the foot length of euparkeria is only about 2 inches.

This settled, Soergel went on, looking for fine detail. Did chirotherium have claws? One print showed one clearly, on digit iv, but when others were examined closely faint marks of claw tips could be found, including one on digit v, the "thumb." In fact, chirotherium had possessed very strong and long claws which were carried in such a way that they were not worn by touching the ground. This strongly suggests carnivorous habits.

The next step was to examine the prints and their casts for skin structure. Folds of the "sole" were quite apparent on some pieces; scaly skin showed clearly on these and on many others. This proved that chirotherium was a reptile. A British zoologist, Richard Lydekker, had always insisted on that and had started writing "chirosaurus" in 1890, but unfortunately he had been unable to break the established habit.

Next step: check the impressions of a number of consecutive tracks for the probable sequence of movement. Soergel concluded that it must have been left foreleg, right hind leg, right foreleg, left hind leg—the normal gait of a four-legged animal. Next step after that was to measure the depth of impression, especially the relative depth of "foot" and "hand" of the same individual. It has been mentioned earlier that the "hand" is much smaller than the "foot." By measuring the depth of impression Soergel also found that the foot carried all the weight, while the hand just touched the ground.

From this fact alone the shape of the unknown animal could be reconstructed. If a four-legged reptile manages to carry virtually the whole weight of its body on its hind feet the body must be built in such a way that it almost balances. This means that chirotherium must have had a long and massive tail, heavy and stiff enough to serve as a counterweight for the body. For the same reason it cannot have had a very long neck, especially since a carnivorous reptile has to have a reasonably large head. This general shape—massive hind legs with large feet, weaker forelegs with small hands, fairly short neck with a relatively large head, and long and massive tail—is very well known to paleontologists. It is the shape of all the later dinosaurs that took to walking upright. Obviously chirotherium was evolving in the general direction of bipedal walk; it did not quite balance on two legs only, but it came close. Of the late forms of chirotherium which left tracks in British Keuper we can be virtually certain that they did walk upright. Of the earlier forms there exist a few suspicious tracks where the small prints of the front legs are un-

Chirotherium as it probably looked

accountably lacking. Maybe chirotherium could do what the Australian collared lizard (*Chlamydosaurus*) still demonstrates. When undisturbed it walks in the same manner as any other lizard, but when angered or frightened it will put on bursts of speed, holding the body stiffly curved backward and running on its hind legs only.

How big was chirotherium? Or, since there were a number of species, how big was *Ch. barthi*? It is easy to measure the length of the stride, but not quite as easy to draw conclusions from it. The length of the stride is determined not only by the length of the legs but also by their angle of "swing." Weighing carefully all the possibilities and especially all the possibilities of error, Professor Soergel concluded that the body of *Ch. barthi* must have been about 3 feet long. The tail, in order to balance the weight in front of the hind legs, must have been equally long or somewhat longer, while neck and head together measured probably a little less than the body. This, then, would make the over-all length 8 feet for *Ch. barthi,* while the total length of the smallest known varieties, *Ch. bornemanni* and *Ch. sickleri,* would work out to 14 inches.

Because it was a carnivore, chirotherium cannot have been very numerous—in any given fauna the carnivores are and must be a small minority. Because of the very numerous tracks, some early paleontologists unthinkingly concluded that it was very common. They forgot that they did not deal with a few hundred fossil foot skeletons but with several hundred footprints, and a single individual can make any desired number of footprints. One Herr Winzer, for many years the owner of the sandstone quarries near Hildburghausen, made himself a large drawing of his quarry in which each footprint was entered as it was discovered. They all fitted the pattern of *four* long trackways and it is not even certain that these were made by four individuals.

After all this was settled, Professor Soergel still had to decide where this family of reptiles belonged in the system, and which other reptiles were its closest relatives. The answers had occurred to Soergel while he was working on the whole complex of problems. The one fossil foot which most closely resembled the reconstructed foot of chirotherium belonged to a pseudo-crocodile. The general proportions of chirotherium, especially the relationship between body length, tail length, length of hind legs as compared to forelegs, all pointed just to these pseudo-crocodiles, the *Pseudosuchia* of the paleontologists, the suborder believed to be ancestral to the dinosaurs and the flying saurians. There was just one main reason for avoiding the outright statement that "the chirotheria are pseudo-crocodiles." Only *Ch. bornemanni*—which Sickler had called *Ch. minus*—was of about the same size as the other known pseudo-crocodiles of European Triassic deposits. All the others are considerably larger.

Soergel's book was received with much surprise, much enthusiasm in selected circles, and without dissent. So it had been possible, by dint of hard work and sound reasoning, to make something out of these tracks which were never joined by any fossil bone. A few dozen handbooks were rewritten and the "family" of the *Chirotheriidae* was established.

More than ten years later an interesting addition to the story was provided by another German paleontologist, Friedrich Freiherr von Huene. He had been in Brazil in the early 1930s with another paleontologist, one Dr. R. Stahlecker. Their interests had been well known, of course, and one day a Brazilian named Vicentino Presto told them about a site of fossils near a place called Chinquá. The two Germans not only found the site promising, they could also determine its age. The fossils belonged to the Upper Rio-do-Rasto formation of Brazil, Upper Triassic and equivalent in age to the German Keuper. The main find was a rather large saurian, which von Huene named, in honor both of the original discoverer and of the place, *Prestosuchus chiniquensis.*

Of course one is quite careful with fossils in the field. Most especially nobody in his right mind will try to separate the fossil bone from the stony matrix to any larger extent than is absolutely necessary for recognition. Fossils are taken out with much of the surrounding stone sticking to them. They are then usually wrapped in burlap that has been soaked in fresh plaster of Paris, more plaster of Paris is smeared on, and the whole is nailed into stout boxes for transportation. The detail work of separating bone from matrix and of mounting the bones (if they are in a shape to be mounted) is decidedly an indoor job and may take years.

Doctors von Huene and Stahlecker packed their prestosuchus and returned home. When the fossil was in a sufficiently advanced state of preparation to be examined it was found to be a pseudo-crocodile, of a size far surpassing all the forms from the same group that had been found in Europe. Its total length was 15 feet 6 inches and it stood 3 feet 6 inches tall. The shape of prestosuchus was almost precisely what Professor Soergel had drawn as the "calculated" shape of chirotherium. And the foot of prestosuchus agreed with the foot of chirotherium as Soergel had reconstructed it from the prints.

Prestosuchus is considerably larger than *Ch. barthi* and it is also considerably later. And, of course, it lived in the Southern Hemisphere, while all chirotherium tracks known were found quite far north of the equator. But it does prove that the pseudo-crocodiles could not only attain the size required for chirotherium but even grow much larger.

As for fossil remains of the European chirotherium, it is still true that there are none. But this is not so disappointing any more, because we can be quite sure that if they are ever found they will merely confirm what could be deduced from patient detail studies and by careful thinking.

4: The Dragon
from the Lias Epsilon

IN MY mind it is literally just one step from chirotherium to another extinct animal which did not resemble it in the least.

This may sound highly illogical, but it is based on a circumstance in my past. In the Berlin Museum of Natural History there was a special hall devoted to paleontology and in that hall there was a whole wall of chirotherium prints. Almost all the way to the high ceiling it was "paneled" with large slabs of red sandstone which was even more intensely red because of the sunlight that struck them slantwise through tall windows. In the days I have in mind Dr. Soergel's book was still in the process of being written and Dr. von Huene had not yet been led by Senhor Presto to the remains of his prestosuchus. One turned away from that wall of red sandstone with a sense of mystery.

And when one had turned away one faced a tall partition, also covered with stone slabs. But this stone was black, black slate, and on that black slate there showed, in beautiful bas relief which yielded even more than every smallest bone, the bodies of fishlike animals, some 7 feet long. To anybody who knew anything about them, these slabs came as a relief from the mystery of the red sandstone. There nothing was known; here it was hard to think of a question for which there was not at least a tentative answer. These slabs showed specimens of ichthyosaurs.

That particular arrangement was probably due to the accident of available space, but it happened to work out into a fine lesson in geology. The few steps the visitor to the Museum had to make in order to

69

progress from the red sandstone to the black slate transported him through a whole geological period, from the Lower Triassic of the chirotherium tracks to the Lower Jurassic of the ichthyosaurs. Expressed in terms of time, these few steps represented approximately 35 million years. They also represented a complete change of environment. It so happens that both the chirotherium tracks and the bodies of the ichthyosaurs were found in the same general area in southwestern Germany. In the Museum they were separated by some 15 feet of distance; the actual localities from which they came are about 100 miles apart. But since Jurassic slate is younger than Triassic rocks, it would even be possible for both to be found in what looks on a map like the same spot: ichthyosaurs near the surface and chirotherium tracks at the bottom of a mine shaft. Because the ichthyosaurs swam in over what had once been a desert.

When the Romans crossed the Alps from Italy into Switzerland they could see, in the distance, still another chain of mountains. These mountains were much lower than the Alps themselves and they were darkly forested. Somebody coined the name which was to be entered on the good Roman road maps. It was *Mons Jura*. It was asserted much later that this name is a Celtic word in Roman garb, namely the word *jor,* meaning forest. Whether this derivation is correct or not does not matter much. "Jura" became the name of these mountains, at first in Switzerland only. A continuation of these mountains, after an interruption, sweeps through German Swabia and then curves up into Franconia. Pliny's Roman knight, when he shipped downriver on the Danube to Carnuntum, had these mountains paralleling his course for quite some time, although not within his range of vision.

In 1795 young Alexander von Humboldt journeyed to Switzerland and saw the *Mons Jura* of the Romans. At first it probably had mostly classical connotations to him, but then he realized two things. One was that this was the same rock he had already seen in southern Germany. The other was that this "Jurassic" rock differed from any other he knew. Presumably it had formed during a specific geological period of its own, different from the other periods that had formed other rocks and other mountains. The name of the mountains was thus extended both to the German mountains and to the geological period during which they had formed. As with the Triassic, there are also three decided subdivisions of the Jurassic. Their names are now in international use, as are the German names of the Triassic subdivisions, but those of the Jurassic are British.

The lowest and oldest of the three is characterized by its decided black color. It can be called either the Lower Jurassic, or the Black Jurassic, or you can use the special name, Lias. The Middle Jurassic, again for reasons of color, is often called the Brown Jurassic, but it too has a special name, Dogger. And finally the Upper Jurassic is either that or White Jurassic or Malm. At some time somebody made the guess that the color shades might simply be the result of difference in age, that the Lias had turned black from sheer age. Well, we now know better, but apparently this simple idea stuck in people's minds. I remember overhearing a man in front of those black slabs in the Museum in Berlin explain it just this way to two boys who were probably his sons. All the time the man was obviously quoting from a book I knew too—but in that book it is stated specifically that one should not ascribe the black color of the Lias to its greater age.

The actual reason involves that change in environment I mentioned earlier. The landscape of the chirotherium sandstones at the beginning of the Triassic was decidedly desert. We are not quite sure how far to the south this desert extended. The Alps, of course, did not exist, they were formed much later, during the Tertiary period, but we do know that there was an ocean in the south. That ocean, a kind of enlarged and glorified Mediterranean, seems to have reached around the whole earth; it is technically known as the Tethys Sea. During the subperiod of the Bunter, something, presumably a coastal mountain chain, kept it out of the "Danube area," which interests us here. I am using the word Danube here in an exaggeratedly broad sense; what I mean is the area just to the north of the present-day Alps, but I don't like to mention their name since they did not exist then.

But whatever restricted the Tethys Sea during the Bunter finally gave way, thereby causing the end of that subperiod. The Tethys broke in and formed a probably shallow local sea, the result of which is the second subperiod of the Triassic, the Muschelkalk—or "clam limestone." But it was a temporary sea only, which in due course of time became land again. In the third subperiod of the Triassic, the Keuper, that area was land again, some of it at least even desert, as the mass death of little aëtosaurus has proved. However, the victory of the land over the "Muschelkalk Sea" hardly counted in the long run. With the end of the Keuper, which marked the end of the Triassic period as a whole, the Tethys Sea won out.

All through the 35 million years of the Jurassic period and the following 65 million years of the Cretaceous period most of Europe was under water. You remember that even the amber forest of the early days of the Tertiary period must have grown on a shore which came down from the north, the southern shore of an enlarged Scandinavia which was not a peninsula then, but a large island. For about 100 million years Scandinavia must have been the largest of the islands of the "European archipelago." Everything from Scandinavia south to about the present-day northern shore of Africa was flooded by the Tethys. The sea, while lasting for a long time, was probably never very deep anywhere, probably even shallower than the present Mediterranean.

The climate was warm and so was the water. The many small islands of the European archipelago must have looked very much like the South Sea archipelagos of today. There were "high islands," remains of former mountains and otherwise solid blocks of land which the sea could not wash away easily. Near them corals built reefs and formed "low islands." On those islands grew tree ferns and the now tropical cycads. On others, the remainders of old land, there grew ginkgo trees and early redwoods—we'll get to all of them in time.

The Jurassic European sea must have started small, a little bay here, a minor breakthrough there, large islands with not too much water between them. The sediments that settled in that sea were essentially mud, now hardened into the black slate of the Lias. As the water surface increased and the land area shrank, the sediments changed character. They were no longer typical black mud, but brown Dogger instead. And finally they were the sediments of the high seas, consisting largely of the hard remains of microscopic animals—white Malm.

As for the ichthyosaurs, their early forms appeared during the Triassic period. As far as time alone is concerned, they might have been found in the South-German Muschelkalk Sea that formed when the Tethys broke in from the southeast, through present-day Bohemia. Actually things did not work out quite that beautifully. In fact most of the early ichthyosaurs now known were found in California. But the first specimen came to light, almost precisely a century ago, in strata from the Muschelkalk level of Spitsbergen, that group of icy islands far to the north of the northernmost capes of the Scandinavian peninsula. The name of the type became *Mixosaurus nordenskjöldi.* By the time mixo-

Mixosaurus nordenskjöldi, one of the early ichthyosaurians

saurus was found, the later Jurassic ichthyosaurs were already well known. One might say that they had become the special friends of many scientists who sometimes became each other's enemies because of them.

Nobody can say whether ichthyosaurs were found, or how many, in times antedating the development of modern science. But for a long time paleontologists believed that the first find of which there is literary mention was made in 1708. However, the late Professor Samuel Wendell Williston, originally an assistant of the famous dinosaur hunter Othniel C. Marsh, and later of the University of Chicago, found a source about twenty years older than the one which was believed to be the first. It is a big and beautifully illustrated book of a Welsh naturalist by the name of Lluyd. The illustrations it contains are mostly those of fossil fishes, and ichthyosaur remains appear among them. Why Lluyd thought them to be fishes is very easy to understand because the vertebrae of the ichthyosaurs have the same typical shape—a bi-concave lens—as the vertebrae of true fishes. This was a mistake for which he can hardly be blamed. What makes a reader of today gasp is the explanation given by Lluyd, but even that was not completely his own invention; he took his pick from a variety of existing ideas.

Fossils, if not specifically ichthyosaurs, had been found all along since
the time of classical Greece. Since they did not interfere with philosophy
they had not caused much of a stir and the worst misinterpretation was
that they were thought to be the bones of former tribes of giants. But
later, during the Christian Middle Ages, somebody had to say something
definitive about fossils. Most theologians seem to have been quite happy
to forget all about them, after stating that these things, which sometimes
looked like bones, and sometimes like clamshells, and sometimes even
like animal skulls, but which were always stone, were merely accidental
formations. Only strangely shaped stones. Others, toying with astrolog-
ical thought, were willing to discourse at length on the influence of the
constellations on inanimate matter. I don't recall right now whether the
devil was ever blamed for their existence, but a few theologians thought
they might have been preliminary models which the Lord created prior
to the creation of the living forms.

Lluyd happened to come in at the tail end of much discussion of this
kind. He apparently did not like any of these ideas but picked up one
more trend of thought which had been handed down from the Greek
philosophers. Theophrastus of Lesbos, who died in 284 B.C., had known
fossil fishes and had also known where they had been found. There were
rivers nearby and Theophrastus considered that these rivers might have
flooded the surrounding countryside some time in the past. During that
flood fish from the river must have swum about over land and laid their
eggs before the flood retreated. For some reason these eggs had not died
off, but grown up in sand instead of water. Hence they were "stony
fishes." Lluyd elaborated only slightly on Theophrastus. He abolished
the river flood. The eggs had been laid in the sea and had been carried
up to the clouds with moisture, ultimately falling on the land as rain.

It was a Swiss naturalist, Johann Jacob Scheuchzer, also a professor of
mathematics and doctor of medicine, who fought against such ideas. To
him a fossil fish was precisely what it is to us, a once-living fish which,
after its death, had been somehow preserved. The only trouble was that
fossil fishes were usually found many miles from the nearest body of
water. But Scheuchzer had an answer: he had his Bible. Didn't the Bible
tell of the Flood? Didn't everybody know this? Didn't everybody know,

too, that this Flood had been caused by the sins of Man? Those fossil fish, which had died in the Flood, had actually lost their lives because of Man. And now Man, in deep wickedness, was not even willing to accept them as visible proof of the Flood and as reminders of the sins of his forefathers, but insisted that these fossils "are engendered by stone and marl." Scheuchzer's convictions took the shape of a book—or should one say a sermon?—entitled *Piscium querulae,* "The Complaint of the Fishes," which appeared in 1708. Among the pictures there are two vertebrae of an ichthyosaur. Strangely enough, the learned doctor did not even make Lluyd's mistake, but described the vertebrae as human, belonging to one of those sinners who had drowned in the Flood. It must have been Scheuchzer's obsession to find the bones of one of these "sinners"; some twenty years later he pictured the skeleton of a fossil giant salamander as *Homo diluvii testis,* adding (in German) "bone-skeleton of a man drowned in the flood."

The way Scheuchzer got the two ichthyosaur vertebrae is known; he himself told the story. One evening in 1708 he accompanied a friend named Langhans for a walk near Altdorf, a village not far from Nuremberg. Philosophizing as they walked along, they came to the local gallows hill, which then was precisely what its name means. Langhans noticed a piece of black slate on the ground and picked it up. Looking at it more closely, he saw eight vertebrae in a row and, struck by sudden panic terror, he hurled the stone away. Scheuchzer, being a physician, was less scared of human bones, which he thought he had recognized. First he walked his frightened friend home, calming him as well as he could. Then he returned for the piece. He kept two of the vertebrae and pictured them on Plate III of his book.

Strangely enough, another picture of ichthyosaur vertebrae appeared during the same year, in a book called *Oryctographia Norica.* It was written by one Johann Jacob Bayer who had found the bones in Jurassic deposits in Franconia and who calmly labeled them "vertebrae from a large fish." Scheuchzer grew indignant. True, Bayer at least had not taken these vertebrae to be mineralogical accidents, and thereby, in Scheuchzer's opinion, acknowledged the Deluge. But Bayer should have seen by their size that they had to be human, coming from a drowned sinner. However, in spite of Scheuchzer's insistence, other anatomists of the time quietly but firmly said "fish" when confronted with the evidence.

Things remained reasonably quiet for a century, as far as the ichthyosaur was concerned. In 1814 there followed the "skull of Lyme Regis," from a coastal town at Lyme Bay of the English Channel. It was a fine ichthyosaur skull and it was described by the Scottish surgeon Sir Everard Home. Other finds followed quickly and after some years Sir Everard began to wonder what kind of an animal it was that kept cropping up down there in Dorset. If he had also concluded that it was a large and peculiar fish, it would not have been too surprising. But he made a different mistake instead, mostly because a peculiar little animal had just then achieved some zoological glory.

Beginning about the year 1700 stories about a strange creature had emerged from Austria, usually originating in the mountains inland from Trieste. The peasants had said at first that the creatures were young dragons. To a calmer observer they could hardly be that, but they were strange enough for anybody's taste; up to 10 inches in length (but usually measuring only 8) they had the general shape of an eel. But instead of fins they had four small legs. They had two bundles of pinkish feathery gills sticking out from their heads. They were blind. And they were pale whitish in color. The mystery of their sporadic occurrence actually had the same cause as their weird appearance. The rare visitor was a newtlike animal which had adapted itself to life in waters in dark caves. Only when the caves were flooded was it occasionally washed up into surface rivers. The first complete description of this animal appeared in 1800 and the scientific name given to it was *Proteus*.

Like the real newts and the salamanders, this proteus is an amphibian. Sir Everard Home thought that the animal from the Lias of Lyme Regis was an amphibian too and, impressed by the recent description of the Austrian mystery, named it *Proteosaurus*. The name was in use—or, let's say, it stayed uncontradicted—for just two years, from 1819 to 1821. Even though Sir Everard became the first president of the Royal College of Surgeons during the latter year, critical characters from other departments of knowledge shelved the name just then. The curator of mineral-

ogy of the British Museum, Koenig by name, had gone over the material
he had received and if there was anything he failed to find it was amphibian characteristics in the skulls or skeletons. The animal, it seemed
clear to him, was either half-fish and half-reptile, or else something with
different proportions of the same ingredients. *Sauros,* as we already
know, is the Greek word for lizard. The Greek word for fish is *ichthys.*
Koenig suggested *Ichthyosaurus.*

During those same years another Englishman, William Daniel Conybeare, had prepared a careful description of the finds. Conybeare (probably predestined to zoology by his name) accepted Koenig's suggestion
and called the animal *Ichthyosaurus communis.* And then the great
French "Father of Paleontology," Baron Georges Léopold Chrétien Fréd-
éric Dagobert Cuvier, began to write *"Ichthyosaurus communis* Conyb."
That made it definite; the name has been in use ever since. Recently
paleontologists have been forced to invent several different names for the
different types, but they still say ichthyosaurs when they mean the whole
group.

Cuvier himself had characterized the old saurian as "a creature with
the snout of a dolphin, the teeth of a crocodile, the skull and the chest of
a lizard, the paddles of a whale, and the vertebrae of a fish"—but in spite
of these various similarities a reptile. Professor Richard Owen in England agreed.

Three years after Conybeare's monograph on ichthyosaurs a small
book appeared in Germany. Its author, one Georg Friedrich Jaeger, was
a man of the old school, who wrote in Latin. And he said that one did
not have to make a trip to England and brave the unpleasantness of a
Channel crossing if one wanted to see an ichthyosaur. They could be
found in fine condition in Swabia, in the vicinity of the places called Boll
and Holzmaden by their vulgar German-speaking inhabitants. They
were located in the so-called Swabian Alb—this, of course, being originally the Roman term *Mons albus,* the "white mountains." Since none
of these names appears on unspecialized maps I may add here that Holzmaden, which was to become the most famous place, is 20 miles from
Stuttgart in a generally easterly direction.

At the same time it became known that a fine skull of an ichthyosaur (probably from Boll) had been kept in the City High School of Stuttgart since about 1750. Nobody connected with the school had any idea what it was; nobody not connected with the school knew it was there.

Careful investigation followed quickly. The white crown of those not very high mountains which gave rise to the Roman name *albus* is, of course, White Jurassic, or Malm. Fossils can be found there, but no ichthyosaurs. They occur in what may be called the foothills, where black Lias forms the surface. The Lias, in turn, rests on Triassic, just as one should expect; mostly on Keuper. Underneath that Keuper there might be, in places, the much older Bunter with chirotherium tracks. It forms the surface 120 miles to the northeast. Examining the black Lias deposits carefully, experts gradually began to discover subdivisions inside the Lias. Of course not every one of them was present everywhere, but one could assign relative ages to them. And it became customary to designate them with Greek letters. The oldest was the Lias alpha. Then followed the Lias beta and gamma, above that the Lias delta. Ichthyosaurus occurred in the Lias epsilon.

The wonder was the quantity. Every visitor to the places where ichthyosaurs could be found returned with the same simile in mind: "They are as tightly packed in that slate as herrings in a barrel." And that held true for other localities too. There was (and is) a pile of ichthyosaurs near Holzmaden. Another one near Castle Banz in Franconia. Another one in Dorset in England. But not a single one in the "original Jura" in Switzerland. That the ichthyosaur came to be identified with Holzmaden in later years is due to several factors. One is that the Holzmaden specimens are especially well preserved—quality always helps. Another is that this particular "ichthyosaur catacomb," as it has been called, was closer than any other to a large city with a natural history museum and a staff of scientists. This was Stuttgart, of course. And finally one of the men whose grounds yielded ichthyosaurs, one Herr Bernhard Hauff, turned into a very specialized specialist and into a craftsman of the very first order. It was no accident that almost every ichthyosaur on exhibit, if only it came from continental Europe, had a little label attached to its frame, reading *"Ichthyosaurus quadriscissus, Dr. B. Hauff. Holzmaden, Württ."* The last word is the abbreviation for the former kingdom, later the state, of Württemberg.

But I am running away from my own story.

There was another factor which contributed to the fame of the Holzmaden deposit. The slate itself was quarried for commercial purposes, for garden walks, for tops of outdoor tables, for blackboards in schools; in general, for all the purposes for which natural black slate was used a century ago. There were numerous small open quarries, and a few of them (those that happened to cut into the epsilon stratum) yielded ichthyosaurs. Two hundred of them per year! Every year. Of course all the workmen knew that they might find slate slabs which were not just sold by weight. Old Professor Oskar Fraas, of the Museum of Natural History in Stuttgart, knew all the details of the "ichthyosaur business" and wrote a report about it in 1866. Before quoting a section in free translation I have to mention that the same Lias epsilon also yields on occasion specimens of *Teleosaurus,* an armored Jurassic marine crocodile. Fraas wrote:

There they lie in their stone coffins of many millennia, wrapped in slate, and one can just discern a rough outline like in a wrapped-up mummy. One may see the head stick out, the spine, the position of the extremities, the over-all length of the animal, and even the workman needs only a glance to see whether it is an animal with paddles or one with "paws" [*Teleosaurus*]. One with "paws" is worth three times as much. But this is not the only criterion for the price . . . a complete animal may bring as much as a hundred guilders. The workman does nothing about selling, he quietly puts his find aside in the secure knowledge that prospective buyers, representatives of scientific institutions, will call every week. No horse trading was ever performed with more zeal, with such an expenditure of eloquence and tricks, and nothing requires as much knowledge and cleverness. Since you buy "packaged goods" to begin with, you can very easily lose a good deal. And then, of course, no sale is ever final, unless the buyer obligates himself, in addition to the cash involved, to throw a wine-drinking party in celebration of the death of the old reptilian hero.

But then comes the most difficult part of the business. It is then necessary to "clean up" the saurian, meaning to free him from his slate wrapping and expose his old bones to the light of the sun. This job can be left only to experienced people, an unskilled hand will "flay" the animal. Occasionally this work takes months and the stone is taken from the bone not by means of hammer and chisel, but with engravers' tools and fine needles.[1] Nobody who

---

[1] Long after Fraas a few progressive technicians began to wield dentists' drills with great success.

has not done it himself can imagine the joy of the expert when he follows the line of a bone in the slate and, every day progressing a little bit, finally can look at the whole.

By the time this was written, scientists had had enough time to study the animal and enough material for their study so that they knew a good deal about it. The original knowledge that this was a reptile which had taken on many of the external characteristics of the fishes did not indicate in what kind of water it swam. The dolphins and the porpoises, mammals by descent and organization, have also approached the fish type in their habits and general appearance. But that does not mean that they have to be marine. Mammals breathe air; hence it does not matter to them whether the water is fresh or salty. A fresh-water dolphin is possible; in fact there *is* a fresh-water dolphin. The ichthyosaurs, being reptiles, were air breathers, as are the water-loving reptiles of today, turtles, crocodiles, and some snakes. Looking at the living water-loving reptiles merely confused the issue. The water snakes of our time live in the Indian Ocean. The crocodiles live in rivers and lakes but don't shun a stretch of salt water. The bigger turtles are marine forms, the smaller ones fresh-water forms.

Whether ichthyosaurs were marine or fresh-water reptiles could be decided only by looking at the fossils associated with them. Of course, teleosaurus, a crocodile, left the question as open as the ichthyosaurs did. But the other fossils were definite. At Holzmaden one can often find "sea lilies," in technical language crinoids. These crinoids are now a rather rare tribe of marine animals. They are related to the sea stars (miscalled starfishes), but while the sea stars are mobile, the sea lilies took to attaching themselves by means of a long stalk to something, in the manner of the present-day sea anemones, to which, however, they are not related. None of the living crinoids can survive in fresh water and all the very numerous fossil sea lilies from all geological periods have always been found in deposits which were definitely marine.

The sea lilies from Holzmaden, usually found clinging to pieces of driftwood, alone decided in favor of salt water. In addition to them, numerous extinct relatives of our squids and cuttlefish have been found. They are mostly forms with shells; of the living octopi, only the nautilus of the Indian Ocean still has a permanent shell. This nautilus is not in any way closely related to the octopi of the Lias Sea, but it demonstrates that octopi can form shells. Again, there is no living fresh-water octopus and no fossil octopus has ever been found in deposits not of marine origin.

The gradual advance of the Tethys Sea, described earlier, has actually been read mostly from the distribution in space and in time of those crinoids and the shelled octopi, the ammonites and belemnites.

The ichthyosaurs, then, were marine reptiles.

The next question was: how did they look?

Conybeare had drawn a nice skeleton with a dotted line around it, showing the probable outline of the missing fleshy parts. Cuvier had reproduced this drawing in his own works with only a few minor changes. It showed the long-snouted head with its hundreds of crocodile teeth and its rather large eyes. The body attached to that head can only be called lizardlike. Of course, instead of four legs it had four paddles, the front paddles quite large, the hind paddles very small by comparison. Then came a long tail, tapering to a point. As for the over-all size, it was usually about 7 feet, some specimens going up to 10 and 11 feet. Smaller ichthyosaurs, of an over-all length of about 3 feet, showed relatively larger heads, and were obviously young individuals. A few vertebrae of much larger size had come to light, presumably of another and much larger variety.

The large number of fossils indicated that the ichthyosaurs probably lived in "schools" like our dolphins, and a few scientists made an additional guess. Being reptiles, the ichthyosaurs were apt to lay eggs, like crocodiles and marine turtles. Marine turtles come ashore for this purpose; the ichthyosaurs probably did too. Of course they would have been quite clumsy on land because of their paddles. But so are the large seals whose legs have almost changed into paddles. And the turtles that do have fully changed paddles somehow manage. So why not the ichthyosaurs?

This about sums up the ideas about the ichthyosaurs as they were held during Cuvier's lifetime (he died in 1832) and for a number of years afterward. The next step was taken by Richard Owen in 1838. Owen, during his long life, repeatedly devoted his attention to the ichthyosaurs, as did most of the German paleontologists during the nineteenth century. In fact one might say that both German and English paleontologists developed a proprietary attitude; the ichthyosaurs were their saurians and if any discussing was to be done they were well equipped to do it, both with material and with eloquence. They fully acknowledged each other and science is, of course, international. But as regarded ichthyosaurs and the paleontology of the Lias formation, Russians, Italians, Frenchmen, and Spaniards were not qualified to butt in. They didn't have any good Lias.

Owen, in looking at the British saurians from Lyme Regis, noted a number of facts. The front paddles were large, the hind paddles small. That reminded him of the whales. The whales, while mammals themselves, resembled the ichthyosaurs in their emphasis on the front paddles. So did, incidentally, the marine turtles. But the whales had gone a long step farther. They had dispensed with their original hind feet completely. To make up for the loss they had developed an enormous tail fin. And from all reports one could find it seemed as if that large horizontal tail fin of the whales did all the propelling, that the paddles in front served for steering without adding a noticeable amount of propulsion. If the ichthyosaurs resembled the whales in habitat and habits—well, of course, they didn't have to. The whales were mammals; the ichthyosaurs had been reptiles. But supposing that they did resemble them, wouldn't it be logical to assume that they might have evolved a tail fin too? Having no bones, the tail fins would not fossilize. But if there had been tail fins, there must have been muscles to move them. And the muscles had to be attached to the bones somewhere. And this will produce very typical marks on the bones and one should be able to find them.

Professor Owen did find them. The marks indicated that the ichthyosaurs had indeed resembled the whales by having a tail fin. But they also indicated that there had been a decided difference. The tail fin of the whales is horizontal; the tail fin of the ichthyosaurs must have been vertical. And there was additional evidence. In almost all specimens found, the pelvic region very neatly marked the halfway point of the total spinal column. The half from head to the pelvic region showed a curvature; from then on it was virtually straight—except that in a good many specimens the last third of the tail appeared to have been broken.

It is always the simple things which require careful thought. The last third of the tail appeared to have been broken. One should have asked, broken before or after fossilization? And if that question had been answered "before," then the next question should have been, before or after death? The men who stripped the superfluous slate from the bones and who had developed a remarkable skill for this job had failed to ask these questions. They had simply assumed that any breaks they came across had happened by pressure in the rock, long after not only this particular ichthyosaur but also all other ichthyosaurs had died. So they had straightened the breaks out, producing the long, straight, tapering tail.

Owen, having found evidence for the existence of a vertical tail fin, had reasons to think differently. That break had obviously occurred before fossilization. But presumably after death. He imagined that an ichthyosaur, having died for any one of a large number of possible reasons, would have drifted at the surface of the sea, slowly decaying. After a while the tissue had weakened enough so that it could no longer support the weight of that large tail fin. Then the tail fin's weight broke the tail. And then the drifting dead body, if luck was with the scientists, fossilized. Fortunately that had happened quite often, because, Owen assumed, the ichthyosaurs probably had habits similar to those of the seals and sea lions of today which spend much of their time at the shore. Being near the shore, a dead saurian, when its body finally sank to the bottom, stood a good chance to be covered by mud from a nearby river.

Now the scene shifts to Germany and more specifically to Holzmaden. I have already mentioned the name of Bernhard Hauff, originally just the owner of a few shallow slate quarries. Hauff's quarries happened to bite into the famous epsilon layer. Hauff became interested. Conversations with visiting naturalists, among them Oskar Fraas, guided him to systematic study.[2] More important for the whole of science, Hauff began to work with his hands on a poor specimen, trying his skill in peeling the slate from the bone. His skill, as became apparent quickly, was simply unheard of. It was not the skill of a man who had mastered a skilled trade, it was the rare skill of an artist which cannot be taught. The fossils of Holzmaden, the beautiful complicated sea lilies, the rare

---

[2] His doctor's degree, however, is honorary, bestowed upon him later with excellent reason.

fishes, the large and delicate shells of those extinct octopi which are known as ammonites, seemed to come to life again under Hauff's hands and tools. Of course they were still just fossilized bone on smooth slate when Hauff was finished. But I remember some slabs with sea lilies that had come from his workshop; it needed little imagination to believe that one saw them alive, attached to a piece of driftwood, floating in black muddy water.

To Hauff all these were incidentals, changes which were welcome because they were changes. His main work was, from beginning to end, ichthyosaurus, his beloved dragon from the epsilon layer. I am not quite sure when he began—it must have been around 1885. But I do know that he finished his three hundred and twentieth ichthyosaur in 1920. This means that he must have judged over three thousand specimens, since it was his own estimate that only about 10 per cent of all the ichthyosaurs found at Holzmaden were worth the large amount of work involved in "cleaning" them. Among the "incidentals" during this period had been twenty-five teleosaurs.

The big discovery was made in 1892. Hauff had a large slab of slate on his work table, broken in two places. That was nothing to worry about; the slabs usually broke in quarrying and as long as nothing was missing it did not matter. But it was practical to ascertain for the purpose of the work itself just where these breaks went through the skeleton. In this case, one break cut through the tail about at the point where the spine might be broken for the reasons which Professor Owen had worked out. The other break was much worse; it seemed to go right through the skull. But since the two pieces fitted together the damage could be repaired. Hauff went to work on the specimen and after about a week's work a good number of the larger bones showed. At that point a glass of water was accidentally spilled on the specimen. No harm done, slate is waterproof. Just wait till it dries. But it did not dry evenly. Hauff saw that the pattern of drying water seemed to suggest an outline around the bones, like the outline of a gigantic fish.

A day or so later some gentlemen from the Natural History Museum in Stuttgart came to Holzmaden. Hauff told them about his experience, asking whether soft parts might have fossilized in some manner and whether he should try to bring them out more clearly. This, the men from the Museum declared, would be a waste of time. They did not see how soft parts could fossilize. They also were very well satisfied with Mr. Hauff's work as it was. The water must have dried in such a pattern by pure chance. Then the conversation turned to business, specimens were nailed into boxes for transportation and gold coins clinked prettily. But after they had left, Hauff decided that he would forget the conversation. He would follow those black shadows which became visible when one spilled water on the slab.

A month later, when Professor Fraas came for another visit, Hauff confronted him with a finished specimen, *complete with skin!* Fraas was enthusiastic. Old Owen (who happened to die during the same year) had been right about his vertical tail fin. Here it was, clearly visible. Detail, however, was different. It was not a symmetrical tail fin like that of the whales. It had not broken the spine by its weight. Instead, that bend in the spine was normal; it supported the lower lobe of the tail fin, which, on the whole, looked like the sickle of the moon just before it has reached the stage of being a half-moon. A fin of similar construction existed in the living world. The shark's tail is built in the same manner, except that in the case of the shark the bone structure supports the upper lobe.

In addition, this extraordinary specimen showed something neither Professor Owen nor anybody else had suspected: a large triangular dorsal fin. All of a sudden, the shape of ichthyosaurus had been changed completely. What had appeared to be essentially a large swimming lizard with paddles instead of feet had turned out to look very familiar. In general appearance it came closest to the dolphin. Of course there are many differences. The dorsal fin, for example, does not have the shape of the dorsal fin of living marine mammals but rather of that of some living sharks. The head is different too. But what one may call the large features, the general shape, the smooth skin, and probably the coloration, too (no doubt dark above and whitish below) are all quite similar to those of the dolphins. If the ichthyosaurs were still alive nobody would mistake one for a dolphin or porpoise when seen close by. But seen from a distance one might not be sure which is which.

Unfortunately the first skin specimen had been somewhat damaged by pressure before it was found. The skin of the back between the large dorsal fin and the tail had been torn to pieces. Hauff could not recover a continuous skin line from this specimen because it was not there. And Professor Fraas, keeping in mind that the ichthyosaurs were reptiles, and probably remembering the dorsal spikes of a number of living lizards, thought that there were six small dorsal fins of irregular shape behind the main fin. That was quickly recognized as a mistake because, fortunately, more skin specimens came to light. In fact every *well*-preserved Holzmaden specimen turned out to be a skin specimen. And because there were younger and older specimens the growth of both dorsal and tail fin could be observed. Individuals which were obviously not only fully grown but old, possibly old males only, showed something else which was as unsuspected as the dorsal fin. They had a rather small throat pouch, or at least a fleshy appendage that is in the place where a throat pouch would be. Whether it actually was a pouch is still uncertain. At any event it was rare.

The skin specimens had definitely killed one of the earlier ideas. With a fish shape like that the ichthyosaurs could not cavort on the shore like seals. They were as decidedly animals of the high seas as our whales, large and small. Ashore they must have been as helpless as our whales— and presumably as doomed. Admitting this, however, produced another difficulty. The original assumption had been that the ichthyosaurs, like our marine turtles, came ashore to lay their eggs. But if they could not go ashore, what did they do?

Fossilized droppings of ichthyosaurs have been found; they have a special scientific name: coproliths. They show that the mainstay of the ichthyosaur's diet was octopods of many kinds. They also show that the saurian's lower intestine had a curious spiral twist. If we are informed about such intimate details we certainly are justified in asking about fossilized eggs. None is known. The lack of fossilized eggs made scientists scan the short list of living marine reptiles once more. The black iguana of the Galápagos islands is called marine, but actually it just swims out to eat seaweed. One could not learn anything from that example. The turtles—well, their method obviously did not apply. The sea snakes of the Indian Ocean? They do form eggs, being reptiles, but they don't lay their eggs. Instead the embryo develops inside the body of the mother and is "born alive," *not* in the manner of the mammals which by way of the placenta furnish nourishment for the embryo. The method of these sea snakes can best be understood if you imagine a bird keeping a ripe egg inside its body until the egg is hatched.

Logic alone decreed that the ichthyosaurs used this method too. The next problem was to find evidence as to whether or not the logic applied.

Bernhard Hauff had done his part. He had not only been able to locate the position of the stomach in some individuals by way of undigested parts of shelled octopi; he had also shown that there were tiny ichthyosaurs inside of big ichthyosaurs. By 1908 he had a total of fourteen such cases. Of these fourteen, seven had one young inside, two had two each. One each had three, five, six, and seven young, respectively, and one had either ten or eleven, depending on whether one wanted to count a very small batch of tiny bones.

The unborn young differed greatly in size. The largest of them was about 2 feet long, which is considerable if you know that the female in question was only an inch or so over 7 feet. The smallest measured around 7 inches and were usually in a curled-up position. The bigger ones were more or less straight. In the majority of cases the heads of the young pointed in the same direction as the heads of their mothers. The large embryos were perfectly clear and sharp, as clear as the bones of the mother. The smaller embryos had often decayed pretty badly before they fossilized.

The preceding paragraph gives the "statement of fact" issued by Hauff and the paleontologists in Stuttgart. But elsewhere that statement was received with a faint sneer. "Decayed?" "Did you say decayed before fossilization? Digested, you mean." These were embryos all right, but they were not unborn embryos. They had been eaten by others, not excluding their own fathers. We know that many fish will gobble up their own young. Some reptiles do it too. Ichthyosaurs presumably lived in the state normal for many marine animals: perpetual hunger. They grabbed and gulped down what they could get, without looking or caring what it was.

Offhand there was nothing one could say against this idea. It certainly was a possibility. Nor was it advanced without some proof. There was, first of all, the predominant position of the embryos: head forward. This did not look like a probable birth position. It looked much more like a "pursuit position": if a full-grown ichthyosaur chased a smaller one which could not swim as fast as the big fellow it would be likely to be caught by the tail and swallowed tail first. Still better proof was offered by one specimen where a young ichthyosaur was lying alongside the hard parts of octopi; obviously it had been in the stomach together with gulped belemnites.

About this last case no doubt was possible. But in the other cases there were no traces of food from which the location of the stomach could be determined. All one could do was to trace, with the aid of those specimens in which the location of the stomach was known, where it should have been and then determine whether the embryos were near that probable position of the stomach or not. At that point the discussion adopted two war cries. One was: too far forward to be an unborn young. The other: not far enough forward to be in the stomach. Of course there were incidental remarks, such as we don't know what allowance to make for individual variations; and, we can't be sure that the location of the stomach of an individual may not change with pregnancy. Much of this fight dealt with one particular specimen in the Berlin Museum. Then somebody had an idea. If an adult ichthyosaur ate a young one it would swallow it whole—reptiles eat that way. But the process of catching and turning it into proper position for swallowing should leave teeth marks. The specimen did not show teeth marks upon examination. But maybe those bones which happen to show also happen not to have marks.

The Museum's saurian was taken from the wall and X-rayed. The photographs were greeted with shouts of triumph: at least some of the embryos were damaged in a way which might be explained by teeth marks. And that proved that!

It is quite easy to lose sight of the whole picture if you find your pet theory confirmed by evidence. The evidence did prove that ichthyosaurs, like fish, occasionally ate their own young. But the young still had to be born first even if they were eaten later. Did anybody know of specimens of young ichthyosaurs unassociated with big ones, either "uneaten" or "unborn"?

Bernhard Hauff had a nice one hanging in his own living room; it was so pretty that he had not sold it. Its length was a little over 2 feet. One or two others like it were in various museums. But nothing smaller was known, except for one piece, in a curled-up position, less than a foot long.

The point was that, with the exception of this one case, all "unassociated" young that were known were quite large. So were some of the "associated" ones. In Berlin there was a 6 foot plus specimen with a young one inside, the latter about 2 feet long. The head of the young one pointed forward but only its head was in a position where the big one's stomach might have been. And the state of preservation of old and young was very much the same.

The solution was finally provided by a Stuttgart specimen and it is possible that commercial reasons had delayed that solution for a number of years. Ever since Hauff had found his first skin specimen the market had been wide open for skin specimens. Consequently Hauff subjected each new find to the water test he had discovered accidentally. If the water test indicated the presence of tail fin and dorsal fin, the specimen had a very high priority in the "cleaning" schedule. This delayed for a long time the cleaning of the Stuttgart specimen I am going to describe, because it had given a negative water test; it had no skin. I don't know when it was found, it did not go on exhibit until several years after the end of the First World War. The specimen is 219 centimeters long, which means 7 feet and slightly above 2 inches. There are three small and very poorly preserved embryos inside the abdominal cavity. And there is a large one, 59.5 centimeters long (half an inch short of 2 feet) with its head in the pelvis of the large one. The remainder of the body is outside. Quite evidently it is in the process of being born, tail first.

Mother and young died together before this birth process was quite finished. Their bodies were covered by a mud which, as that type of mud is even today, was virtually free of bacteria. They fossilized without decaying in the usual sense of the word. But the three very young embryos inside, probably still in their egg sacs, were not in a sterile environment and did decay to a considerable extent before fossilizing. One could read these things off that specimen without needing any additional information. But there happens to be a parallel among living animals. I am quoting the following from a work by Dr. Othenio Abel of the University of Vienna:

According to information received from Chr. Lütken it is well known to the Greenland Eskimos that in the case of the white whale (*Delphinapterus leucas*) the tail of the unborn young will protrude from the vagina of the

mother four to six weeks prior to actual birth. During this whole period
the pregnant mother will carry its young with the tail hanging for a considerable length from her body. At first the tail of the young is still curled but
soon straightens and when it is strong enough so that the young can maintain
itself swimming the real birth takes place. The birth, therefore, takes place
not head first but tail first.

The ichthyosaurs, being adapted to the same environment, obviously
functioned in a similar way. This, of course, completely collapses the idea

Ichthyosaur with young: *Stenopterygius quadriscissus* from Holzmaden in
Württemberg

This is a restoration of the "Stuttgart specimen," which fossilized during the long-drawn-
out birth process.

of "pursuit position." It explains why "unassociated" young are always
fairly large, 2 feet long or more, because that was their birth size. It may
be that one mating fertilized several ova which then developed to full
birth size one by one. On rare occasions there may have been an abortion
of a true egg, which would account for the single small curled-up specimen known. And the X-rayed teeth marks in the Berlin specimen may
not be teeth marks after all. Or else a few ichthyosaurs tore up a pregnant
female which had died from some other cause.

All along, scientists who investigated the ichthyosaurs and tried to
piece their life history together were, needless to say, greatly pleased with

the excellent material that came from Holzmaden. But its very excellence, both in quality and in quantity, brought up another question: what had happened at Holzmaden? How had this wonderful deposit formed?

A few facts were clear. The European Lias Sea must have had a shore nearby when the epsilon deposits formed. The type of sediment speaks in favor of this. So do occasional plant fossils, which are remains of land plants such as may be torn off by wind and blown out to sea. So does the fossil of a small flying saurian which may have been out fishing. Scientists, in fact, speak of the Bay of Holzmaden. Fishes seem to have been rare in that bay; the few that were found—in an excellent state of preservation—are of the type of our living sturgeon. The field is dominated by the large fossils. Ichthyosaurs by the ton. The skull of a much larger type of ichthyosaur, called *Leptopterygius,* which must have measured 40 feet over-all length. Considerable numbers of the marine crocodile teleosaurus. An occasional long-necked plesiosaur. And, of course, those shelled octopi. Also one small shark, which, to Hauff's satisfaction, turned out to be a skin specimen.

The generally excellent state of preservation is explained by the nature of that black mud which enshrouded its specimens about as effectively as the amber rosin entombed its insects a 100 million years later. The mystery is that the black mud almost invariably had sound specimens to enshroud. Those which we now consider poor turned into poor specimens afterward, torn apart, broken and ground up by pressure in the stone. But even these, as far as it is possible to judge, were fine specimens when they fossilized.

And that is unnatural, because among animals death is normally violent and does not leave unmutilated bodies. Also one would expect that a dead ichthyosaur that drifted ashore would have been torn apart at the seashore by large numbers of small carrion eaters, especially crabs. Well, that probably happened all the time elsewhere. But not at Holzmaden. With understandable reluctance scientists had to assume that there was something in the Bay of Holzmaden which killed the larger visitors without mutilating their bodies and which at the same time was inimical to crabs; crabs are very rare in the Holzmaden deposits.

There is only one answer: poison. Just such "foul mud," as the Germans call it, is apt to form a rather potent poison, hydrogen sulphide. Of course no crabs or marine worms would or could live in such mud, which made the carcass of a larger animal safe for fossilization. We not only have examples of such hydrogen sulphide mud now, we also know that the slate of the Lias epsilon contains considerable quantities of sulphur compounds. So do the similar deposits of Boll and of Castle Banz. The evidence for a submarine death trap is quite strong.

Now we don't have to imagine that the shallow waters of the Bay of Holzmaden were poisonous all the time. It was not necessarily a dead sea. There probably was life all the time for 10 feet of depth or so from the surface. But when a storm broke or when a large "school" of ichthyosaurs, in pursuit of a swarm of fishes or darting octopi, thundered into the bay, the thick layer of poisonous bottom mud was disturbed. The gas was released in large quantities and the bigger intruders were overcome by the poison. Those that did not accidentally escape died and finally sank to the bottom to be covered by the settling mud. The mud was impartial. It killed and preserved without discrimination: fish and ichthyosaurs, plesiosaurs and marine crocodiles, sea-lilies and sharks.

In this story of the life and death of the ichthyosaurs I could and did behave as if there were only one kind. That, of course, is not the case. I simply related the researches into the life history of the best-known form. And because Koenig and Conybeare originally called it *Ichthyosaurus communis* I have used the term ichthyosaur. Its scientific name is now *Stenopterygius quadriscissus*. There was a good reason for the change, too.

I have mentioned that an early type of ichthyosaur was found in Triassic deposits of the Muschelkalk level of Spitsbergen, the small three-foot mixosaurus. Several decades later an early type of ichthyosaur, from levels of corresponding age, was found in Nevada. It was named *Cymbospondylus* for reasons which will become understandable when the name is translated. The Greek word for "boat" is *kymbion,* while *spondylus* is Greek for vertebra. If the early type from Spitsbergen was rather small for an ichthyosaur, the one from Nevada was exceptionally large; its over-all length must have exceeded 33 feet. But in general appearance the two resembled each other. Additional fossil finds made it clear that there had been quite a number of quite different marine reptiles of the order *Ichthyosauria* when the Jurassic period began. They entered the Jurassic with at least three sharply distinct "tribes." But paleontologists had fallen into the habit of naming anything Jurassic ichthyosaurus, behaving more or less as if the existing differences were merely the differences between closely related species.

Quite some time ago, in 1904, Professor O. Jaekel began to say that things could not go on in this manner. He set an example by coining a new name for a new type. But a revision of the existing names involved a thorough study of all the available material and literature. To say that this was a formidable job is using gentle language and it was not until 1922 that another paleontologist, Friedrich Freiherr von Huene, got it done.

The best and easiest way of telling the ichthyosaurs apart was to examine the skeleton of the paddles. In the course of adaptation to life in the seas the ichthyosaurs, originally land reptiles, had changed the construction of their extremities considerably. The originally elongated bones of the fingers had turned into small round thick disks. They had also increased in number: where there should have been three bones there were ten or more disks in a row. And when you started trying to label the fingers by the I, II, III, IV, V method, you saw that even that had been changed. The numerous Holzmaden type, for example, had four fingers in the front paddle but only three toes in the hind paddle. That was bearable, but in one type you could count to eleven "fingers."

Since the paddles served as a criterion the new names referred to them. There is a Greek word *pteryx* which means both "wing" and "fin"; it could serve for "paddle" too. And "broad" in Greek is *europs,* "narrow" is *stenops,* and "slender" is *leptos.* Consequently the names of the three main types became *Europterygius, Stenopterygius,* and *Leptopterygius.*

The last of the three is the 40-foot giant from Holzmaden which has been found in England too. The second is the well-known original "ichthyosaurus," the first the one with multiple "fingers." Of this type there existed a strange offshoot, called *Eurhinosaurus,* for which one need only point to the illustration on page 94.

Of course the end of the Lias formation did not mean the end of the ichthyosaurs. There just doesn't seem to have been any more such reliable death traps as the Bay of Holzmaden. But such ichthyosaurs as have been found in more recent deposits show interesting trends. There is one from the White Jurassic of England which has been named *Nannopterygius* (Greek, *nanodes,* "dwarfish") because of its tiny paddles, the hind paddles being so small that they look useless. But it has

Eurhinosaurus longirostris, a late form of the ichthyosaurians

an exceptionally long tail. Apparently one trend was to increase speed, which could be accomplished by a more elongated shape. Another ichthyosaur, also from the White Jurassic of England, had a more conventional shape, with two outstanding characteristics. One is expressed in its name, *Ophthalmosaurus. Ophthalmos* (Greek again) means "eye"; it had enormous eyes, indicating, probably, that it hunted at night and hid during the day. Its other characteristic was that it was virtually toothless. The shelled octopi of the early Jurassic had mostly died out for unknown reasons and for eating the soft octopi teeth were unnecessary. The soft octopi were also faster.

It looks as if the ichthyosaurs had adapted themselves to speedier prey. Their early Triassic forefathers had entered the seas well armed and with considerable armor. In the early Jurassic the armor had been shed, the armament was still there. In the late Jurassic the armament was gone too, which is probably the reason why we have no ichthyosaurs left in our oceans. In the early Cretaceous the sharks, themselves a far older type than any reptile, produced a number of very large, speedy, and heavily armed forms. The ichthyosaurs, having specialized on a diet of small and speedy squids, had in the process become helpless prey themselves.

Sharks are still with us. But the last of the ichthyosaurs lived during the Cretaceous period.

5: The Mammal from the Permafrost

O F ALL the animals of the past none is better known by name to a wide public than the woolly elephant of the Pleistocene: the mammoth. And of all the animals of the past there is none which has so persistently intruded on human history as this very mammoth. The resurrections of other extinct animals, like the gigantic dinosaurs of the Atlantosaurus beds of Wyoming, or the fish-shaped ichthyosaurs of the German and English Lias, were purely intellectual adventures, requiring an advanced science to accomplish. But the mammoth was always part of human history, even when people had no conscious idea of its existence. Because of that ignorance it sometimes appeared in strange disguises. Or it cropped up in a curious roundabout manner. Or it appeared in places which were so far outside the realm of normal activities that even professional geographers had to consult maps to identify the strange place names with which it was associated.

At first the relationship between mammoth and man was simple and direct. Primitive men of the type we now call Neanderthal men hunted it. It must have been a difficult and dangerous hunt, but no other animal rewarded success with such mountains of meat and fat. A less primitive type of man which came somewhat later, the small and graceful Aurignac people, not only hunted it, they also left its portrait on cave walls. There is no disagreement about the reasons for these paintings; they figured in ceremonial rites which were to assure hunting luck in days to come. The animal which had been "captured" in a picture would not escape in the flesh. But it is quite difficult to date these paintings, even ignoring the obvious fact that they certainly are not all of equal age. A reasonably well-founded estimate for the best of these artistic efforts seems to be 50,000 B.C.

But from then until modern historical times there is an enormous gap in the direct relationship. When the famous Cro-Magnon men appeared in western Europe the mammoth apparently was no longer there, although another race of mammoths still inhabited the tundra of northeastern Siberia. The successors of the Cro-Magnon, the ancestors of the modern peoples of Europe, never knew the mammoth.

Yet they were haunted by it all through recorded history. When a river changed its course, large bones were likely to come to light. The people in the vicinity presumably kept quiet about the occurrence and avoided the spot for a while until erosion had done its work and made the bones disappear again. But that was not always easy; often there were too many witnesses present. A king ordered a palace built, and large bones were found in the ground when the foundations were put down. Monks broke the ground for an addition to the monastery and their shovels struck big bones. Many an abbot was faced with the decision of whether these bones deserved Christian burial, or should be quietly thrown away—or whether they should be saved.

One that was saved is still in Vienna, with a date inscribed on it. The date is 1443, which is the year during which excavations for an addition to St. Stephen's Cathedral were begun. This particular bone was taken to be that of a giant, as were most of the others.[1] Sometimes they were even recognized as elephant bones, especially when the geographical location was such that they could be explained as the remains of one of Hannibal's war elephants.

But not only large bones came out of the ground as mysterious reminders of something past and unknown. Many an old chronicle or description of a town or landscape contains a remark about fossilized hands of monkeys. If some accounts did not include pictures, or if the "stone hands" themselves had not been saved, we could never puzzle out just what the chronicler meant. The stone hands were mammoth

---

[1] I have told of a number of specific cases in *The Lungfish, the Dodo, and the Unicorn,* chapter 2.

molars, found separately because the jaw bone in which they had grown
had eroded. The strange designation was caused by the fact that such
a mammoth molar has several roots, often five, which were taken to be
the fingers.

And then there was the *unicornum verum,* the "true unicorn" which
was dug from the ground and which was so named to distinguish it
from the *unicornum falsum* which was traded by Norse fishermen. This
unicornum falsum appeared as a long straight staff, white or yellowish
and curiously twisted. It was relatively cheap but it lacked the fabulous
curative powers of the true unicorn and was said to be merely the tooth
of a fish.[2] The "true unicorn" was different, less hard, usually darker in
color, and a sure protection against poisoning, both deliberate and accidental. It was the highest-priced medicine there was. It was the ultimate
remedy for any sickness. It also was mammoth tusk.

There came a time, of course, when the big bones dug from the ground
no longer frightened people, when it was considered doubtful whether
those things that looked like small stuffed gloves were actually fossilized
monkey hands, and when the remaining specimens of *unicornum verum*
began to gather dust in dark corners of old pharmacies because both
doctors and patients had lost faith in their remedial value.

Just at this time the mammoth began to appear in a new form, this
time coming from the east. In 1611 a British traveler, Josias Logan, returned to London, bringing with him the tusk of an elephant. That
would have been commonplace if Logan had been in India or Africa.
But he had been in Russia, and the tusk was not a hunting trophy, but
had been bought from Samoyede tribesmen who lived near the shore
of the Arctic Ocean (more precisely the Barents Sea) at the mouth of
the river Petchora. It was not the tusk itself which was marvelous, it
was the climate of the area from which it had come.

Almost precisely a century later a Dutchman, Evert Ysbrandszoon
Ides, came with a similar tale. He had journeyed across Siberia and a
member of the party, a Russian, had told him that he had once found
the frozen head of an elephant and also a frozen elephant's foot, which
had been taken to the village of Turukhansk on the Yenisei River. From

---

[2] Actually it was the ornamental tusk of the male narwhal, a marine mammal of the
northern seas.

more recent and better-authenticated experience one may conclude that the find was probably made on the banks of the Yenisei itself.

There followed confused reports about ivory found in Siberia and large bones sticking from the frozen ground. The reason these reports were so confused is now easy to explain: mammoth and walrus were mixed together and described as one and the same animal. But the tribesmen, mostly Tunguses and Yakuts, not only failed to distinguish between the two animals, which had in common only that they both furnished ivory, they also added their own reasoning. When they came across one of these beasts it was always partly in the ground. And it was invariably dead. Their conclusion was that the animal lived underground like a gigantic mole, burrowing all its life. But sometimes it burrowed up instead of down, or it came out on the bank of a river. When it saw the light it died.

The hodgepodge of several sets of facts and native legends was not accepted in full by the scientists of the western countries. But it did indicate that there was something large and interesting in Siberia. A name had filtered through too. It was *maman, mamont,* or something like that. Englishmen, Germans, Frenchmen, Dutchmen, and Swedes decided that it had to be a Russian word. The fact is that it isn't, at least not originally. It was the name given by the tribesmen and just possibly means something like "large," though it is probably safer to say that the meaning is unknown. The reason the word was believed to be Russian was that the Russians, in referring to the indubitably existent Siberian ivory, had adopted the name in a Russianized version and called the ivory *mamontova-kostj.* The last syllable means bone as well as ivory, but when used in such a construction it usually refers to ivory.

In 1722 a Swedish officer, Baron Kagg, colonel of the Royal Swedish Cavalry, returned home from Siberia, where he had been not as an explorer but as a prisoner of war. One of his fellow prisoners, Ph. J. Tabbert von Strahlenberg, had spent whatever time he had in inquiring about those rumors of a large ivory-bearing creature, possibly of subterranean habits, and had found a Russian who claimed to know about it and who drew him a picture which is reproduced on page 100. It was this picture which von Strahlenberg handed to Kagg to take with him to Sweden, where it is still preserved in the library of Linköping. It is hard to decide whether the Russian who drew this clawed and twisted-horned super-cow was sincere in his belief or whether he was indulging in a heavy-handed joke on his imprisoned enemy.

Baron Kagg obviously believed in the picture. Scientists didn't.

"Russian mammoth" of 1722

This is a copy of the picture the Swedish Baron Kagg brought with him from Russia.

Nor were the Russians themselves too sure about those Siberian rumors. Czar Pyotr Alekseyevitch, known as Peter the Great, had sent a naturalist, Dr. D. G. Messerschmidt, to Siberia for general exploration, but with the injunction to keep his eyes open for those supposed elephants. The Czar knew about Ides' story, for Ides had been a member of his own ambassadorial party to China. Doctor Messerschmidt was lucky. A mammoth had come to light in the steep banks of the river Indigirka in eastern Siberia and he came in time to examine it before wolves had devoured all the fleshy parts and the rapid decay of the hot Siberian summer dissolved what even the wolves did not want. He reported on the large bones and on big pieces of skin with long hair, resembling the fur of a goat, if different in color. "No doubt," Messerschmidt ended his report, "no doubt this is the animal mentioned in the Bible as behemoth."

Since the Biblical behemoth is actually the hippopotamus, Dr. Messerschmidt very nearly succeeded in adding a third ingredient to the mixture that already included an extinct elephant and the living walrus. That danger was avoided mostly because few people then believed in the identification of the behemoth and the hippopotamus. But another confusing element was added by a generally very reliable man, the German explorer Peter Simon Pallas, who traveled through Siberia in 1768–74 at the expense of Catherine II of Russia. In 1771 Pallas came across an incomplete skeleton and large pieces of heavy fur of an animal which had thawed from the banks of the Vilyui River, a tributary of the Lena River, a number of miles to the west of the village of Vilyuisk. The fur consisted of thick woolly hair, "of conspicuously dark coloration." Protruding from this woolly hair there were bunches of stiff bristles, about three inches long, almost black in color. On the head of the animal the fur was reddish brown and in places a brownish-black. But this animal—and it did not need Pallas's training and experience to recognize it—was most certainly a rhinoceros.

The one thing which prevented western scientists from giving up in resignation was the fact that they could find the same animals on their home grounds, in Germany and France. The Siberian finds were superior in producing whole carcasses which had frozen when the animals had succumbed in treacherous muck or broken through thin layers of new snow covering rifts in the ice. In Germany and France the dead animals had been covered by sand and had decayed, so only bones and teeth were left. But they had some advantages just the same. They were not 4000 miles away. And one did not have to carry a shovel in the right hand for the work and a rifle in the left for the wolves.

The first European rhinoceros bones had been collected from Pleistocene deposits in England in 1701. They had been turned over to Professor Nehemiah Grew, who had recognized them for what they were and put the case on record. But since he was a botanist he had not pursued the matter any further. Precisely half a century later, in 1751, a similar collection of bones was handed to Professor Samuel Christian Hollmann of the University of Göttingen. They had been found at Grubenhagen near Herzberg in the Hartz Mountains. Professor Hollmann saw quickly that they too were rhinoceros bones and described them in detail. But he also refrained from drawing conclusions. That was left to his younger colleague, Johann Friedrich Blumenbach, who became professor of medicine at the same university after Hollmann's retirement.

Blumenbach began to collect large bones from the sand pits, which were a special kind of sand that later received the name of loess. Some of the bones were certainly rhinoceros bones, just as Hollmann had said. Others just as certainly were not. They were elephant bones, but not quite the same as the bones of the two living types of elephants. In 1799 Blumenbach felt that he had his evidence complete and he announced that there had once been a kind of elephant in Europe which was different from the living types. And it was also, obviously, much older. Hence he proposed the name of "first" elephant or *Elephas primigenius*. The name, we now know, was a bit enthusiastic—the mammoth was by no means the "first" elephant. Blumenbach also could not know that it had had a heavy fur. But he traveled around and looked at various "giant's bones," preserved in churches, castles, town halls. All *Elephas primigenius*. He ferreted out old pieces of *unicornum verum—Elephas primigenius,* too.

Then he turned his attention to the rhinoceros bones. They too closely resembled those of living species of rhinoceros, but again were not quite the same. In 1708 Blumenbach was sure that this was a species apart and he named it the "old rhinoceros," *Rhinoceros antiquitatis* (now *Tichorhinus antiquitatis*). A little later a second type of extinct rhinoceros was identified; in honor of Goethe's friend, the privy councilor, writer, and literary critic Johann Heinrich Merck, this was named *Rhinoceros merckii* (now *Coelodonta merckii*).

Meanwhile another mammoth had thawed from a river bank in Siberia, in the delta of the Lena River. This was found in 1799, the same year in which Blumenbach proposed the name *Elephas primigenius*. A Tungus ivory collector, Ossip Shumakhoff, saw it first, but he did not know at once what it was. It looked like a small dark-colored icy hillock. But it also looked unusual, so that Shumakhoff returned to the place in the following year. He still could not be sure. But one year later, in 1801, one of the tusks protruded from the ice. Shumakhoff was much less happy than one would think. The Tunguses think nothing of picking up tusks which they find lying around by themselves. But to find a whole *mamont* is, for some reason, bad luck. Indeed it prophesies the death of the finder and of all his family. And Shumakhoff actually fell sick; he had worried himself into a psychosomatic condition of some kind. But matter triumphed over mind in his case, and he recovered, from his illness and also from the superstitious fear. He had not died, in spite of everything people always said. Now for some money.

There was a Russian in a neighboring village, one of the men who traveled through Siberia for the purpose of buying *mamontova-kostj,* also furs on occasion, from the tribesmen. The Russian, whose name was Boltunoff, followed Shumakhoff to the place which the latter had kept carefully secret. Now, during the third summer, the carcass had really thawed. The two men pried the tusks loose and then Boltunoff handed the tribesman fifty rubles. He also made a drawing which a few years later was acquired by Blumenbach, was seen in Blumenbach's study by Cuvier some time prior to 1812, and later belonged to Ernst Haeckel. Blumenbach made a notation at the bottom of the picture which reads (translated): *"Elephas primigenius,* which in Russia is called *Mammut,* dug up with skin and hair in 1806 at the mouth of the Lena River at the Ice Ocean. Badly drawn, just as it was found, mutilated and all dirty."

The date 1806 refers to the year when a special expedition under Professor Adams reached the place to salvage the whole skeleton and much of the pelt. The drawing itself does look funny, mostly because there is no trunk and the tusks are in an impossible position. But one should not judge too harshly. Boltunoff most likely had never seen an elephant and the mammoth's trunk probably had been torn away by wolves before Boltunoff got there. Presumably the whole face had been torn away, because Boltunoff placed the eyes of his drawing in what must be the ear opening. There were probably no ears left—the mammoth has rather small ears anyway—and the remaining holes looked as if they might be the eye sockets. I believe that Boltunoff was as careful as he could be under the circumstances, because above his picture he placed a sketch of the grinding surface of the mammoth's molar.

This find, often called the "Adams mammoth," converted Blumenbach's "first elephant," assembled from bones only, into the "woolly mammoth." The skeleton which Adams had salvaged was mounted in the museum in St. Petersburg (now Leningrad) with the skin on the feet and a number of tendons still attached to the skull. Cuvier printed a picture of this mammoth in his large work on fossil bones. With that the mammoth finally and definitely entered the world of science.

Nevertheless, there was still some feeling of uncertainty. Thanks to Mr. Boltunoff of Yakutsk and Professor Adams of St. Petersburg on the one hand, and Professor Blumenbach of Göttingen and the Baron de Cuvier of Paris on the other hand, the woolly mammoth was nicely nailed down. So was the woolly rhinoceros, thanks to Pallas and Blumenbach. The other rhinoceros, which had been named after Goethe's friend Merck, was summarily taken to be woolly too. From all we know now this was a mistaken conclusion, but what applied to the one was logically thought to apply to its contemporary too. The question was, why had they been woolly? By then scientists had good pictures and descriptions of the elephants and rhinoceri of Africa and India, and many of them were even in a position to visit the steadily improving and growing zoological gardens where they could see these animals alive. The modern animals were not completely hairless: the rhinoceros had some few hairs on face and ears; the elephants had some around the mouth, on the trunk, and on the tail. Indians who had domesticated elephants even said that a very young elephant had something like a sparse fur which did not last long and of which the few hairs one could see later were the remains.

All of which showed that it was not impossible for an elephant or a rhinoceros to grow a fur. The living types just didn't do it; the extinct types, as was established beyond any doubt, had done so. Why?

To this question a troublesome Frenchman added another. It was now known that the mammoth had, without being recognized, intruded on human history as far back as there were records. Even the Romans had found elephant bones occasionally. This Frenchman, Jacques Boucher de Crèvecœur de Perthes by name, claimed that at one time in the past man had intruded on the mammoth. Monsieur de Perthes, in his younger years a diplomat in the service of Napoleon I, later economist, playwright, novelist, and self-styled archaeologist, had dug up things fashioned of stone. They were really just pieces of flint, chipped around the edges. Such things were no novelty in themselves.

They had "always" been found, and the population had called them "thunderbolts" and many other names. Oh no, one didn't know what they were. One had to admit that they did resemble some implements which travelers had brought back from certain backward tribes beyond the seas. Monsieur de Perthes insisted that they were tools and weapons of a primitive race of man which had once inhabited France.[3] Maybe so, maybe so, but he certainly went too far. He said that those primitive men, our own ancestors, had hunted mammoths with such weapons!

Of course not! That was just the kind of idea one could expect from a man who had written novels, not even using a pen name, a man who had written stage plays and probably even associated with actors and actresses. What Monsieur de Perthes apparently did not know was that the mammoth and the woolly rhinoceros and primitive man (whatever *that* term was supposed to mean) had not been contemporaries. More, that they could not have been contemporaries, because the mammoth and the various European rhinoceri had lived during the preceding geological period. In that period there had been no men because men belonged to our period.

The name most frequently quoted in all attacks on Boucher de Perthes' *chimères* was that of Cuvier. Cuvier had said that the various geological periods had been separated by world-wide catastrophes which had killed all life, necessitating a new creation for each period. He had said it because he had never found a fossil animal in more than one period. Sometimes similar forms, yes. The mammoth had existed in one period, while the Indian and the African elephants lived in another. They were similar. But they were not the same. And most especially, Cuvier had emphasized that no fossil man had ever been found. Considering that Cuvier died in 1832, this seemed to be true, though actually one Cro-Magnon skeleton had come to light in England, on the seaward side of Bristol Channel, in 1823. But it had been taken to be the skeleton of a Briton lady of the Roman period of Great Britain.

Boucher de Perthes kept quiet. He was not looking for a professorship

---

[3] Boucher de Perthes arrived at that idea independently, but he was not the first. Some decades earlier a British antiquary, John Frere, had anticipated him. Frere had collected such flint implements in England and sent a selection to the Society of Antiquaries in 1797, accompanied by a letter in which he wrote: "I think they are evidently weapons of war fabricated and used by a people who had not the use of metals."

anywhere, he had some income, derived in part from those novels and plays that were cited against him. He went on collecting his chipped flint implements, meanwhile resolved not to believe in Cuvier's world-wide catastrophes. Johann Wolfgang von Goethe in Germany did not believe in them either, but he was another playwright and novelist and one did not have to believe his scientific reasoning even though he also held a high position in society and in politics. But somebody else who did not believe in them was Sir Charles Lyell in England, a professional geologist. He collected all the geological evidence he could find. But he could not find any evidence for world-wide catastrophes. Tectonic forces built mountains; rains and rivers washed them away again. Rivers filled seas with sediments and made them shallower and shallower. On the other hand the surf nibbled at coastlines and slowly moved them inland. Wherever Lyell looked, he saw only those forces which are still operat-ing, day and night, day after day and night after night, through weeks, months, years, centuries, and millennia.

Thoughts always become books. Lyell's thoughts, observations, and conclusions turned into a book of three volumes, entitled *Principles of Geology*. The volumes appeared from 1830 to 1833, just at the time Cuvier died. Young Charles Darwin carried the first volume in his suitcase when he boarded the H. M. S. *Beagle* for a voyage of exploration around the world. They were carefully read by geologists everywhere. And they were, with only very minor objections on a few points, unani-mously accepted. Cuvier's world-wide catastrophes did not survive the death of their originator. His good work on fossils did survive.

There was no longer any reason for disbelieving that a species of animals or plants had survived from one geological period into another. In fact later on scientists began to look very avidly for such "living fossils." There was no longer any reason why the mammoth should not have survived into the present geological period (then called the Alluvium). Conversely, if the mammoth had died out with the end of the Pleistocene there was no reason why Man should not have lived *then*. Sir Charles Lyell himself considered this not at all improbable. And one day, in 1859, old Boucher de Perthes, living reasonably con-tentedly at Abbeville in the beautiful valley of the Somme, received a visitor, an English gentleman by the name of Sir Charles Lyell. He wanted to see the stone implements which Monsieur de Perthes had collected. After that he wanted to see where they had been found. He checked carefully, not saying much. But when he did open his mouth he began with the words, "Monsieur de Perthes, you are correct."

With that, one of the two questions which had been answerless in 1830 had been disposed of. Theoretically, at least, man and mammoth could have been contemporaries. It took the remainder of the nineteenth century to show that they actually had been, and also that they had lived in the same place at the same time. This was not as easy as it sounds nowadays. Fossil remains of man not only had to be found, which in itself was mostly a matter of luck, they also had to be established as unmistakably fossil. That took time, and many people did not want to go along with these new ideas. Not only that, some individual scientists, being human, were reluctant to abandon theories which they had treasured as valuable property. They were even justified in being skeptical; skepticism is a prime requirement in scientific work. To us, who see everything brightly illuminated in the light of after-knowledge, some of the skepticism looks exaggerated, stubborn, and blind. All that was the case on occasion, but essentially the skeptics were merely wrong.

I'll just touch upon a few cases. When the first skull of Neanderthal Man was found (in a valley, *Thal* in German, near Düsseldorf, named in honor of the religious poet Neander), Rudolf Virchow tried to show that its differences from a modern skull might be explained as pathological differences, caused by battle wounds in youth and by *arthritis deformans* in old age. It was nonsense, but as long as only one such skull was known the possibility existed. When a place where ancient man had obviously eaten mammoths was discovered near Předmost in Bohemia, the Danish professor Japetus Steenstrup said that this still was no proof for contemporaneous existence; the men might have found frozen carcasses, as Tunguses and Yakuts still do. When the first cave paintings came to light in France, they were suspected of not being genuine. But fossil man, or his modern champions, won all along the battle-line.

Before that victory could be complete, something fundamental had to be learned, which had to do with that other question already posed:

why had the mammoth been woolly? The Siberian finds indicated a
fur from 6 to 9 inches thick.

It was a question about which one could think in circles for any length
of time. If one took the fur to be a special adaptation to Siberian conditions, from the example of the Siberian tiger which has a heavier fur
than his Bengal brother, one got into the dead-end problem of why the
mammoth no longer walked the Siberian tundra. If one did not take
the fur to be a Siberian specialty, one had to assume Siberian climate in
Europe, all the way from England to Bohemia. There was one suspicious indication in Switzerland, relating to the glaciers, which became a
tourist attraction after the invention of the railroad simplified travel. A
glacier is essentially a slowly flowing river of compacted snow and ice.
When rocks are dislodged by the glacier itself, or by other causes, they
are carried by the glacier. If it should at some later time melt faster than
it can advance, these rocks are left as a telltale mark, called a moraine.
But a glacier not only carries rocks on its back, it also moves them with
its sole, scraping another telltale mark into the rock over which it flows.
Nobody who had looked at the evidence could doubt that the glaciers of
Switzerland had been much larger in the past. Goethe himself, after
looking at them, stated thoughtfully, "For all that ice [of the larger gla-
ciers] we need cold. I hold the suspicion that a period of great cold has
passed at least over Europe." [4]

But the scientific world did not pay too much attention to the Swiss
glaciers. It had another and geographically larger puzzle on its hands.
All over North Germany and the corresponding areas of Poland and
Russia one found large blocks of stone, from pieces a man could still
move to boulders weighing hundreds of tons. They were scattered without rhyme or reason over a landscape which was largely sand, with
bedrock hundreds of feet below the surface. Nor did that bedrock correspond to the boulders on the sand. Geologists comparing rock samples
had established something at least as surprising as the presence of the
boulders themselves. Their material perfectly matched the mountains
on the Scandinavian peninsula. How did large pieces of Scandinavian
mountains get to Pomerania and Poland?

Lyell's answer, incorporated in his big work, seemed to explain all

---

[4] November 5, 1829.

this nicely and was fully accepted for about half a century. Let's assume, he began, that all of Europe north of the Alps was lower by a certain and comparatively small amount. Then a shallow sea would cover the plains of Germany quite far inland, at least to the Hartz Mountains. The Scandinavian glaciers would then have flowed directly into the sea. When a glacier flows into the sea its end breaks off periodically to form icebergs. Drifting southward, these icebergs, probably smaller to begin with than the monsters which float down into the Atlantic from Greenland, would slowly melt. The rocks they had scooped up as glaciers would drop to the bottom. As the European mainland slowly rose, the sea became shallower and shallower and simultaneously iceberg production in the north would stop because the Scandinavian glaciers no longer reached the shoreline.

Building on the foundation of that theory one could even explain the larger size of the Swiss glaciers. If the sea was that much larger, a lot more water could evaporate from it, causing more snow in Switzerland in winter and thereby increasing the size of its glaciers. That that sea apparently had not covered France was somewhat awkward, but France did not seem to have any of those boulders from Scandinavia, so obviously it had not been flooded.

Any doubts anybody might have harbored could not be voiced for lack of evidence. But in 1875 there was a meeting of the German Geological Society in Berlin. Among the invited guests was the head of the Swedish Geological Survey, Otto Martin Torell. Torell did not just come, deliver a speech, and rush home again; he made a few excursions, looking at boulders from Scandinavia resting in the rye fields in the vicinity. And there is a place named Rüdersdorf, about an hour's train ride from Berlin, where bedrock actually breaks through the sand and forms very modest mountains. The bedrock is Muschelkalk. Torell had to see that. When he did, he also saw the typical glacier scrapes which he knew so well. (Later a boulder from Sweden was placed near that spot as a memorial.) The same night Torell spoke to the assembled geologists. Europe had not been covered by a shallow sea with icebergs from the Scandinavian glaciers, he said. Europe had been covered by the Scandinavian glaciers. Wherever there was bedrock at the surface their marks would be found.

Goethe's forgotten remark of more than forty years before about the period of great cold that had passed at least over Europe suddenly seemed prophetic. The idea of a large portion of a continent flooded by a shallow sea was not a rare concept to geologists. Europe had been flooded like that during the Jurassic and Cretaceous periods. And during the Cretaceous at least, the North American continent had been split in two in the same manner by a shallow sea extending from the Gulf of Mexico through the central plains to Hudson Bay.

It was a different proposition to be asked to imagine large portions of a continent buried under glacier ice. That concept could not be assimilated quickly, not just because it was new, but because it seemed to involve a very profound climatic change. You could imagine a sea breaking through from the Gulf to Hudson Bay, or one connecting the North Sea with the Adriatic Sea, without a climatic change at the outset. Of course the presence of the sea, once it existed, would influence the climate. "But for all that ice we need cold." It was received with something like relief when Melchior Neumayr of Vienna published a calculation which said that the whole Ice Age could be explained by a reduction of the average year-round temperature of from 8 to 10 degrees Fahrenheit. If every day and every night, Neumayr said, were 8 degrees cooler than it is now, the snow and ice of winter would fail to melt away as completely as it does now. The snow line of the mountains would be lower, for one thing. Next winter more ice and snow would accumulate in these places. If this went on for a sufficiently long time the glaciers could grow large enough to cover all of Europe.

Meanwhile the glacier scrapes which Torrell had so confidently predicted had actually been found. Once geologists knew what to look for, it seemed a wonder that they had ever been overlooked. From a mass of data maps were made, showing the extent of that past glaciation. There was one large area of which so little was known that one could not tell. That happened to be Siberia. We still don't know about Siberia, but the expedition under Roy Chapman Andrews established definitely that the ice shield did *not* reach the Gobi and the high land of Tibet. But from the Ural Mountains west, the picture was quite clear. The glaciers had covered Russia to points south of Moscow, Poland to south of Warsaw, and Germany to Berlin and beyond. From there on the "glacier line" ran through Belgium, crossed the Channel, cut across the southernmost portion of England to the vicinity of Bristol, and then ran westward through the Irish Sea. Everything north of that line was covered by the ice shield, including all of Ireland. That is the reason there are no snakes in Ireland. Probably there were some before, but after the glaciers which had killed them had melted away, no snakes could get back.

In the Western Hemisphere the glacier line began at the shore of the Atlantic Ocean somewhat south of the fortieth parallel, ran west south of the Great Lakes to the Dakotas, turned north there, and then followed approximately the present United States–Canadian border to the Pacific Ocean. Naturally it was not quite as straight as that political boundary. Here in America the areas not covered by the ice shield were comparatively large, including everything south of Pennsylvania in the east and everything south of the state of Washington in the west. In Europe the Mediterranean countries and all of France had escaped. So had the extreme south of England, much of the area of the English Channel (then probably dry land), western and southern Germany, southern Poland, and southern Russia. Austria and Czechoslovakia had not been reached by the Scandinavian glaciers. But the Alps, as Swiss guides had pointed out to the visiting Goethe, had produced large glaciers of their own.

The evidence seemed to leave little room for early men and mammoths, but there was an ameliorating factor. It was a pardonable mistake of the geologists to have thought at first that there had been just "the Ice Age." Then, they discovered evidence that two glaciations had successively gone over the same spot, with an interval during which plants grew there which can now be found in Italy. With eyes sharpened once more, they continued to search, finally arriving at the conclusion that there had been about four glaciations, with "interglacial periods" between. The "glacier line" first established belonged to the time of the maximum glaciation, the third. The others had been of somewhat lesser extent; it is hard to say just how much less. For easier reference the glaciations have received names which as names mean very little, because they are actually just the names of small rivers. In chronological order, the names are Günz, Mindel, Riss, and Würm, and the majority of the experts believe that the last of the four, the Würm glaciation, had two distinct phases.

How much the glaciers receded during the warmer interglacial periods is an especially hard question to answer. Since the first of these warmer periods was quite long in duration one may be justified in thinking that the glaciers had receded to at least their present status, which leaves only the extreme north of America, Greenland, and the Siberian rim still in the Ice Age. As for the recession in the other warmer periods, almost any guess will do, but it must have been a good deal, because one can clearly see that each time a fauna geared to a somewhat warmer climate moved in. When the glaciers advanced, spreading tundra and cold steppes ahead of them, cold-proof mammals appeared on those tundras. The mammoth itself. The woolly rhinoceros. The heavily furred musk ox. The reindeer. The gigantic cave bear. Wolves.

When the glaciers receded and the steppes warmed up, forests spread and with the forests came a different group of animals. There was the "old" elephant, the majestic *Elephas antiquitatis* with its long tusks. (Because it was not particularly old, scientists later referred to it as the "forest elephant," in spite of the meaning of its Latin name.) There was Merck's rhinoceros, most likely a hairless form. There were bears, lions, lynxes, stags, fallow deer, deer, and wild hogs.

This seesaw between a temperate forest fauna and a cold-resistant tundra fauna had started with a fairly stable condition in the late days of the Tertiary period. At that time the area which was to be invaded by the northern cold had a fauna which, if anybody saw it now, would make him think that he had been transported to Africa. In fact, in a manner of speaking he would have been transported to Africa's fauna, except that it was not yet on African soil. The north European fauna of the late Tertiary, leaving the slowly cooling continent, largely escaped via the Balkan peninsula (which had somewhat different geography then) into Africa, where they survived with comparatively little change. During the time when the first glaciation was slowly building up there were only a few apparently more hardy forms left.

A species of hippopotamus was still around for a while and so was a rhinoceros which is called the Etruscan rhinoceros. There was a large elephant, called the "southern" elephant (*Elephas meridionalis*). There was a type of moose which is considered to be the direct ancestor of the living form, and another which was the ancestor of a form that flourished all through the Pleistocene but became extinct in very early historical times; it seems to have survived longest in Ireland. There was a very large beaver which has been named in honor of Cuvier and there were large numbers of a wild horse, possibly zebra-striped.

In putting down these names I am relying on a list prepared by Professor Wolfgang Soergel of *Chirotherium* fame. Professor Soergel had long been interested in a specific problem. Because of animal bones burned in fires, large bones split open for the sake of the marrow, and lots of similar evidence, everybody was sure that primitive man had been largely a hunter. The problem which busied Soergel was no longer *whether* the men of the Old Stone Age, the Neanderthalers and the later men of the small Aurignac race, had hunted. The problem was *how* they had hunted their game. But that problem, in turn, rested on the question of what kind of game was available. By about 1910, when Soergel started this work, enough material had been amassed to enable him to draw up tables showing which animals had occurred when. Some ten years later he brought his tables up to date once more; the adaptation on pp. 114–16 is based on his second table.[5]

The tables show clearly how that "temperate forest fauna" which was to become so typical for the interglacial periods moved in during the first of them. The earliest known fossil of a man, the so-called Heidelberg jaw, indicating a 6-footer of the Neanderthal type (the later "true" Neanderthalers were a good 6 inches shorter), is also dated as belonging to the first interglacial period. During the second glaciation, the mammoth's ancestor (*Elephas trogontherii*) appeared on the scene, along with the reindeer, an early form of the cave bear, and so forth. The transition from the remains of the Tertiary fauna which somehow managed to hold on for a while to the fauna that "belongs" to the Ice Age was complete.

---

[5] In translating Soergel's table I had to make up a number of popular names in English; the animals can be identified by the subsidiary list of scientific names. I doubt whether so complete a table could yet be compiled for the glacial period of America. In the Western Hemisphere we are dealing with far larger areas which are also less densely settled, which were settled later, and in which scientific investigation also started later.

ANIMAL LIFE AND CLIMATE CONDITIONS IN

Adapted from *Die Jagd der*

SUBDIVISION	PROBABLE DURATION (THOUSANDS OF YEARS)	CLIMATE AND LANDSCAPE
Pliocene Preglacial	400	Mild climate with seasonal changes; open forest and prairie
Nebraskan Günz glaciation	20	Cold and dry; steppes; tundra near glaciated areas
Aftonian First interglacial	50	Mild climate, probably slightly warmer than now; mostly forest
Kansan Mindel glaciation	35	Cold and dry; steppes; tundra near glaciated areas
Yarmouth Second interglacial	150	Mild climate, probably slightly warmer than now; mostly forest
Illinoian Riss glaciation	30	Very cold and dry; extensive cold steppes; large tundra areas
Sangamon Third interglacial	20	Mild climate with large forests
Wisconsin Würm glaciation, first part	20	Very cold and dry (maximum extent of glaciation in Switzerland); cold steppes and tundra
Interval between the two Würm glaciations	25	Fairly mild; forest locally; prairie
Würm glaciation, second part	25	Very cold and dry; extensive cold steppes and tundra
Post-glacial	30 +	Gradually warming; gradual advance of forests into steppes and tundra
Historical time (Pliny and Tacitus)		Extensive forests

NORTHERN EUROPE DURING THE PLEISTOCENE PERIOD

Vorzeit by W. Soergel, 1922 edition

CHARACTERISTIC LARGE MAMMALS
(SEE PAGES 116–17 FOR SCIENTIFIC NAMES)

South elephant, Etruscan rhinoceros, zebra, old wisent, old moose, old giant moose, hippopotamus, giant beaver

South elephant, Etruscan rhinoceros, zebra, old wisent, old giant moose

Forest elephant, Etruscan rhinoceros, Merck's rhinoceros, hyena, old horse, old moose, stag, deer, old cave bear, lion, wild hog, panther, old wisent; only known fossil of *Homo heidelbergensis*

Old mammoth, Etruscan rhinoceros, zebra, western horse, old wisent, old moose, musk ox, old giant moose, reindeer, stag, old cave bear, wolverine

Forest elephant, Merck's rhinoceros, old wisent, stag, giant moose, lion, bear —probably cave bear, hippopotamus in western sections; first appearance of *Homo neanderthalensis*

Mammoth, woolly rhinoceros, old wisent, western horse, musk ox, ibex, giant moose, reindeer, cave bear (?)

Forest elephant, Merck's rhinoceros, old horse, old wisent, urus, moose, giant moose, stag, deer, fallow deer, wild hog, beaver, dormouse, bear, cave bear, cave lion, panther, lynx, cat, wolf

Mammoth, woolly rhinoceros, eastern horse, western horse, wild ass, old wisent, musk ox, reindeer, giant moose, lemming, lesser hare, cave bear, northern fox

Mammoth, woolly rhinoceros, Merck's rhinoceros, wild ass, western horse, stag, reindeer, dormouse, bear, cave bear, wolf; small Aurignac race of man

Mammoth, woolly rhinoceros, old wisent, eastern horse, western horse, urus, musk ox, moose, giant moose, reindeer, lesser hare, lemming, cave bear, wolverine

Wisent, urus, eastern horse, moose, stag, deer, snow hare, lesser hare, bear, wolf, fox, northern fox, wolverine; *getting rare:* reindeer, giant moose, cave lion, mammoth *very* rare if present; Cro-Magnon man

Urus, wisent, moose, stag, deer, beaver, bear, wolf, fox, lynx; in north only: reindeer, wolverine; in east only: western horse, possibly eastern horse

Mammoth	*Elephas (Mammuthus) primigenius* (and *Fraasi*)
Forest elephant	*Elephas (Loxodon) antiquitatis*
South elephant	*Elephas (Archidiskodon) meridionalis*
Old mammoth	*Elephas (Mammuthus) trogontherii*
Woolly rhinoceros	*Rhinoceros (Tichorhinus) antiquitatis*
Merck's rhinoceros	*Rhinoceros (Coelodonta) merckii*
Etruscan rhinoceros	*Rhinoceros etruscus*
Bear	*Ursus arctos*
Cave bear	*Ursus spelaeus*
Old cave bear	*Ursus deningeri*
Small bear	*Ursus arvernensis*
Panther	*Felis pardus antiquus*
Lion	*Felis leo fossilis*
Cave lion	*Felis spelaeus*
Lynx	*Felis lynx*
Cat	*Felis cattus ferus*
Wolverine	*Gulo borealis*
Wolf	*Canis lupus*
Fox	*Canis vulpes*
Northern fox	*Canis lagopus*
Hyena	*Hyaena mosbachensis*
Wild hog	*Sus scrofa ferus*
Hippopotamus	*Hippopotamus major*
Wisent	*Bos bison europaeus*
Urus	*Bos primigenius*
Old wisent	*Bison priscus*
Beaver	*Castor fiber*
Giant beaver	*Trogontherium cuvieri*
Musk ox	*Ovibos moschatus*
Moose	*Alces palmatus*
Giant moose	*Cervus eurycerus*
Old moose	*Alces latifrons*
Old giant moose	*Cervus verticornis*
Stag	*Cervus elaphus*
Deer	*Cervus capreolus*
Fallow deer	*Cervus dama*
Eastern deer	*Cervus pygergus*
Reindeer	*Rangifer tarandus*
Ibex	*Capra ibex*
Eastern horse	*Equus przhewalski*

SCIENTIFIC NAMES OF ANIMALS LISTED IN TABLE ON PAGES 114–15

Western horse	*Equus germanicus*
Old horse	*Equus abeli*
Zebra	*Equus suessenbornensis*
Wild ass	*Equus hemionus*
Dormouse	*Miaxus glis*
Snow hare	*Lepus variabilis*
Lesser hare	*Lagomys pusillus*
Lemming	*Myodes torquatus*

Man did not have easy hunting in these surroundings, which he could endure only because of his possession of fire. There was much competition from carnivorous mammals, some of them of considerable size. The hunter often enough became the hunted. Even more often he must have lost to wolves game which he could not kill at a stroke.

And, as the remains of his meals show, he was handicapped in other ways too. We do know that the forests of the interglacial periods, as well as the tundra and steppes fringing the glaciers during the glaciations, were inhabited by many small mammals which, being rodents, were probably numerous. There were also flocks of birds, many of them types still living in the northern countries. But in the refuse heaps of ancient man the bones of small mammals are a great rarity, and there is not a single well-established case of bird bones as remains of a meal. This seems to indicate at least that the men of the Old Stone Age had not yet learned how to build traps and snares, and that he had no missile weapons—slingshots, bows and arrows, etc.—with which he could kill a bird. He probably relied entirely on what are known as impact weapons: spears, clubs, and related armament which required a close approach. Small animals were difficult to approach and not worth the trouble. With equal effort the hunter could kill a reindeer or a horse.

Anthropologists have often tried to give helpful hints to paleontologists by pointing out the methods of hunting used by primitive tribes in comparatively recent times. They have told how natives use brush fires to stampede animals in a certain direction so that they are forced to jump down steep cliffs. They have told how natives, armed with several spears per man, isolate a single animal from the herd, corner it, and then dispatch it either by means of thrown spears or by using the spears as close-range weapons.

Such hints are helpful, but whether or not they are applicable is another question. The so-called fire drive requires not only fire (and a suitable locality), but also large numbers of hunters. The anthropologists who told about such hunts stressed that hundreds and sometimes even thousands of natives took part in them, with enough yield for every hunter and his family. But primitive man, at least during the Old Stone Age, simply was not numerous enough to conduct such hunts. Later, in Cro-Magnon times, the fire drive was probably used; in fact, there is one place in France where everything speaks in favor of the theory that herds of animals (especially horses) were stampeded over a cliff, not just once, but many times. Neanderthal man, however, did not live in tribes, in our meaning of the word. There were just large families; maybe two or three families getting together on occasion. They were not numerous enough to stampede herds, either by means of the fire drive or by plain noise-making.

Separating a single animal from a herd and cornering it was probably practiced, but what weapons they used was another problem. Those natives about whom the anthropologists told had already acquired iron; their spears were tipped with pointed and sharp blades of considerable size and fatal power. Stone blades of equivalent deadliness were a late invention. A German archaeologist, Otto Profé, borrowed a number of stone artifacts which were indubitably "Neanderthal," attached them to wooden handles in a manner probably superior to what the Neanderthal men could have done, and then tried to "kill" a freshly butchered calf with these weapons. Try as he might, he could not even penetrate the thin skin of the belly. Only where the skin was underlaid by strong muscles did the flint implements break through the skin at all. Even if wielded by a powerful man, these weapons could not have inflicted fatal wounds. They were just not sharp enough.

It was a different matter to use the Neanderthal implements to cut the carcass apart. For operations like separating the skin from the flesh, splitting the flesh off the bone, and even for cutting the tendons from the bone, these stone knives were almost as effective as modern tools. One could not cut across the muscle, but Neanderthal man probably did not care whether his meat was sliced into steaks or roasted as chunks. Profé concluded from this experiment, and Soergel agreed with him, that the stone weapons were not hunting weapons at all, with all due respect for Boucher de Perthes' pioneer work. The stone weapons were household tools. They may have been weapons of war, where the situation is different, but they were useless for hunting.

Then what did they use for hunting? They needed a weapon which would penetrate deeply with relative ease, causing a wound that did not permit the animal to get far away. Soergel concluded (in 1922) that Neanderthal man's hunting weapon was probably a spear not tipped by anything. Just a straight stick, either a straight branch or more likely a sapling tree, with the tip hardened by fire and then sharpened. Such a spear would be effective in a more or less individual hunt on reindeer and horse and animals of similar size, and with luck even on larger game. Soergel's prediction was borne out in 1948 when such a wooden spear was actually found near the Aller River in northwestern Germany. It was broken into ten pieces, but nothing was missing. It had been 8 feet long, fashioned of the tough and heavy wood of the European yew (*Taxus baccata*), and examination of the tip showed that it had been hardened by fire. It was pointed and showed no traces of having anything attached to it, but clear traces of the strokes of stone knives that had been used to sharpen it.

The spear could be dated as having been made and used during the last interglacial period, and it was found imbedded in the rib case of a forest elephant. Nearby a dozen flint scrapers were lying about. The whole effect was precisely like a hunting method still in use in Africa by the pygmy tribes of Cameroon. There, a solitary hunter, armed with a spear longer than himself, carefully approaches a solitary feeding or dozing elephant from behind. If his approach fails to be noiseless enough, the elephant usually just moves on. If the hunter does succeed in getting close, he pushes his spear into the elephant's abdomen from below and behind. The animal, fatally wounded, rarely seems to turn around for an attack on the hunter but races away in terror and pain. Finally it breaks down exhausted, often a considerable distance away. It worked that way with the African elephant early in this century; it worked that way with the forest elephant during the last interglacial period in Europe.

But it could not have worked that way with the mammoth. The skin of the elephant, while thick, has soft spots. So, presumably, did the skin of the mammoth. But the long hair protected those softer areas. Before a spear could touch the inch-thick skin it had to penetrate some 8 inches of wool. And under the skin there were some 6 inches of fat. A high-powered rifle bullet would be needed to get through all this to the vital organs. No spear could ever do it; no man could put enough driving force behind it.

The only thing we can think of now—and primitive man certainly thought of it too—is the pit. That had always seemed the most likely method, but it was one about which quite a number of archaeologists were very skeptical. They said a pit large enough to catch a mammoth was impossible for primitive man to make. The only digging tool Neanderthal man could have had was the so-called digging stick. It would take a whole tribe many weeks to dig a large enough pit.

It sounded like a very strong argument, but in view of the evidence it had to be wrong. There were several answers. One was that the men would not have dug all the hole; they would have started with a natural hole of some kind. Another was that it was not necessary to make a hole into which a full-grown mammoth would disappear; it was enough to render it helpless. If only the forelegs or the hind legs were caught, even a mammoth could be clubbed to death by incessant attack. I may add here that I personally doubt very much that the digging stick was the only digging instrument of Neanderthal man. He dealt with fairly loose sand and for such material nature provided a ready-made digging tool: moose antlers. They may be somewhat awkward to handle, but I can testify that they work in loose sand.

Still and all, the mammoth probably was exceptional game which was hunted only under special circumstances. But there was Předmost in Bohemia, where, as mentioned earlier, man had evidentally eaten mammoths. This place, like so many such finds, was an accidental discovery. The ground belonged to a Czech landowner who could not help noticing that his farm hands quite often came across large bones. To the mind of the landowner there was just one use for old bones: he had them ground up as fertilizer for his fields—until one day somebody who knew better saw what was going on and screamed for help, invoking the Academy of Science, the police, the Ministry of the Interior, and everybody else he could think of in a hurry. The practice of fertilizing fields with mammoth bone meal was stopped and an investigation started.

There were numerous remains of people. There were also numerous remains of mammoth. And the people, it could not be denied, had had some sense of order. Here was a pile of shoulder blades, there was a pile of leg bones. Over there some skulls. Since nobody could tell how many bones had been ground up there was immediate disagreement on the number of mammoths that had been eaten there. First estimates said "at least a thousand"; that was revised downward to about half in the course of time. Soergel, on the other hand, at first refused to believe in a number higher than about three hundred, but doubled his estimate later on, so that we can't be far wrong in saying that the Předmost site contained the remains of about six hundred mammoths.

As I mentioned (p. 107) the Danish zoologist Japetus Steenstrup (justly famous for other work) held that all these mammoths had just been frozen carcasses, such as had been found in the Lena delta and along the Indigirka River. If he had stopped at that point we would now say, "Old Steenstrup was a good judge." But he elaborated on the case, "proving" that primitive man had never hunted or killed a mammoth. Very soon afterward overwhelming evidence that primitive man had hunted and killed mammoths was found in many places. Steenstrup's reputation collapsed, he was ridiculed, and those who had originally sided with him kept very quiet about it. Primitive man was acclaimed as a great hunter.

But it is now accepted that in the specific case of the Předmost mammoths primitive man actually had stuffed himself with the flesh of dead animals. No doubt he could kill 600 mammoths in time. But he could not have dragged the heavy bodies to the same place. And if he made a mammoth trap of some kind near Předmost, the animals would not have patiently walked into the same trap year after year. Obviously something, probably a blizzard of unusual severity, had killed the mammoths there. Only a natural catastrophe can account for the presence of 600 mammoth carcasses in one place.

Six hundred elephants, however, is a very large herd. And that naturally brings up the question of how numerous the mammoth was. It cannot have been rare. The teeth (molars) of more than 200 individuals have been found in a most unlikely spot: they were dredged up with

Mammoth

oysters from the Dogger Bank in the North Sea. In the German state of Württemberg alone, remains belonging to about 3000 individuals have been found during the time interval from 1700 to 1900. The number of remains from Austria and Czechoslovakia must be about the same. And the total of the tusks found so far in Siberia, where the mammoth lasted longest, points to 50,000 individuals. Even if that estimate is wrong by 10,000 in either direction, it remains an impressive number. Of course, all these bones represent accumulations over long periods of time.

A comparison with the African elephant shows that elephants tend to occur in large numbers if they occur at all. For the year 1800, prior to the mass hunts with high-powered rifles which decimated the herds, the number of living individuals of the African elephant is estimated at 4,000,000. The area over which the African elephant could live and that useful to the mammoth may be taken to be about equal. On that assumption the African elephant was the more numerous, which is easily explained by adverse conditions and lesser food supply for the mammoth.

As to the appearance of the mammoth, there are absolutely no doubts left. We have numerous complete skeletons, we have the Siberian specimens preserved by what engineers now call "permafrost" (permanently

European mammoth, Cave of Font de Gaume, Dordogne, France

frozen ground), and we have, almost more important, the very lifelike drawings left by men of the later Stone Age. These show something one could not have deduced from the skeleton: the mammoth had two humps, like the Bactrian camel. These were indubitably humps of fat for the foodless season. One of these humps was placed above the shoulder blades, as one should expect; the other, strangely enough, was on top of the head. These two humps, combined with the long fur and the enormous tusks which apparently never were put to any use, made the shape of the mammoth quite different from that of living elephants. The color of the fur looks quite red now, but it is supposed that it has faded, so that in life the mammoth was probably clothed in reddish-black. One special adaptation to the cold climate, revealed by the Siberian finds, is worth mentioning. The mammoth carried, at the root of its tail, a strange skin flap which protected the anal opening against the cold. Its tail was quite short and the ears were small, smaller even than those of the small-eared Indian elephant.

And not all mammoths were of "mammoth size." There is really only one type to which this word would properly apply: the race or sub-species which occurred in Württemberg and which has been named after Professor Fraas. "Fraas's mammoth," as it may be called, stood a full 3 feet taller than the largest African elephant known. And that measurement disregards the hump, which may have added another foot or two. The most common type was somewhere between the African and the Indian elephant in size, and the Siberian species was smaller than the Indian elephant, just half as tall as the mammoth's ancestor, the admittedly enormous *Elephas trogontherii.* Whether that Siberian spe-cies—named *Elephas beresovkius* for reasons which will quickly become apparent—is to be considered a degenerate version of the European species is an unanswered question. But it probably was.

It is usually said that the European mammoth "died out" at the end of the glacial period. But it is more likely that it did not die out but moved out. As soon as the last glaciation in Europe had come to an end the forest moved in again—look once more at the tables on pages 114–115. And apparently the mammoth just did not like forest. It probably behaved much the same as did another typical animal of the glacial periods—the reindeer. The reindeer also just moved away, with the one difference that it stayed alive in the extreme north and the mammoth did not. One may imagine, therefore, that the mammoth, like the rein-deer, stuck to the cold steppes and tundra, following them northward as they receded, and then going east, to Siberia, where conditions were still most like those to which it had adapted itself.

How those Siberian permafrost mammoths which started all the excitement had found their individual end became clear in 1901. During that year the Russian Academy of Science in St. Petersburg received news from Yakutsk that another mammoth had come to light, this time in the extreme northeast, near the Beresovka,[6] a tributary of the river Kolyma. Because of an old ukase originally issued by Peter the Great, the Czar had to be notified about the find and he ordered an expedition

---

[6] The name signifies "Birch River" and the proper pronunciation is Berózovka, with the accent on the "ro."

to go after the mammoth. Leader of the expedition was Dr. Otto Hertz.

When the expedition arrived, wolves and dogs had already done their work, and much of the skull was bare of flesh. But it was still a virtually complete mammoth, since everything but the head was still solidly frozen. The decayed portions of the flesh emitted such a terrible stench that the scientists more than once felt that they might have to give up. But they always succeeded in persuading themselves to stand it for a few more days. And as the work progressed, their professional enthusiasm dulled their noses, to the great benefit of science.

The mammoth apparently had been feeding in freshly fallen snow which covered a deep crevasse in its path. When it fell in it was fatally injured, having broken both the right foreleg and the pelvis. It is quite probable that it struggled for some time in spite of the injury, pulling down tons of loose snow under which it finally died. There was still food in its mouth, and from the frozen stomach the scientists extracted 27 pounds of chewed but undigested food. Botanists could still classify the food: it consisted of larch, fir, and pine, some ground-up fir cones, sedge, wild flowers of various kinds, wild thyme, and two kinds of moss. Except on the head and one foreleg, the fur was complete, consisting of a thick yellowish undercoat and a thick mass of guide hairs, up to 14 inches long. There were manelike patches of long guide hairs on cheeks, chin, shoulders, flanks, and belly. The fat layer under the skin was pure white and on the average 4 inches thick. The meat was dark red, suggesting horse meat, and marbled with fat. The dogs ate it avidly; the men could not quite steel themselves to try it too. Some of the dark frozen blood was saved; a serological test made later indicated the Indian elephant as the closest living relative.

The scientists who did the work were not only hampered by the stench of the decayed parts, but after they had skinned the mammoth and cleaned up the skeleton they were faced with distance. It took ten sleds to carry what they had salvaged, for a 2000-mile journey over a snowy landscape, ending with the city of Irkutsk and the Trans-Siberian railroad. Both skeleton and skin were finally mounted in the museum in St. Petersburg, the skeleton in normal position, the skin in the half-sitting position in which the animal had died.

The mammoth was an American animal too in its time. Together with other elephants, it had crossed over from Asia into Alaska and found its way south. But it was not very numerous in the Western Hemisphere, much less so than the American mastodon which, in spite of early guesses to the contrary, was probably a hairless type.

For a long time there was a rumor that the woolly mammoth might still be alive in Alaska. Nobody knows just when or how that rumor originated but it is more than a century old. And every once in a while something happened to strengthen it. One of the most widely believed props of the rumor was a piece of fiction describing the "killing of the last mammoth," which appeared in *McClure's Magazine* in 1899 and was taken seriously by a large percentage of the magazine's readers. Obviously it is an appealing idea that the mammoth of the Ice Age, unwilling companion of Man since the earliest days of recordless prehistory, is still alive somewhere. Unfortunately it is not true.

But there must be mammoths in Alaska—frozen mammoths, undisturbed in permafrost like their Siberian kin. A tiny one was found two years ago and made the journey to New York in a deep-freeze unit. It is a promising beginning. Scientists are eying the frozen muck of Alaska. Somewhere in it there must be specimens which will teach us a lot about the mammoth in America—and possibly about early man in America too.

Part Two

THE LAST
OF THEIR KIND

6: The Story of the Milu

'*Mes préparatifs de voyage sont terminés depuis plusieurs jours,*" the missionary wrote in his diary, adding, "*je pourrais me mettre en route dès le fin de février.*" Or, in translation: "My preparations for the journey were completed several days ago and I could have gone ahead by about the end of February."

These lines were written in March 1866, possibly in Peking, or else somewhere en route between Peking and a place their writer called Suen-Hoa-Fou (Suan-Hwa), the first stopover on a long journey of exploration. The writer was a French missionary of Basque ancestry, Jean Pierre Armand David by name. When he wrote those lines he was Père David; later, after his final return from China, he became the Abbé David. But the fact that he was the Abbé David in the latter years of his long life is important only to clerics and to historians. Naturalists cannot help thinking of him as Père David, because it was under this designation that he took his extended trips and made the discoveries for which he is famous among naturalists. Before discussing the numerous and varied contributions of the naturalist-missionary to the natural history of the Far East, let's go on with his diary, because the delay in departure implied in the lines already quoted had a good reason.

"Because of this intention"—that of leaving Peking by the end of February—"I hurried to have my last shipment for the Museum packed up; it consists of the skins of mammals and birds and a few live plants which I have entrusted to the intelligent care of Monsieur Alphonse Pichon, attaché of the French Legation, who is going to return to Paris."

The importance of that particular shipment was well known to Father

David. He probably did not expect that it would make him famous for many years to come, but he did call it *la pièce principale,* writing:

"The principal item in this shipment is the *sse-pu-hsiang,* a kind of large reindeer of which the female is antlerless. For a long time I have tried to obtain a specimen of this interesting variety of the *Cervidae,* still unknown to naturalists, which I know to exist in large numbers and for centuries in the Imperial Park Haé-Dze, a few Chinese *li* to the south of the capital."

The name for the park used by Father David is not the one used by Sinologists, but there is no doubt about the locality to which he referred. Several miles south of Peking was the Imperial Hunting Park called Nan Hai-tzu, which at the time of Father David's visit was considerably larger in extent than the city itself. The area which later became a park seems to have been a kind of hunting and/or pleasure ground for the emperors of China for many centuries, but most of the time it was more or less open ground. About 1400 it was probably walled in; in any event the wall surrounding the park was centuries old when Father David saw it. Needless to say, nobody was permitted to enter it—especially no foreigner.

Having heard that animals were kept inside the park under the guard of soldiers (mostly Tartars), Father David decided that he would at least look at them, even though there was no way of wangling a permission to enter. Early in 1865 he climbed the wall and saw several game animals which he knew well, but also a large herd—he estimated it at 120 head—of large staglike animals which he had never seen before. He was also certain that no other naturalist had seen them, and it naturally became his ambition to place this unknown large animal in the catalogs of science. His diary contains some information which must have been supplied by native friends. He was told that there was a death sentence waiting for anybody who dared to kill one of these animals. But it was also said that the Tartar guards violated that law themselves on occasion when their rations grew too short or too monotonous. However, their fear of the law was strong enough to prevent them from selling anything that might be evidence; they would part neither with a skin nor with the bones nor even with the antlers. As regards the antlers, there seem to have been some exceptions to the rule: Father David reported that the insides of those antlers resembled ivory so closely that pieces of antler were sold as ivory (presumably after the outside had been ground off) and transformed into various utensils by Chinese craftsmen. Many collections of Chinese ivory probably contain pieces which are not ivory at all but parts of illicitly acquired antlers of "Père David's deer."

Naturally Father David inquired for the native name of the animal. His friends could tell him. It was *sse-pu-hsiang,* the name he put into his diary. He also knew what the name meant. It is literally "not like four." Somewhat more elegantly, it might be translated as "four dis-similarities." It is supposed to express the idea that the animal in ques-tion does *not* look like a stag, does *not* look like a goat, does *not* look like an ass, and does *not* look like a cow. But there also seems to be an implication that the animal does suggest each of the four in some aspect or feature.

Later a more handy name became known, *mi-lou* or milu. It is men-tioned in the first scientific description of the animal but apparently was unknown to Father David. In any event he did what he could to obtain more tangible evidence of the existence of this animal, evidence which could be nailed into a box to be sent to the Museum in Paris. He prob-ably postponed his planned trip into the interior repeatedly just for this reason. But for a long time his quest remained, to use his own term, "unfruitful." At long last, in January 1866, he got two complete skins *en assez bon état* (in passable condition), probably by devious and slightly fantastic dealings which he unfortunately did not record in detail. Shortly thereafter the French Legation obtained three live *Sse-pu-hsiang* through the good offices of the Imperial Minister Hen-Tchi. Unfortunately they did not survive the trip, but Alphonse Milne-Edward in Paris had the material needed for the first scientific description.

It appeared in the *Comptes rendus des Séances de l'Académie des Sciences*.[1] As is customary, the first describer also has to propose a scientific name and Milne-Edward chose *Elaphurus davidianus*. In English-speaking countries, "Père David's deer" has become the usual

---

[1] *"Sur le Mi-lou ou Sseu-pou-siang, mammifère du nord de la Chine, qui constitue une section nouvelle de la famille de Cerfs. Note de Monsieur Alphonse Milne-Edward,"* vol. 62, 1866, p. 1090.

appellation, which is nice in that it honors the discoverer who may have had to pay dearly for his scientific curiosity, but is not quite as short and simple as milu, which is the commonly used name in continental Europe.

After that description had been published, the directors of zoological gardens all over the world had a brand-new dream—the future exhibition of a pair of milus. The various legations in Peking suddenly began receiving surprising mail, which dealt, not with trade and tariffs, mili-

Milu (Père David's deer)

tary matters of hush-hush nature, or trips of dignitaries, but with animals in the Imperial Hunting Park. The diplomats, presumably after shaking their heads in complete and assured privacy, went to work, and they were usually successful on a small scale. After all, the Imperial Hunting Park was not actually used for imperial hunts, and Father David himself had pointed out that according to his best information no hunt had ever taken place there, not only for as long as anybody could remember, but as long as the records accessible to historians went back.

In 1869 two live specimens were presented to the Royal Zoological Society of London by Sir Rutherford Alcock. Some years later, in 1883, the same Society bought two more in China. One specimen arrived in the Berlin Zoological Garden where it lived, lonely and unhappy, for many years and indoctrinated many Berliners with the belief that "stags in China look like that."

Even at first glance Père David's deer appears as peculiar a creature as further study proved it to be. It is rather large: a full-grown stag will stand 4 feet at the withers, about the same as a red deer. But its general carriage is quite different from that of the red deer, a fact that was not always known to taxidermists who mounted specimens. Instead of carrying its head high like a deer, the milu usually carries its head low, more like a cow. Its whole attitude has been termed "slouching" by Lydekker. The tail is unusually long for a deer and equipped with a hairy tassel like the tail of a donkey. The animal has both neck and throat manes. It has rather large wide-spreading hoofs which fall together with a loud clicking noise when it walks slowly. The antlers are especially strange; they are large and at first sight look as if they had been put on wrong. The main fork curves forward, dividing at least once, while the rear prong is undivided, very long, and directed backward in a way which is unlike any other antler known.

Usually only one young is born, in May. The fawns are heavily spotted with white but as the animal grows up the spots vanish, though the females seem to retain them a little better than the males. In summer the adults have a grayish red coat shading to whitish tints on the under side. In winter the coat is a grayish buff. The call of the adults is more like a bray than like the typical call of deer.

While naturalists were recording these facts in zoological gardens, the Duke of Bedford, father of the present Duke, decided to add the milu to the collection of rare mammals which he kept on his estates at Woburn Abbey in England. Of course nobody could possibly have guessed it then, but this decision kept Père David's deer alive. After the Duke of Bedford had decided that there should be milus at Woburn Abbey, they had to be obtained. In all probability he hoped to get some directly from China, but in the meantime he bought as many milus from zoological gardens in continental Europe as the directors would sell. At

Woburn Abbey, during the years 1893–1896, the surprising discovery was made that the milu sheds its antlers twice a year, instead of yearly like other deer.

Other zoological institutions, interested though they were in the reports coming out of Woburn Abbey, preferred to get first-hand knowledge. They wanted more milus themselves, and they kept writing letters which were routed by train and by steamship to wind up in the post-office of Peking, unless they traveled in diplomatic pouches. But while many of these letters were still traveling in a ship's hold, the milus of Nan Hai-tzu Park suffered a catastrophe. In 1895 a disastrous flood on the Hun Ho River sentenced thousands of peasants to death from starvation. The same flood also undermined the ancient brick wall of the Nan Hai-tzu Park, and many of the animals penned up there, including the rare milus, escaped and were killed and eaten by the starving populace.

Still, that cannot have been the end of the whole herd. Some must have survived, because it is reported that "the Imperial Hunting Park was thrown open in 1900 and all the deer in it killed by the International troops." In 1901 only one milu, a female, still existed in Peking, and she stayed alive until 1920.

This was the last Chinese milu, for the major mystery surrounding this animal is that it has never been found elsewhere. When Père David's discovery was reported in Europe, most naturalists began to wonder about the milu's normal habitat. Since none was known from the reasonably familiar areas of China near the coast, its habitat was probably to be sought in the interior. The idea that it was otherwise extinct and existed in the Park only was sufficiently "wild" not to occur to anybody. The natural assumption that there had to be wild milus somewhere was strengthened by travelers' reports that native guides, especially from the northern parts of China, had told them about occasional small herds of *sse-pu-hsiang*. But all these reports were mistaken. The Chinese really meant reindeer, as was dramatically demonstrated in 1904 when a hunt undertaken by Chinese netted eleven *"sse-pu-hsiang"* to be shipped to Woburn Abbey. Ten of the eleven died during the journey to the coast and the eleventh proved to be a reindeer. Some entries in Père David's later diaries must be founded on the same mistake; it is important to note that Père David never saw any of the animals he was told about.

Possibly native Chinese, living a considerable distance from Peking and knowing nothing about the real milu, took that term "four not alike" and fitted it to an animal they knew, and the reindeer qualifies reasonably well.

Slowly even the most careful naturalists, as well as the most hardened skeptics among them, had to admit that there were no wild milus. Even then they qualified the admission by the addition of a date of some sort. Obviously there were no wild milus in 1905 or 1906 when that fact had finally to be admitted. Most likely there had been no wild milus when Père David obtained his first information about the animal. And it was probable that there had been no wild milus even in 1800, 1700, or 1600. But at one time, somewhere in East Asia, there must have been wild milus. The question was when and where.

Where there are no facts, hypothesis is called upon to fill the gap. One of the more fanciful ideas was that the milu was not really Chinese at all but had been brought to China by the Manchu. This sounds rather romantic, but has nothing else to recommend it. In fact this particular hypothesis was mainly based upon those faint rumors of *"sse-pu-hsiang"* in North China and in Manchuria, rumors which were mistaken in themselves. The more likely theory is that the original home of the milu was the large plains of Chihli province which in former centuries were immense reed-covered swamps. As agriculture spread, the reeds were cut or burned and the swamps were drained; the milus gradually became homeless, dwindled in numbers, and finally survived only in the area which became the Imperial Hunting Park.

The idea that the milu preferred such areas as the former swamps of Chihli province is bolstered by observations of the Woburn Abbey specimens. "In England during summer they are very partial to water, often wading out as far as they can go, and sometimes swimming; at this season they feed largely upon water plants, especially rushes. The long and widely expanding hoofs, which form one of the characteristic features of this species, are evidently adapted for walking on marshy ground" (Richard Lydekker, *Deer of Many Lands,* 1901).

After the destruction of all Chinese milus except that one female the picture looked quite bleak. A number of zoological parks still had a specimen or two. But even if they did have two and if these two (quite important when you come to think of it) were of different sex, no offspring were forthcoming. I read somewhere a long time ago that "the milu does not breed when removed from his native soil." Well, it wasn't quite as noble as that; the specimens were mostly simply too old for breeding. If all the specimens in existence had been pooled at that time, at least a few fawns would have been born.

Some were born at Woburn Abbey, the only place where milus can still be said to live. And the Woburn Abbey herd slowly increased in size. Since there is little information available on the growth of the herd, or on what special care it receives, I wrote to Woburn Abbey and received a prompt reply, dated April 19, 1949, from the present Duke of Bedford, son of the founder of the herd. His Grace informed me that the number of milus at Woburn Abbey as of that date was 242: 45 stags, 119 hinds, and 78 last year's calves of as yet undetermined sex.

Eighteen Père David's deer were originally imported from various continental zoological gardens, but of these at least three never bred, so that the present herd is descended from not more than 15 animals. By the end of 1913, 137 had been born, 48 had died and 35 had been killed owing to old age or diseases, and one had been sent away. During my father's lifetime, I think, only two stags were sent away, one to Karl Hagenbeck in Germany and one to the London Zoological Gardens. During the summer of 1914, 20 calves were born and there were 88 animals in the herd. During the First World War, however, quite half of the herd perished of starvation, as the authorities insisted on sheep and cattle being turned into the Park and did not allow enough hay to be provided for winter feeding. I had to put up a great fight to prevent official folly from having similar disastrous consequences in the last war.

As for special care, the survivor from Old China turns out to be rather hardy.

The deer here run in the open Park, where they have access to open-fronted sheds, which are used a good deal by the adult animals, but rarely by the young ones. The sheds are unnecessary from the standpoint of giving protection from the cold as the deer are able to stand very severe weather and even the growing antlers of the stag do not seem to suffer from frost bite. . . .

The only artificial food which is necessary in winter is hay, but of this there must be an ample supply, as if there is any shortage and the young animals are allowed to get into a low condition, a number are lost from parasitic worms. Unlike most deer, Père David's do not care for the branches or fruit of trees, nor do they eat turnips. Apart from grass, the only natural food for which they show any fondness is certain water plants.

Since the herd is now so large it has been possible to restock zoological gardens from Woburn Abbey. Seven milus have been given to the London Zoological Society, but for natural reasons the Society now has eight. New York received four and now has five, the fawn having been born on April 10, 1949, the first in the Western Hemisphere. During 1949 four milus were shipped to Taronga Park near Sydney, Australia, and four to Dr. Heck in Munich, in exchange for Mongolian wild horses (*Equus przhevalski*).

In the course of time more and more people in various corners of the world will be able to see live examples of the milu, discovered not quite a century ago near Peking, extinct in nature and almost extinct in captivity, but saved at a time when to any "sane" observer the case must have seemed hopeless.

7: *Stronghold of the Pandas*

WHEN the Abbé Jean Pierre Armand David died in 1900 at the age of 74 years, he was world-famous in scientific circles. His various expeditions into the interior of eastern Asia, subsidized by the French government, had yielded large collections of all kinds of plants and animals. Even though he had worked almost alone—sometimes accompanied by two Chinese Christians—the fact that he was virtually the first to collect in a new territory resulted in a large number of discoveries of new species. And since scientists are grateful when handed a new discovery and since most of the time the only way in which they can express their gratitude is by naming the species after its discoverer, there are quite a number of scientific names, both botanical and zoological, which contain Father David's name. There is the tree *Davidia involucrata* and the lily *Lilium davidi,* the flowering peach *Prunus davidiana;* there is *Clematis davidi* and the lilaclike *Buddleia davidi.*

It would require a special and involved study to state how many varieties of plants were actually seen first and collected first by Father David, but ten score is likely to be a very modest guess. And while he discovered about a hundred new insects (several butterflies also bear his name), it is safe to say that the bulk of his discoveries was botanical.

Zoology benefited by three major discoveries from the life work of the Abbé David, the son of *le docteur* Fructueux Dominique David, *maire,* justice of the peace, and also physician of the little town of Espelette in the Basses-Pyrénées. The doctor David had probably assumed that his son would become a doctor too and he taught him much medical knowledge. While the son did not become a doctor, that medical knowledge often proved valuable; both missionaries and explorers can make good use of it, and a missionary-explorer needs it twice as much. The doctor David had also taught young Armand to recognize plants and birds. This probably was just part of general instruction; later on it turned out to be almost the most important part.

Father David's three major discoveries were all mammals. Needless to say, they were known to the Chinese, but that did not make them "known." The Chinese boasted of their old and elaborate culture—with much reason but also with a good deal of patriotic exaggeration which has made the life of historians difficult. But they did not have science in our sense. They also were remarkably reluctant to indulge in international cooperation, without which science is impossible. The only Chinese that fraternized easily were merchants and traders.

One of the three mammals discovered "in the flesh" by Father David was the Roxellana monkey, now known to zoologists under the sonorous name of *Rhinopithecus* (*Semnopithecus*) *roxellanae*. It had figured in some Chinese paintings, especially on vases, but had been taken to be an artistic convention, something like the Chinese dragon. But it was real, a fact which caused some special trouble in scientific circles, as we shall see later.

The other two discoveries, one of which was the milu, have a curious twist to them, slightly reminiscent of Madame Curie's "mistake" in naming her discoveries. Madame Skladovska-Curie, working in collaboration with her French husband, was Polish and a very patriotic Pole at that. Consequently, when she found a new chemical element, she named it polonium. It was something which was then of interest to chemists only, and even now, when the interested chemists have changed their title to "nuclear physicists," the element polonium is still just one of the "stages of radioactive decay." Some time later Madame Curie discovered another element which became known by name to everybody who can read and to quite a number of people who can't. But Madame Curie had already allotted the name of her native country. The new element was named radium.

Similarly, Père David's earlier discovery, the milu, is named after him, but the animal itself is not well known outside professional circles. The next one, which is known to everybody, does not bear his name; in fact most people don't even know who discovered it. It is the giant panda.

The Chinese knew that somewhere in the west of their immense country—the province of Szechwan, it turned out later—there lived bears. They knew of two kinds of bears, one which was dark in color and one which was mostly white. The latter was called "white bear," or, in Chinese, *bei-shun*. Mention of this *bei-shun* is said to occur in Chinese chronicles as far back as our year 650 A.D. But beyond the rumor that there existed a white bear in the mountains of the west nothing was known. A western scientist of a century ago, if queried about these rumors, could only have pleaded ignorance and might have added that such rumors are not necessarily true. And if he had been given more detail about the landscape where that white bear was supposed to exist— perfectly correct detail but coming from an untrustworthy source—he would have insisted that none of this could be true.

What he would have been told, and what scientists slowly had to learn and digest later, all seemed to add up to a collection of climatic impossibilities. The area in question, Szechwan, is located roughly under the thirtieth degree of northern latitude. A European or an American automatically associates this parallel with a torrid and dry climate. The thirtieth parallel runs south of Europe through Morocco, Algeria, Libya, Egypt, and Saudi Arabia, all of them spelling sand and heat. In the Western Hemisphere St. Augustine, Fla., is about on the thirtieth parallel. So is New Orleans. And so is Austin, Texas. The thirtieth parallel cuts across the Rio Grande and runs through northern Mexico, across the Gulf of California and the peninsula of Baja California.

No doubt about it, it is warm under the thirtieth parallel. A semitropical landscape, with magnolias and rhododendron and bamboo, seems quite indicated. If someone reports that there are monkeys in such a forest, there is no reason off-hand to doubt it. Monkeys are tropical, as everybody knows. Their habitat is everywhere centered on the equator, from about the Tropic of Cancer in the north not quite to the Tropic of Capricorn on the south. And in places monkeys go beyond the Tropic of Cancer northward, the northernmost natural colony being the famous herd on the Rock of Gibraltar, under 36 degrees northern latitude.

So much for general impressions based purely on the geographical latitude. But the few people who had been in these sections of inner China reported that warmth did not trouble them; in fact, that it was quite often quite cold. The reason was that the land was generally high above sea level. Of course that was entirely possible. The South American Andes, more precisely the *Cordillera Occidental* in Ecuador, shows snow-capped peaks in the immediate vicinity of the equator itself. An area, although situated in the tropics, might not be tropical in appearance because of high altitude.

The reports from China said, however, that although the area was cold, with frequent snow, it had some tropical characteristics just the same. Bamboo, for example, the epitome of wet-warm jungles, was said to climb up to 11,000- and even 13,000-foot altitudes, its long reedy stems on occasion bending under loads of snow. Among this impossible high-altitude bamboo, pretty rhododendrons were said to grow and to flower, also some varieties of magnolia. All this did not seem to make much sense.

The case was rendered even more weird by Father David's Roxellana monkey. Almost at first glance it was obvious that the Roxellana monkey had to be a close relative of the famous proboscis monkey, or *Semnopithecus nasicus,* of the moisture-dripping hot jungles of Borneo. That proboscis monkey, while not differing too greatly in size and shape from other tropical monkeys, has a simply fearsome long nose. Usually monkeys have rather short and small noses. But the nose of the proboscis monkey goes far beyond the biggest olfactory appendage any human being ever sported. In fact, with the proboscis monkey it *is* an appendage. Old males, when they want to eat, have to hold their food in one hand and push their nose aside with the other. Young females, as if to make up for it, have tiny turned-up "Little Lulu" noses which would be a surprising sight even if not contrasted with those of the old males.

The Roxellana monkey resembles the young females of the related proboscis monkey, as far as the nose is concerned. Needless to say, its fur is much heavier than its relative's, as one would expect from a variety of monkeys which has taken to snow and to mountain forests 2 miles and more above sea level. The fur, unkempt in appearance and uneven looking, boasts a rather unusual coloration. The back is gray with a pronounced golden sheen, snowy white farther down. Belly and chest, neck, ears, and the section fringing the face are a mixture of yellow and rusty red. The hairless face, with that turned-up miniature nose in the center, is blue-green in color. Small wonder that Chinese paintings, which exaggerated the colors only slightly, were not regarded as portraits of an actually existing animal. But to the zoologist this coloration did not seem too unusual, once it had been shown to exist. But it was unusual to have a member of a typically tropical tribe sporting about in a snow-covered landscape.

Father David's "snow monkey," as it was actually called for a while, got in the way of many later arguments, since without it, any find of fossil bones of monkeys would automatically have spelled a very warm climate for the area and time in question. After its discovery, such generalizations were unsafe.

The accepted explanation for the whole case, from monkeys to bamboo, is that this area was once actually a semitropical plain before tectonic forces started building mountains. Presumably many of the tropical plants and animals could not adapt to the gradually cooling climate and either emigrated in time or became locally extinct. The ones that could adapt did so and stayed on. And among them was that legendary *bei-shun* of the Chinese, the "white bear" of the bamboo forest in the snow mountains.

It is not quite clear from Father David's diaries [1] whether he had doubted the story of the "white bear" before he obtained evidence or whether the evidence, when obtained, confirmed his hopes. He just wrote down what he experienced and saw. The giant panda first appears under the date of March 11, 1869. Père David had gone on an excursion, and when he and his companions returned, they found themselves invited for tea and *sucreries* (candies) *chez un certain Li* whom he characterized as the principal landowner in the valley. In Li's house he saw a pelt of a giant panda. Père David did not use that name, of course; he referred to it as *le fameux ours blanc et noir* (the famous white and black bear). He noted happily that his hunters had promised that they would certainly obtain one for him very shortly.

---

[1] The travel diaries of Père David were reissued under the title of *Abbé David's Diary* by Harvard University Press in 1949, but in a rather unfortunate form. Numerous minor and major cuts have been made in the text but are not marked, so that one has to keep going back to the original if one wants to make sure not to miss anything. As for the translation itself, I can only say that the diaries were "done into English" in a manner which eliminates all the flavor and most of the style.

"Very shortly" can mean a lot of things in China; in this case it meant twelve days, a rather reasonable interval of time. All the more reasonable in that particular case because the hunters had been gone for ten days. They had caught a young giant panda alive, but had killed it so that they could carry it more easily. Père David noted that the colors were the same that he had observed on the fur of the adult specimen in the home of the landowner Li. Color generally white, with black hind legs, fore-

Giant panda

legs also black but the black color extending ribbonlike across the shoulders from foreleg to foreleg, with black ears, black muzzle, and black "spectacles." Père David also noted that the soles of the feet were hairy, which is not typical for bears, but he thought that it was a different kind of bear. He did regret that the hunters had killed it and he remarked slyly that they sold it to him "dearly" (entry of March 23, 1869).

On April 1 another giant panda was brought in, this time one which the hunters claimed was fully grown. Unfortunately Père David did not record its weight. We now know that a strong male can weigh up to 300 pounds. He noted that the black was not quite as black as in the young specimen and that the white was more soiled.

On April 6 he got, not a giant panda, but a lesser panda, but since he still took the *bei-shun* to be a bear he was unaware of the relationship. He knew that the "panda" ("lesser panda" in our terminology) was already known to science, but he wrote down what his hunters told him, that it lives in holes and on trees, that its food is "vegetable or animal, depending on occasion," and that the Chinese call it "mountain child" because of its childlike cries.

Another lesser panda came in the following day, alive. Père David noted that its paws and head were like those of the *bei-shun,* except in size, of course; a lesser panda never measures more than 2 feet from nose to the root of the tail. The tail itself is from 12 to 16 inches long. "Its stomach is full of leaves."

I now leave Père David's diaries, and temporarily the giant panda too, because by a strange coincidence the first lesser panda to get to Europe reached the London Zoological Garden during the same year in which Père David obtained one along with the giant panda from his native hunters. The lesser panda had been known for some time, and descriptions had been given, most of them comparing the lesser panda with the European fox. This was due, no doubt, partly to the fact that the European fox was a familiar animal to the describers, and partly to the thick furry "fox tail" and general coloration. The fur of the lesser panda is a golden red. The inner surface of its large ears is a beautifully contrasting snow white, as are its cheeks. The four legs appear to be black at first glance, but in reality are just a blackened version of the same red. And while the typical "shoulder strap" of the giant panda does not appear in a pronounced blackish-red, it can be seen on caged specimens as a slightly deeper tone of red. The tail shows a number of rings, like that of the raccoon. In fact the Englishmen who talked about the lesser panda, while comparing it with the fox, called it the Himalaya raccoon.

How it came to be called "panda" is an open question. One explanation is that it is a corruption of a native name *niyalya-ponga,* which is said to mean "bamboo eater." I can't vouch for the translation, but if it is correct, it is also factually true, for both pandas. They are both vegetarians and the statements like the one by Father David's hunters about "animal food on occasion" have not been borne out by subsequent observation.

The original discoverer of the lesser panda was the British naturalist

Hardwicke. Because he delayed publication of his description a number of older books attribute the discovery to the explorer Simpson, but the latter was "merely" the man who brought the first live specimen to London. Three lesser pandas had been caught but only one of them survived the long trip. And when Professor Bartlett in London caught the

Lesser panda (also called Himalaya raccoon)

first glimpse of the new and precious arrival he was justified in doubting whether any visitor to the Zoological Garden would ever see it. The animal was in a deplorable condition, too weak to stand on its legs, barely capable of crawling on the floor, sick and dirty. During the long sea voyage it may have been seasick; many animals can resist the motion of a ship for a much shorter time than the most sensitive of human passengers. And its food had consisted of dried grass, fresh grass on occasion, boiled rice and milk.

Professor Bartlett could not do anything about past seasickness, but he could try to improve the diet at once. Since nobody had ever kept a lesser panda as a pet, the nature of an improved diet had to be found by trial and error. He tried boiled chicken and boiled rabbit; the panda did not accept either. He tried milk, sweetened with sugar and with an egg yolk or two mixed in. That worked. He tried tea with sugar, with the addition of cornmeal or ground green peas. The panda took that too and improved visibly. After a few days Bartlett dared to let it out into an enclosed garden. The panda at once pounced upon some rosebushes, ate a few young shoots and leaves, then found some unripe apples on the ground and ate those, and began looking, successfully, for berries.

Professor Bartlett's fears that the animal might have a relapse because of this sudden spree of feeding on things which certainly did not grow on Tibetan mountains were completely unfounded. The panda, eating roses and unripe apples, improved beautifully, grew new fur, and seemed, in general, in the best of health. But it never became really "tame"; it was always on guard, nervous, and given to sudden violence. The other lesser pandas which have been imported by various zoological gardens since then sometimes showed a similar behavior, sometimes not. Apparently it is mostly a matter of individual temperament, not a characteristic of the species.

I have neglected so far to mention the scientific name of the lesser panda. It is *Ailurus fulgens*. The first part is simply the Greek word for "cat," and the second means "shiny" or "glossy," so that one could translate the whole as "shining cat." That, of course, is nonsense. The lesser panda is not a member of the cat family—but for quite some time scientists were puzzled about the problem of just what it is. Somebody, going by the established scientific name, dubbed it "cat-bear," and for some time one could find in books that "the range of the cat-bear extends from Nepal in the west to northern Burma and the Chinese province of Yunnan in the east."

But meanwhile Père David had discovered the *bei-shun* or, as the word was also rendered, *pei-ssewn,* our well-known giant panda. There were four skins in the museum in Paris and for more than a decade all scientific knowledge rested on these four skins. Some time later a fifth skin was mounted in Europe, in the museum of Stuttgart, Germany. Its origin is somewhat mysterious. It seems that this specimen was shot by a native hunter who then traded the skin to a Chinese merchant who, in turn, sold it to a German. Its existence did not increase scientific knowledge to any great extent. The *bei-shun* was still taken to be a bear and the Germans began advocating "harlequin bear" as a popular name for the animal. Anybody who has ever watched a giant panda clown for hours in its enclosure in a zoological garden will have to admit that the name would have been highly descriptive. But it failed to be generally accepted; there were not enough people then who knew about the animal. The scientific name had become *Ailuropus melanoleucus*. The first part of that name actually means "catlike," but it was given with reference to the lesser panda *Ailurus* and intended to mean "panda-like." [2] The second part of the name just consists of the Greek words for black and white.

As the name indicates, the relationship between the two animals had been recognized, but that did not solve the chief problem. In spite of a generally bearlike appearance, the pandas were obviously not bears. Their dentition proved what was known anyway, that they were vegetarians. But, it could be argued, the true bears are a rather diversified group as far as diet goes. Many bears subsist on a part vegetable, part meat diet. The polar bear is exclusively on a meat diet, surely because its environment has no edible plants to offer. So why not assume that some bears, in a suitable environment, may become outright vegetarians? Well, that is possible, of course, but such reasoning did not change anatomical features that have nothing to do with diet habits. And these features simply were not "bear."

The problem of the panda's place in relationship to other present-day mammals could be settled in only one manner: by the discovery of fossil forms which represented "bridges" between pandas and other mammals. Well, one can't discover fossils to order, as the case of the chirotherium has shown. But for some time suspicion centered on a fossil mammal which was probably ancestral to the present-day bears and which appeared first during the Miocene subdivision of the Tertiary period. When it came to light in Upper Silesia it was thought first to be a wolf-sized carnivore somewhere between present-day bears and present-day hyenas. Consequently it was called *Hyaenarctos* or "hyaena-bear." The same type was subsequently found in Austria and Italy and in Spain and the idea that it might be a connecting link between bears and hyenas was slowly dropped.

Then a much larger form of the "same" animal was found in Tertiary layers in India and China and when that happened Professor Max Weber

---

[2] It has since been changed to *Ailuropoda* or "panda foot."

felt certain that he had found the solution. The giant panda was apparently just a surviving hyaenarctos, a kind of ancestral bear which had somehow succeeded in staying alive in its mountain retreat in western Szechwan. A comparison between the molars of hyaenarctos and giant panda seemed to clinch the case; both indicated a predominantly vegetarian diet. Apparently the whole bear tribe had started off essentially vegetarian and the giant panda had continued the tradition, becoming wholly vegetarian in the course of time. The other bears, by adapting themselves to different conditions, had become more carnivorous or even completely so.

It was an interesting hypothesis, but it happened not to be correct. Whether hyaenarctos is an actual ancestor of the living bears is still debatable and with it the question about the original diet of the bear tribe. But the living pandas, and especially the giant panda, have no direct connection with either fossil or living bears.

While paleontologists were wondering just what animals might be related to the pandas and what connecting links might be known but not recognized as such, the experts on living mammals and most especially the directors of zoological gardens had another approach. If I were director of a zoological garden I would keep in my desk drawer a list of all the animals which I would like to exhibit but which are not in the garden.

The giant panda must have been among the high-ranking zoological daydreams for decades. The lesser panda could be kept in captivity, as Bartlett had proved first. It should be possible to keep the giant panda too. The main problem was to get one. Not only was an expedition to western Szechwan an expensive venture, one could not even be sure that it would be successful. The giant panda seemed to be very rare even in its own small habitat. Père David had succeeded in obtaining four skins. Then one more had been brought to Europe. In 1916 a white man saw one giant panda alive. That was the whole record. It was not until 1929 that a panda was even shot by a white man. More precisely it was shot by two white men, Kermit and Theodore Roosevelt, the sons of President Theodore Roosevelt. They had set out on an expedition and panda hunt with the understanding that the one who saw a panda first would notify the other, if circumstances permitted, so that both could fire together.

It happened just that way, impossible though it may seem to any hunter, especially since the two brothers were not even together when Theodore saw the first and only giant panda they encountered. The specimen which was shot literally by the brothers Roosevelt is now on exhibit in Chicago. Another giant panda was bagged by the Marshall Field Zoological Expedition to Southeast Asia in 1930–32 which was led by Floyd Tangier Smith.

These two expeditions not only yielded a museum specimen apiece, they established definitely where the giant panda could be found. The habitat of the lesser panda had been known to be just south of the Himalaya range. The giant panda had been taken first at the eastern end of the lesser panda's habitat but nobody could be sure where else it might be found. In 1932 it became a certainty that the giant panda occurred only in western Szechwan province; the total habitat is a mountainous district, measuring some 75 miles from west to east and about 400 miles north and south.

The problem then was to get one alive. Floyd T. Smith seemed to be the first to succeed. In 1936 he captured a giant panda which was destined for the London Zoological Garden. But the specimen died in Singapore.

The developments that followed make a picture which is not only crowded by the rapid sequence of events but also slightly confused by rivalries among individuals and institutions. After reading my way through a stack of newspaper clippings, statements in the publications of the institutions involved, and a book written too early, I got the following impression of the sequence of events:

It seems that Floyd T. Smith, who had headed the Marshall Field Expedition, had been associated with William H. Harkness, Jr., who suddenly died in Shanghai early in 1936. His widow, Mrs. Ruth Harkness, then decided to carry on the work and went to China in 1937. She not only succeeded in obtaining a female panda cub, named Su-lin, but she got it safely to the Brookfield Zoo in Chicago. When this feat was publicized, Floyd T. Smith issued a statement saying that he had had his eye on Su-lin for a long time and had just waited for her to grow a little older.

Su-lin did not live very long in captivity; she died in March 1938.

Meanwhile Mrs. Harkness had gone back to China and had obtained another female panda cub which was named Mei-mei. Mei-mei was also shipped to Chicago. And a few days after Su-lin's death, Floyd T. Smith came back from an expedition which had obtained four young pandas, three of them males. He arrived in Chengtu with his catch on April 3, 1938.

All along, the New York Zoological Society had been of the opinion that if the Brookfield Zoo in Chicago exhibited a live giant panda the Bronx Zoological Park in New York was at least equally well qualified. Smith's arrival in Chengtu with the four pandas seemed the proper moment for New York to acquire one. But the price asked by Smith was "far above and beyond" what New York was willing to pay. New York then began to negotiate in great secrecy with the West China Union University in Chengtu, Province of Szechwan, the only learned institution located close to the panda country. Early in the summer of 1938 Frank Dickinson, a missionary attached to that university, cabled to New York that he had obtained a panda cub from natives. Almost on the spot the cub was named Pandora and it arrived safely in New York on June 10, 1938, later becoming a major attraction at the New York World's Fair in 1939–40.

Some time later, in April 1939, the Chinese Foreign Office notified all governments that it intended to keep the giant panda alive on its home grounds and that further attempts to secure giant pandas would not be encouraged by the Chinese government. But, it was added, an exception might be made in the case of a reputable scientific institution.

In August 1939 permission was given for a panda to be shipped to the zoological garden in St. Louis.

In October 1939 the "last permit" was given for the export of a panda cub, destination Chicago.

And in 1941 there was something like an absolutely final permit: two panda cubs were given to the New York Zoological Society as a present of the Chinese government to express China's appreciation for American United China Relief.

Since then, to the best of my knowledge and ability to find out, no giant panda has left China. Nor has there been any news about the fate of the panda in its native habitat.

But meanwhile the old stumbling block of the panda's relationship to other present-day mammals has been removed by a careful study made by Professor William K. Gregory of the American Museum of Natural History.

You remember that Professor Max Weber had tried to establish a relationship between the living giant panda on the one hand and the fossil hyaenarctos from the Miocene subperiod and the whole bear tribe on the other hand. To Professor Weber the giant panda had seemed an almost unchanged survivor from the early days of the bears. The lesser panda, in his scheme, had been merely an unimportant offshoot of the bigger panda.

The truth proved to be an almost complete reversal of Professor Weber's ideas. An American expert, H. C. Raven, claimed that the lesser panda was the older form. The giant panda, although more impressive in size and coloration, and on account of rarity, was an offshoot of the lesser panda—one might say a lesser panda grown large and spectacular. And since the lesser panda was, in a manner of speaking, the "original," any connection of the pandas with other mammals had to be made with the smaller of the two. The big ones, far from being "living fossils," belonged to a relatively recent species.

Professor Gregory's study confirmed this point of view. If one looked for relatives of the pandas, one had to look for relatives of the lesser panda. And that did not prove to be so difficult, once the fairly wide-spread idea that the giant panda was a "distant bear" had been dropped. The nearest well-known living relative, although some distance removed, was our American raccoon. The search then went on via living relatives of the raccoon, extinct relatives of the raccoon, extinct ancestors of the raccoon, down to an animal which was the ancestor not only of the raccoons—and the pandas—but of other animals as well.

The results of the study are best told in chronological, or rather geological, sequence. The story begins in the days of the amber forest, during the subperiod of the "dawn of the new," the Eocene. At that time there lived a group of small, rat- or squirrel-sized mammals which had carnivorous habits but which were not yet any of our well-known groups of carnivorous mammals. They were neither cats nor dogs, nor bears nor martens; they were just unspecialized carnivores. During the latter

part of the Eocene some of these animals began to show a little more
specialization. They are known to paleontologists as the "miacids." If they
still existed, they would probably be thought at first to belong to a group
of carnivorous mammals that still thrives in the warmer sections of

American raccoon

modern Asia: the civets. But while they must have looked like the
modern civets, they were not the same.

One subperiod later, these miacids had clearly split into two groups.
Both had a doglike appearance but one might be tempted to call the one
group "heavy" dogs and the other group "light" dogs. A typical representative of the "heavy" dogs has received the name of *Daphaenus;* a
contemporary (i.e., Oligocene) representative of the "light" dogs has been
called *Cynodictis*.

Daphaenus can be dismissed with a few words; its line is the direct
line of the present-day bears. After the Eocene there is no connection between the bear tribe and the raccoon tribe. As for cynodictis, the lighter-

boned offspring of the miacids, it led to two groups of modern animals. By the end of the Oligocene subperiod the cynodictislike animals had already separated into two lines. One of them goes straight to the present-day dogs and wolves, naturally through a large number of intermediate forms.

The other strain, during the Miocene subperiod, produced an animal which might well be called an ancestral raccoon. It has the scientific name *Phlaocyon,* and if it were alive today completely unchanged, it would be considered another variety of lesser panda by anybody but an expert. This, at least, is what the bones lead us to believe; it is just possible that phlaocyon sported a coloration and markings which would destroy the resemblance. It is not very likely, though, because the animal which appears to be an almost unchanged phlaocyon has a coloration which even enhances the resemblance to the lesser panda. This animal occurs in Mexico, where it is known as *cacomistle,* but can also be found in some of our southwestern states, where it is called "ring-tailed cat." The scientific name is *Bassariscus.* While bassariscus did not change much during 15 million years, the raccoon did, mostly by growing bigger and heavier. The coati-mundi of the tropical sections of the New World is also an offspring of phlaocyon, but the kinkajou or "honey bear" of Mexico and Central America is not. The kinkajou belongs to the raccoon family all right, but its evolutionary line did not pass through phlaocyon, it goes back to phlaocyon's ancestors.

All this can be made a little clearer if we do pay attention not only to the relationships but to the geography involved. Phlaocyon's habitat, as far as known, was about the center section of the North American continent. From there it and its offspring spread. Some of them went south and either stayed almost unchanged (cacomistle) or grew bigger (raccoon and coati-mundi). Others went north and invaded Asia via the land bridge over the Bering Strait. They became pandas, lesser pandas. Apparently they skirted the big Asiatic mountains to the south of the mountains where the lesser pandas still live. But they must have proceeded westward from there; we know fossil lesser pandas from the Balkan peninsula and from England.

The giant panda is known in a fossil state only from western China and from Burma. It must have originated, in rather recent times, in about the same place where it still lives, and it never became numerous enough to migrate far from its home.

Because of these studies we know now not only what pandas really are but also how they got where they are. And we know that the giant panda was found in its original home.

The question which remains is, does it still live there?

8: A Bird Known as Takahe

IT WAS during the summer of 1642–43—Southern Hemisphere style —that the coast of New Zealand was first seen by a white man. The Hollander Abel Janszoon Tasman, having sailed the seas south of Australia, had pushed to the east, wondering where and when he would find land again. As was logical considering the course he sailed, he made his landfall on the South Island of New Zealand, and, because an orderly log was kept on board the ship *Heemskirk,* we even know the precise date: December 16, 1642.

Since Tasman made no attempt at exploration it is a matter of taste and inclination whether this date should be considered the date of the "discovery" of New Zealand or whether that term should be reserved for the landing of Captain James Cook's *Endeavour* in November 1769. However, the islands had been discovered and even settled by the Maoris at a much earlier date. Some two hundred years before Columbus sailed for America the Maori canoes had reached New Zealand's North Island. They came from a place which in Maori legends is called "Hawaiki"— which was not Hawaii but a different island much farther to the south. In New Zealand, the island of Raiatea, a little over 100 nautical miles to the northwest of Tahiti, is generally accepted as "Hawaiki."

While naturally we don't know the dates, the experts agree that the Maoris must have arrived between 1300 and 1350 A.D., and that during that period there were several waves of Maori immigration to *Aotea-roa* ("Long white cloud"), meaning New Zealand. All landed on the North Island and spread to the South Island later. By the time Tasman saw the snow-covered peaks of the gigantic mountain chain that is called the Southern Alps, the settling of both main islands was completed.

The Maoris must have been greatly impressed by their new land. They might have seen towering mountains before, but not eternal snow. There were also glaciers, slow-moving rivers of hard ice. There were mighty forests with enormous kauri trees. There were active volcanoes with smoke pennants hanging from their summits. There were boiling springs, but also ice-cold rivers. There were rocky islands off shore cut by deep bays, and inland there were large plains. And on the mountains and plains there lived strange birds, like the small hen-sized kiwi which has hairlike feathers, no wings at all, and nostrils at the tip of its long bill instead of at the base as all other birds have. And there were wingless and flightless bird giants, the moas. These resembled the African ostrich, though the Maoris would not have known that, but surpassed it in size—at least some species did, among the score discovered by scientists from about 1840 on.

At that time there still lived a few old Maoris who said they had helped to hunt moas when they were boys. At first all these statements were collected avidly, mostly in the hope that they might lead to the discovery of a living moa. When none was found, some scientists began to think that the Maoris had not told the truth. There was no doubt that such birds had once existed on New Zealand. Scientists had found their bones. While a few of these bones were decidedly fossil, most of them were in what is technically known as a "subfossil state." That means old, but not yet old enough to fossilize as, for example, the bones of dinosaurs or of the large mammals of the Tertiary period had done. The trouble with the term "subfossil" is that it is not very specific. In certain surroundings a subfossil bone may be 200 years old, and one in other surroundings 2000 years old. In fact, the expert has no trouble in imagining conditions in which a bone may be 30,000 years old and still "subfossil."

Some skeptical scientists wished to push all moas back to the period before the Maori immigration, in a kind of reaction from the earlier hopes of still finding them alive. Later and more balanced judgment tended, however, to believe the stories of the old natives and to assume that moas were probably still alive, if rare, in 1800.

Zoologists noted another strange fact about New Zealand. There was an exceptionally varied bird life, having representatives of exceptional size (the moas, especially the variety called *Dinornis*), of exceptional strangeness (*Apteryx,* the kiwi), and of exceptional beauty—too long a list to mention here—but *there were no mammals!*

We now know the reason. During the Cretaceous period, which ended some 60 million years ago, New Zealand was still connected with the rest of the world, specifically with southeastern Asia, by a land bridge via New Caledonia and New Guinea. But that land bridge collapsed before the end of the Cretaceous period. New Zealand became isolated a good 80 million years ago. At that time mammals existed, but only in small numbers and comparatively few varieties. It happened either that none ever got to New Zealand or that the few types which became isolated there died out afterward.

If the Maoris had been professional zoologists, they would have noticed that there were two kinds of bats, but these were evidently late arrivals like the Maoris themselves. The Maoris brought two more types of mammals with them: a dog, now extinct, and a black rat, now very rare.

Indigenous land mammals are represented by one rumor only. One may put it paradoxically by saying that the only native mammal to exist before the Maoris arrived may never have existed at all. When, in about 1850, one Mr. Walter Mantell, son of the then very famous British geologist and paleontologist Dr. Gideon Algernon Mantell, was collecting zoological material in New Zealand, he heard about this animal. Mantell wrote down its name as *kaureke*. Others have given it as *waitoreke*. Mantell, camping at Arowenua in the vicinity of the present coastal city of Timaru, talked to local natives who assured him that the *kaureke* could be found some ten miles inland. He at once offered a reward and a number of Maoris made their way into the interior. The natives returned after some time, crestfallen and empty-handed. Walter Mantell wrote to his father that he did not distrust the native accounts, even though this particular attempt had failed. He did say that the animal might be extinct, but that he thought that, if so, "its extermination is of a very recent date." Even today the problem of the *waitoreke* or *kaureke* is not settled; not only has it not been found alive, but we still don't know whether there ever was such an animal.

Of course Walter Mantell had a valid reason for being optimistic about the quest—which brings us to the bird now known as takahe.

When the new settlers from England, insofar as they had any scientific interests, were all excited about the big moa bones and were questioning all natives who claimed to have even the slightest bit of information, they often came across a certain story.

In addition to the large moas, the natives insisted, there had been another large bird, not as large as the moas but larger than any bird that flies, which provided exceptionally good eating. They had hunted it and feasted, but now there were none left. The whites listened with interest; at first they had no reason for doubt. But their belief and with it their interest in the stories slowly dwindled; the bones and eggs and occasional feathers which they found all belonged to different varieties of moas.

But in 1847 Walter Mantell acquired near Waingongoro on the North Island a bird's skull, breastbone, and a few other parts of the skeleton, which decidedly did not belong to a moa. First guess was that it was a very large rail. Mantell packed and boxed the bones with great care and shipped them to his father in London. He wrote that this was in all probability the bird which the natives called *moho* or *takahe,* the latter name being used on the South Island, the former on the North Island where the bones had been collected. Doctor Mantell gave these bones, and a lot of moa remains which had been in the same shipment, to the famous Professor Richard Owen who had been the first to describe a moa bone in a scientific journal. Professor Owen could only say that the Maoris had spoken the truth. There had been a rather large, goose-sized, flightless but not wingless bird on the islands. He called it *Notornis,* and in order to honor the collector the name of *Notornis mantelli* was proposed and accepted.

So far things were going as might be expected, but two years later the first big surprise came. It came from the South Island, more specifically from the extreme southwestern portion which on maps printed in New Zealand is usually called "West Coast Sounds." There are a number of fiords which cut deeply into the land, forming a number of islands. Most of the islands are small, but some, like Secretary Island and Resolution Island, are quite large.

In 1849 a group of sealers camped on Resolution Island, hunting seals. Snow had fallen the previous night and one of the men noticed the footprints of a large bird in the new snow. Being curious, a number of them followed the footprints with their dogs and after some time saw a large bird in the distance. The dogs pursued it at once. The bird ran away with unusual speed. But the dogs finally caught it and brought it back to their masters. The bird screamed loudly when it was taken away from the dogs and fought with bill and claws as best it could.

Notornis mantelli

The extinct variety of takahe from the North Island of New Zealand, as reconstructed in a book by Professor Richard Owen, published in 1879. When the drawing was made, only the fossil remains from the North Island and two unskillfully taken skins from the South Island were known. This picture is redrawn from the original lithograph prepared for Professor Owen.

The sealers were no naturalists, but this bird was something to behold. To begin with it was quite large, with a comparatively short neck, but with long strong legs and strong feet. The heavy sharp bill and the strong legs were bright red, the feathers of head and throat bluish-black—purplish-blue on the back of the neck. The back and most of the rather small wings were dull olive-green, the larger feathers tipped with verditer green; while the breast, the sides of the body, and the flanks were of a very beautiful purplish-blue. The larger wing and tail feathers showed a more metallic blue while the underside of the tail was white. Presumably impressed by the glitter of its plumage, the men did not kill the bird instantly but put it aboard their ship where it was kept alive for three or four days. Then, not quite knowing what else to do with it, the sealers killed the bird, roasted it, and ate it. But they saved the skin and offered it for sale or trade when they landed again.

By one of those incredible coincidences the skin was secured by the same Walter Mantell who had purchased the remains at Waingongoro on the North Island. He shipped it to his father in London and there excitement ran high. The bird which had been found in "subfossil state" on the North Island was evidently still alive on the South Island. Scientists compared the drawings of the probable appearance of the bird which had been made from those few bones with the shape demonstrated by that skin and felt even more elated. It matched wonderfully; about the only thing the experts had not been able to guess was the coloration.

Specimen number two followed in 1851. It came from almost the same locality, from Secretary Island, where it had been captured by a Maori. The circumstances of this capture do not seem to have been recorded, but apparently the Maori did what the sealers had done: ate the bird and saved the skin. The skin passed through the hands of two generations of the Mantell family and ended up in the British Museum, literally alongside the first.

So far the story of notornis had been exclusively, if not too firmly, in the hands of New Zealanders, Maori or white. But in the latter years of the 1850s foreign explorers began trying to get into it. An Austrian vessel, the *Novara,* in the course of a voyage round the world and to the southern seas, lasting from 1857 till 1859, landed in New Zealand ports in 1858. One of the scientists aboard was Professor Ferdinand von Hochstetter, a geologist by specialization, but also greatly interested in geographical, zoological, anthropological, and ethnographical problems. Professor von Hochstetter did what he could, considering the circumstances and the limited time at his disposal, to obtain a notornis. He had very little to go on, since up to that time only the Waingongoro bones and two skins had been seen by scientists. Most of the skeleton and all of the intestinal organs were still missing. Nobody could tell what the bird's habits were, except that it was obviously elusive, or very rare, or most likely both.

Scientists did guess that the bird ate plants, but could not be sure even about that. In spite of concentrated efforts Professor von Hochstetter had no success in finding a takahe, though he did important work in other fields.

Nor did others do much better. Sir James Hector explored the southwest coast of Otago Province (the second southernmost province of the South Island) in 1863 and succeeded in locating the Maori who had caught the second specimen. The Maori did not consider the bird rare; he assured Sir James that there were plenty of them at the head of the northwest arm of Lake Te Anau, near a small lake in the valley that leads to Bligh Sound. Sir James did hear some strange noises—"a boom followed by a shrill whistle," and another exploring party confirmed this experience. But neither party found out what produced these sounds.

In 1866 the chronicler of New Zealand birds, Sir Walter Lawry Buller, received a letter from a Dr. Hector, who told him that he had come across "tracks of the takahe near Thompson Sound and the middle arm of Lake Te Anau in 1861–1862." This occurrence had not prompted the doctor's letter, however; what he really wanted to report was the experience of a Mr. Gibson. Mr. Gibson, a botanist, was a newcomer to New Zealand who, in August or September 1866, had seen a large bird near Motupipi. The bird had been only a few feet from Mr. Gibson in the tall swamp grass. The description given by him tallied in every respect with notornis. Doctor Hector stressed two points. One was that Mr. Gibson did not know about the takahe and had never seen a picture of it. Secondly, Mr. Gibson *did* know the swamp hen, the *pukeho* of the Maori and *Porphyrio melanotus* of the scientists, which looks somewhat similar.

This swamp hen, which is actually distantly related to the takahe, resembles it in coloration of plumage, but has a smaller bill, somewhat longer and slenderer legs with much longer toes, and a lighter build generally. Moreover, it can fly and it is not rare. Nor is it restricted to New Zealand but occurs in New Guinea, New Caledonia, Australia, Norfolk Islands, Lord Howe Islands, both main islands of New Zealand, and on many of the small islands off New Zealand.

In 1868 Sir Walter Buller heard an even more astonishing account from Sir George Grey, who had been Governor of South Australia, twice

Governor of New Zealand, and Governor of the Cape Colony, and who later became Prime Minister of New Zealand—not a man who was likely to make up tales.

Sir George Grey tells me that in 1868 he was at Preservation Inlet and saw a party of natives there who gave him a circumstantial account of the recent killing of a small moa (*Palapteryx?*), describing with much spirit its capture out of a drove of six or seven. The same natives pointed out to him a valley where the *Notornis* was said to be still plentiful. This was at the head of Preservation Inlet. Besides being swampy, the ground was covered with vegetation so close and thick that it was impossible to penetrate it on foot, and under this cover the *Notornis* might roam about in perfect security.[1]

But while the travelers who actually got to New Zealand wrote optimistic letters and told tales like the ones just reported, some experts in Europe grew doubtful. These assertions quoted "only natives," and did not produce any proof. Maybe the takahe had disappeared from the main islands first, to survive precariously and for a short time on adjacent islands. Maybe it was altogether wrong to contrast the "living form" of the South Island with the "extinct form" of the North Island. Maybe takahe had ceased to exist under the eyes of the white man, as had the dodo of Mauritius and the great auk of the small islands off Iceland. Takahe even got written up in a book devoted exclusively to extinct birds.

While that book was being written in Europe, a rabbit hunter with his dog camped in the open in the province called Otago on the South Island, near the Mararoa River and some 9 miles away from the southern end of Lake Te Anau. One day in December 1879 the dog brought him a large bird, still alive, still struggling. The rabbit hunter killed it and hung it up on the ridgepole of his tent. It so happened that the station manager, a Mr. J. Connor, visited the rabbit hunter's camp the following day. He was given the dead bird, which he immediately suspected of being a takahe. He took it to the station, skinned it carefully, and boiled the flesh off the bones, saving every bone. It was the first complete skeleton of notornis to arrive in London.

There follows a financial interlude.

---

[1] Sir Walter Lawry Buller, *A History of the Birds of New Zealand* (London, 1888), vol. 11, p. 88.

The third takahe was auctioned off in London. A representative of the British Museum was present and carried instructions in his head allowing him to bid as much as 100 pounds sterling for it. A representative of the Dresden Museum was present too, with instructions to go as high as necessary. Following orders, the man from the British Museum dropped out when the price of 100 pounds was reached; the man from Dresden bid another 5 pounds and returned home in smug triumph. In Dresden they went over their loot virtually with a microscope and discovered that there were a number of small but definite and pronounced differences between the living South Island form and the North Island specimen from Waingongoro. It was a notornis, to be sure, but a different variety. This called for a new name and the Dresden specimen was called *Notornis hochstetteri* in honor of the Austrian explorer.

Again year after year passed without a single takahe and again there were voices prophesying that the specimen that had given rise to the new and distinct name had been the last one. For a while the news was rare and what there was, dismal. In November 1884 a Mr. R. Henry discovered an incomplete skeleton near the shore of Lake Te Anau, and eight years later a Mr. A. Hamilton came with two almost complete skeletons from the same locality. All three skeletons were put on exhibit in New Zealand museums and there was, needless to say, some faint teeth-gnashing that they were only skeletons. It seemed as if New Zealand would be left without a stuffed specimen, the few existing ones having been shipped off to Europe before there were any museums in the Dominion.

At about this point another Austrian enters into the picture, one Andreas Reischek. Reischek was deeply impressed with New Zealand, but in a way which, in view of subsequent developments, appears more than mildly silly. The Maoris were a dying race which would not exist much longer. The natural beauty of the islands would soon be ruined, sacrificed to British commercialism. The strange fauna and flora were doomed to extinction. Whatever knowledge could still be gathered in New Zealand had to be gathered at once, before it was too late. One has to admit that he actively helped to gather such knowledge; he became one of the most tireless explorers of New Zealand, and then wrote a book called *Sterbende Welt* (*Dying World*).

Andreas Reischek spent more than a decade, on and off, hunting for takahe, but never did get to see one, and probably died in the belief that the bird was extinct. We now know why he failed; he stayed too far north. The place where he could have found the elusive bird was precisely the place the natives had pointed out to Sir James Hector, the shores of Lake Te Anau.

I mentioned that the New Zealanders had been made quite unhappy

The takahe of the South Island

by the fact that all three specimens of their rarest bird had left their country for places of honor in European museums. But they did get a specimen at long last, again by accident. One Mr. Ross was walking along the shore of the Middle Fiord, Lake Te Anau, in the evening hours of August 7, 1898, when his dog suddenly darted off into the bush and returned with a takahe, still feebly struggling. The bird died soon after, but fortunately Mr. Ross recognized it at once. He and his brother rowed the dead bird to the southern end of Lake Te Anau—a trip of some 25 miles—and sent it to Invercargill. This time not only skeleton and skin, but even the internal organs could be salvaged, and the bird was bought by the New Zealand government for 250 pounds sterling. The skin was mounted and is on exhibit in the Dunedin Museum. And there the matter rested for another half century.

Because no other takahe came to light during all the years that followed, most writers began to conclude the notornis chapter of their books with the statement, "quite rare, possibly extinct," or something similar, indicating that the author refrained from saying "extinct" only because that fact was after all not proved. Only the incurable type of optimist might mutter that the bird had been believed to be extinct several times before. Rumors about footprints in snow came in from time to time, but they were not too definite. The Maori who claimed to know anything about takahe—very few of them now—also claimed that the bird lived high up in the mountains and came down to the lake shore only rarely.

Whether that was correct or not, one could always point out that Lake Te Anau was no longer remote territory, nothing like, say, the interior of Greenland or the Australian Central Desert. I have in front of me a beautifully illustrated travel booklet, issued by the New Zealand Government Tourist Department, entitled "Milford Sound." Milford Sound is the northernmost of the fiords of southwest New Zealand and the booklet recommends an especially scenic route for a trip to it. The tourist first goes to Lumsden, either by rail from Dunedin on the east coast (136 miles) or from Invercargill on the south shore (50 miles); from there a bus brings him to the Te Anau Hotel. Then a trip of 40 miles on Lake Te Anau itself—it is stressed that the ship *Tawera* is a modern oil burner which requires about three and one-half hours for the trip—brings you to Glade House, situated at the northernmost point of Lake Te Anau. From there you start out, on foot, along a highly picturesque route called "Milford Track," to the Milford Hotel on Milford Sound.

The booklet indicates that the *Tawera* must keep rather close to the eastern shore of Lake Te Anau. For its whole trip, the place where the takahe is still very much alive, if hiding in the dense underbrush, is theoretically in sight. It probably is below the horizon most of the time, but it is around the western arm of that lake which is really a drowned valley between the mountains.

It was in 1947 that Dr. Geoffrey B. Orbell, a physician of Invercargill, struck out into the dense forest of the west shore of Lake Te Anau. On

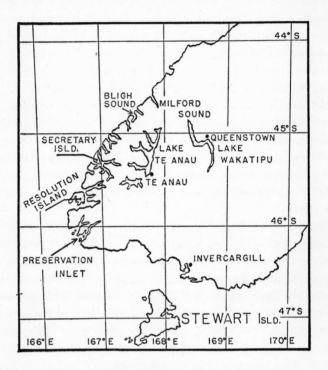

The takahe country

the east shore the forest had been felled and grazing land created. The west shore is untouched. Doctor Orbell worked his way up the mountains to an altitude of almost 3000 feet. That the many stories he had heard earlier were not completely without foundation became clear on that first trip. There was a small lake about which frontiersmen had told but which was not on any map. Doctor Orbell and his party heard strange bird noises, but also found something more definite: a print of a bird's foot in mud. Whether this was actually a footprint of takahe could not be stated definitely at that time, but later it was found to be.

The discoveries of the uncharted lake and the footprint were enough encouragement for Dr. Orbell; he returned to the scene during the southern spring of 1948, in November. He was well equipped with cameras, even a movie camera with color film, and with nets for catching the birds. A takahe was seen and one of the members of the small expedition threw a net. It caught not one but two takahes. The birds were tied to a stake, photographed, and then released, and Dr. Orbell and his party returned to Invercargill to tell the tale and to show their pictures.

In January 1949 Dr. Orbell went back again, this time setting up camp in what he now knew to be the takahe country. The expedition was a great success. Not only did it establish that the takahe is a complete vegetarian, as had been suspected earlier, but it also found nests. Naturally these nests are situated on the ground since the heavy bird cannot fly. Some thirty nests were examined. It seems that a takahe pair raises only one chick every year—detail still remains to be investigated. The chicks show none of the gaudy coloration of their parents but are simply black. About a dozen adult birds were actually seen by the party and indications were that there are two colonies in two adjacent valleys. The two colonies together are believed to comprise between fifty and one hundred birds. Of course there may be more colonies in the area.

When Dr. Orbell's third expedition returned, the New Zealand government took steps. The area actually investigated by Dr. Orbell and found to harbor "lost colonies" of takahe is only about 500 acres in extent; the government declared an area totaling 400,000 acres a closed sanctuary for takahe. This area includes all the spots where takahe *may* exist. In addition, a campaign is in progress against predatory animals which may reduce the numbers of the rare bird. The New Zealanders are determined to keep the bird which was several times thought to be extinct. And judging from what they did for their unique Hatteria lizard—also called *Sphenodon* or in Maori *tuatera*—one may expect them to succeed.

9: Green Fossil

WHEN I lived in Washington, D.C., just after the war I had a large flower pot on my back porch in which five small trees were growing prettily. They had been grown from seeds which had literally been picked up from the street. To be precise about it, the seeds had been scooped up from the ground near a park bench on Scott Circle.

They were ginkgos.

Visitors never gave them more than a passing glance, if that. They were just five small green things in a large pot on a porch, and beyond the porch there was a garden with spectacular tall sunflowers and an enormous spreading castor-bean plant. If the pot had been a terrarium and if there had been five small but growing dinosaurs in it I wouldn't have had a quiet minute in the day. And yet the comparison of those small ginkgo trees to small dinosaurs is not even farfetched. When, during the so-called Age of Reptiles, in the Triassic, Jurassic, and Cretaceous periods, the large reptiles of the dinosaur tribe wallowed in streams, wandered ponderously across the land, swam in the seas, and even flew through the air, there were ginkgo trees growing along the banks of those ancient streams and in sight of the seas. The plant-eaters among the dinosaurs no doubt made meals of the leaves of the ginkgo trees. The first birds which appeared during the Jurassic period may have been essentially insect eaters, but at least some of them probably feasted on the "nuts" of the ginkgo. And the early mammals, then hiding in the forests, no doubt did the same.

To the best of our knowledge, the ginkgo "nuts" that were eaten by some of the smaller dinosaurs, by the pouched tree-dwelling mammals which lived then, and by the first birds in the history of our planet, were the same kind which I picked up on Scott Circle and which without any special care produced little "fossil" trees. Identifiable remains of ginkgos have been found in all three of the geological periods mentioned, but

Leaves of *Ginkgo biloba*

we happen to know more remains from the Jurassic period than from the Triassic which preceded it and the Cretaceous which followed taken together. Of course we also know ginkgo remains from the Tertiary period, but they are not too numerous. Personally I am always surprised that the ginkgo seems to have been missing from the amber forest; everything else seems to have grown there, but the tree for which Charles Darwin himself coined the term "living fossil" apparently did not.

As regards geographical distribution in earlier geological periods we have ginkgos from Bavaria, from western Greenland, and from the Yukon Territory. We have some from England and from Washington State, from Italy and from Turkestan, from Scandinavia and Australia, from Mongolia and Patagonia. Evidently the ginkgo was as widely distributed as the dinosaurs which went with it.

As you proverbially recognize the fish by its scales and the bird by its feathers, so you recognize the ginkgo by its leaves. Before the now generally accepted name of ginkgo became common, it was also called "elephant ear tree," "fan leaf tree," and, with reference to a superficial resemblance to the maidenhair fern, as "maidenhair tree." "Fan-leaf tree" was probably best, because the leaves look like an old-fashioned fan; most of them are cleft in the center, almost down to the leaf stem, so that the leaf has two lobes, accounting for the botanical name of *Ginkgo biloba*. My little flower-pot ginkgos were still four-lobed, since every lobe had a secondary cleavage. This is a feature which is now restricted to young seedlings, but some of those old ginkgos which were contemporaries of the dinosaurs seem to have had four-lobed leaves all through their lives.

If you look closer at those leaves you'll see that the leaf differs from the leaves of such everyday trees as maple or ash or oak not only in shape but also in structure. Instead of the dense network of veins which characterize more "modern" tree leaves, all the veins of the ginkgo leaf radiate from the stem, like the ribs of a fan. There are no cross connections. The structure of the leaf is like a flat cluster of pine needles grown together. Primitive in a similar manner is the shape of the tree itself. The customary scheme of large branches growing from the trunk, smaller branches from the main branches, and twigs from the smaller branches, does not quite hold true. The slender tapering trunk of the ginkgo tree develops a number of large branches, but smaller branches are usually missing. What we may call twigs grow directly from the large branches. And both branches and "twigs" are covered with numerous little barrel-shaped "short shoots," an inch long or less. The leaves, and the fruits, grow in clusters from these "short shoots."

The result is that the tree looks somewhat stiff, like a formalized design, with a long branch, densely covered with clusters of foliage, sticking out here and there. The full wavy bough of other trees is merely approximated in very old specimens; as long as the tree is less than half a century old it shows a somehow dignified design of straight lines that makes it easy to recognize a ginkgo a quarter-mile away.

And unless an earthquake or a roadbuilder interferes, a young ginkgo has an excellent chance of growing up. It does not mind the change of the seasons; it is resistant to fungus diseases; insect pests fail to bother it. Even Japanese beetles take off again after the first tentative bite. Smoke from coal fires does not seem to harm it noticeably and the same is true for gasoline fumes. "Nobody has ever seen a dead branch on a ginkgo tree," as one expert put it in his recommendation to the city planning board which employed him.

In spite of these excellent qualities for survival the ginkgo might well be extinct by now, as are the animals which lived in the original ginkgo forests of the Jurassic period. Once of world-wide distribution (Africa is the only continent from which no fossil ginkgos are known, and that may be purely accidental), three centuries ago it was restricted to a few small areas in the Far East.

The first white man to look at a ginkgo with the eyes of an expert was a German physician and traveler named Dr. Engelbrecht Kaempfer. Born in Westphalia in September 1651, a son of a pastor, young Engelbrecht soon began to lead an international life. He studied at Hameln, the town of the legendary pied piper, then at Hamburg, Lübeck, and Danzig. Then he went to Cracow in Poland where he got his Ph.D. After that he moved to Königsberg to study medicine and natural history at the university there, then still called the Collegium Albertianum after Albert I, Duke of Prussia, who had founded it in 1544 with the stern admonition that this was to be a Lutheran university. In 1681 Dr. Kaempfer went to Uppsala in Sweden for further study, and incidentally was open to job suggestions. The King of Sweden had some use for him. He was about to send an ambassadorial party to Persia and Dr. Kaempfer was offered and accepted the job of confidential secretary to that party. He traveled to Isfahan, then the capital of Persia, via Moscow, Kazan, and Astrakhan, with side trips on the Caspian Sea and to the Baku peninsula, reaching his destination in 1684. When, after a little more than a year, the Swedes prepared to return home, Dr.

Kaempfer took service, this time as a doctor, with the Dutch East Indies Company. Their ships first brought him to Batavia in September 1689 and in May of the following year he started out for Japan, arriving in Nagasaki in September 1690. He stayed there as physician to the Royal Dutch Embassy for two years, then returned home to Westphalia where he died in November 1716.

Doctor Kaempfer "discovered" the ginkgo tree within a month or two after his arrival in Nagasaki. The tree was grown in the vicinity of sacred shrines. It was clearly a tree of religious significance and we now know that some of these "holy" Japanese ginkgos are many centuries old. One especially large and old specimen at Sendai in Japan, 97 feet tall and 27 feet around the trunk near the ground, is estimated to have an age of 1200 years.

The first description of the ginkgo tree, written by Kaempfer, was published in 1712. Additional information was incorporated into a manuscript called *History of Japan and Siam* which was found among his papers after his death. The manuscript was sent to London where it was translated into English and published in 1728.

Ever since Dr. Kaempfer informed botanists of the existence of the tree an energetic but generally fruitless debate about "wild ginkgos" has been going on in professional journals. The Japanese have always claimed in more or less clear language that there never were any wild ginkgos in Japan and that they existed only as Temple Trees. Some dating is possible because of the religious significance and especially in connection with that very old ginkgo at Sendai. The Emperor Shome of Japan issued an imperial message in about 700 A.D. ordering the establishment of Buddhism throughout Japan. Accordingly, Buddhist temples were built and several court ladies begged the empress to permit them to become priestesses of the new religion. Among them was the Lady Naihaku-Kojo, who had been the wet nurse of the emperor. When she was near death, she decreed that no monument should be erected over her grave, but that a ginkgo tree should be planted on it instead, so that her soul could continue to live in the tree. The reason for choosing a ginkgo was that the Lady Naihaku-Kojo had been a nurse and that old ginkgo trees develop growths like pendulous breasts (these growths will, in time, reach the ground and form something like secondary trunks). The tree planted on her grave is the old giant of Sendai.[1]

This indicates that the Japanese knew ginkgo trees in about 700 A.D. and must even have seen very old specimens or else they would not know about the growths which they compared to women's breasts. Apparently they did not start planting ginkgos systematically until after the conversion to Buddhism.

The assertion that there are no wild ginkgos in Japan *now* may be accepted at face value and it is possible that there never were any. The Japanese probably got their first ginkgos from the Chinese, who also planted the tree around temples. So if wild ginkgos exist we would have to look for them in China. But it is at least doubtful whether any have been found so far. Ginkgos are not rare in China, but wherever they grow there is either a settlement, or a former settlement, or at least rumors of a former settlement. Even the most recent professional works state the case carefully by saying that there are "probably" forests of wild ginkgos in the interior of China.

It may be remarked in passing that the name "ginkgo" is not a genuine Chinese word, even if it sounds like one. Doctor Kaempfer knew that the Chinese word *gin* means "silver," and he thought that ginkgo meant "silver apricot," a name which might well be given to the seed of the tree. But there is no such word in Chinese; in fact the Chinese poets of the Middle Ages used the rather unpoetical name of "duck's foot tree." Possibly Dr. Kaempfer's name is the result of misreading the word *sankyo,* which means "hill apricot." That word has been found in one of his manuscripts, as well as the Japanese names *itsio* or *itcho* for the tree and *ginnan* for the fruit. But whatever its origin may be, the name is as firmly established by now as the tree itself.

One might say that the ginkgo, after a temporary withdrawal into the interior of China, is now re-establishing its original world-wide distribution with the aid of man.

Probably because Dr. Kaempfer was attached to the Dutch Embassy, ginkgos were first brought to Holland. A ginkgo tree was planted at Utrecht in about 1730. The precise date is not known but it can be deduced from various sources as not earlier than 1727 and not later than

---

[1] As related in a letter to the editor of *American Forests* (April 1948), from Professor Florence B. Robinson, University of Illinois.

1737. There is still an old ginkgo growing in the Botanical Garden of the University of Utrecht and while there seems to be no definite proof that this is the first ginkgo to grow in Europe since the Tertiary period there is also no special reason to doubt it.

Some fifteen or twenty years later, in about 1752, a few small ginkgos began to grow in England, from seeds obtained directly from Japan. And in 1768 a ginkgo tree grew in Vienna. It later turned out to be a male. Ginkgo trees are either male or female, having either male flowers only or female flowers only. As long as the tree was very rare this sometimes posed a problem.

Karl von Linné received ginkgo material from the British botanist Gordon in 1771, described it, and gave it the name *Ginkgo biloba*. That an English botanist named Smith wanted to change this name to *Salisburia adiantifolia* some twenty-five years after Linnaeus is a historical fact but does not rate more than bare mention. Fortunately all of Smith's contemporaries felt about this proposed change as we do now.[2]

Although the ginkgo's European history started in the Netherlands the tree gained its firmest foothold in England and from there spread over most of the civilized world. England was the one place in Europe where ginkgos could be *bought*. British scientists also made presents of ginkgos to scientists from the Continent. Sir Joseph Banks, for example, gave a ginkgo to the French Professor Broussonet when the latter visited him in London. This particular tree was planted in the famous garden at Montpellier in France and attracted more attention than most others.

But it was not, as is sometimes stated, the first ginkgo in France. Five others had preceded it by about a decade, in a rather peculiar manner. The story of the first ginkgos that went to France has been put on record by the Scottish horticulturist John Claudius Loudon in his book *Arboretum et Fruticetum Britannicum* (1837). In about 1770 several British gardeners engaged in correspondence with Japan in order to

---

[2] Later, however, a number of so-called "horticultural varieties" were distinguished: *pendula*, characterized by pendant branchlets; *fastigiata*, characterized by upright branchlets; *variegata*, which has leaves blotched and streaked with yellow at any season of the year, while normally the leaves turn yellow only in autumn and have a very definite glossy green otherwise; *macrophylla*, which has larger leaves. Except for the interesting blotched leaves of *variegata*, these differences are not important to the layman.

obtain ginkgo seeds. After due lapse of time, a considerable lapse from our point of view, they got their seeds and the one who became the unwilling hero of the peculiar story planted his share in a large pot. It is not reported how many seeds he planted, but five of them sprouted. (My own five were the outcome of planting seven seeds, but of course my seeds were much fresher.)

In about 1780 the gardener's five ginkgos were well established and he was probably delighted with them. They were still quite small and still growing together in the same pot (they may have been four or five years old, since the ginkgo is a comparatively slow-growing tree) when his establishment was visited by a Frenchman by the name of Pétigny. Monsieur Pétigny made up his mind that he had to have those ginkgos. The Englishman asked an enormous price, swearing quite untruthfully that nobody else in Greater London had any ginkgo trees. Monsieur Pétigny took him to lunch and made frequent reference to the wine list in the long discussion that followed. Finally he bought the pot with the ginkgos for 25 guineas, paid at once, and took them with him. The next morning, after the alcoholic fumes had cleared away, the Englishman waylaid him in the lobby of his hotel. He was willing to return the 25 guineas for just one of the five ginkgos. But Monsieur Pétigny refused. He took all of them with him to Paris, and later many Frenchmen believed that all the ginkgos in France were descended from Pétigny's five.

That, of course, was not quite true, because there was also the Montpellier ginkgo. It was a mature tree in about 1812, but it was a female, and there was no male ginkgo anywhere near. The nearest male mature ginkgo on record for that time was the one in the botanical garden of Kew Gardens near London, which had flowered for the first time in 1795. Then one of the botanists at Montpellier thought of a way out. He secured a live branch of a male ginkgo and grafted it to the female Montpellier tree. While Nature did not make ginkgos bisexual, she apparently has no objection to supporting them that way once they have been created artificially. A few decades later the same thing in reverse was done in Jena, where a female branch was grafted to a male tree.

The Jena ginkgo has been linked with literary history for a long time, although not completely successfully. In those days Johann Wolfgang von Goethe was Privy Councillor in Jena. He spoke the decisive word

not only in literary matters but also in matters of state. Goethe was an
amateur botanist with ideas of his own which contained some germs
of the theory of evolution. Goethe had been in Montpellier. He had
seen the Montpellier ginkgo and had been moved to write a poem about
it which millions of future German school children have had to learn
by heart. Wasn't it logical to assume that the Jena ginkgo had been imported because Goethe wanted a ginkgo tree?

But to find proof for the assumption was a different matter. Patriotic
Germans, literary Germans, and scientific Germans did their best, searching old books, pamphlets, newspapers, and correspondence for such
proof. The Goethe Society turned all available archives upside down,
but to date no documentary evidence has been found for the idea Goethe
was actually responsible for the Jena ginkgo.

Now, more than a century later, there are quite a number of ginkgos
flourishing in Europe. The ginkgos of Locarno are famous for their
decorative effect, but they are just one group among many. But although
you can find a ginkgo tree in many places in Europe if you look for it,
the tree can still be called comparatively rare.

In America it is almost common.

In spite of what a certain novel may lead you to believe, many Brooklyn
streets are lined with ginkgos. One of them, located on Clinton Avenue,
measures a good 3½ feet in diameter a foot from the ground, is about
70 feet high, and at least as many years old. There are ginkgos in
Prospect Park, and also in Central Park and on many Manhattan streets.
In Washington, D.C., ginkgos, at a rough guess, constitute about one
quarter of the tree population of that exceptionally green city. But neither
New York nor Washington can boast of having been the home of the
first ginkgo in America.

The first ginkgo in America was planted on the estates of William
Hamilton on the west bank of the Schuylkill River, in what is now
Philadelphia's Woodland Cemetery, in 1784. It was imported from England. Mrs. J. M. Stetson of Williamsburg, Virginia, kindly informed
me that Hamilton wrote from London on November 2, 1785, to his
secretary in Philadelphia, instructing him about the care of the tree.
Some twenty years later (on July 7, 1806) he wrote Thomas Jefferson
that he would send him several trees for his garden, one of them a ginkgo,

"said to produce a good eatable nut." He added that his ginkgo had weathered hard winters in open ground without protection.

A few more ginkgos were planted in America in the decades following the War of 1812. One of the oldest is the Boston Common ginkgo, which was transplanted to that location from an estate in about 1835 and which is still alive, although it is not doing too well.

But these early ginkgos in America were "hobby trees," imported from Europe, mostly from England, by wealthy individuals, and planted as curiosities. Large-scale planting did not start until commercial interests became involved: in this case nurserymen who provided trees for the growing parks and lengthening streets of American cities. Most of the ginkgos in the New York area were ultimately derived from a nursery established on Long Island Sound by a German named Siebrecht. It seems to have been a kind of chain reaction, the park commissioners of the eastern cities passing on young trees and seeds among themselves. Every once in a while, too, somebody went back to the nursery.

In an attempt to trace the wanderings of the ginkgo across the Western Hemisphere, I wrote to some thirty city park departments, asking whether they had planted ginkgos, when they planted them, how the trees were doing, and where they got the seeds or saplings. While I received many and courteous replies they failed to shed light on the main question, namely, where the trees came from. City after city reported that they had ginkgo trees, that the trees were doing fine—except in cities in the northern part of the Middle West, where the winters seem to be too severe—that they were highly satisfied with them, and that they planned to plant more. But as for the source the records usually just stated that the trees had come "from an eastern nursery." The city of Boston, for example, has a number of ginkgos which most likely came from the Siebrecht nurseries and a few others which the officials believe were imported directly from Japan. But this is an exceptional case. Most ginkgos in American cities came originally from Europe, with intermediate stops and sometimes intermediate generations in American nurseries. The city of Montreal got its ginkgos from Belgium.

Under these circumstances I was naturally especially interested in the question whether the ginkgos in our West Coast cities had been imported directly from Japan or China or whether they too had traveled the long way around the world. The matter was cleared up by a letter from H. M. Butterfield of the College of Agriculture at the University of California. The California ginkgos—all planted since 1850—came from the eastern states, probably through the agency of an Irish family by the name of Saul. It seems that this family took over the Downing Nursery at Newburgh, N.Y., after A. J. Downing died in an accident. John Saul established a nursery in New York in about 1852; his brother James Saul started one in California two years later. His catalog, of which a copy is still preserved in Berkeley, listed ginkgos. Another nurseryman in California who sold ginkgo trees during the same period was one William C. Walker, who had come to California from the southeastern states. His stock must have been derived either from Long Island or directly from Europe.

The West Coast ginkgos, therefore, had traveled the long route via Europe; at least, if there are any which came directly from the Orient they did not leave a record.

In short, the green fossil from the days of the dinosaurs before the amber forest is doing well in our world of today. It is doing well even in cities which are deadly to many more modern trees. The next thing to do, obviously, is to make clear just where the ginkgo belongs among trees, living as well as extinct.

But at this point we get into a difficulty of a special kind. The layman —which means everybody except the professional botanist—is well acquainted with plants but not with plant sciences. Acquaintance with plants is unavoidable and except for such special cases as poison ivy on this side of the Atlantic and the burning nettle of Europe (where poison ivy does not grow naturally), nobody tries to avoid it. But the plant sciences have a habit of being discouraging to the layman. What I mean by that can best be shown by a comparison.

If a zoologist tells a layman that the horses and donkeys of civilization, the wild asses of India, the Przhevalski horse of Mongolia, and the zebras of Africa form a zoological "family," the layman is not much surprised. It is a relationship which is quite visible. Likewise, the relationship between the American bison, the water buffalo of India, the yak of Tibet, the gaur, the zebu, and domestic cattle is believable at the surface. Nor does it cause great wonderment that the two Old World camels, the one-humped dromedary and the two-humped camel, are considered to be related to the llama and the vicuña of South America.

Now, in the botanical field, it is likewise believable that rye and wheat and oats and barleycorn and so on are grasses like the grasses in the field and on the lawn. But the layman who admires a banana "tree" in the botanical garden and is then told that it is merely the world's biggest herb is likely to shake his head in a mixture of wonder and subdued doubt. That the bay tree and the avocado are relatives is something he will accept because, after all, *he* is no botanist. But the going gets difficult when he hears that the deadly nightshade, the versatile tomato, and the useful potato belong to the same "family." When he finally makes up his mind that this may be so he will then expect to include the sweet potato. But then he is told that the sweet potato is a *Convolvulus* or morning glory. He learns in greater and greater astonishment that strawberries and raspberries are members of the rose family, that apples and pears are not only related, as one might suspect, but that they also belong to the rose family. So do the quince and the almond. And the cherry. He learns that the vanilla is an orchid. That the milkworts, the tapioca plant, and the castor-oil plant all belong to the geranium family. That asparagus is a member of the lily family and that the grotesque Joshua tree of the southwestern deserts is a lily too.

This, of course, may help explain why zoological handbooks usually range from 300 to 350 printed pages, while a botanical handbook of less than 500 pages is an uncommon sight.

At all events, the reader should now fail to be surprised when he learns that botanists place the ginkgo with its beautiful full foliage alongside (although no longer among) the pines and firs, and that they refer to its "fruit," which looks like a wrinkled apricot about an inch in diameter, as a "naked seed." For the explanation of this, see the discussion of seed-bearing ferns and cycad trees, Chapter 11.

The ginkgo's fruits hang in clusters like cherries from the "short shoots" from which they grow. Their numbers are such that fallen fruits will form a thick carpet under a group of female trees. Because they are almost perfectly round they roll easily, and if a female ginkgo is growing on a hill one can usually discover seeds or growing seedlings at the foot of the hill. A single fruit consists of a rather thin layer of pulp which covers a rather large "nut," like an overgrown cherry pit. The "nuts" are eaten in China and in Japan, and by Chinese and Japanese living in other countries where ginkgos will grow.

While I naturally hesitate to contradict the printed opinions of a large number of men, most of them professional botanists, who have written about the "fruit" of the ginkgo, my personal experience just doesn't corroborate their loudly expressed views. The British botanist A. C. Seward, for example, said that the fruit pulp of the ginkgo is "nauseous." It isn't, it just fails to compete with other tree fruit. The fruit pulp of the ginkgo, the little of it there is, is perfectly edible; it just isn't very interesting. It tastes like a watery plum. It is sweetish, but not sweet, resembling a fruit, but not "fruity." In short, at the risk of repeating myself: edible but uninteresting. As for the "nut" inside, when eaten raw it resembles almond to about the same degree that the pulp resembles plum. The general texture is about the same, but "taste" is virtually absent. Roasted, as the seeds are served in Japan, the taste is somewhat improved, but even so it remains unimpressive.

I also find myself in disagreement with the oft-expressed statement that the odor of ginkgo fruit is "unbearable." Newspapermen have implored their city park departments to plant male ginkgo trees only and have pictured the female tree as a kind of vegetable skunk which has to be passed up wind at a safe distance. This, to me, seems to be more in the nature of a literary convention than a fact of nature. I have plucked fruit which seemed about ripe from trees and by virtually stuffing them into my nostrils I did succeed in detecting a faint odor of rancid butter. Of course, after the fruit has become overripe, fallen off the tree, and begun to rot on the ground, its odor begins to be noticeable. An overripe ginkgo fruit does not smell sweet, any more than an overripe apple, a rotten plum, or a decaying peach, does. The "offensiveness" of the ginkgo is, in my opinion, largely a matter of sweeping the streets.

The really important fact is that the living fossil from the Jurassic and Cretaceous periods, which somehow survived into our time in the

Far East, is doing so well along our streets. It does not show the faintest trace of either senility or weakness. Its recession into a few Far Eastern hiding places must have been caused by a series of accidents about which we would like to learn more, but which are unlikely to happen again, because by now there must be more ginkgos in the United States alone than existed in eastern Asia at the time Linnaeus gave it its scientific name.

10: The Forest of the Dinosaurs: Sequoias

THIS chapter also brings us in the end to China's western provinces, because of a discovery which Père David might easily have made. It also resembles the story of the ginkgo in that at one point a number of small trees growing in large pots are to play a role. But most of it is an American story. And the trees are not small trees at all. On the contrary. We are going to deal with the redwoods. The precise date of discovery of the redwoods happens to be known. It was in 1769 that the first expedition of Europeans moved up along the California coast by land. Because its leader was one Gaspar de Portolá, this is usually referred to as the Portolá Expedition. The thoughts of the members of that expedition most likely revolved around gold, which they did not find. Instead, the expedition clarified the geography of California—many geographers then still thought and spoke about the Island of California—and made two interesting scientific discoveries. One was the tar pits of what later became known as the Rancho La Brea and is now Hancock Park in Los Angeles. The other was the coastal redwoods.

Fray Juan Crespi, the diarist of the Portolá Expedition, recorded under the date of Tuesday, October 10, 1769, that the expedition, having left its camp on the Pájaro River (near Watsonville, on a present-day map), traveled "over plains and low hills, well forested with very high trees of a red color, not known to us." Because nobody knew the name of these trees, the expedition decided to name them. And because of the bright pink or red color of the freshly cut wood, they chose the name "red tree," or, in Spanish, *palo colorado*.

The second mention of these trees also appeared in the travel diary of a Franciscan monk, Fray Pedro Font, who accompanied the Anza Expedition to San Francisco Bay in 1776. Under the date of Tuesday, March 26, he wrote that they saw a few trees of the kind "which they call redwood, a tree that is certainly beautiful; and I believe that it is very useful for timber." Three days later Fray Pedro Font saw "a very high redwood—rising like a great tower." The following day he came closer to it and made some measurements from which he could calculate its height and wrote down that it was "some fifty *varas* high, a little more or less." Since a *vara* is 3 inches short of a yard, 50 *varas* work out to 137.5 feet. We now know that this is not a very tall redwood, but it impressed the Spaniards into recording it as a landmark. They labeled it "tall tree," in Spanish *palo alto*. It is still standing and its designation has become the name of the locality.

While the record of the discovery of the coastal redwoods is clear, there is less certainty about the discovery of the Sierra redwoods of the interior. Of course we know who found them eventually, but there are some earlier rumors. One can be suspicious, for example, about the remainder of the entry about the *palo alto* in Fray Pedro's diary. After giving his calculations of its height, he stated that its trunk measured 5½ *varas* in circumference, and added that "the soldiers said that they had seen even larger ones in the sierras."

Since we have no way of knowing whether that referred to bigger coastal redwoods a little farther away from the coast or actually to the different species in the Sierras, no valid conclusion can be drawn from this entry. But as regards the next story in chronological sequence, we don't even know whether it is true at all. In about 1820, it was said later, some men pursuing fleeing Indians came across gigantic trees in the mountains. This may be true, but the story may also have been made up later, after the pattern of the discovery of what is now known as the Calaveras Grove. That grove (and this story has been verified) was found in 1852 by a miner named A. T. Dowd, while he was pursuing a wounded bear.

The report of the discovery of the Sierra redwoods which is accepted by historians is the one written by Zenas Leonard in 1833. Leonard was a clerk with the expedition of Joseph R. Walker which crossed the Sierra

Nevada in that year. "In the last two days' travelling," Leonard wrote, "we have found some trees of the Redwood species incredible large; some of which would measure from 16 to 18 fathom [a fathom equals 6 feet] round the trunk at the height of a man's head from the ground." The Walker expedition must have found either the Merced or the Tuolumne Grove, both of which are now included in Yosemite National Park.

But the largest grove was found comparatively late, by Hale D. Tharp in 1858. Soon afterward it was visited and explored by John Muir, who called it the Giant Forest. It is now known as Sequoia National Park.

Stories about the existence of the "redwood belt" along the shore and of the groves of the trees in the Sierras spread quickly. Many descriptions were published during the second half of the nineteenth century, most of them emphasizing the enormous size of the trees. But there were some misunderstandings. Sometimes the accounts were simply disbelieved. Sometimes, as a later writer phrased it, "where the explorers talked about feet, their readers thought they meant inches." But those who knew the trees and who wanted to save them for posterity persevered. As far as saving the trees for posterity goes, the men who devoted their energies to this task succeeded admirably. As far as literature is concerned, there is probably no other tree about which so much has been written. But reading about them is not quite enough. I found that out for myself.

I had read a great deal about them before I saw them in 1941. I had seen enough pictures of the big sequoias to be sure that I would recognize them at a glance, even disregarding their size. But I did know that a really big tree measures some 90 feet in circumference near the ground. That its weight is more than 3,000,000 pounds. That it is clothed in 2 feet of virtually fireproof bark. That its wood, paradoxically for the world's biggest tree, is not particularly hard. That it produces some two hundred seeds per cone on the average, the actually counted numbers ranging from about 90 to a little over three hundred. That only about 15 per cent of these seeds are viable—which doesn't matter much with thousands of cones every year during most of the tree's life span. I had read all that when still in Europe. And in spite of all my reading I had formed a wrong conception which was so much in the back of my mind that it did not even emerge clearly until I was almost face to face with the trees.

Maybe because I had once imagined that Alexander the Great might have marked the route of his conquests by planting such trees which would still be alive, maybe because I had known that this type was in vigorous existence since the days of the dinosaurs—in any event I had somehow associated a tropical climate with the giants. I had pictured a moist warm forest, a near-tropical splendor, culminating in groves of the great relics of the past.

It was Robert A. Heinlein, the writer, who drove me from Los Angeles to the forest of the giants a decade ago. We stopped for the night in Visalia and all through the night there was a howling storm with sleet and rain. I should have expected that from latitude, altitude, and season. But reasoning needed some time to overcome an established mental picture; for hours I was experiencing a kind of prolonged wondering surprise.

The next day, too, was a cold and unfriendly day with intermittent rain. The sky was gray, the clouds thinned out by altitude just enough to betray the position of the sun as a bright spot. Even when the rain did not actually fall in small hard cold drops, water continued to drip from the tall trees.

It was a kind of weather and a kind of day that would have been abominable in either the city or the country and all the more so in other mountains. It was a kind of weather and a kind of day that one would have tried to forget as quickly as possible—if one had experienced it anywhere else. But in that forest of the red and green giants—in spite of my initial surprise—the cold rain enhanced the quality of timeless vitality which surrounds the sequoias. They did not, like other trees, seem to cower under the clouds, waiting for them to disperse. They reached up and supported them. The gigantic columns of living wood, their green boughs partly obscured by the cloud veils, seemed to create a strangely roofed island. Not an island of mountain forest up in the Sierras—but an island in time, an island in the time stream which flowed around them. And also an island of silence.

One does not speak loudly in the forest of the giants. And if something which is not subject to emotions—the engine of a car, say—makes its customary noise, the sound seems to be swallowed up in some manner. It may have been the moisture-saturated air, or else the fact that the bark of the big trees and the other plants absorbed the sound. Or it may have been simply an illusion, caused by the size of the trees, which makes the distance between two of them appear much shorter than it actually is—in fact, like the distance between two ordinary trees—but the fact remains that there was silence. Silent too were the footsteps on the forest floor because of the thick carpet of fallen needles.

Except for a most incongruous squirrel and a few subdued human visitors the trees were alone on that day. In retrospect one puts a few figures and comparisons into the memories. There were enormous old trees along the road, trees which germinated when Cornelius Tacitus wrote down hearsay of the amber coast or which were only ripe seeds at the time Imperator Marcus Aurelius wrote his *Meditations* in Carnuntum. The visual picture of the massive trunks in the cold rain produced a mental picture in which the forest of the Californian Sierra coalesced with the descriptions of the Hercynian Forest of Gaius Julius Caesar and recalled visions of the forest of the Nibelungs. It felt—yes, it felt as if by a special permit one was granted a few hours in the past, in the forests in which much of later civilization originated and which became the unavoidable background of all folklore.

And then—the rain happened to get stronger at that moment—we came to a clearing, and in the clearing stood The Tree. The one which has been named General Sherman. The clearing may be due to many, many centuries of shade cast by the tree, or to other circumstances that I do not know—and for all I care it may have been improved somewhat with an ax—but it looks as if everything else had retreated to a respectful distance from the place where the Big Tree is standing.

I thought of Yggdrasil later, as a comparison which did not seem quite good enough and which needed some kind of an apology—that was later. When I saw it, standing massive and motionless in the cold rain, no comparison existed. There was not even any thought; there was only the Big Tree. It needed no looking at all to see that the tree did not "resist" the weather. Rather the weather resisted the tree. The tree permitted cold rain to fall from the clouds it supported, it did not endure the rain. And it looked so alive and vigorous that one expected it to radiate warmth.

Of course trees do not radiate warmth, even though they are alive. But since to a mammal like man the ideas "warmth" and "life" are closely synonymous—no reptile and no mountain fir would ever think such

Sequoiadendron

nonsense—it looked as if it should. Just a little more imagination and somebody would swear that he felt the tree's warmth.

The imagination is supplied with fuel by the knowledge that the General Sherman tree is "the oldest living thing." Factually that is true in the sense that there is no other old and large tree known which can be proved to be even of equal age with the General Sherman. There exist some famous old trees in various parts of the world. None of them is much more than 1000 years old; I think that the highest sober estimate for some of these others which are not redwoods goes to 1500 years.

We know that the General Sherman is much older, without being able to say precisely how much. The minimum is around 3600 years, the maximum 500 years more. A careful but not too conservative estimate would therefore say "slightly short of 4000 years."

Once it must have been a sapling which a man could have pulled from the ground with his bare hands. But that man would have had to live at a time prior to the First Dynasty of Babylon. He would have had to be a contemporary of the Egyptian pharaohs who built the pyramids. "And the king caused his deeds to be inscribed in stone." No doubt, such an inscription will last a long time, but there are many inscriptions in granite which have weathered to illegibility, even though they were made at a time when the General Sherman was already one of the biggest trees in the Sierras.

The oldest fallen sequoia of the Sierras is known to have lived 3126 years until the day it fell, a few decades ago. Estimates may go wrong; here we have an actual count of rings. At the time when the Greeks fought Troy near the present hill of Hissarlik, that tree was still small; large enough for an oar, maybe large enough even for a mast—the ships of that day were not very big ships. Some three centuries later, when the story of the fight for Troy became the *Iliad,* the tree had grown much larger. Ships probably had grown in size too during those 300 years, but by that time the tree, instead of providing an oar or a mast, would have been more than sufficient to build a whole ship.

But we are not so sure about the date either of the actual battle for Troy or of the composition of the epic poem which has kept its memory alive. At that point the early youth of that tree literally reaches into periods which are only partly known historically. In any event, by the time of Pliny the Elder the tree was more than 1000 years old, and in size and majesty it was such that Pliny would by no means have believed it. But the tree was only in early maturity. It was still in early maturity when the Roman Empire collapsed. A few centuries later there came the year when Charlemagne died. The tree was mature, producing thousands upon countless thousands of seeds with every cycle of the seasons. The Crusades came; the tree had grown a little older in the meantime, by about one-tenth of its life span. That was the time when the Vikings reached America from Greenland. Another tenth of its life span and a little more, and an Italian navigator called Cristoforo Colombo, having been rejected by Portugal, sailed for the Spanish king and reached the New World. Because of him the first expedition up the coast of California was a Spanish-speaking expedition; when Portolá discovered the coastal kin of the old tree in the mountains, it had passed maturity. While still vigorous, it was growing old. But it would be alive today, had not water washed the soil from under its roots so that it fell.

In order to go on with the story of the redwoods I have to return to its beginning. The Spaniards who first saw the coastal redwoods realized at once that they had never seen anything like them before. But they also wanted to give some impression of the *palo colorado,* aside from saying that it had red wood and was very tall and straight. So they wrote that it was a kind of spruce, which is about what most modern travelers would write, unless they had some botanical training. And it happened to be a long time before a professional botanist said anything about the trees. Twigs and cones and samples of wood were brought to England by Menzies in 1795, fairly soon after the original discovery, but nobody paid any attention to them. It was not until 1823 that the English botanist Aylmer Bourke Lambert examined the specimens. It seemed to him that this was a tree very much like the bald cypress (*Taxodium*) of Florida and since reports said that it did not shed its needles in winter, Lambert named it *Taxodium sempervirens,* the "evergreen taxodium."

The first part of this name was wrong and the second was not a very happy choice. Lambert could not know it, but the related trees of the Sierras are "evergreen" too, so that *sempervirens* was nothing distinctive. To increase the confusion a little more, somebody later began to explain to the public that *sempervirens* means "always living." If it did, that would be a good descriptive term for the redwoods, which have been known to sprout new foliage from logs that for some years had been used for gate posts. But while *semper* means "always," *virens* does not come from *vita,* the Latin word for "life," but from *vireo* meaning "to be green" (verdant).

Several decades after Lambert, redwood specimens were examined again, this time by an Austrian botanist, Stephan Endlicher. Endlicher (and this is important for what follows), when not working in his field as a botanist, was fascinated by linguistic studies. He loved languages and phonetics and had been deeply impressed with something that had happened in America when he was a young man: the feat of the Cherokee Indian Sequo-yah.

Sequo-yah was born in about 1770 in Georgia and was Indian by ancestry only on his mother's side. But since his father, a German trader named Georg Gist, had abandoned his mother, Sequo-yah was brought up as an Indian. He was a silversmith and, when necessary, a blacksmith. He also busied himself as a trader, but in spite of that occupation he never learned to speak English. The white man's speech apparently did not interest him, but he was fascinated by something else the white men did: they read newspapers and books and wrote notes and letters to one another. Sequo-yah wanted to give writing to his fellow tribesmen. He spent his time thinking of signs that would be easy to write and easy to recognize. However, his early efforts miscarried because he had made the obvious and fallacious assumption that there was a written sign for each word. This led to impossible complications and he gave up until he learned that letters represented sounds and not words. He then began anew, inventing signs for the sounds of the Cherokee language, some forty or fifty at first. In the end the total number of signs increased to eighty-five.

In 1821 he had progressed far enough to submit his idea to the tribal council. Sequo-yah's alphabet was accepted and only seven years later there were two newspapers printed in the new alphabet. There also existed several books, among them the Gospels. White men were not able to judge for themselves how well Sequo-yah's phonetic alphabet worked, because their knowledge of the Cherokee language was poor or at best incomplete. But Indians said that they could master the alphabet in a single day and were able to write and read after a few days of study. Sequo-yah was made an honorary chief by his tribe, and received a monetary appropriation from Congress to further his work, which had been begun with no other information than the knowledge that it could be done.

Stephan Endlicher, the Austrian botanist, knew about Sequo-yah.

And when his work on the specimens of the *palo colorado* of the Span-iards convinced him that this was not a new species of *Taxodium* but a new genus, he decided to name the red tree after the red man and pro-posed *Sequoia sempervirens*. The name was accepted. That was in 1847.

Five years later an English botanical collector, William Lobb, took specimens of the trees of the Calaveras Grove in the Sierra to England where they were handed over to the botanist John Lindley for study and classification. Lindley decided that this was a new genus and, ap-parently in all innocence, decided to honor the Duke of Wellington by proposing the name of *Wellingtonia gigantea*. That did not please American botanists at all. They did not like the idea of having *their* big tree from the Sierra Nevada known as the tree of the Iron Duke. As much as they had applauded Stephan Endlicher's graceful and friendly gesture, so much were they incensed at Lindley's "patriotic skulldug-gery." While they were still gnashing their teeth, a French botanist, Joseph Decaisne, proved that Lindley had not even been right with his new genus. The tree from the Sierras was a member of the same genus as Endlicher's *sempervirens* and Decaisne therefore proposed (in 1854) to call it *Sequoia gigantea*. Those American botanists who were still in-censed about "Wellingtonia"—a rather small minority—welcomed the proof that both trees belonged to the same genus but disregarded the name. They called the tree *Sequoia washingtoniana* instead, intending to honor both the red man and the "white father" of the country.

Their name caught on best in continental Europe; the connotation was easy—the big tree that grew only in America and the name of the first American president. But they were not very consistent in their usage. One might even say that they developed a method of consistent inconsistency. When using the Latin names they spoke of *Sequoia gigantea* and *Sequoia sempervirens* like good pupils. But when they did not use the Latin names, they called *S. gigantea* the "Washingtonianas" and decided that *S. sempervirens* might just as well be spoken of as "the Wellingtonianas." That they occasionally got mixed up between the two types did not really improve matters. The term "Mammoth Trees," which had meanwhile made its appearance in America, was also taken over from the English. But whereas Americans used Mammoth Tree (and later Big Tree) as a popular designation for *S. gigantea* only, the Europeans used it for the genus *Sequoia,* for both trees.

In order to avoid things like that—since even the best-established confusion is still a confusion—later American writers suggested dropping all popular designations except the very descriptive term "redwood" and distinguishing the two trees as coastal redwood and sierra redwood. Since the habitats of the two trees do not overlap—the coastal redwood grows only in a belt some 30 miles wide and 450 miles long near the coast, and the Sierra redwood only in scattered groves in the mountains quite some distance from the coast—this was a fine suggestion. But it is no longer needed.

Because quite recently botanists have decided that Decaisne made a mistake and that the two trees are not just two species of the same genus. The case was re-opened by Professor J. T. Buchholz of the University of Illinois in 1939. That there are numerous differences between the two trees has, of course, been known for a long time. Whether one considered the differences sufficient to allot the two trees to two different genera or thought them small enough for the trees to be called just two different species of the same genus was mostly a matter of taste. Scientists are people too, and some delight in making fine distinctions while others are generous in "lumping." But with species, say of pines, one usually has the following picture: fully grown trees show considerable differences; younger trees of different species resemble each other more closely; very young saplings are hard to tell apart. In short, the differences show with age. But in the case of the sequoias Professor Buchholz found that there were considerable differences in the development of the embryo and even in pre-embryo development. This not only justified regarding the two trees as not sufficiently close to be called species, but actually compelled separation. Other botanists had to admit that Professor Buchholz was right and in spite of an understandable reluctance acclaimed the separation.

Sequoia sempervirens, the coastal redwood, still bears that name. But for the big trees of the Sierras, by using the Greek word for "tree," Professor Buchholz coined the new name *Sequoiadendron giganteum.*

As regards over-all dimensions, sequoia (coast) grows taller; sequoiadendron (Sierra) is more massive. The following four sequoiadendrons are considered the biggest:

NAME AND LOCATION	HEIGHT (FEET)	CIRCUMFERENCE (FEET)
General Sherman, Sequoia National Park	272.4	101.6
General Grant, General Grant Grove	267.0	107.6
Boole Tree, Converse Basin	269.0	112.0
Grizzly Giant, Mariposa Grove, Yosemite National Park	209.0	96.0

The first of the five *sempervirens* in the following list is considered the tallest tree on earth.

NAME AND LOCATION	HEIGHT (FEET)	CIRCUMFERENCE (FEET)
Founder's Tree, North Dyerville Flat	364	47.1
Big Tree, Bull Creek Flat	345	72.0
Santa Clara, Big Basin	340	65.6
Big Tree, Mill Creek Park	340	62.3
Big Tree, Prairie Creek Park	300	90.0

Only one other tree can compete in height with sequoia, and that is the Australian eucalyptus. Quite a number of eucalyptus trees 300 feet high or thereabouts are known; the tallest of which there is a reliable and authentic record was felled about 1890 near Colac, Victoria, and measured 346 feet.[1] But our own Douglas fir (*Pseudotsuga taxifolia*) lags not far behind. One standing near Little Rock, Washington, is 330 feet high with a circumference of 19 feet. And the sugar pine (*Pinus lambertiana*) which grows associated with sequoiadendron on the western slopes of the Sierra Nevada can be a most respectable tree too, reaching a height of 240 feet and a circumference of 36 feet.

The most obvious difference between sequoiadendron and sequoia is the foliage. The leaves of sequoiadendron are rather small green scales, "closely appressed," as the botanist says—which means that they do not

---

[1] Heights of 400, 450, and even 525 feet have been reported for eucalyptus, but are considered doubtful. No tree higher than 320 feet is now standing.

"stick out." While sequoia shows similar foliage at the tips of the twigs, it normally has larger needles, lining the twigs in two ranks. The cones of sequoiadendron are about double the size of those of sequoia, and hold three to six times as many seeds, the cones of sequoia holding only about fifty to sixty seeds each. That same pattern of similarity with differences applies to the wood too. The woods of both are similar in color, unlikely to decay, fully proof against insects, very hard to ignite, and easy to quench when burning. But the wood of sequoia is heavier and tougher; its dry weight is 26¼ pounds per cubic foot, while that of sequoiadendron is only 18¼ pounds per cubic foot.

Another difference which is not well known is that sequoiadendron reproduces by seeds only, while sequoia will also reproduce by root sprouts. Sequoia forms its typical burls which can be very large, and it is possible to grow a sequoia tree by planting a burl. The knots of sequoiadendron, superficially similar, are just wood.

As of 1850, sequoiadendron grew only in California and sequoia virtually only in California—a few outposts of the northern end of the redwood belt belonged to Oregon. This situation has changed, confounding some naturalists who made philosophical speeches about "last relics from former ages, unable to compete in a modern world, precariously hanging on in only a few places in California." It is, of course, true that they were just hanging on in California, but the situation is very much like that of the ginkgo. Accidents of geological and climatological developments did restrict the trees to one area, but when transplanted they do well elsewhere too. Especially sequoiadendron. A fine big specimen, planted as a seed in 1857 at Statfield Tage, England, was 114 feet tall with a circumference of 21 feet at 5 feet from the ground when it was 75 years old. Another, near Aurora, N.Y., was nearly a century old when it perished after a succession of severe winters.

Sequoiadendron is also doing well in the Black Forest of western Germany, where there are quite a lot of specimens. Their large numbers are partly due to a mistake. When the news of the discovery of the Giant Forest spread, King Wilhelm I of Württemberg grew curious and wanted to grow a few trees in one of his forests. His chief forester ordered a small quantity of seeds, requesting only 20 grams (1 ounce equals 28 grams), from somebody in California. That unknown individual felt sure this was a mistake and sent 20 pounds. As a result there are several hundred 80-year old trees near Stuttgart and in various other localities in Württemberg.

Sequoia sempervirens is not so easy to transplant. It does not tolerate cold as does the other and seems to require fog coming in, preferably every day, from the ocean. As an ornamental tree it has been planted with success in many other localities in California near the coast, but the only place outside of America which so far has been found to offer good living conditions is New Zealand. In another hundred years there will be tall redwood forests in many places along the New Zealand coast.

Visitors to Yellowstone National Park can see sequoias too, but they are sequoias of the past, fossilized stumps. One of the largest yet known, found by Professor Henry N. Andrews, Jr., a few years ago in the northwest corner of the Park, measures over 14 feet in diameter. But the bark did not fossilize, so the living tree must have had a diameter of 16 to 18 feet. The core had decayed prior to fossilization, but a count of the remaining tree rings revealed a minimum age of 1600 years. Many of the fossilized sequoias of Yellowstone National Park belong to a species which was named *Sequoia magnifica* and which is quite similar to the living *S. sempervirens*. Other fossil sequoias, both from North America and from Europe, belong to a species named *Sequoia langsdorfii*—though many of the experts agreed privately and even in print that this name was "merely convention." What they meant was that examination of fossilized leaves, twigs, and even cones of the extinct *Sequoia langsdorfii* had not convinced them that the tree was really distinct from *S. sempervirens*. The name *S. langsdorfii* was retained merely because it saved specifying every time whether the extinct or the living tree was meant.

The oldest known sequoialike trees appeared during the Jurassic period when the dinosaurs ruled land, sea, and air and when the first birds began to diverge from their reptilian ancestors. Sequoias and closely related forms seem to have become more numerous during the succeeding Cretaceous period but as far as we can tell they did not yet form continuous forests. This conclusion is based on lack of evidence rather than on evidence, and it is still possible that somebody may un-cover a redwood forest from the Cretaceous, complete with dinosaurs on the one hand and early marsupials of the type of the so-called "dawn opossum" on the other. But as far as we know the sequoia forests are typical for the Tertiary period—those ancient Yellowstone Park forests belong to the Miocene subperiod.

Many books and pamphlets on the sequoias contain a little outline map of the world, with circles marking the places where fossil sequoias have been found. This map shows that, at one time or another, such trees lived in America up to the farthest north, and in Alaska; that they lived on the west coast of Greenland, in England, Ireland, and central Europe; at the coast of the Black Sea and in central Asia; in Manchuria and on the Japanese Islands. The map is correct in itself but it can be highly misleading, because of a fact pointed out by Professor Stanley A. Cain in his excellent *Foundations of Plant Geography* (1944):

The widespread occurrence of fossils of *Sequoia,* even in Tertiary time, has led to the false impression of a widespread occurrence of redwood forests. In the North American Tertiary, redwood fossils are known through over 40 degrees of latitude, from Ellesmere Island in Arctic America to Colorado. At no one time, however, was redwood known to have lived over even one-half of this latitude. Eocene fossil localities for redwood are all north of the United States boundary. It was not until Late Oligocene, and principally Miocene, that redwood fossils were found south of Canada. When figs and palms lived in Oregon, the redwood and its associates lived far to the north. It is the telescoping of geological time that gives the appearance of extremely widespread vegetational types. During the ages, the forests have wandered over the earth in response to changing climates.

It was literally the whole forest that wandered and not just the se-quoias, as Professor Cain shows by means of tables of which the one on p. 197 is an example. The common trees now growing at Jasper Ridge, Palo Alto, Calif., are listed in one column, and the common trees of the so-called Mascall Flora, dating back some 15 million years to the Miocene subperiod, in the other. I give the table without change, except that I have inserted a center column with the common names.

Only one of the twelve trees now common near Palo Alto did not have an opposite number in the Miocene forest. It is hard to think of a better proof for the wandering of whole forests than this short table.

JASPER RIDGE FLORA	COMMON NAME	MIOCENE MASCALL FLORA
Sequoia sempervirens	Redwood	*Sequoia langsdorfii*
Salix laevigata	Willow	*Salix varians*
Salix lasiolepis	Willow	*Salix varians*
Populus trichocarpa	Poplar	*Populus lindgreni*
Alnus rhombifolia	Alder	*Alnus sp.*
Quercus kelloggii	Oak	*Quercus pseudo-lyrata*
Quercus agrifolia	Oak	*Quercus convexa*
Quercus lobata	Oak	*Quercus duriuscula*
Umbellularia californica	California laurel	*Umbellularia sp.*
Arbutus menziesii	Madroña	*Arbutus sp.*
Acer macrophyllum	Maple	*Acer bolanderi*
Aesculus californica	Horse chestnut	absent

As has been partly said and partly implied in the foregoing, the majority of the fossils resemble the living *sempervirens* more closely than they resemble sequoiadendron. Perhaps Professor Buchholz's separation of the two living forms prompted paleobotanists to go over their fossil material once more. The paper which made sequoiadendron a genus of its own appeared in 1939, and in 1941 a Japanese paleobotanist came up with still another genus. He was Shigeru Miki, instructor at Kyoto University, and his paper bore the title *On the Change of Flora in Eastern Asia since the Tertiary Period*. Miki made special reference to two old sequoias from Pliocene deposits near Tokyo. One of them had been known for a long time and had been named *S. disticha* by old Heer in Switzerland. The other had been found more recently and had been named *S. japonica* by Miki's compatriot and colleague Professor S. Endo, who was just then busily at work describing still another sequoia (*S. chinensis*) from Eocene deposits of the Fushun coal mines in southern Manchuria.

Shigeru Miki noticed that the cones of both *disticha* and *japonica* differed considerably from those of *sempervirens*. They had a much longer stalk and their scales were placed opposite each other, instead of spirally as in *sempervirens*. Once the eye had been sharpened for differences more could be seen. Miki decided that these ancient trees should not be called sequoia. They clearly belonged to a different genus for which he suggested the name *Metasequoia*. The Greek prefix *meta* really means "next to" or "among," or it may denote "change"; as a name metasequoia is useful but does not carry much inherent meaning. The English name that has been introduced for metasequoia is much better: it is dawn redwood.

In spite of the war a copy of Miki's paper reached Dr. Hsen-hsu Hu, director of the Fan Memorial Institute of Biology in Peiping. Doctor Hu, professionally a botanist and paleobotanist, realized that Miki was right, and that both *S. disticha* and *S. japonica* should be called metasequoia. He also saw that Endo's just-named *S. chinensis* from Fushun was a metasequoia too. He then wrote to Professor Ralph W. Chaney of the University of California, who had not seen either Miki's or Endo's papers. Whereupon Professor Chaney went over other fossil sequoias and decided on a kind of wholesale transfer to *Metasequoia*. There was *S. macrolepis, S. concinna, S. nordenskioldi,* and *S. reichenbachii,* all named by old Heer, all metasequoia. Even *S. langsdorfii,* also named by Heer, was a metasequoia. So was *S. heerii,* named for Heer by his French colleague Lesquereux.

If Dr. Hsen-hsu Hu had only announced the establishment of the new genus *Metasequoia,* considered ancestral to *Sequoia,* it would have been just professional news, indubitably an advance, but of little interest outside of botanical circles. But in addition, Dr. Hu announced the discovery of metasequoia as a living tree in Szechwan Province!

It had been discovered just three years after the establishment of the new genus from fossils. Actually it could have been discovered during the same year that Shigeru Miki wrote his paper, because it was established later that during the winter of 1941 Professor T. Kan of the Forestry Department of the National Central University (of China) had seen a large tree near the village of Mo-tao-chi. It was the one now recognized as the largest of the living dawn redwood trees, but, unlike the two American forms, metasequoia sheds its needles in winter, and for this reason Professor Kan had not collected any specimens.

The whole area is known as the Valley of the Tiger and is located where the two provinces of Szechwan and Hupeh adjoin along a meandering border line resembling the customary shape of jigsaw puzzle pieces. In 1944 the forester Tsang Wang traveled through the Valley of the Tiger, came to the village of Mo-tao-chi, and saw a large tree growing there. It is 110 feet tall, measuring 11 feet in diameter near the ground and about 7 feet at eye-level height. There is a small shrine at its base. Wang asked the villagers what kind of tree it was and was told *"shui-sa,"* which, elsewhere in China, is the name for the so-called water pine called by botanists *Glyptostrobus pensilis*. Wang accepted the name and the implications, but took some twigs with needles and a few cones and

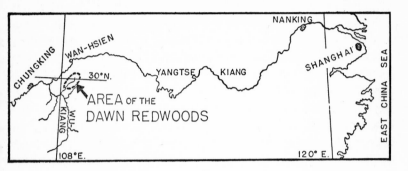

The Dawn Redwood country

surrendered them to the Forestry Division of the Ministry of Agriculture in Nanking. The botanists at the Foresty Division were puzzled and took the material to Professor Wan-chun Cheng of National Central University, knowing that Professor Cheng was the outstanding authority on the trees of Szechwan.

This fact helped him only insofar as it enabled him to say at once that he had never seen anything like that. He decided to hear the opinion of Dr. Hsen-hsu Hu. Doctor Hu, who had by then read Miki's paper, must have felt somewhat like the younger Mantell when he obtained the first skin of a takahe. A fossil had come to life in front of his eyes. Metasequoia still existed in the interior.

But Tsang Wang, not knowing the importance of his accidental discovery, had done little more than report the existence of that tall tree and two much smaller ones like it nearby. It was necessary to go there and to *look* for metasequoia. Professor Cheng had already sent his assistant, C. Y. Hsieh on two trips (February and May 1946), which resulted in more specimens and a report of the existence of an additional twenty-two trees.

At this point America entered the picture. Professor Cheng sent a specimen to Dr. E. D. Merrill of the Arnold Arboretum of Harvard University. Simultaneously Dr. Hu wrote to Dr. Merrill, telling him of his identification of this tree as a living metasequoia and asking for $250 to send Hsieh back to Szechwan to collect seeds for distribution to scientific institutions. Doctor Merrill sent the money. Hsieh boarded an airplane for Chungking from where he proceeded to Mo-tao-chi. He returned with a large quantity of seeds which Professor Cheng sent to Dr. Merrill. He, in turn, distributed them to seventy-six different institutions and individuals, all of whom began trying to grow metasequoia from seeds, mostly successfully. During that seed-gathering expedition it was also discovered that several hundred dawn redwoods were growing among the rice paddies to the south of the place where the tree had first been seen.

Some of the seeds received from China by Dr. Merrill traveled back across the American continent to Professor Ralph W. Chaney, of the University of California. Professor Chaney had done much of the work of determining metasequoia in the fossil state. When he saw the seeds of the living tree he was so impressed that he decided to go and see the trees in their original habitat. An arrangement was made with the San Francisco *Chronicle* and in March 1948 Professor Chaney and Dr. Milton Silverman of the *Chronicle* left San Francisco by air. They flew across the Pacific and then to Chungking. There modern transportation methods deserted them. Their next stop was Wan Hsien, some 175 not very comfortable miles by river boat. At Wan Hsien the real expedition began, going almost due south for another 115 still more uncomfortable miles. At the end of that route there was the small village of Shui-hsa Pa, situated at an altitude of about 4000 feet in the province of Hupeh near the Hupeh-Szechwan border. It was in the vicinity of Shui-hsa Pa that the largest number of living dawn redwoods had been discovered.

Professor Chaney brought back numerous specimens, not only twigs and samples of wood, cones and seeds and samples of bark, but also four small seedlings which are now growing at Berkeley. Other metasequoias, grown from seeds, are at the Arnold Arboretum, in the Brooklyn Botanic Garden, and at the United States Plant Introduction Garden, Glenn Dale, Md. At Glenn Dale the botanists began to test something which had been mentioned in passing by Dr. Hu. He had written that the peasants in the metasequoia area transplant the tree by means of cuttings.

A limited number of cuttings were made from the young lateral shoots of these 5-months-old plants. These cuttings were handled in a routine fashion; that is, the basal leaves were stripped from the stems and the cuttings inserted into a bed of moist sand. Because the stems of these cuttings were very delicate, care in removing the leaves and inserting them in the sand was necessary. Only 2 cuttings of the entire lot died, and the remaining 13 cuttings rooted successfully. At the end of 3 weeks an examination of the cuttings indicated that roots were forming. The cuttings remained in the sandbed for 5 weeks, at which time they were removed and potted. When it was obvious that the original lot of cuttings was rooting successfully, a second, larger propagation was made. These have begun to root in a comparable manner, with roots appearing in three weeks. Apparently, cuttings made from lateral shoots when the plants are still in the seedling stage root easily and rapidly.[2]

While small metasequoias were growing in pots in a number of institutions in the United States, the assistants of Dr. Hu and of Professor Cheng finished a census in the Valley of the Tiger and adjacent areas. They reported that the total number of naturally growing dawn redwoods slightly exceeds one thousand. About a hundred of them can be called large—around 100 feet tall; the others are fairly young trees. Along with this pleasing report, however, the Chinese scientists sounded a warning: the local inhabitants felled trees for timber indiscriminately; one of the largest at Shui-hsa Pa had been felled just before Professor Chaney arrived.

True, the Nationalist Chinese government made the dawn redwood area the first "Chinese National Park" in May 1948. But a year later that government had to leave China. What happened to the dawn redwoods since 1949, if only through lack of protection, is anybody's guess. To be safe, we should go on the assumption that the small potted trees in our institutions are the last of their kind.

Why metasequoia survived only in that particular area, some 400 miles east of the stronghold of the giant pandas, is a different question. Professor Chaney, the only American expert who has been there, offered

---

[2] Dr. John L. Creech, Division of Plant Exploration, USDA, Beltsville, Md., in *Science*, vol. 108; Dec. 10, 1948.

an interesting tentative answer. The trees associated with the dawn redwood are all trees which grew farther to the north in Asia during the
Pliocene subperiod. Presumably the forests moved south in Asia too—as
forests—just as they did in North America. Professor Chaney believes
that they were accustomed to rather wet summers, alternating with
winter seasons that were cooler but as a rule had temperatures above the
freezing point. But this combination is rather rare outside the tropics.

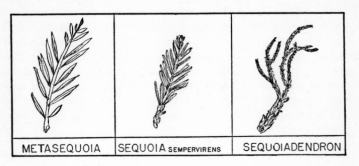

Leaves of living redwoodlike trees

In the southern United States, for example, where the swamp cypress,
related to the metasequoia-sequoia-sequoiadendron group, grows, the
summers are wet enough, but the winter temperatures go below freezing
point with fair regularity. In California, on the other hand, the winters
are mild, but the summers dry. You find either the wet-summer—cold-
winter or the dry-summer—mild-winter combination practically everywhere in the temperate zones, no matter whether you think of Europe,
Asia, or even the Southern Hemisphere. The exception from this rule is
the Valley of the Tiger.

"If it were not for the ranges of mountains that surround Mo-tao-chi
and Shui-hsa Pa," Professor Chaney wrote (*Natural History,* December 1948), "the winds from North China would come down during the
winter and make these valleys too cold for the Dawn Redwood. And the
hot summer winds from the north and west would make them too dry.
These mountains were built during the Pliocene epoch, when metasequoia was disappearing from other parts of the world. They have preserved in this limited area the climate on which the existence of the

Dawn Redwood depends. If for any reason the climate here were to change, they would probably become extinct in these valleys, as they have in all other known parts of the world."

And here the story ends for the time being. We were lucky to have discovered the dawn redwood when we did. At least, we know a great deal about it that we never knew before. As for its chances for survival, they are the same as were the milu's in 1900.

11: *The Forest of the Dinosaurs: Cycads*

EVEN before I knew that the redwood forest of Jasper Ridge is to all intents and purposes a surviving Miocene forest, I had occasionally toyed with the idea that it would be nice if some zoological or botanical garden were to make up a few paleobiological exhibits. The customary and time-honored method of arranging exhibits is "systematic"; it has found its expression in terms like monkey house, reptile house, and so on. A more modern version is the geographic exhibit: one can and does have exhibits which are condensed versions of, say, the African plains, showing the animals occurring there with the plants that grow there. To carry out my idea, one could start with the natural Miocene forest of Jasper Ridge. By putting animals from the same era into it (tapir and rhinoceros come to mind first, but the list can be lengthened), one could reconstruct a Miocene landscape. Not necessarily American Miocene, but alive. Of course the further back one goes in geological history the less material there is to work with. One would, of necessity, have to be content with very narrow segments of the older periods. Still, a saltwater tank with sharks in the water, horseshoe crabs on the bottom, certain clams in the sand, and a few living crinoids on the rocks would be a piece of pretty ancient sea, say, early Triassic.

For lack of living ichthyosaurs we could not reconstruct a piece of the European Lias Sea. But we could produce a very reasonable replica of the forest that grew on the islands in the Lias Sea. China has preserved both the ginkgos and the metasequoias that grew then. We have tree ferns from Australia and Tasmania. We have araucarias from Norfolk Island, popularly miscalled Norfolk pine. We have the smaller ferns for underbrush. And we could gather cycads from all over the earth—I mean that a scientific institution could; personally I have been singularly unsuccessful in my private attempts to buy a small cycad tree.

Most people will be ready to swear that they have never heard of cycads; that they do not now and never did have anything to do with such a tree; that, if the tree produces anything, it produces something not known to them.

They would all be swearing falsely, because one product of one species of cycad tree is known to everybody, if not in substance, at least by name. The tree which botanists call *Cycas revoluta* is called the sago palm by those who grow it. It has been under cultivation in Japan for a long time, presumably growing "across the road" from a group of ginkgo trees. The two have grown together for a long time. They did when the ichthyosaurs swam in the sea and early small mammals hid in their crowns and under their roots, waiting for the night when the flesh-eating dinosaurs would not be active.

The reason why the interesting cycads are so little known is that they are usually taken to be palm trees. Ever since Christian missionaries came to Guam, cycad leaves have done duty as "palm fronds" on Palm Sunday. In Florida, where the trees have been planted for ornamental purposes, the same thing happens. In Germany cut cycad leaves were imported in large quantities for use in funeral services, the reason being that cycad leaves are glossier and of stiffer texture than true palm fronds and keep longer. All the popular names somehow involve the word "palm." The genus *Cycas* extends from Japan to Australia. *Cycas revoluta,* as has been mentioned, is called sago palm. *Cycas media,* which grows in Queensland, Australia, is called nut palm. *Cycas circinalis* is known as the fern palm. Even the scientific name fails to avoid this comparison, because the Greek word *kykas* (pronounced *kee-kas*) also means "palm tree."

Like the ginkgo, the cycads are not molested by plant diseases and, when transplanted, are not carriers of plant diseases. Like the ginkgo, they are not bothered by insects. Unlike the ginkgo, they often contain poison, either in their leaves or in their otherwise edible starchy substance. It is known that during the Civil War a number of soldiers died because they ate the root of the only cycad native to the United States (*Zamia*). They knew that the root of this plant produces an edible substance which is said to make very nice puddings. They also knew how to recognize the plant. But they did not know that a poison has to be washed out of the starch first, or else they did not have the patience, or the time, to do it properly.

There are quite a number of cycads left on earth, all growing in warm climates. Botanists distinguish nine genera with a total of eighty-seven species. For convenience's sake the genera can be divided into three groups; the various genera are kind enough to stick to certain geographical areas. The first of these geographical groups is the Western Cycads, growing mostly south of the Rio Grande but north of Honduras. The one genus that occurs naturally in the United States (in southern Florida) also occurs naturally in South America and in Puerto Rico and other Caribbean islands. Cuba has another genus of its own. But since the whole area from the extreme south of the United States to Rio de Janeiro and beyond is suitable for cycads, they can now be found in plenty of places where they don't belong naturally. And since people don't always keep records about who planted what tree when, there has been a large number of confusing reports about their occurrence.

The second geographical group is the Australian Cycads. These, however, must not be taken to be limited to Australia itself. If it were not for the clumsiness of the term one might do better to label them the Far Eastern and Australian Cycads. The third geographical group is quite clear-cut as to habitat. It is the African Cycads.[1]

Most cycads, though the species native to the United States happens to be one of the exceptions, form heavy columnar trunks which also look at first glance like the trunks of palm trees. But they are far more mas-

---

[1] The following is a tabulation of the genera for quick reference:

WESTERN CYCADS	AUSTRALIAN CYCADS	AFRICAN CYCADS
Zamia	*Macrozamia*	*Stangeria*
Microcycas	*Cycas*	*Encephalartos*
Ceratozamia	*Bowenia*	
Dioön		

sive and encased in a very substantial armor formed by the bases of old leaves that have fallen off. Usually such cycad trees show several crowns of leaves: the youngest crown stands stiffly upright, the next older crown sticks out from the trunk at an angle, the oldest droops. These drooping leaves are several years old, two, three, or even more; it depends partly on the species, partly on growing conditions. They first lose their leaflets, so that for a while the strong center rib is left, slowly decaying. Finally it breaks off, leaving an inch or so attached to the trunk. The point at which it breaks is not accidental, as it is when a dead branch breaks off an apple or maple tree. The process is comparable to the breaking off of a single maple leaf in the fall; the place for the break has been prepared by the formation of protective tissues so that the resulting wound is actually healed before it is made. But the old leaf bases remain clearly visible for the whole long life of the cycad tree. They can therefore be used to determine its age.

But there are some difficulties. Counting the leaf bases is both easy and monotonous. And it is only one part of the job of estimating the age of the tree. One has to know, too, how many leaves are formed each year. Some cycads produce a "crown"—or maybe it would be better to call it a new crop of leaves—every year. Some form two crops per year. Some others produce a new crown every second year. And, of course, the number of leaves in a new crown varies from species to species. One has to have observations extending over a considerable period of time before one is in a position to state that a certain cycad tree is so and so many years old.

The late Professor Charles Joseph Chamberlain of the University of Chicago produced the only reliable estimate that has come to my knowledge. It is contained in his book *The Living Cycads*. Professor Chamberlain traveled over most of the globe in a search for living cycads, but those growing in Mexico were most easily accessible to him, and the estimate I mentioned therefore concerns the Mexican species *Dioön edule*. Professor Chamberlain had satisfied himself that that species forms a new crown every other year. The number of leaves in a crown is about twenty. This led to the nice round figure of ten leaves per year on the average. But when he counted the leaf bases on a beautiful specimen with a trunk about 6 feet tall he found them to number ten thousand. Which made this comparatively small, if impressive, tree a thousand years old.

And he pointed out that that was "very conservative, for seedlings have only one or two leaves the first year, and at ten years they are not likely to produce more than four or five leaves at a time, and the crowns are not likely to contain as many as twenty leaves until the plant is at least fifty years old. Besides, when a cone is produced there may be no new leaves in that year. And further, after bearing a cone the plant may be exhausted and may go into a prolonged resting period of three or four years, during which neither cones nor leaves are produced." One is obviously justified in adding about a century to the thousand-year age derived by pure arithmetic.

The cones mentioned in the previous quotation are very large and very conspicuous in all species and are the one feature which would make even a casual observer stop and wonder whether the tree he took to be a palm tree really is one. Not only are the cones large, but the seeds too; in fact the scientific name of that Mexican species is derived directly from the appearance of its seeds. Each scale of the female cone bears two seeds; hence *dioön,* which means "double egg." And because the Mexicans use the seeds for flour from which to make tortillas the species designation *edule* (Latin for edible) has been added.

Another Mexican species has been named *Dioön spinulosum* because of its spiny leaflets. It is the tallest of the living cycads, with the exception of the Australian *Macrozamia hopei* which will grow to a height of 60 feet. The spiny dioön of Mexico reaches a little more than half that, say 35 to 40 feet in especially splendid specimens. But all the other cycads are much smaller. A female cone of the spiny dioön, when fully developed, will be close to 2 feet in length and weigh as much as 30 pounds. While it stands erect like a young leaf when young, its great weight makes it hang down through the crown when ripe; it may even bend the trunk itself. Although the scientific name of this species does not indicate it, the two to three hundred seeds of the cone also furnish flour for tortillas. The Mexicans who eat them have no idea that the same flour could have been obtained about a hundred million years ago.

In some areas of Mexico, in the country beyond Tuxtepec not far from the banks of the Papaloapan River, the spiny dioön is the only large plant. In places it forms real cycad forests, to a naturalist the backdrop for the saurian life of the Jurassic period. But the spiny dioön is of interest to a naturalist also because of the rather strong possibility that the two species of dioön in Mexico may be much more directly related to each other than had been suspected at first.

That they were closely related had been known all along, the main differences being the greater height of the spiny form and the spiny leaflets for which it is named. But then Professor Chamberlain observed that very young speciments of the "edible" dioön have spiny leaflets too. They lose them later. All scientists know that the development of an individual repeats, in a hurried and concentrated manner, the evolutionary pattern of its species. Young individuals of the tailless amphibians, frogs and toads, do have a tail for a while, as everybody knows. Its existence indicates that the tailless amphibians of today are the more recent form and that their ancestors were tailed like salamanders. This so-called "biogenetic rule," while most frequently mentioned with reference to animal evolution, naturally applies to plants too. Very young ginkgo trees, remember, have four-lobed leaves for a while, like Jurassic ginkgos. The fact that the cycad *Dioön edule* starts out with spiny leaflets proves that its ancestor sported spiny leaflets. It does not in itself prove that *Dioön spinulosum* is that ancestor. But that looks rather probable.

Mexico is much more of a cycad country in our age than is any other part of the planet. Not only does the spiny dioön form forests, there are also more genera of cycads in Mexico than in any other region of comparable size. I chose dioön as the first example because it is more typical of the appearance of a cycad tree than is *Zamia floridana,* which in Florida is called a coontie. Several species of the genus *Zamia* grow in Mexico too, and its name must be explained here.

The Florida zamia differs from the Mexican dioön and from the Far Eastern cycas by the absence of the columnar trunk. It does have a short trunk, but that is underground. Zamia prefers dry and well-drained soils. Its underground trunk reaches for some distance in the direction of the water supply. The remaining distance is negotiated by a deep tap root and by long slender roots. What shows above the surface are only a few leaves, half a dozen or less, and the male and female cones. *Zamia*

floridana was named by Linnaeus, who introduced the systematic use of
Greek-Latin double names. When he received a specimen of the Florida
cycad it happened to be one with a small male cone. Linnaeus thought
that it was sterile and chose the Latin word which means "loss" or

A living cycad

"damage," *zamia*. That, of course, was a mistake, but it made a name
just the same.

Besides several species of zamia, Mexico also has *Ceratozamia*, so
named because *kerastes* (again a Greek root) means "horned" and each
cone scale of this plant bears two spikes which look like horns. The
story of the way Professor Chamberlain found ceratozamia in Mexico
is an example of ingenuity with a very typical Mexican flavor. During
his first trips to Mexico in quest of cycads, Professor Chamberlain had
found dioön, both species, in quantities. He had also stumbled, some-

times literally, across various zamias. But no ceratozamia. He had been introduced earlier to Señor Teodoro A. Dehesa, then governor of the state of Veracruz. The governor had helped him greatly with introductions and written recommendations. Naturally Professor Chamberlain, before returning to the United States, went to pay a farewell call on the governor. In the course of the conversation Professor Chamberlain mentioned that he had also searched for ceratozamia which was said to grow in that state but had not found it.

Governor Dehesa asked for a description of the plant. This happened to be very simple, because a specimen was growing in the park near the governor's palace. But that one had been planted there, which reduced Professor Chamberlain's interest in it. He knew that this genus of cycads existed, and how it looked; the question was where it grew naturally. The governor told Professor Chamberlain that he would find out for him. He did.

Barely a month after Chamberlain's arrival in Chicago, he received a parcel containing some very fine cones of ceratozamia. More came a while later. Through intermediaries Chamberlain learned how the governor had done it. Very simple indeed. He had stationed relays of policemen near the specimen in the public park. The policemen stopped anybody who looked as if he had come from the country, pointed to the park specimen, and asked him whether such plants grew where he came from. After about two weeks they found somebody who knew the plant and who could dictate information on how to find it. Its habitat was not even far from Veracruz. There is an extinct volcano in the general vicinity. Its name is Naolinco and it is closer to Jalapa than to Veracruz. A valley with rather steep slopes leads to the volcano, and ceratozamia grows abundantly on these slopes. It is a small plant; a specimen 3 or 4 feet tall is definitely large, and 6 feet is the maximum.

There is one more genus of the Western Cycads, which grows in Cuba. Cuba, like most islands in the Caribbean Sea, has zamia too, but it is also the home of a cycad with a columnar trunk. This does not even occur everywhere on the island and is probably the least numerous of all living cycads. It was described for the first time from a few leaves only, and the botanist who did the work did not know the appearance of the whole plant. The leaves reminded him of the Japanese cycas but the Cuban form seemed much smaller. Hence he called it *Microcycas*. Actually the Cuban microcycas is not much smaller, on the whole, than the Far Eastern cycas.

The reason that botanists and especially paleobotanists have such an intense interest in cycads is the same as that for the zoologist's preoccupation with platypus. No zoologist would be surprised if platypus were extinct. No botanist would be surprised if he knew cycads only as an extinct form of plant life. It is the fact that they are still with us that makes them special.

To elaborate on this a bit we have to go back into geological history. The plants which, like the animals, had originated in the seas, began to climb the land at about the middle of the Paleozoic Era, during the Devonian period, some 350 million years ago. It caused considerable surprise when fossils of Devonian trees came to light in New York State some time ago. There had been many indications that land plants had existed during the Devonian period, but whether there had been actual trees then had been debatable.

The Carboniferous period which followed was the period of the enormous forests. We now have a good mental picture about the nature of the forests which produced our coal seams. But a word of caution has to be inserted here. The forests which our experts know so well—in the Chicago Museum of Natural History they built a Carboniferous landscape—are all of one type, a swampy lowland forest. These swampy lowland forests finally became coal seams. But we can't very well assume that all of earth was swampy lowland during that period. There must have been extensive highlands too. Presumably there was also a dry highland type of forest during the Carboniferous period, but that suspected highland forest is not known to us.

As for the swampy lowland forest, we have the good luck that some of it still exists, literally in miniature. Several of the tree types which must have dominated the coal forest can be called clubmoss trees. The clubmoss trees are gone, but the clubmoss is still with us, and in New England you can find places where you can look at a clubmoss forest, by lying flat and assuming frog perspective. Another tree type of the coal forest was related to the present day *Equisitum,* the horsetails and scouring rushes. And then, of course, there were ferns in the coal forest. They were not the ferns of today; even our present-day tree ferns of the tropical areas are not straight survivors from the coal forest, though for some time they were believed to be, but our ferns do indicate what the coal forest must have looked like in certain places.

All the plants mentioned in the preceding paragraph fall into one classification to the botanist, who calls them the leafy spore plants. There is emphasis on both words. There are other spore plants, the fungi, for example, but they are not leafy. On the other hand, the vast majority of the leafy plants of today do not form spores, they produce seeds. It was obviously a long step forward when plants changed from spore production to the formation of seeds. Considering these facts one can understand why botanists are so happy about a group of extinct plants called the seed-bearing ferns.

The Carboniferous period had both spore-producing ferns—that type is still with us—and seed-bearing ferns, of which one form is rather thoroughly known from fossils in the English coal fields. In fact, fossils found in Scotland prove that there were seed-ferns during the early part of the Carboniferous, and they may have originated during the latter part of the Devonian.

The seed-ferns, apparently having served their purpose, died out; in their time they were a truly intermediate form. The seed plants of today fall into two groups, one which is comparatively small, even though the numbers of individuals of some species may be large. The seeds of plants in this group do not have any special protection; the little winged seeds in a pine cone are an example. The vast majority of living plants have thoroughly protected seeds. Think of the nursery rhyme of the little green house in which there is a little brown house and in the little brown house there is a little yellow house—only then do you get to the kernel of the walnut. These higher plants with well-protected seeds are the angiosperms, *angeion* being Greek for a vessel. The naked-seed plants are called gymnosperms from *gymnos,* Greek for naked.

The most advanced group among the gymnosperms is the conifers, our familiar pines, spruces, cedars, and also the redwoods. This conifer group is still going strong and may be said to belong to our time. The other gymnosperms are rare, isolated relics of the past, not related either to each other or to the conifers. One of them is the strange Welwitschia of the Southwest African deserts which would look like an enormous wooden carrot if it were pulled from the ground. The top of this "carrot" protrudes, some 18 inches high. It measures more than a yard across. It forms just two leaves, ribbonlike in shape. They are over 2 feet wide and over 10 feet long, and are usually torn into many narrower ribbons. Welwitschia seems to have been around, virtually unchanged, since the Permian period when the ancestors of the later dinosaurs walked about.

Another group of ancient gymnosperms is the Gnetum plants, of which there are three living representatives, one of them in the United States. The scientific name of the American representative is *Ephedra;* the people who live where it grows (New Mexico and neighboring states) call it Mormon tea. It is a shrubby woody plant without true leaves, but with stiff green stems which serve the functions of the leaves of other plants.

Another group of ancient gymnosperms has only one representative: the ginkgo. That is why the ginkgo's "apricots," in spite of their pulpy covering, are called "naked seeds." The fruit pulp is a kind of secondary addition; the bearer of the fruit is one of the gymnosperms.

And the last group, the closest thing we still have to the old seed-bearing ferns, is the cycads.

One of the places where fossil cycads have been found for more than a century is the British Yorkshire coast near Scarborough. The general situation resembles that of the amber coast: an almost vertical shoreline that is slowly receding under the pounding of the surf, and at the foot of that coast, below sea level at high tide (this is the North Sea, not the tideless Baltic), there is a dark gray clayish layer, full of fossils. But this fossil-bearing layer is of Jurassic origin and the fossils are mostly land plants. It has yielded numerous Jurassic ferns, and ginkgos in almost equal numbers. But there are also many cycads. The one which is found most frequently has been called *Nilssonia*. This is the name given to the fossil leaves. Fossil seeds have also been found, and were called *Beania*—in both cases personal names. More recently botanists have begun to nurse the suspicion that leaves and seeds belong to one and the same plant, a cycad resembling our zamia though much larger. The case is not yet proved since leaves and seeds have not yet been found connected. Well, one can't expect the perfection of the Lias epsilon everywhere.

The most famous site of fossil cycads is in the United States and has been protected as the Cycad National Monument, located in the southern Black Hills of Dakota. There, in a whole fossil forest, cycads are really numerous. But while the best preserved and in some respects the most astonishing fossil cycads come from that area, it is not the only place in the United States where they occur. Workmen building the road from

Fossil "flower-bearing" cycad

Washington to Baltimore found them in large numbers, and many homes around there still contain specimens, usually thought to be "petrified wasp nests" or beehives. They have also been found in Texas, California, Colorado, and Wyoming; in the West they are dubbed "petrified pineapples."

As these popular terms indicate, these fossil cycads have a different shape from the columnar trunks with which we are familiar. Their shape is reminiscent of cacti; even some fossil collectors, although scientists have told them that they are dealing with cycadlike plants, refer privately to "stone cactus." Botanically speaking, these fossil American forms, plus a few fossil forms from England and elsewhere, do not belong to the botanical "family" of the living cycads. They are *Cycadeoidea* or cycadeoids, "cycadlike"; some experts prefer the term *Benettitales* to make a stronger distinction.

It was the late Professor G. R. Wieland who discovered that these fossil cycadeoids had done something which gymnosperms, by definition, should not do. Gymnosperms produce male and female cones. Angiosperms produce flowers. But the cycadeoids also produced flowers. At least that is the only word which describes the result; you are, of course, at liberty to invent a special name for a gymnosperm flower. These cycadeoids produced buds, not only on the top of the trunk where cycads form their cones, but almost anywhere on the trunk between the old leaf bases. And not just one or two, but literally hundreds of them. Such a flowering cycadeoid at full display must have been a very strange and in all probability a very beautiful sight. No fully opened flower has been found so far, but the buds, protected by the typical cycad armor, have fossilized in all stages of development.

We have no cycadeoids any more, just cycads, survivors from the Jurassic. And when a scientist hears that term he automatically looks in a certain direction on a modern map. In the days before the Jurassic the map of the earth showed three main continents. One was essentially the North American continent of today. The other was the Asiatic land mass, at certain times minus its southern portions, India and Thailand-Burma. The third was a southern continent, comprising more or less the East India of today, Australia in the east, and the African land mass in the west, with even a temporary connection to South America.

During the Jurassic period many changes took place. Europe, as we already know, was flooded and changed into an archipelago. A little later the sea also made considerable inroads into Asia and later still split the North American continent in two, flooding the center section from the Arctic to the Gulf of Mexico. During the Jurassic, Australia became an independent continent and Africa followed suit. But while Africa was reconnected repeatedly with either Europe or Asia or both, Australia stayed isolated. Australia, therefore, is the oldest existing isolated land mass on earth. The South Polar continent may be able to compete in that respect, though we don't know enough about it yet to be sure, but in its present stage it is not too exciting, from a biological point of view.

But Australia, by virtue of the events described, maintained an older fauna. Its dominant type, prior to settlement, was the pouched mammals or marsupials. It preserved for us the ancient egg-laying mammals platypus and echidna. It kept the lungfish *Neoceratodus* alive. If ancient plants like the cycads survived anywhere, Australia would be the logical place to look, with Africa as second choice.

It has already been mentioned that there are cycads both in Australia and in Africa. Queensland in Australia has three genera, as many as Mexico. There is *Macrozamia,* one species of which is the biggest living cycad.[2] There is *Bowenia* which, being quite short, in places forms the sole underbrush in a sparse eucalyptus forest. And there is *Cycas* which also occurs in the East Indies and as far north as Japan. Cycas differs from the other cycads in not forming female cones. It forms male cones like the others, but its seeds are borne on what is a modified leaf, technically known as a sporophyll. Sometimes this looks even more impressive than the big cones of the other cycads. In *Cycas revoluta* (sago palm) the sporophylls are densely covered with hair; the large seeds are bright red. In *Cycas circinalis* (fern palm), the seeds that sprout from the sporophyll are as large as goose eggs. "The earliest seed plants . . . bore their seeds on the margins of more or less modified leaves, so that in this respect *Cycas* shows the most primitive condition to be found in the plant kingdom. In all the cycads the 'scales' of both male and female cones are modified leaves, but all have digressed farther than *Cycas* from the primitive condition." (Chamberlain.)

The African cycads are concentrated in the southeast section, Zululand and the area south of it. The first African genus, named *Stangeria*

---

[2] By a curious accumulation of mistakes, an example of *Macrozamia* has also been claimed to be the oldest living individual plant. What happened, as explained by Dr. Scheinfeld, who first repeated the mistake in his book *You and Heredity,* was this: Dr. A. O. Herbert of the University of Queensland had found an especially impressive specimen of *Macrozamia* on Tamborine Mountain. Presumably applying Professor Chamberlain's method, he estimated its age as 500 years minimum, 1000 years maximum. A reporter of a Brisbane newspaper wrote an account of this discovery, stating that the age had been estimated as 1000 years. The typesetter, however, made that 10,000 years. Another Australian newspaper changed the figure to 15,000 years. Ripley's *Believe it or Not,* which has repeatedly shown itself to be weak in the field of natural history, uncritically accepted the largest figure available.

after the botanist Stanger, is a trunkless form and its leaves are so fern-
like that it was first described as a fern. Only when a specimen of the
supposed fern suddenly developed a cone did the truth dawn. The plant
is now called *Stangeria paradoxa* because it looks like a fern but is
something else. Professor Chamberlain reported that it is easy to collect
because in the open veldt the grass is dry and yellowish in midsummer,
while the leaves of *Stangeria,* like those of all other cycads, stay fresh
and green no matter what the temperature or the percentage of humidity.

The other African genus of cycads is named *Encephalartos;* named
by somebody who combined a knowledge of Greek with a sense of
humor. The African natives, like the Mexicans, make meal from the
seeds, and the name means "cake in the head." This genus has not
only a considerable range but its dozen species also show a great diversity
of form. Some have trunks like cycas, others have only a subterranean
stem like zamia. One will form as many as three cones simultaneously,
weighing together 140 pounds. But that had to be established in a botanical garden, because the specimens in the open are regularly robbed
of their cones at just the proper stage of ripeness by baboons who also
appreciate the "cake in the head." And there is one trunkless species
which can be safely approached only with a tank. Each of its leaflets
is a hard and sharp spine, and these spines grow out from the midrib
in several directions—its name *Encephalartos horridus* is quite understandable.

Probably because they are resistant to disease and to drought, un-
attractive to insects, and often poisonous to bigger plant-eaters, the cycads
are still with us. The worst harm that seems to befall them in the normal
course of events is for somebody to steal their seeds. But since they are
long-lived and can produce very many seeds over long periods, that has
not proved fatal. Cycads are still available for a reproduction of the
forests that grew on the islands of the Lias Sea. But there is no one locality
where the elements which composed that forest now grow together.
They managed to survive into the age of man in widely separated areas.

Part Three

WANDERERS
ACROSS
THE PLANET

12: The Story
of the Fish Anguilla

IT SEEMS that one cannot say "fish" without evoking the reaction "Izaak Walton," and this chapter, for this reason, may as well start with a reference to the famous Izaak Walton and his equally famous book *The Compleat Angler,* written some three hundred years ago. As regards the fish *Anguilla,* the common eel of rivers and lakes, Walton wrote:

It is agreed by most men, that the Eel is a most dainty fish; the Romans have esteemed her the Helena of their feasts; and some the queen of palate pleasure. But most men differ about their breeding: some say they breed by generation, as other fish do; and others, that they breed, as some worms do, of mud.

The first of these two sentences may astonish American readers somewhat, since the eel, probably just because of its serpentine shape, is not valued highly as a food fish on this side of the Atlantic Ocean. Europeans, however, are in full agreement that the eel is superlative as a food fish, provided it has been well prepared. There are some differences of opinion as to what "well prepared" means. In the North European countries, especially along the seashore, smoked eel is preferred, while farther inland eel is either boiled with dill or served cold in aspic. The fishermen along the amber coast go everybody else one better: they smoke it first and then fry the smoked eel in butter. It may have added to the eel's popularity that it is never a rare fish. Where eels occur at all, they occur in large, sometimes incredible, numbers.

So much for Izaak Walton's first statement.

As for the second—that is a long and complicated story full of surprises.

Since the earliest times fishermen, when preparing caught fishes for
consumption, have been used to coming across roe or semen in their fish
when the season was right. But with eels there seemed to be no season.
Nobody could truthfully claim to have seen eel roe, and Aristotle, some
two millennia ago, summed up popular experience when he stated that
"the eel has no sex, no eggs, no semen, and originates from the entrails
of the sea."

Pliny the Elder said surprisingly little about eels: his three most positive statements are that the eel lives eight years, that it can survive on
land for as long as six days, and that it is the only fish which does not
float up to the surface when it dies. The first statement seems to be about
correct, although in isolated cases eels have lived much longer. The
second statement has to refer to very wet grass or moss to be true; of
course, nobody ever measured the time precisely, but my Samland eel-
fisherman agreed with it "if packed right." The third statement is true
too, if you cross out the word "only."

It was probably the fact that eels can survive for a very considerable
time outside of water, provided only that the surroundings are wet,
which gave rise to the story that the eel will leave the rivers at night.
This belief acquired a definite shape in the book on animals which Albert
von Bollstädt (Albertus Magnus) wrote during the second half of the
thirteenth century: "The eel is also said to leave the water during the
nights and to slip onto the fields, where he'll find peas, lentils, or beans
growing." The peasants, especially in southwestern Germany, believe
this even today and strangely enough they tell it in almost the words
used by Albertus. It probably is a piece of folklore which has been passed
on through the generations from the late Middle Ages. But when a
skeptic dares to doubt its truth he is solemnly assured that so-and-so
knew a man who had told him that he had seen it with his own eyes
when he was a boy.

The stories were so persistent that scientists repeatedly started in-
quiries to track down a definite and well-documented case. But they
never succeeded. So-and-so did assert that he had found eels in his field

on one occasion, but when the time was nailed down it turned out to have been shortly after a small and harmless, local flood. Another one had a similar story to report, but investigation showed that there was a poorly fitted sewer running along the edge of the field. One Dr. Emil Walter, a German fisheries expert, who devoted a whole book to the eel (*Der Flussaal,* Neudamm, 1910), came to the conclusion that a number of the reports were simply the result of confusing a common and harmless snake for an eel. This may seem incredible at first glance, but this snake, which grows to a length of 3 to 4 feet, resembles a river eel in size. Moreover—and this fact is well known—this particular snake likes water and swims well and often. Doctor Walter was probably correct in the belief that somebody saw such a snake disappear into the water and assumed that it must have been an eel, especially when this happened at night. If it happened in daylight, the snake was recognized and the incident did not cause a story.

It may be useful to say that the performance would not be completely impossible just because the eel is a fish. Of course, the eel probably would not try to steal green peas or young lentils, since it doesn't eat anything vegetable, but it might go after insects or earthworms. There are several varieties of fish that do go on land without hesitation. There is the so-called "climbing perch," a fish which lives up to its name only in part: it does climb, but it is not a perch. It grows to a length of 8 inches (6 inches, however, is more usual) and it inhabits most of India and almost all of West Africa in a number of closely related species. This climbing perch, or, to give it its scientific name, *Anabas,* does move considerable distances over land in a jerky and clumsy manner but at a rather fast rate. It does climb steep banks, and at least the Indian variety, *Anabas scandens,* has been seen to climb up the trunk of a palm tree to a height of about 5 feet. As far as is known, *Anabas* indulges in this peculiar habit in order to reach another body of water. It has evolved a special organ to breathe air temporarily and since this organ seems to work rather well the fish is in the strange dilemma of needing both air and water to breathe. If it does not get water it will die after some time, like any other fish. But if it cannot get air it will drown.

Along Africa's east coast there is the better-known mudspringer (*Periophthalmus*) which habitually climbs up on tree roots. It also is about

6 inches long, and while *Anabas* has a typical fish shape, *Periophthalmus* (the name means "he who looks around") reminds the onlooker of a tadpole. His jumps also have been compared to the jumps of frogs. And it does seem as if the mudspringer might be hunting insects on land.

The story of the eel's excursions onto dry land is, as these examples show, not impossible *per se*. It just seems to be erroneous. Italian naturalists, among them the famous Lazzaro Spallanzani, have pointed out that occasionally large numbers of eels have died in Italian waters when they could have reached fresh river water by an overland trip of a few hundred yards. But eels do show up in strange places (that they enter city water supplies and clog the household plumbing is not too strange, considering their shape) and occasionally baffle even naturalists. The Dr. Emil Walter previously mentioned reported a case which he had learned from a professional naturalist, even a fisheries expert. This was a Professor Frenzel who ran an experiment station near Berlin. The station was situated close to a fairly large lake, the Müggelsee, but had its own ponds, mostly artificial, several hundred yards from the lakeshore. Near one of those ponds a small dead tree was uprooted. Under its roots was a small eel, 5 inches long and a little less than a ¼-inch thick, covered with sand but very much alive otherwise. The scientists first took some measurements to be sure of their facts. The eel was slightly more than a foot below ground level. The place was 12 feet from the rim of the pond and 5 feet above water level. The ground below the 1-foot hole where the tree roots had been was dry and hard.

It was several days before a gardener remembered that they had taken water from that pond in buckets to water the young trees during dry weather. They had stopped when a rainy period set in. The last watering had taken place a full six weeks before the eel was found. This, of course, affords a clue as to how eels might be found in fields. While there are fish that do go on land, the eel is not one of them. But it does manage to stay alive on land for a long time if conditions are at all favorable.

But while the idea of the eel's "excursions" did not cause too much discussion because it was simply accepted, the problem of propagation was a different matter. That, everybody agreed, was the real mystery. And because it was such a deep mystery and because the eel is such a common fish, it is not at all surprising that everybody who wrote a book produced his own pet theory. Doctor Konrad Gesner of Zürich, writing in 1558, still tried to be impartial, saying that "those who have written about their origin and procreation" hold three views. One is that eels form in mud and moisture, "as has been written about some other aquatic animals too." Doctor Gesner apparently did not think too highly of the idea. The next opinion he reported was that eels rub their bellies against the ground and that the slime from their bodies causes the mud or soil to form more eels, "wherefore the eels are said not to have a distinction in sex, neither male nor female." The third opinion was that the eels propagate with eggs like other fish, but he added that "our fishermen" say the eels bear living young.

Next after Gesner, another Swiss, Mangolt (in *Fischbuch,* Zürich, 1565), sided with the fishermen without reservations:

This fish has a special propagation since it has neither milt nor roe but gives birth to live young. At first they are small like a piece of string. They don't give birth at any specific season, but in all seasons. They are best for food in May . . . hate muddy water and are afraid of thunder.

The fishermen thought they spoke the truth. Unfortunately the "tiny eels looking like twine" which were found inside large eels were neither eels, nor fish, nor even vertebrates. They were intestinal parasites, worms (mostly nematodes), which infest all kinds of fish with complete impartiality. But if such worms were found inside a pike or a carp nobody thought anything about it; if they were found inside an eel it was another story. Occasionally somebody also found "proof" that the eel laid eggs like other fish, swearing that he had found fish eggs inside a large eel. That was true, too, even more literally true than the teller of the tale believed. He *had* found fish eggs inside a large eel, eggs of other fish. The eel has the bad luck of combining a large appetite with a small mouth; fish eggs are one of the things it can swallow best.

While the professional fishermen did assume a natural cycle of large eels, small eels growing up, large eels, small eels growing up, others formed weird and wonderful superstitions, which, handed on, took deep root in the course of time. German folklore, put on record in the sixteenth century but probably centuries older, provided a simple recipe for increasing the supply of eels in a given locality: "Take hairs from the tail of a horse, cut them into finger-long pieces and throw them into a clear river; after some time they will swell up, come to life and in due course be transformed into eels."

That folklore and men of learning were in close agreement is shown by a similar recipe, advocated in about 1600 by no less a person than the Flemish physician and chemist Jan Baptista van Helmont: "Cut two pieces of grass sod wet with Maydew and place the grassy sides together, then put it into the rays of the spring sun, and after a few hours you'll find that a large number of small eels have been generated."

If propagation were that simple it posed a major puzzle: why, for example, did the Rhine and all its tributaries swarm with eels while the Danube and its tributaries were void of them? Konrad Gesner had decided that the water of the Danube must be "inimical" to eels and stated that eels thrown into the Danube would die soon. It was an explanation which was probably accepted by his contemporaries; and it is a safe bet that they would have disbelieved the real explanation, had anybody been able to give it.

Zoologists did the logical thing; they dissected eels in the hope of finding, if not milt or roe, at least the organs which might produce them at the proper time. An Italian by the name of Mondini in 1777 found what he believed to be the female organ. It was, as a matter of fact; but the famous Spallanzani did not believe it. Since Spallanzani was the great crusader against the belief that anything living could come into existence without parents, his word was accepted. If the doubts of Mondini's discovery had been expressed by any of the professors who still believed in "spontaneous generation," the vote would probably have gone in favor of Mondini almost automatically. But if Spallanzani doubted it—well, Mondini must have been mistaken. Then, when a German, Otto Friedrich Müller, made the same discovery independently three years after Mondini, he was told that the mistake had already been refuted in Italy. Finally, in 1824, Professor Rathke of the Albertus Universität in Königsberg again discovered the eel's female sex organ, and this time the discovery was accepted.

The male organ was found half a century later, in 1874, by Syrski of Trieste. And in the meantime the seacoast branch of the fishing trade had reported additional and apparently quite simple evidence. Every year in the fall, more or less fully grown eels were seen coming downriver and disappearing into the sea. And in the spring swarms of small 3-inch eels came out of the sea and gradually worked their way upriver. Because of their transparent appearance these young eels were called "glass eels" along the European continental coast. British fishermen referred to them as elvers.

After careful comparing of notes, scientists about a hundred years ago began to consider the question nicely settled. Some well-known fish, like salmon, shad, and others, went upriver for spawning but were not really river fish otherwise. The eel reversed the process; it was a fresh-water fish that went to the sea for spawning. That was true for *Anguilla anguilla,* the European eel, and it was also true for *Anguilla chrysypa,* the American eel.[1] And the Danube river system did not harbor eels because the Danube empties into the Black Sea where eels probably could not breed. It was already known that the water of the Black Sea is "clean" only in its surface layers; the bottom layers are poisoned by hydrogen sulphide (H_2S). Why this is so has still not been explained to everybody's complete satisfaction, but there is no doubt about the fact, and it is also definitely established that no life above the level of bacteria exists in the Black Sea below the 80-fathom line. That solved the "Danube problem": it was not the water of the river that was "inimical," but the water of the sea beyond the mouth of that river. That water was decidedly "inimical"—it was poisonous.

Beginning in about 1830, that was the way the case was presented. The books of 1850 were still saying the same [2] and so were those of 1880, 1900, and 1905. But meanwhile a quiet revolution had taken place which went unnoticed for several decades.

It had begun in 1856.

---

[1] Older books use *Anguilla vulgaris* for the European form and *Anguilla rostrata* for the American.

[2] Nevertheless, I recently found a book entitled *The Origin of the Silver Eel,* by one David Cairncross, published in London in 1862, which left me breathless with surprise. It was dedicated to "the President, the Vice-President and the Members of the Blairgowrie Angling Club," and the author said about himself that he "had been reared near the mouth of the Tay; [where] education was small in quantity and inferior in quality; little of it came my way." His thesis was that the parents of eels are—*beetles*. He had seen small black beetles go into water and small eels come forth from them; the beetles then died. In one of his cases, "two beetles appeared in the well and gave birth to two eels each." Although he never succeeded in raising young eels from the things that had come out of the beetles, he attributed his failure to the need for flowing water to effect the transformation. Of course, the "eels" were intestinal parasites. I read through half of the small book in anticipation of a joking disclaimer of some kind, but its author was deadly serious.

During that year a naturalist, our old acquaintance Dr. Kaup, who had named chirotherium, had caught a very curious small saltwater fish. It was interesting mainly because of its appearance. If some of these fish were in a saltwater aquarium, at first glance the aquarium would appear to be empty. Looking more closely, you would see a few pairs of tiny dark eyes swimming around by themselves. Intent watching would disclose watery shades trailing the eyes. Out of water the fish looked like a laurel leaf, but larger, 3 inches long—a laurel leaf made of flexible glass, thin and fragile and transparent. You could place the fish on the page of a newspaper or a book and read the type through its body without trouble.

Doctor Kaup followed the usual procedure of searching the literature for an earlier description of that fish, and finding none, described it himself. Following scientific custom he also selected a name. It was *Leptocephalus brevirostris*.

Nothing more occurred for some time. But two Italian ichthyologists, Grassi and Calandruccio, read Dr. Kaup's description and decided to investigate leptocephalus a little further when they got around to it. In retrospect, they said that they would not have waited so long if they had known what they were to discover. But they did not know and there always was other more pressing work; the investigation of leptocephalus was postponed from year to year. They had learned, meanwhile, that the fish at least was not rare; they could get examples from Messina if they needed them.

The long-postponed investigation began in 1895. At first it was still routine. The fish were caught near Messina, and an aquarium which should please an inhabitant of the waters near Messina was prepared. Several leptocephali were put into it and Grassi and Calandruccio began their work by trying to find out what leptocephalus would eat. Many an investigation of living animals has come to an end because of feeding problems. But there was no trouble on that score; the little fish ate about what Grassi and Calandruccio expected them to eat. They fed and swam around and looked—what was visible of them—as if they were in good health.

But they shrank!

The largest of the leptocephali had been 75 millimeters (3 inches) long when caught. It lost a full 10 millimeters of length while under observation. It also shrank in the other direction, getting narrower and losing that typical leaf shape. And then, with fair suddenness, leptocephalus became an elver, a "glass eel."

When they had recovered from their surprise Grassi and Calandruccio announced that Dr. Kaup's genus *Leptocephalus* was invalid. Leptocephalus was merely a kind of larval stage of the elver, which, as everybody knew, was the youthful stage of the eel. The river and lake eel then became the adolescent stage which, upon maturing, returned to the sea, unless prevented from doing so by artificial means or by accident. The mature eel, Grassi and Calandruccio concluded, lays its eggs at the bottom of the sea and presumably dies, since nobody had ever seen large eels returning from the sea and going upriver. The eggs hatch into the larval stage, Dr. Kaup's mistaken *Leptocephalus,* which stays near the bottom until it is either changed or about to change into the elver stage. The elvers then swim for water of less and less salinity, finally entering the rivers.

Grassi and Calandruccio also had an explanation for the rarity of the leptocephalus stage. It was rare, they said, because it stays near the sea bottom. They had just been lucky enough to get their eel larvae from the Strait of Messina where currents often swept deep-water forms to the surface. Thus, modestly ascribing their own success to their advantageous geographical position, the two Italian scientists concluded their report, which constituted one of the great advances in a zoological field. They even made an additional contribution which was not to become really important until later.

When you make a leptocephalus reasonably visible by placing it on black paper, you find that its body is built up of a number of segments. The technical term for these segments, which might be compared to the links of a chain, is myomeres. Grassi and Calandruccio suspected that the number of myomeres might correspond to the number of vertebrae in the finished eel. They proved that this suspicion was correct: if you have the necessary patience to count the myomeres of a leptocephalus you can tell the number of vertebrae that will form.

All this was fine, but it was not yet the end of the story. The scene shifted once more, to another year, another sea, and another expert. The

year was 1904, the sea the Atlantic Ocean between Iceland and the
Faeroes, the expert Danish biologist Dr. Johannes Schmidt, attached to
the Royal Ministry of Fisheries and at that time aboard the small Danish
steamer *Thor.*

From aboard the *Thor*, Dr. Johannes Schmidt caught, *by means of
a surface net,* one of the transparent laurel leaves the two Italian scientists
had made so famous. The catch was *Leptocephalus brevirostris* beyond
doubt. It was as long as the longest specimens from Messina—75 millimeters. Dr. Schmidt was mildly elated: a case of leptocephalus having
come to the surface for some unknown but probably interesting reason.

Only a few months later a Mr. Farran caught another leptocephalus
from the research steamer *Helga,* based in Ireland. Again a surface net
had been used, and again the specimen was some 75 millimeters long.
The place was the Atlantic off the Irish coast. It became clear that there
was still a lot to be learned. So far all the work had been done in the
Mediterranean, now there was a chance to carry the same work through
for the area to the west of Europe.

A nautical chart of western Europe shows a line out in the sea where
the depth is 3000 feet; sailors refer to it as the 500-fathom line. West
of that line there is the deep Atlantic, east of it the shallow sea which is
a flooded section of the continental land mass itself. Schmidt found that
the 500-fathom line marked, approximately of course, the area of 75-
millimeter leptocephali, and that they stayed that distance from land at
the time, in late summer, when they began to undergo the changes
described by Grassi and Calandruccio. By the following spring they
had become elvers and had reached the mouths of the European
rivers.

Schmidt drew up a tentative chart of the eel's spawning grounds.
They seemed to have three characteristics: a depth of 500 fathoms or
more; a rather high salinity, 35 parts in 1000 parts of water, or higher;
and a temperature of 48 degrees Fahrenheit or higher. The last was
presumably the difficulty, because in depths greater than 500 fathoms
the temperature of the water, while tending to be uniform and unchang-
ing through the seasons, is usually less than 48 degrees Fahrenheit. But
a chart could still be drawn up, showing probable spawning places running straight north to south off the Irish coast, then dipping eastward

into the Bay of Biscay, following the Spanish and Portuguese coasts at a respectful distance, and going through the Strait of Gibraltar into the Mediterranean for a hundred miles or so.

All this was still based on the assumption which Grassi and Calandruccio had made: that the eggs hatched at the bottom of the sea and that the leptocephalus stage also grew up near the bottom until it had reached the famous 75-millimeter length, when it came to the surface, ready to change. If you wanted leptocephalus of a smaller size and of an earlier stage you had to fish in deep water. There existed special nets for this kind of research work, nets which stay closed until a certain depth is reached, open at that depth, and then close up again as soon as the people aboard the research vessel begin hauling them in.

Unfortunately the *Thor* was a small ship, which could not very well cruise for long beyond the 500-fathom line. Doctor Schmidt returned home—and then he got a report from the *SS Michael Sars,* a Norwegian survey ship, that a much smaller leptocephalus had been caught far out in the Atlantic. Not having a ship comparable to the *SS Michael Sars,* Dr. Schmidt did the next best thing. He soon got in touch with all the captains of Danish vessels that sailed the Atlantic, asking them to assist in the search. He gave classes to the old salts, telling them what to look for. He promised to furnish special nets. And he begged them, for the sake of science and the Danish fisheries, to make stops in midocean and see what they could catch.

Twenty-three captains promised to cooperate. Among them they made 550 stops en route from and to America and fished for eel larvae. Among them they caught 120, a very small figure indeed, but a significant result if you entered the successful stops on a chart. They showed that leptocephali seemed to have definite travel routes.

By 1912 Dr. Schmidt knew that his first guess about the spawning grounds near the 500-fathom line had been wrong. Most of the larvae that the Danish sea captains had brought back from their commercial trips had been caught at or near the surface. The original idea of "the deeper the smaller" did not hold true; instead it was clearly a case of "the farther out the smaller." The travel route which showed up faintly on the chart on which the catches had been marked seemed to run with the Gulf Stream; the eel larvae were helped along on their trip to Europe by that warm current. And the place from which they came was in all probability the Sargasso Sea.

The Sargasso Sea, far from being a graveyard of lost ships held immobile in a floating tangle of tough decaying weeds, is actually just an area of the Atlantic Ocean where a specific kind of seaweed grows in the warm waters of southern latitudes. Being of the shape of an egg, the Sargasso Sea, measuring about 1000 miles from north to south and 2000 miles from west to east, slowly turns, receiving a steady push by ocean currents, especially the Gulf Stream. The center of that turning area is a few hundred miles southeast of the Bermudas. The islands themselves are at the fringe of the Sargasso Sea. How close to the fringe depends on the year, for the amount of seaweed varies. In poor years only a few floating bunches can be seen here and there. An old Navy man told me once that as a young man he had sailed through the Sargasso Sea without knowing it. In "good" years it looks from a distance as if the weed formed a solid carpet, but when you approach closely you find that there are yards of water separating the bunches, even in the densest areas. Sampling of the weed enabled oceanographers to make the calculation that the total amounts to about 10 million tons.

Ten million tons of seaweed sounds like a very large amount and in a sense it certainly is a large amount; it is more than doubtful that any other single plant on earth occurs in such quantities. But if the 10 million tons of weed were distributed evenly over the whole area of the Sargasso Sea, each acre would contain just 24 ounces.

At the time that Dr. Schmidt learned that his eel investigations led in the direction of the Sargasso Sea, a good deal was already known about it. As for the weed itself, *Sargassum bacciferum* (the second part of the name refers to the "bladders" which keep it afloat), Dr. Schmidt's compatriot Winge had just proved that it occurred in the Sargasso Sea only. It had been thought that it grew somewhere on submarine banks, was torn loose by storms, and then drifted around for some time in the Sargasso Sea area. Winge (and before him others) had looked around for such submarine banks, without finding any. The Atlantic Ocean is especially deep just under the Sargasso Sea, so the weed could not possibly come from the bottom. Its whole organization is such that it would have to grow in shallow water. Winge (Danish Oceanographic

Expedition of 1908–1909) found that the strands of weed which drifted around decayed at one end and grew at the other. He felt justified to conclude that the sargassum weed had adapted itself to a pelagic life on the high seas, even though originally it may have grown on the bottom in shallow water like other seaweeds of its kind.

There was also known to be a numerous and interesting animal life associated with the sargassum weed. There were two very typical crabs; one was called "little wanderer," or *Planes minutus,* while the other has an even more impressive name: *Neptunus pelagicus,* "the drifting crab of the sea god." Then there is the sea slug *Scyllaea pelagica,* all decorated up with folds and flaps of skin which make it look as if it were a piece of the brownish weed itself. There are little octopi in large numbers; there are tiny crabs like the *Daphnia* which is used to feed tropical fish in home aquaria. There is the strange *Halobates,* a water strider, the only real marine insect. It scurries across the water by means of six hairy legs and it lays its eggs not on seaweed which may sink, but on floating bird feathers. As for fishes, there are sea horses and little zebra-striped yellow-jack (*Caranx*) which hide in tangles of weed. There is the sargassum fish, *Pterophryne,* which has camouflaging fins and bumps and when taken out of the Sargasso Sea looks in general as no fish should look, but at home, in the weed, doesn't look at all, being almost invisible.

Just to inject a little mystery, pterophryne is always female. Scientists are still puzzling about the whereabouts of the males or wondering whether pterophryne has learned how to do without. As Dr. Schmidt probably knew, fish eggs are often found clinging to the weed, but he doubtless took for granted, as everyone else had since these eggs were found for the first time, that they were eggs of pterophryne. Much later, in 1925, William Beebe found that they were not; he hatched a string of them under careful observation and from the eggs emerged little flying fish (*Exonautes*). The eggs of pterophryne do not even resemble those of the flying fish; the sargassum fish produces a long string of gelatinous matter which contains about 2000 eggs. The gelatinous string absorbs water rapidly and thirstily and swells to over ten times its original volume. It then is a lump of quivering jelly which can float without the aid of the air bladders of the sargassum weed.

The expedition which was to track the eel down to its real spawning grounds sailed in 1913 on the small schooner *Margarete*. Johannes
Schmidt and his assistants, at first A. Strubberg, later Peter Jaspersen
and Åge Vedel Tåning, found that theory began to agree well with
practice. The farther they progressed along the Gulf Stream—if it were
a river one would say that they sailed "upstream"—the smaller the leptocephali became. The spawning ground was the area of the Sargasso
Sea; the expedition settled that problem definitely. Unfortunately, after
only about half a year of service, the *Margarete* ran aground in the West
Indies. And then the First World War came.

In 1920 Dr. Schmidt went back to work, on the four-masted engine-
powered schooner *Dana*. In the meantime several American ichthyologists had proved what had been suspected all along: that the American
eel not only went through a leptocephalus stage, but that it too went
for spawning to the Sargasso Sea.

The expedition could work on both, but it had the problem of distinguishing "American" leptocephali from the European type. At this
point Grassi's and Calandruccio's observations about the number of
myomeres proved useful. It is impossible to tell a fully grown European
eel from an American eel just by looking at it. Outward appearance
doesn't count because eels show a good deal of individual variation,
presumably caused by environment and food. And to try to tell an
American leptocephalus from a European one by appearance was even
more hopeless. But it could be done by counting vertebrae. Doctor
Schmidt got himself 266 eels from Danish waters and found that they
had from 111 to 119 vertebrae. In that batch there was just one with 119
and five with 118. Likewise at the lower end of the range there were
only a few: two had 111 vertebrae, nine had 112. The majority had
between 113 and 117, and more than half of the total had either 114
or 115. After that he obtained 266 eels from Massachusetts and counted
their vertebrae. It turned out that the vertebrae of the American eels
ranged from 104 to 111. Again the majority was, as one should expect,
in the middle of that range. One of the Americans had 111 vertebrae,
seven had 110. There were two with as few as 104, a dozen with 105. The
majority had either 106, 107, or 108. The critical figure was obviously
111. If an eel had less, it was an American eel; if it had more, it was

European. The occasional specimens with 111 vertebrae were nuisances. Fortunately there were only a very few of them.

The counting of myomeres sounds like tedious work, even if you know only that counting to figures above 100 is involved. But remember that a leptocephalus is transparent when in water and still almost transparent when in air, and the specimens caught en route to the Sargasso Sea grew progressively smaller; for a while they were 2 inches long, later only 1 inch. The counting had to be done under a strong magnifying glass, and later even under low-power microscopes. And the myomeres of 7000 specimens had to be counted. That this was mostly done on board the *Dana* did not really facilitate matters.

Of those 7000 specimens precisely five had the critical number of 111 segments; nobody can tell whether they would have ended up in the Rhine or in the Hudson, if they had been left alone. All others were clearly either *Anguilla anguilla* (European) or *Anguilla chrysypa* (American).

When Dr. Schmidt had all his facts neatly entered on large charts one could see what happened. The eels that leave their rivers in Europe (Schmidt, of course, was mostly interested in the European variety, for good sound commercial reasons) in the fall seem to travel with steady high speed, arriving in the Sargasso Sea around Christmas and the New Year. Where they lay their eggs is still not quite certain; it is *not* among the drifting weed at the surface, which is weighed down with fish eggs as it is. But it does not seem to be at the bottom of the sea either, because the ocean is so deep under the Sargasso Sea. At any event the smallest larvae, only 7 millimeters or about ¼ inch long, were caught at a depth of about 1000 feet. During the first summer they grow to a full inch or 25 millimeters; during the second summer they double that length, and during the third they reach 75 millimeters. Then, after the change, they enter fresh water and go upriver. During the three years before changing, they travel at the rate of about 1000 miles per year, evidently "riding" in the Gulf Stream most of the way.

The American eels lay their eggs under the Sargasso Sea too, but not quite in the same place. The spawning area of the American eels is closer to the American shore and seems to be a little more to the south, in about the latitude of the Florida Keys. The spawning area of the

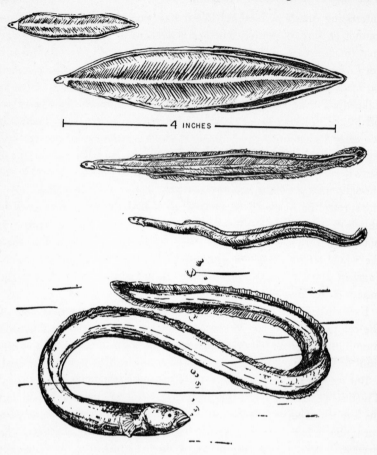

The development of the common eel

European form is in about the latitude of Florida proper and more to the east. There is an overlap of the areas, but it is no "melting pot." It couldn't be, because the rates of growth of the two kinds are entirely different. The American eel also travels at the rate of about 1000 miles per year but it grows to the full leptocephalus size of 3 inches in one year. It does not need a longer time because it is so much closer to the rivers where it is going to stay for most of its life.

Whether some eel larvae occasionally get "on the wrong track" is an interesting question. Nothing like it has been observed so far and we cannot be sure, of course, whether it happens at all. But if it did one may imagine that an American eel which started to ride the Gulf Stream for Europe by mistake would be killed by the sea water because it would be ready to be a "river eel" when still in the middle of the Atlantic. Likewise a European eel which went west by mistake might be killed off by the brackish water outside of river mouths which it reached at too early a stage in its development. Something similar may be the real solution of the "Danube problem." The strange chemistry of the Black Sea's deeper layers could be accepted as an explanation when it was still thought the the eels wanted to breed there, but for a mere passage at the surface the Black Sea that would be no obstacle. The answer probably is that the trip is too long; in just three years the leptocephalus cannot travel from the Sargasso Sea through the Strait of Gibraltar, then the whole length of the Mediterranean, through the Sea of Marmara (against a fairly strong current) into the Black Sea, and then to the mouth of the Danube.

Ever since Dr. Schmidt and his assistants uncovered the true story of the eel, people have asked why eels do what they do. So far I haven't found an answer which does not have to be classified as "wild speculation" or worse. For the present, that question has to be left unanswered.

But we can tie up a few loose ends and mention a few specific facts. The discoveries of Grassi and Calandruccio enabled both the Italian and the French fishery commissions to do what had once been tried with cut-up horse hairs and grass sods: to restock water depleted of eels. The French especially kept careful books about their work; they reported that each kilogram of elvers seeded into swamps and small waters off the River Aisne resulted in 2500 kilograms of food in five years.

Pliny may have been right with his "eight years" as the average time which the eel needs to reach maturity: the females seem to need from eight to twelve years and the males from five to eight. Then they go on a complete fast. Aquarium specimens have kept this up for six months and then died, which is the reason for the belief that the eel spawns only once and dies soon afterward. But some individuals do not mature sexually; they have been found to live more than twenty years and to reach a length of 6 to 8 feet and a weight of 30 pounds. I do not know which particular eel established a weight record or what it was. But the age record for the common European eel is a celebrated case. An eel known as the Eel of Ross was caught as an elver in a small Scottish river in 1895 and kept in an aquarium until it died in 1949, at a total age of 57 years.

The conger eel, which spends all its life in salt water, goes through the same transformation as the common eel. Its larva is called *Leptocephalus morrisii* and can be told from the others when still quite small.

And now I have one more eel mystery to report.

The ship *Dana* made another expedition after the trip to the Sargasso Sea. It was an expedition around the world, made in 1928–1930. The collection of specimens made during this expedition is now at the Marinbiologisk Laboratorium in Charlottenlund, Denmark, under the care of Dr. Åge Vedel Tåning who accompanied Dr. Schmidt on his later trips. And in this collection is a leptocephalus taken, according to a letter from Dr. Tåning, on January 31, 1930, from a depth of about 1000 feet west of the Agulhas Bank, off the southernmost point of Africa. Doctor Tåning supplied me with the precise location: 35 degrees 42 minutes south and 18 degrees 37 minutes east. *This leptocephalus is 184 centimeters long—6 feet and ½ inch!*

Nobody knows the adult form.

It may be a kind of salt-water eel which grows to its full size as a leptocephalus and changes into an adult form which is not appreciably larger. If it grows in the same proportion as the ordinary eel, the result would be a monster between 60 and 70 feet long. I don't suggest that this is the "great sea serpent." But, like everybody else who knows about it, I wonder what it would have grown into.

13: The Return of a Native

DURING the decade which preceded the outbreak of the Civil War a native returned to North America. It was the occasion for many columns of type in the daily press and became the subject of several Executive Documents published by the Thirty-third Congress. But nobody spoke of the event as the return of a native. The native in question was the camel and at the time it was not known that camels, the proverbial ships of the desert of Biblical lands, had originated in North America.

Mostly because of the war which was soon to break out, the homecoming of the camel was a failure. The reasons are known in detail. The attempt just happened to be made at an unfavorable time. The mystery is that the camel had to be reintroduced at all. At the time when the oldest living sequoiadendrons were seeds, still protected in their cones, a few small herds of a sturdy native variety of camel, known to paleontologists as *Camelops,* were probably still around, and the animal might as well have survived on the continent of its origin.

For unknown and unguessable reasons it didn't. It became extinct and we can't even tell precisely when. We do know now that the early American Indians of the southwest hunted it on occasion. But before this camelops had even come into existence other members of the camel tribe had left the North American continent via the two exits that existed during the Pliocene. One group went south via the isthmus and established itself in South America. Two representatives of these emigrants still exist and even flourish: the guanaco and the vicuña.[1] Another group went west via the "Bering bridge" and made its home in Asia. Fossils

---

[1] It has become customary to refer generally to the little South American cameloids as "llamas," but the llama itself is a domesticated form, as is the alpaca. Both were probably derived from the guanaco.

of both groups have been found which date the emigrations nicely: the earliest llamalike cameloids in the Pliocene of South America, the earliest ancient camels on the Asiatic mainland in the Pliocene of India.

Of the emigrants to Asia there is also a remainder left. Because of its remote habitat it was unknown for a long time. Books on zoology had evolved a kind of routine beginning for the camel chapter, which read: "There are two kinds of camels, the two-humped true camel, also known as Bactrian camel (*Camelus bactrianus*), and the one-humped dromedary (*Camelus dromedarius*). Both are domesticated. No wild form of camel is known." When the news came from Russia in about 1880 that wild camels had actually been found, it was greeted with mixed emotions. Some were happy that wild camels did, after all, exist. They provided a kind of firm ground for the domesticated versions which had been dangerously dangling in thin air. But a good many took the news as a kind of personal insult. Every zoologist of note had written that wild camels did not exist and one had grown used to the idea. It merely brought the camel in line with the great majority of other domesticated animals whose ancestors did not live any more either. And now this Russian explorer, what was his name, oh here, Nikolai Mikhailovitch Przhevalski (*Pshe-vall-skee*) claimed that there was a *Camelus bactrianus ferus* in Inner Asia in the area of Lake Lob, or Lob Nor. And he said that he had interviewed the people living around there—he called them the Lob Nortsi—and they had told him that these animals had been numerous only a few decades earlier. Well, Colonel Przhevalski certainly did not lie, but he did not furnish any proof either. He said the animal was "ferus" (wild) but it was much more likely that it was merely "feral"— the wild offspring of domestic animals that escaped or were abandoned.

Skeptical grumbling of this kind, quite justified in itself, went on literally for decades until it was finally generally accepted that the wild camels of the Lob Nor region are really wild and not feral, with a provision that Przhevalski himself had made. He had written, in 1879:

According to the unanimous testimony of the Lob Nortsi, the chief habitat of the wild camel at the present day is the desert of Kum-tagh, to the east of Lake Lob; this animal is also occasionally found on the Lower Tarim River in the Kuruk-tagh mountains. . . . Twenty years ago, wild camels were numerous near Lake Lob, where the village of Tchargalik now stands,

Bactrian camel

and farther to the east along the foot of the Altin-tagh mountains, as well as in the range itself. Our guide, a hunter from Tchargalik, told us that it was not unusual in those days to see several dozens, or even a hundred, of these animals together. He himself had killed over a hundred of them in the course of his life (he was an old man) with a flintlock musket. With an increase of the population of Tchargalik, the Lob Nor hunters became more numerous and the camels rarer. Now, the wild camel only frequents the neighborhood of Lob Nor and even here in small numbers. Years pass without a single one being seen; in better years the native hunters may kill five or six during the summer and autumn. The flesh of the wild camel, which is very fat in autumn, is used for food, the skins for clothing. . . . During the excessive heat of summer the camels are attracted by the cooler temperature of the higher valleys of the Altin-tagh and make their way there, going up to 11,000 feet or even higher. In winter the wild camel keeps entirely to the lower and warmer desert. . . .

When caught young, wild camels are easily tamed and taught to carry a pack. Enemies are very few in number in the localities which it inhabits; man and wolves being the only ones. . . . Wolves are rare in the desert and would hardly be dangerous to a fully grown camel.

It seems possible to me to arrive at the conclusion that the wild camel of the present day is the direct descendant of wild parents, but that from time to time escaped domesticated animals probably became mixed with them.

Later travelers corroborated Przhevalski in almost every respect, the main point of disagreement being the question of whether a caught camel can be trained. The Mongol informants of several travelers were unanimous in saying that a wild camel can never be trained to carry a burden, but that it might be tamed for riding and that, when tame, it will be able to go 200 miles a day for a whole week.

Although a skin of an old male which has been measured carefully showed roughly the same dimensions as an average specimen of a domesticated two-humped camel, most travelers agree that the wild camel is generally smaller. Especially, the humps are smaller; the hair is finer, closer, and shorter, and shows the same color variations that occur in the domesticated species.

Where was the camel domesticated?

A general answer to that question is easy. It must have been somewhere in Asia, but where in Asia is impossible to say. Or when. Most likely it happened in different places at different times. Most likely it was done by illiterate tribes that could not leave any records and did not even pass on stories to other peoples where they might have been written down. There is some reason for this belief. The oldest record-writing peoples of the Near East have left a very few records pertaining to camels. Apparently these records first deal with wild camels, then, all of a sudden, they deal with domesticated camels. But there is nothing that even faintly indicates that these people themselves domesticated the camels. The logical conclusion, to my mind, is that while there were wild camels around, the domesticated camels were brought in from elsewhere.

It seems that the camel never went very far west in Europe, as distinct from that other adventuresome American, the horse. The horses had spread from North America too, of necessity following the same paths that the camels took. They had rolled through Asia like a living wave, had crossed over into Europe, and gone west in Europe as far as it was possible for a horse to go, stopping only at the shores of the ocean. And these wild horses had been around in Europe all through the Ice Age into early historical times. A last living remnant of them can still be found in the Gobi desert area, discovered in 1880 by the same Przhevalski who found the last wild camels. Another branch of that flood of horses had poured south from European Russia, finding its way into northeast Africa, and conquering the African continent, where they astonished explorers and early settlers by their numbers. As far as the eye could see, there were herds of black-and-white striped wild horses.[2]

The camel never attained such an extensive habitat. It never seems to have gone into Africa, except later when prodded by drivers. It never reached northern and western Europe. Its snooty face and its humped back do not appear on any of those examples of ancient art which we mentally lump together as "caveman drawings." Its unmistakable bones were not found in northern Europe; no camel or camel relative appears anywhere on those tables on pp. 114-15. I know of only two fossil camels which are of European origin and belong in the post-Pleistocene period; they are *Camelus knoblochi,* found in Russia, and *Camelus alutensis,* from Rumania. Both were closely related to the present wild type from the Altin-tagh Mountains.

Apparently there was one feeble advance through southern Russia into the Balkan peninsula which did not come to anything. The bigger advance seems to have proceeded south to and through Afghanistan, through Iran and Iraq, into the Arabian peninsula. It is interesting that the bones of fossil camels have been found, associated with the bones of fossil horses and fossil men of the Neanderthal type, in Palestine. This seems to mark the "farthest west" of the camel's wanderings.

All these camels were two-humped. The somewhat better-known one-humped "version," the dromedary, really does not exist in the wild state. It is generally conceded that it was, somewhere and at some time, bred from the two-humped camel. If the two are hybridized nowadays, the offspring tends to the general type of the dromedary but also tends to show a second (smaller) hump. It is one of those sad cases where one has to accept the lesser mystery as an explanation. Nobody can say why the domestication of the wild camel should have resulted in one type which is hard to distinguish from the original *and* in another type with only one hump. On the other hand, it would be pure fantasy to assume that there once existed a wild dromedary which became domesticated as a whole species.

The earliest "civilized" record of the camel, as often happens with earliest records, presents a mystery. The record consists of pottery from tombs of the Fourth Dynasty of ancient Egypt, dated cautiously "not later than 3500 B.C." Just how this pottery could "happen" is mysterious

---

[2] More about the history of the wild horses in *The Lungfish, the Dodo, and the Unicorn.*

in view of the fact that the camel definitely was not known in the Nile
Valley until about thirty centuries after that. Was it inspired by a straying
group of wild camels which wandered into the Nile Valley either from
Palestine or from Arabia? Or did a caravan of "foreigners" crossing
through Egypt use camels? The former is, of course, far more likely, but
why didn't it happen again? But there is no doubt about the long dearth
of camels in Egypt afterward. The climate of Egypt has preserved almost anything about as well as it could have been done with the greatest
of care over an equal interval of time. However, none of the many classical monuments of Egypt shows a camel. And it would not even have
been necessary for the camel to be an "Egyptian animal" to be represented. If the Egyptian armies had encountered an enemy using camels,
battle scenes would have been depicted, showing victorious Egyptians
stepping on dead enemies and over dead camels.

The next oldest record comes from Assyria and is by contrast wonderfully simple and plain. It consists of monuments from the time of
Tiglath-pileser I of Assyria, who reigned from 1115 to 1102 b.c. The inscriptions on those monuments tell of the king's deeds: "Wild oxen,
dangerous and immense, he killed . . . their live young he caught . . .
elephants he killed with his shaft, living elephants he caught and brought
to his city of Assur, 120 lions he killed . . . all kinds of beasts of the soil
and birds of the sky he brought to his place." The published translations
of the inscriptions do not mention camels, but two-humped camels are
pictured; probably they had been lumped in the text among the beasts
of the soil. There can be no doubt that they were wild, not part of the
king's household, but part of his menagerie.

Similar monuments were erected 150 years later during the reign of
Ashur-nasir-pal II, who is known to historians as one of the great con-
querors of Assyria. The inscriptions telling about his hunts read very
much like the one just quoted, but one of them contains a listing:
"Lynxes I caught with my hands, herds of wild oxen, elephants, lions,
ostriches, *pagu,* wild asses, gazelles, antelopes, wild hogs, panthers, and
sikurru; animals of the deserts and of the mountains I brought together
in my city, the city of Kalakh, and let the people of my lands see them
all." Certainly neither of the two unidentified names, *pagu* and *sikurru,*
means "camel," but it probably was included under animals of the desert.

The menagerie in Assur still existed in 670 B.C., although in a deteriorated state. A source stating the contents specifically lists camels, along with horses, asses, goats, gazelles, etc. These may still have been wild camels, but meanwhile the domesticated camel had come to that general area. The Queen of Sheba, when she visited King Solomon in Jerusalem (955 B.C.) had camels as beasts of burden. And from that time on the camel is a kind of "staple animal" in the Bible; it occurs again and again, both in the flesh and in metaphorical use. The domesticated camel was known to the Assyrians too, a panel in Nimrud's palace (about 750 B.C) shows a battle between Assyrian warriors mounted on horses and Arabs fleeing on dromedaries. And in the palace of Ashur-bani-pal, king of Assyria from 669 to 626 B.C., at Nineveh, there is a mural showing an officer returning to his tent for rest, and outside are two kneeling dromedaries snapping at each other.

One can't say that the camel is a "good" domesticated animal. It is not trustworthy at any time and during the mating period its temper differs from that of any carnivorous "wild beast" merely by being far worse. And unfortunately it has weight and bulk and four completely unjustified doglike canine teeth for unreasonable use. For a camel to try to bite its rider after having "faithfully" carried him all day long is not a rare occurrence; it is something which is expected and for which an experienced man watches out. In the days before Przhevalski made his trip to Lob Nor the statement that there are no wild camels was often countered jokingly with the remark that there are no tame camels either. Later a famous utterance by Sir F. Palgrave could be quoted in support: "He is from first to last an undomesticated and savage animal, rendered serviceable by stupidity alone, without much skill on his master's part or any cooperation on his own, save that of extreme passiveness. Neither attachment nor even habit impress him; never tame, though not wide awake enough to be exactly wild." And even the German zoologist Dr. Alfred Brehm, who embraced everything with equal love, provided only that it was alive, exclaimed on occasion, "It is incredible how a dromedary manages to annoy its driver, all day and all night long without any let-up at all, in the most fantastic variety of ways."

Stupid, unwilling, recalcitrant, obnoxious, untrustworthy, and on occasion openly vicious, but also strong, enduring, satisfied with vegetation a horse would pass by even when hungry, naturally constructed to be desert-proof, the camel met urgent needs admirably and its deficiencies could be coped with. Your camel will bite you and most likely mangle you permanently if you don't watch out. What of it? Your knife will cut you, if you are clumsy. If it does, do you throw it away? Your home fire can burn you—do you prefer your food uncooked for this reason?

The Arabs and the Hebrews gratefully accepted the camel from whomever brought it to them—not, admittedly, in a "tame" condition, but in a condition where it could be prodded into work. Its very name designated it. There was a Semitic word meaning "carrying a burden." The word was *gamal*. It became a noun as far as grammar was concerned, and a name for everyday purposes. The Jews—but not the Arabs—invented an additional protective measure. Twisting and stretching religious argument they discovered that it was "unclean"; it could not be eaten. That effectively eliminated a danger which threatens any animal of large size; I have been assured by people with experience that the religious verdict also saved the reputation of the Jewish cuisine from a serious danger.

Whenever I come across a combination involving animals and Judaism I hopefully turn to that book which Dr. L. Lewysohn, "Preacher of the Israelitic Congregation of Worms," had printed at his own expense in 1858: *Zoology of the Talmud*. Nor did Dr. Lewysohn disappoint me on old Hebrew camel lore. There was, he reported, a special term for the dromedary. It was "flying camel" since it is so much faster than the two-humped camel. (Our own word dromedary is derived from the Greek *dromaios* which means "running at full speed.") Apparently the Jews had been surprised about the small size of the camel's ears, because there was a legend that the camel wanted horns and because this was an impudent wish the Lord took away its ears.

Since one camel is stronger than another, a proverb originated: "The camel determines its burden," meaning that one should not ask more of anybody than he is able to do. The Romans later phrased the same idea more directly by saying *ultra posse nemo obligatur* (nobody is obligated beyond his powers). Since the camels were valuable property they had to be marked. Branding apparently was still to be invented, and even if it had been one may have doubts about both the wisdom and the effectiveness of this procedure when it comes to camels. Therefore a colored flag was tied to the camel's tail. If the idea of camels shuffling about with colored flags tied to their tails does not stimulate your imagination sufficiently, Dr. Lewysohn can supply something better. It also was customary to tie a string from the tail to the hump and to attach the ownership flags to that string. This, I maintain, was the ship of the desert fully rigged. Ever since I read this I have been thinking of a pennant tied to the head and red and green running lights on the stirrups, a white "tail" light, and a Plimsoll mark painted on the rump.

Four hundred years after the Queen of Sheba went north to visit Jerusalem, the burden-carrying camel was pressed into a new task: it became a war camel. The occasion was the battle of Sardis where the armies of Cyrus and of Croesus were facing each other. The great event, which took place in 546 B.C., has been described by the Father of History, Herodotus himself, in his book *Clio,* the first of his nine books of history.

This is what happened:

When Cyrus beheld the Lydians arranging themselves in order of battle on this plain, fearful of the strength of their cavalry, he adopted a device which Harpagus, one of the Medes, suggested to him. He collected together all the camels that had come in the train of his army to carry the provisions and the baggage, and taking off their loads, he mounted riders upon them accoutred as horsemen. These he commanded to advance in front of his other troops against the Lydian horse; behind them were to follow the foot soldiers, and last of all the cavalry. When his arrangements were complete, he gave his troops orders to slay all the other Lydians who came in their way without mercy, but to spare Croesus and not kill him, even if he should be seized and offered resistance. The reason why Cyrus opposed his camels to the enemy's horse was, because the horse has a natural dread of the camel, and cannot abide either the sight or the smell of that animal. By this stratagem he hoped to make Croesus's horse useless to him, the horse being what he chiefly depended on for victory. The two armies then joined battle, and immediately the Lydian war-horses, seeing and smelling the camels, turned round and galloped off; and so it came to pass that all Croesus's hopes withered away. The Lydians, however, behaved manfully. As soon as they understood what was happening, they leaped off their horses, and engaged the Persians on foot. The combat was long; but at last, after a great slaughter on both sides, the Lydians turned and fled. They were driven within their walls, and the Persians laid siege to Sardis.[3]

---

[3] Rawlinson translation.

That camels and horses are natural enemies is of course untrue, even though Aelian, Aristotle, and Pliny asserted the same thing. But there can be no doubt that horses do behave peculiarly when camels are around. William Beebe suggested that it may be essentially a question of the camel's smell. "After a night spent in an Arab caravanserai surrounded by camels, my entire sympathy goes out to the horses." It is also possible that the camel's loquaciousness is annoying to horses. There is just one time during the life of a camel when one can count on its being quiet, and that is when a female gives birth to the single young. Otherwise there is a steady succession of moans, shouts, grunts, snorts, and fifteen other unnamed kinds of annoying sounds, indicating hunger or pleasure or thirst or annoyance, wakefulness or sleepiness, or any other sentiment; also for no reason whatever. As Beebe put it: "A dozen camels, stimulated by as many different sentiments, can produce a dissonance which should end all human attempts at swing." But, as far as its relation to the horse is concerned, many horses apparently learn to tolerate whatever the camel does that annoys them normally. All over Egypt you can see horses paying no attention whatever to camels they meet on the road and there are even numerous horse-camel teams working together.

Although the camel did not reach Africa by itself, the majority of the living camels, estimated at over three million, are now on African soil. But they are only where there is desert or a reasonable facsimile of desert. All attempts to introduce the camel into equatorial Africa have ended in failure. Having originally adapted itself to a dry landscape, caring little whether it was warm or cold, the camel just can't cope with jungle. And there seem to be some other limits to its endurance, though these are hard to define precisely. In 1622 one of the Medici, Ferdinand II, had the idea that camels ought to do well in Tuscany. Several dromedaries were bought and brought to Italy. They proved to be far superior to horses as burden carriers on the sandy plains near Pisa; they stayed in good health and propagated too. In 1738–39 another fourteen were imported. Since then there has been an independent and self-sufficient herd of dromedaries on Italian soil. By 1810 their numbers had grown to 170 head and all through the nineteenth century it stayed between 170 and 200, even though there was a steady drain because carnivals, circuses, and even zoological gardens got their dromedaries from that herd. There are fewer since the beginning of the present century, but they are still there.

The owners of sulphur mines on Sicily quickly came to the conclusion that camels were superior to donkeys and mules and brought them to Sicily. Not just once, but repeatedly. None survived. Spanish land-owners looked at the Tuscany herd and thought that camels might be useful in southern Spain. They imported some and are now practically independent of supply from either Italy or Africa. The latest country to consider camel raising is Australia and it looks as if the camel may be able to compete with the tractor.

Now that we have brought the history up to date, except for the American experiment of a century ago, let's have a closer look at the camel's anatomical peculiarities. Its magnificent eyelashes are part of its adaptation to desert conditions; in addition to looking glamorous on an otherwise completely unglamorous animal, they are sand filters. Functionally these eyelashes are the same as the muscles around the camel's enormous nostrils which can close them "sand tight."

More unusual from the anatomical point of view are the camel's feet. A sufficiently long time ago, say in the early Paleocene, all mammals had five fingers and five toes and very many of them still do. Others, in the course of evolution, lost some fingers and toes, the most extreme case being the well-known one of the horse. The horse's ancestors, becoming more and more specialized runners, shed their fingers and toes one by one in the course of the Tertiary period. Their ancestors entered this period with the full set of i to v; at the end of the Tertiary the true horse was finished, having only number iii, which had not only grown strong and heavy but had also acquired a solid hoof to cover and protect it. The camel did not go quite so far; it still has iii and iv. So do a lot of other animals whose "cloven hoofs" have become proverbial; of course they are not really cloven, they are two hoofs, fitting against each other and covering two toe endings.

The camels did a very peculiar thing. Their two toes did not evolve hoofs; even now they only show blunt nails. Nor did the bones of these toes grow particularly strong—if it were not for a special feature, they would hardly be strong enough to carry the weight of the heavy animal. But the toes, assuming a kind of semireclined position, are supported by a large and tough tissue pad underneath. This is such an unusual design that it has given its name to the suborder to which the family of the *Camelidae* belongs: the *Tylopoda,* or "cushion feet." The two knuckle-bones from which III and IV spring start separately in the fetus, but then grow together so that both toes branch from a single "cannon bone."

This construction of the foot, while strange, has some obvious advantages. But the construction of the dentition contains a feature for which the reason is so obscure that nobody has found it yet, if indeed it has a reason at all. In the back there are solid molars which do not interest us particularly. In front there are six incisors in the lower jaw. The upper jaw shows, in the fetal stage, the corresponding six upper incisors. In the half-grown and especially in the adult animal, the upper incisors are not present. This lack is customary with a number of other plant-eating mammals. But what is special about the camel is that the outer two incisors do develop, only they don't look like incisors, but like curved canines. Behind them are the two real canines; it is the four together that render the camel's bite so dangerous.

As regards the hump or humps, they are simply storage vaults for the lean days which a camel expects as a matter of course. In good times the hump is stiff and hard, well-filled with fat. When times are not so good the hump begins to wrinkle and sag, a sure sign that the animal is in poor condition. As a feature the hump is not unique. The mammoth carried a hump on its head and a secondary hump on its shoulders. And the bison's hump is as responsible for the bison's typical appearance as is the camel's hump for its appearance. The interesting difference between the bison's hump and that of the camel is that the existence of the camel's hump could in no way be guessed from the skeleton. The bison's hump is supported by a number of elongated vertebral spines so that it could be predicted by somebody who only had a skeleton from which to judge. A new-born camel has no hump and for that reason alone one suddenly sees a resemblance to the South American cameloids which the adult doesn't show. But at any age the skeleton of a dromedary resembles the skeleton of a llama much more than the two living animals resemble each other.

There are a few other soft parts of the camel's anatomy which are surprising. The camel's placenta has been labeled "diffuse"; no other mammal has one of like construction. And the camel's blood is unique. In any mammal, the red corpuscles, which carry oxygen from the lungs to the tissues, have a cross section like a bi-concave lens, thick around the rim, thinner in the middle. The red corpuscles of the various mammals are of course of different sizes, but they are all perfectly circular. All except those of the camel. The camel's red corpuscles are oval.

The camel's stomach has three sections, two of which are lined with strange large "cells," pockets for water storage. (The llamas have these too, although they don't need them.) And that brings me to the theme about which more nonsense has been written than about any other. That is the camel's relationship to water. Generations of travelers have told how the camel abhors the touch of water. They have described in great detail what enormous trouble it is to get a group of camels across even a narrow river. If you can ferry them across on rafts it is comparatively easy. But if they have to go into the water themselves, there is a violent scene of men pushing and pulling madly in one direction, with the animals as madly resisting and struggling to get away. After a crossing both men and animals are exhausted, bruised, and sometimes bitten. It is an undertaking requiring about as much preparation and courage as an assault operation. The Arabs have even developed what might be called life jackets for camels to keep them afloat, while a boat tows them across. But there are reports of camels going into the water with hardly any coaxing and swimming across the river by themselves. Apparently they can swim. They just don't want to.

As regards what may be called the "internal relationship" between camels and water, there are even more stories, most of them wildly exaggerated. "A camel can go for weeks without water." "A camel drinks only when the moon is full." "A camel has to have salty water; fresh water will make it drunk." "If a camel rider is lost in the desert and there is no other way out, he might survive by sacrificing his camel. In its stomach he'll find several gallons of clear and cool water, even if the animal took its last drink weeks ago."

That a camel can go for weeks without water may be true if a number of conditions mesh properly. If it started out with its customary full-size drink—some 15 gallons, if the vegetation is green and fresh, furthermore if it does not have to work too hard, and if the air is not too hot—if all these conditions are fulfilled, as they sometimes are, three weeks may go by until the animal needs another long drink. But it most decidedly does not wait for a full moon; thirst knows no lunar phases. That a camel cannot drink fresh water is also nonsense. The story may have originated from the fact that the Bactrian camel can and does drink brackish water, which is quite remarkable in itself, but essentially another adaptation to desert life, in this case to the specialized desert of the Asiatic salt steppes. However, even those camels prefer fresh water if they can get it.

As for that famous reservoir of clear cool water I only need to quote a few lines from Dr. Brehm:

I did, although I doubted the story from the outset, take pains to question camel drivers who had grown old and gray in the desert. Not a single one knew anything about it, not a single one had ever heard anybody tell this enormous lie. And later I watched the slaughtering of camels that had been given water only the previous day and have convinced myself that it is completely impossible to drink water which had been mixed with the chewed cud and the digestive juices of the stomach. The camel as a whole has a repulsive odor; such stomach juice must cause insurmountable nausea even to a man half dead of thirst. The stench of a freshly opened stomach of a camel is absolutely unbearable.[4]

The distance from Mecca to Medina is about 240 miles. And the Arabs say that a good dromedary will carry its rider from one of these holy places to the other in the time from sunset to sunset. Considering that this refers to animals bred especially for speed and carrying only the weight of a single rider, the claim is in all probability true.

But such figures do not apply even remotely to the average load-carrying camel of the poor man. We, to whom the camel is an animal we read about and occasionally see in a zoological garden, are apt to forget that there are differences between strains fully as important as those between Percherons and race horses. The Arab distinguishes not less than twenty-three strains of dromedaries. "Seventeen of them," an educated Turk once told me, "are imaginary." He recognized only six types: the heavy Nile Valley dromedary which does not do well under true desert conditions, a heavy desert type, two somewhat lighter desert types which

---

[4] Alfred Brehm, *Tierleben*, 1900 ed., vol. III, p. 145.

he called "family camels," the true riding dromedary, used by police forces and some military units, and finally the racer, the rich man's showpiece.

In Egypt the legal limit for loading a camel is slightly short of 600 pounds. With such a load a healthy animal will maintain a steady pace of 30 miles a day for about a week. If necessary, it can carry twice as much, but then the daily journey is cut down to 10 or 12 miles. The camel not only determines its burden, as the ancient Hebrews said; it also determines the pace. The Arab camel drivers are equipped with an astonishing vocabulary of praising and ingratiating terms, and with an even more astonishing vocabulary of abuse. They use both with great and practiced eloquence, switching from the one to the other as they think the occasion warrants. But neither makes any measurable difference.

True, it was Man who put the camel caravan into the desert. But the camel determines how fast it will go.

Let's return now to the Western Hemisphere where the tylopods, the "cushion feet," originated. Their past on the North American continent is characterized by a large variety of forms and shapes, as one would expect it to be on the continent of origin. What is a bit surprising is how early they achieved diversity. In mammalian evolution the beginning of the Oligocene is a pretty ancient period. But one of the most eminent experts on fossil North American mammals, the late Dr. W. D. Matthew, was convinced that the ancestors of the camels entered even this early period with three clearly distinct groups.

One of them has been called the main stem because it ends up with the camels and llamas of today. Another group, which must have looked especially incredible, is referred to as the giraffelike camels. The term does not imply any relationship to the giraffes, for there is none, but was coined merely with regard to external appearance. The third group is the gazellelike camels; again the name does not imply relationship but only appearance. And not all the fossil camels of North America fit into these three groups. There are a number of isolated forms which may or may not belong to one of the three and which probably were side branches.

Fortunately one of the earliest tylopods is quite well known: *Protylopus* of the Upper Eocene. It was a small animal, about the size of a jack rabbit. The shape of its skull clearly forecast the shape of camel skulls to come. But it still had all its teeth, top and bottom, with canines only very slightly enlarged. Its hind feet were already reduced to two functional digits, iii and iv, but there was not yet a cannon bone. And small bone "splints" show that its ancestors had digits ii and v too. There is no trace of number i, but naturally a sufficiently remote ancestor must have had it. The forefeet of *Protylopus* are even more interesting. There is no trace of number i on them either, but the other four toes are all functional, and iii and iv are not much larger than ii and v.

It is suspected that the whole group of the browsing giraffelike camels, as well as the main stem, came from *Protylopus*. There is an Oligocene type (*Paratylopus*) which is probably ancestral to the later giraffelike camels, but forms connecting it with *Protylopus* are still missing. The earliest well-known giraffe-camel is a form that has been called *Oxydactylus,* dating from the Lower Miocene. Having a body about the size of a sheep, it stood on legs long enough for a horse but very slender. It still lacked the cannon bone and, as the shape of the toes indicates, did not have the pads of the later camels. This *Oxydactylus* is considered the direct ancestor of the grotesque *Alticamelus* which appeared first in the Middle Miocene and lasted without change into the Lower Pliocene, when it died out without leaving descendants.

Alticamelus was a large animal. But it was mainly tall. It had an elongated neck like the giraffe's and legs so absurdly long and thin that the whole must have looked stilted and rickety in the extreme. Unlike the legs of the giraffe, the four legs of *Alticamelus* were of about equal length, so that the body did not slope like that of the giraffe, but was balanced horizontally at a considerable altitude.

The design, one is tempted to say, worked. But production of the model and of the whole series of giraffe-camels was discontinued.

The main stem, however, continued from *Protylopus* to the sheep-sized *Poëbrotherium* of the Oligocene. *Poëbrotherium's* skull can be described as an enlarged version of that of *Protylopus*. Elsewhere there was progress. Both forefeet and hind feet now consisted of only two functional digits, but there were still very small traces of ii and v in the form of tiny nodules. There was no cannon bone yet. Nor pads. They don't fossilize directly, of course, but their presence or absence can be deduced from the position of the bones. *Poëbrotherium* still retained all its teeth.

Since we know how the evolution of the camels ended up, we know what had to happen later. Some teeth had to be lost; some had to change their shape. The two "metapodials," as they are called, had to consolidate for the formation of the cannon bone. The pads had to evolve. But for a long time evolution lingered around the *Poëbrotherium* shape as if reluctant to do away with something which apparently was quite successful. The small *Protomeryx* of the Middle Miocene had not progressed much. Still the same size. Still no cannon bone. No pads. No missing teeth—but a space had begun to form between the canines and the first pre-molars.

Protomeryx of the Lower Miocene slowly developed into *Protolabis* of the Middle Miocene. Slightly larger over-all size. No pads yet. No cannon bone. No missing teeth, but the size of the upper incisors is clearly reduced. Then, with the next in line of succession in the Upper Miocene, evolution had finally moved on. The name proclaims it: *Pro-camelus*. The middle incisors are lost. The unreasonable caninelike teeth, plus the true canines, are there, though not yet in the modern form. The face was much longer than that of the modern camels and llamas, the brain case smaller. Foot pads have appeared. So has the cannon bone, with the "seam" slightly more visible than on the modern forms.

The last subdivision of the Tertiary period, the Pliocene, is characterized by a tylopod extravaganza. One of the little gazellelike camels which had been quite numerous during the Miocene was still around. But for that one exception it was now all main stem. They began to indulge in large size. *Colossocamelus* from Nebraska and *Megacamelus* from Arizona towered over the elephants and mastodons present, standing 15 feet at the shoulders. *Megatylopus* also surpassed any living camel and so did one which has been named *Pliauchenia*—the latter cannot have been ancestral to any living form but probably was an isolated offshoot from the main stem.

When the Pleistocene began, the giants had passed away again, but there were still numerous forms, with sizes ranging up to that of a large dromedary of today. They ranged from Alaska to Florida but seem to have been more numerous in the west. Some paleontologists also think they can recognize certain features of distribution: forms more like the Asiatic camels in the northwest, forms somewhat more like the llamas in the southwest.

Their remains are widely scattered and as a rule quite fragmentary. But one of these late American camels is perfectly known because it was found in those La Brea tar pits discovered by the Portolá expedition on August 3, 1769. During the eighteenth and nineteenth centuries people had noticed repeatedly that animals were sometimes trapped in the tar. The reverse, that the tar which was taken from the pits for commercial purposes yielded bones on occasion, had been noticed too. But it was not until 1906 that large-scale excavations for scientific reasons were undertaken.

These excavations, conducted for more than ten years, produced more than a hundred thousand bones of mammals and birds that had lived in California during the later portion of what was the Ice Age farther north. While the finds were deeply appreciated later, it cannot be denied that at first there was some disappointment. As long as only single bones had been recovered in commercial operations, one could hope for more complete and more interesting finds, if only the investigations were done scientifically. Probably complete cadavers of extinct animals might be recovered from the tar, similar to those mammoths that had been chopped from frozen mud in Siberia. One could live in hope of dissecting the jaw and neck muscles of the extinct saber-toothed near-cats of that time, or of determining the color of the fur of the big extinct so-called short-faced bear of California. But as soon as it was "done scientifically," it became evident that none of these hopes would ever be realized. The fleshy parts of all trapped creatures quickly dissolve in the tar and become one with their surroundings. Nothing recognizable is left except bones and teeth. And the whole mass of the tar seems to be in steady if gradual flow, so that the bones do not even hang together. Once the tar has dissolved the muscles and tendons, the bones drift apart. Vertebrae are invariably separated from one another. Lower jaws are in one place, the skulls from which they were pulled in another. But fortunately each single bone is in fine undamaged condition.

Another "drawback" is that the pits have been open for a very long time. Hence the fact that a bone has been recovered from the La Brea tar reveals practically nothing about its age. Among the bird bones there are, for example, two condors; they have been named the La Brea condor and the California condor, respectively. At present most condors occur only in South America. Obviously these condors are quite old. But among the bird bones there are also some from birds you can watch flying around in California now. When did these bones get in? Five thousand years ago? The week before Señor de Portolá passed the spot? Or during the presidency of Theodore Roosevelt? The bones of *Mastodon americanus* and of the gigantic Archidiskodon elephant are obviously old. But a few human bones which have been recovered unfortunately do not prove that their original owner was on a mastodon hunt. In fact these human bones have been estimated to be about three centuries old. Purely geological evidence (as distinct from paleontological evidence) suggests that the tar pits formed not earlier than 100,000 and not later than 30,000 years ago. Late to very late Pleistocene, in short, and post-Pleistocene.

The camels recovered from the pits are in fine condition. Two of them stand mounted in the Los Angeles County Museum, 7 feet tall measured to the highest point of the back which is located somewhat behind the shoulders. Their name is *Camelops hesternus,* the syllable *ops* in the first part of the name meaning "looking like" (Greek), and Latin *hesternus,* meaning "of yesterday." As specimens they are beautiful. It would be so nice if we knew when they perished in the tar.

The dating of just these skeletons of *Camelops* is made a virtual impossibility because of other finds made elsewhere afterward. At Fillmore, Utah, a skull of *Camelops* has been found with dried flesh still sticking to it. In such a case it is hard to believe in an age of much more than a thousand years. And in the central San Joaquin Valley, near Tranquillity, Fresno County, California, definite evidence was discovered in 1939 that the Indians at one time did hunt *Camelops*.[5] The place, about 30 miles west of the foothills of the Sierra Nevada, is a typical campsite, to which the hunters brought the carcasses of their prey. Broken tools are there (stone and bone tools), traces of old campfires, animal bones, blackened and broken. Many of the bones are of animals still living in

---

[5] *Science,* no. 2519, April 9, 1943.

the San Joaquin Válley. But there are also bones of bison, probably the kind which still exists but which has never been seen by white men in that valley. There are bones of the extinct Pleistocene horse of the Pacific states. And bones of *Camelops*.

How long ago? We don't know yet.

But by the time the tar pits were formed, the llamalike forms of the camel were already firmly established in South America. They were discovered when Pizarro conquered Peru, and first mentioned by his secretary Francisco de Xerez. "Six leagues from Caxamalca," he wrote, "Indian shepherds lived near a lake in the woods with sheep of different kinds: small ones like ours and others, large enough to be utilized for carrying burdens." Obviously llamas and alpacas—it was probably the long fur of the latter which made Xerez think they were sheep.

Francisco de Xerez wrote in 1534. Only seven years later another Spanish soldier-historian, Pedro de Cieza de León, produced a few pages on the South American cameloids in his *Crónica del Perú,* which show that the animals have not changed since then. The llamas, he wrote, resemble both sheep and camels; they have the size of a donkey, are tame, and carry loads. The guanaco roams around in the open in large herds and is so fast that a dog can hardly catch it. The vicuñas are smaller and even faster, their wool is better than that of the best breed of sheep. Then there is another one which is tame and is called a "paco" (alpaca), smaller than the llamas and with very long wool. "Without the aid of all these sheep it would be impossible to transport merchandise."

For a long time it was taken for granted that the domesticated alpaca had been derived from the wild vicuña, while the domesticated llama had been bred from the guanaco. It seemed a reasonable view, because vicuña and alpaca are both small forms, while guanaco and llama are both large, comparatively speaking. But the ones who ought to know best, the South American zoologists, always tended to the belief that both domesticated versions have been bred from the guanaco and that the little vicuña has never been tamed, except, maybe, for a few individuals in isolated cases. During the last few decades this point of view has been more or less generally accepted.

At present the little vicuña—it stands only $2\frac{1}{2}$ feet high at the shoulders—is very decidedly an animal of the mountains and the elevated plains. Its range extends from the southernmost tip of Ecuador southward in the high Cordillera through western Peru and western Bolivia into northwestern Argentina. The southern end of its range is marked approximately by Mount Aconcagua. Although much hunted for its fine fleece, the vicuña manages to hold its own.

Llama

The larger guanaco—about 4 feet tall at the shoulders—is essentially an animal of the mountains too, but not so exclusively as is the vicuña. Its present-day natural range begins in southern Peru, in the region of Lake Titicaca, and extends southward, following the mountains, through Bolivia into Argentina and Chile. Following about the line of the Rio Negro, its range runs east to the Atlantic and includes the whole southern tip of South America, from Bahía Blanca down to Tierra del Fuego. The guanaco is therefore largely an Argentine animal, and its protection in Argentina is subject to much legal confusion. There are game laws which are meant to protect it. But Argentina is a federal republic and the game laws can be enforced only on federal territory. The states do not have to go along and usually don't, because to the sheep ranchers the guanaco is mainly an animal that takes up space where sheep could be put.

Still, there is no reason to worry. In 1948 official Argentine sources published estimates of the number of wild cameloids in their country. The figure for the vicuña read "over 10,000," and Argentine territory forms only a small section of the vicuña range. As for the guanaco, the Argentine government estimated that there were 400,000 of them on the plains of Patagonia alone.

The attempt to bring camels to America was not just the thought of one man, although the most important phase of that attempt, the phase which almost succeeded, can be pinned to the name of Jefferson Davis. There had been a few private actions earlier, the earliest in South America. Around the middle of the sixteenth century a Spaniard, one Juan de Reineza, decided that camels could carry heavier loads than those "sheep" of the natives. He brought camels to Peru. At some time or other they escaped and were occasionally seen until the end of that century. Apparently they just lived out their normal life span of about forty years. If Juan de Reineza had brought Bactrian camels to Patagonia instead of to Peru, the southern end of South America might look entirely different now.

The earliest importation to North America is dated 1701, when a slave trader landed some camels in Virginia, hardly the proper place for this animal. Moreover, in colonial times, with all the colonies strung out along the seashore, there was really no need for camels. That aspect changed slowly, later on, after the United States had become independent. Expansion meant transportation and communication. The territory of the United States began to include dry areas. It was in 1836 that one Major George H. Crosman, after having served in Florida, began to wonder whether the United States Army should not have a camel corps. He went to Washington, where all schemes, good or bad, land in the end, and talked about his idea. Official enthusiasm ran a little lower than low ebb, but in Washington Major Crosman met Major Henry C. Wayne, who thought the idea sound. But he apparently also thought that the time was not quite ripe, since his next move came a full twelve years later.

In 1848 Major Wayne approached the Senator from Mississippi, Jefferson Davis by name, and began to extol the usefulness, if not the virtues, of the camel. Jefferson Davis not only listened politely, he became enthusiastic himself and called everybody who could be expected to know anything about camels to his office. He read whatever he could find and was, in the end, firmly convinced that the time for acclimatization of the camel had come. Five years after Major Wayne had brought the idea to his attention, Jefferson Davis wrote a report to the President, dated December 1, 1853. And he now really had a large number of good arguments. Gold had been found in California, which was in the extreme west, and had attracted large numbers of men who had made their way to California with great hardship, crossing arid deserts, climbing through mountain passes, fighting Indians all the way. It was now up to the government to establish good communication with the west coast. There had to be roads. The roads had to be protected. The job involved very long distances. Much of the intervening country was dry. Later the railroad might tie the East and the West together. In the meantime the camel was the best bet. He urged congressional action and federal funds for the importation of camels: "For military purposes, for expresses, and for reconnaissance, it is believed, the dromedary would supply a want now seriously felt in our service; and for transportation with troops rapidly moving across the country, the camel, it is believed, would remove an obstacle which now serves greatly to diminish the value and efficiency of our troops on the western frontier."

It should be mentioned that Jefferson Davis wrote these lines, not as Senator from Mississippi, but as Secretary of War, a position to which he had been appointed in the meantime by President Pierce.

But Congress was not impressed. About the only result of the report, as far as the government was concerned, was to put the case for the camel on public record. A few people in New York listened, however. If camels really were so useful and if the Secretary of War was in favor of a camel corps, this might be a good business opportunity. They founded the "American Camel Company" which was to take care of the demand and especially of probable government contracts. It must have been a badly underfinanced company because it dissolved before it had even bought and imported a single camel.

Jefferson Davis did not give up. He used the opportunity of the annual report for the following year to go on record once more: "I again invite attention to the advantages to be anticipated from the use of camels and dromedaries for military and other purposes, and, for the reasons set forth in my last annual report, recommend that an appropriation be made to introduce a small number of the several varieties of this animal, to test their adaptation to our country.

Congress, as a whole, was still unimpressed. The Appropriations Committee did not think highly of camels, or did not think of camels at all. But suddenly Senator Shields of Illinois came up with an amendment, proposing the appropriation of $30,000 "to be expended under the direction of the War Department in the purchase and importation of camels and dromedaries to be employed for military purposes."

Meanwhile, Davis had found a fellow enthusiast, Edward Fitzgerald Beale, originally a lieutenant in the Navy, who had fought in the Mexican War, had explored Death Valley with Kit Carson, and had been appointed Superintendent of Indian Affairs in California and Nevada in 1852. Beale had conceived independently the idea of a camel corps and camel caravans in the Southwest; when he learned about Davis's enthusiasm, he went to Washington. At the time the legislation was passed, Beale happened to be vacationing in Chester, Pa. One may imagine that he would have liked to go on a camel-purchasing expedition himself, but he probably felt that he could not leave his post in the West for any extended length of time. He urged a relative, Lieutenant (later Admiral) David Dixon Porter, to apply for the command of the purchasing expedition. Porter was appointed, jointly with Major Henry C. Wayne who had approached Davis originally. The store ship *Supply* had been selected for the job and sailed for the Mediterranean in 1855. Lieutenant Porter commanded the ship; Major Wayne was entrusted with the purchasing.

They did not sail together, however. Major Wayne first went to London, for a special reason. He had read everything printed and available about camels, but he had yet to see one alive. He went to the London Zoological Garden to study them. From London he went to Paris and from Paris to Genoa. Porter meanwhile visited the then well-established herd of the Grand Dukes of Tuscany. In Italy the two joined forces and went to Tunis, where they bought their first camel in August 1855. A few days later the Bey of Tunis presented them with two more.

The expedition then sailed for Malta, Smyrna, Salonica, and Constantinople, eagerly collecting, if not camels, at least camel lore, in every port. In December they arrived in Alexandria, Egypt, only to learn that a law had recently been made forbidding the export of camels.

The reasons for that law presumably did not apply to faraway America, since a special permit was obtained without trouble or delay and half a dozen camels were purchased. Other camels were waiting for them when they got back to Smyrna in January 1856. Loading the animals aboard was not easy, but it could be managed. Accommodating the prize purchase was somewhat more difficult; it was a 2000-pound beast, 10 feet long and 7 feet 5 inches in height. Lieutenant Porter finally cut a hole in the deck to make room for the hump. All in all, there were 33 camels aboard when they weighed anchor in the morning hours of February 15, 1856. Most of them were dromedaries. A few Arabs who knew how to take care of camels were taken along.

The voyage lasted three months, the *Supply* finally landing at Indianola, Texas, about 120 miles south of Galveston, on May 14, 1856. Most of the time there had been storms. The camels had spent weeks tied down in a kneeling position on deck, which strangely enough did not seem to harm them much. The Arabs had been seasick all the time; the crew had to care not only for the camels but also for their caretakers. Thirty-three camels had left Smyrna; thirty-four arrived in Indianola. One had died en route; two had been born.

Most of the Arabs deserted just as soon as they were convinced that they were on land again. Only two of them stayed on loyally and became well-known characters in the West later on. One of them, called "Greek George" (he had taken the name of George Allen when he became naturalized in 1866), lived well into the new century; he died in California on September 2, 1915. The other, Hadji Ali (called "Hi-Jolly"), died in Arizona in 1902, and his grave is marked with a quartzite monument erected by the State of Arizona.

After landing his first load of camels, Lieutenant Porter was ordered back to Smyrna at once for a second batch. He brought another forty-four to Indianola in February 1857. The first load had meanwhile made a leisurely if hot trip overland to San Antonio where they were put into a camp for recovery, rest, and training. The second load followed to the same camp in due course. By then the Army knew that the camels did well in Texas, thrived on native vegetation, and were not subject to unexpected diseases. But the main test was still ahead—to find out how they would do in the area for which they had been meant in the first place, the southwestern desert.

In the fall of 1857 the new Secretary of War, John B. Floyd, ordered the survey of a wagon road to California along the thirty-fifth parallel. Camels were to be used on that survey, in addition to horses and mules, and Lieutenant Beale was placed in command. Several young men, the sons of friends of Beale, joined in the expedition and one of them, May Humphreys Stacey, wrote a colorful and interesting "Journal" of the trip, which was first published in 1929.[6]

The expedition started from the camp near San Antonio, then commonly called Camp Verde, going first west, then north, and then west again until it reached the Rio Grande. Following the course of the river it reached El Paso. Then it turned straight north for Albuquerque. There, having now attained the thirty-fifth parallel, the real survey began. Beale's camelcade headed west, through the Zuñi village, to Navajo Springs, Arizona, then on to the Colorado River which was reached near the present Mojave City. The river was crossed and the survey continued until Fort Tejon, California, was reached. There everybody had a long rest.

Beale wrote a long and enthusiastic report. The camels had done very well, much better than horses and mules. Considering the fact that they are naturally adapted to land which horses and mules would naturally shun, this was only to be expected. Beale had expected it and Secretary of War Floyd apparently had caught some of Jefferson Davis's enthusiasm. He officially recommended the purchase of one thousand camels. But Congress took its time, presumably in anticipation of the trouble that was brewing at home and which erupted into open war soon afterward.

Because of that survey, the Civil War split the government camels into two groups. The majority were still at Camp Verde near San Antonio; the others were in California. The Camp Verde animals were

[6] *Uncle Sam's Camels,* edited by Lewis Burt Lesley (Cambridge: Harvard University Press, 1929). The book also contains a reprint of Edward F. Beale's report, originally published as Executive Document No. 124, 35th Congress, 1st Session, May 1858.

taken over by the Confederates and used mostly for carrying the mail between Camp Verde and San Antonio, a distance of about 60 miles. It happened quite often that an animal made a full round trip in one day. Every once in a while a few wandered off; Union soldiers caught some as far away as the Dakotas. But because of natural reproduction the total number did not drop as sharply as a simple adding up of escapes would indicate. In 1866, when the federal government was in control again, all the camels at Camp Verde were auctioned off, mostly to traveling circuses.

The camels in California, some of which had been taken to Los Angeles, were turned over to the quartermaster at Los Angeles and used for carrying freight between Los Angeles and San Pedro. But their drivers were inexperienced and had a tough time. Some camels escaped; others were sold to mine owners in Nevada. In Nevada there were already a number of other camels, two-humped Bactrians, which had been brought by the schooner *Caroline E. Foote* in 1860 from the Amur River in Manchuria and sold in San Francisco. Most of the camels carried salt to the mining camps of Austin and Virginia City; the salt was needed for the treatment of ores by the chlorination process. But the citizens and the legislature of Nevada did not take kindly to the camels. They stampeded horses and cattle and while their usefulness could hardly be questioned their nuisance value was also beyond doubt. The 1875 state legislature pondered the problem of the camels. It would have been awkward to legislate against camels generally. A compromise was reached by making it unlawful to let camels run at large or to use them on any public road or highway. That law remained on the books until 1899. In view of the fact that the camel is, after all, of American origin, to a naturalist that old state law sounds a bit like a "Natives Keep Out" sign.

Meanwhile the camels, law or no law, did run at large, in Nevada and even more so in Arizona. They were ownerless camels, camels which had escaped, camels which had been born in the Arizona desert. In 1877 two Frenchmen rounded up thirty such ownerless camels near Tucson, Arizona, took them to Virginia City, and sold them to the Comstock Mine, which employed them as carriers for wood and salt. Some of them escaped again and for a number of years there was a center

of wild camels along the Gila River. The engineers who laid out the line
of the Southern Pacific Railroad saw wild camels quite often; they were
the teamsters' pet hate.

During the early nineties the United States Boundary Commission
saw small groups of camels in many places along the Mexican border.
In 1894 a local character known as Uncle Dan Noonan captured a considerable number at Gila Bend and sold them to circuses at $25 a head.
The Indians had, quite naturally, become acquainted with the camel
too; they had seen them first when Beale made the survey. They hunted
them, trying to catch them alive since they knew that the white man
would pay them. If they could not catch them alive they killed them
and then ate them, a late repetition of the old day of *Camelops* hunting.
The camel considered to be the very last was buried in Indian stomachs
in 1899 near Yuma.

But after the appropriate obituaries had been written it turned out
not to have been the last. Reports about camels have been coming out
of Arizona almost ever since. A camel cow and calf were seen near a
water hole near Quitovaquita in 1901. Two camels were seen near Quartzite in 1909. A railroad surveying party was startled at the sudden appearance of camels, also in Arizona, in 1913.

This is the last well-authenticated report on the actual sighting of
camels in Arizona. But it is not the end of the story. An Arizona writer,
Sherman Baker, in an article on the camels of the West published in
1941,[7] stated that two old-time prospectors had told him they had seen
camel tracks along the Mexican border in Pima County, Arizona. Mr.
Baker ended his article with the words: "One cannot help wondering
whether it is not within the realm of possibility that a few roving camels
. . . are alive today in this arid and almost unknown part of the United
States."

It is certainly well within the realm of possibility that there are still
some feral camels in Arizona and possibly in adjacent parts of Mexico.
No one has reported any recently, but there would be little reason for
surprise if such a report were made.

---

[7] "The American Camelcade," *Frontiers*, Academy of Natural Sciences, Philadelphia,
Pa., June 1941.

14: Wanderers Across the Planet

ONE SUMMER evening in 1766—the year is important chiefly because it indicates that streets were illuminated by moonlight, if at all—Parisians received a considerable fright. "Something" was flying through their streets, to all appearances a flying lantern. How easily it might cause a conflagration! And what made it fly? Some stout-hearted men, possibly spurred by the hope or promise of reward, set out to capture the menace. This was not too difficult, because it turned out to be merely a large luminous beetle of a brightness beyond the experience of any ordinary Parisian. The savants of the Jardin des Plantes were not ordinary Parisians, of course. They knew that this beetle came from Cuba and that its native name was *cucujo*. It had probably arrived with a shipment of fine woods.

Something similar, if less spectacular, happened again in Paris about a century later in Les Halles, those big roofed-over market places which, for reasons I fail to understand, are shown to visitors with obvious pride as one of the sights of the city. Night watchmen told that in the evening, after both vendors and customers had gone home, a small dark ghost emerged from a hiding place, rushing around and making strange noises. After a few hours it disappeared again, without trace.

In about 1850 general skepticism had already advanced to the stage where anybody telling about a ghost underwent pointed questioning about the kind of wine he had imbibed for supper and especially about the quantity of it. *Naturellement,* the night watchman had had his wine with his *dîner,* but not more than usual, perhaps even less. But while he had been sober, *absolument sobre, Monsieur,* he had not been able to see well. It is, as everyone knows, dark at night. And the something was dark, too. Hence it was hard to see. But it was there.

It was. One morning it was caught: it was a kiwi, one of those strange flightless birds which occur naturally only in New Zealand.

Not only Paris was afflicted with strange visitors. Something peculiar literally cropped up about sixty years ago in the Saar Territory. Workers walking to their factories in the morning noticed, as soon as spring had sufficiently advanced, that plants grew in places where ores had been piled up outdoors during the previous year. That plants should grow there, now that the ore piles had gone, was in itself not strange. But as the year progressed these plants did not seem to stop growing; they went on, being taller than a man by summer, with large deeply indented leaves which nobody had ever seen before. The workers told their foreman, the foreman passed it on to the engineers, and the engineers, being puzzled themselves, reported to management. Management called in a botanist who needed slightly less than half a glance; the mysterious plants were *Rhizinus,* the castor-oil bean plant, which had come with ores from Spain.

In the Principality of Luxembourg an International Exposition was held in 1909, the place being a former drill ground. A professor of botany who had gone there for strictly nonscientific reasons suddenly found himself professionally interested and occupied. A plant he knew grew there. It looked at first glance somewhat like *Camomila officinalis,* the well-known medicinal camomile. But it was not a European plant at all; it was the flower *Matrisaria discoidea,* which had been discovered in California in 1814 and had traveled to Luxembourg in less than a century, nobody knows how.

Again a number of years later, in the fall of 1932, a Miss Kappus walked in the woods along the Rhine River in the German province of Baden. There were tall annuals growing near blackberry bushes and it suddenly occurred to Miss Kappus that she had never seen this rather conspicuous weed which grew as much as 6 feet tall and was covered with beautiful yellow flowers looking at first glance like small orchids. Ripe seed capsules which burst suddenly seemed to proclaim it to be one of the "touch-me-not" varieties. Having tried to establish its identity from books and failed, she finally mailed a description of the plant with some samples to a Professor Oltmanns who had written a book about the plants of the Black Forest region. Professor Oltmanns was not only able to supply the name, *Impatiens glanduligera;* he also knew some details about the plant. It was a native of India, growing normally in a hot and moist climate. But apparently it could do with less heat, provided that air and ground were moist enough. It had appeared in the vicinity of the city of Basel in Switzerland around 1910. During the following twenty years it must have spread downriver along the Rhine without being noticed. The only clue to its appearance in Europe was the fact that a Swiss Mission Society had its headquarters in Basel; beyond the logical suspicion that a missionary returning from India had been an unknowing carrier the mystery remained unsolved.

By the time the Indian flower showed up along the Rhine, botanists had developed a special term for such an occurrence. They spoke of *adventive flora;* zoologists adapted the term to their own field by speaking of *adventive fauna.* It was not only a necessary term but a nice one, suggesting "arrival" as well as "adventure" (the latter inadvertently), but unfortunately the experts were not in complete agreement on how it should be used. Some were rather generous, applying it to the case of the Parisian beetle from Cuba, and the "ghost" of the market halls, as well as to the Luxembourg drill-ground flowers from California and the Rhine forest immigrants from India. Some even went so far as to advocate its use for everything not strictly autochthonous, including conscious introductions like rye in American fields and ginkgos in American cities, potatoes and tomatoes in Europe, and rabbits in Australia.

That, of course, made no sense. Any large-scale migration of historic and prehistoric times had also resulted in the introduction of plants and animals to places where they had not existed before. If one wanted to consider such changes, the terms "adventive flora" and "adventive fauna" would have to be hinged to an arbitrary dateline like a legal document. And just what should be picked for a dateline? The birth of Christ? Or the death of Charlemagne? The First Crusade, the discovery of America, or the Declaration of Independence?

Logic demanded that the use of the term be restricted by the imposition of two conditions: one negative, one positive. The negative condition was that the plant or animal must not be a conscious introduction, that any human agency involved must have been so unknowingly. The positive condition was that the wanderer must have succeeded in establishing itself more or less permanently in the new habitat. Even with these limiting conditions the number of known cases of adventive life forms is enormous. And in addition to all these true cases you still get a very large number of cases which are intermediate. For want of an accepted term they might be called the "escapes."

A fine example of an "escape" is a plant closely related to the one from India which showed up on the banks of the Rhine. Its name is *Impatiens parviflora,* and it is now virtually a common weed in Austria, Bohemia, Germany, and parts of Switzerland. The original home is Nepal and the southern portion of Siberia. It was brought as a rare specimen to the Botanical Garden in Dresden. That was in 1837. In 1838 it was growing in the public park of the same city, in larger numbers than in the Botanical Garden. In 1842 the farmers in the vicinity of Dresden began to complain about it. In 1869 it could be found for a hundred miles around, following the valleys of the Elbe River and its tributaries. In 1873 it had reached Stuttgart in the west, and in 1881 Berlin in the north. When the plant was new, the director of the Dresden Botanical Garden sent seeds to his colleagues in Prague and in Geneva. By 1880 it had spread over most of Bohemia and was well established in Switzerland too.

What is still a fairly rare and hence noticeable exception in Europe has become almost the rule in the northeastern states on our side of the Atlantic Ocean. Human immigrants came and brought seeds for their flower gardens. And with the forget-me-not they brought shepherd's purse. Rich people imported roses for their gardens, and with the soil came earthworms which were not on the program but which were at least welcome. It is strange but true that most of the earthworms in the American Northeast are "adventive." The glaciers of the Ice Age pushed the native varieties of earthworms southward and although, when the glaciers vanished, they began to make their way back northward, they simply were not fast travelers. They had not quite made it to the New England area when European earthworms were introduced accidentally, and now the boundary between native and adventive earthworms is roughly the Mason-Dixon line. West of the New England area the distribution is not as clear cut. The praying mantis is also adventive; it too came with plants that were introduced for gardens. There are native praying mantises in America too, on the west coast. The ones you catch from Maine on southward along the shores of the Atlantic are the European version.

For reasons which don't need explaining the number of adventive forms is largest in New England, although the farmers don't know it; they are likely to consider any flower and any weed with which they became acquainted in childhood as "native."

Even people with a science background often fail to realize the extent of the change which has come about since colonial times. I do know of several scientists (not professional botanists, of course) who were struck speechless by two pages in Lewis Gannett's *Cream Hill* (1949) which I'm going to quote here because they contain such a fine list:

Drive along any New England road today, and note the "wild" flowers that give it character: most of them are immigrants from Europe, strangers who arrived and made themselves at home with the white man. We recognize the pale pink bouncing Bet and the abundant banks of tawny day lilies as "escapes" from vanished gardens—partly because they tend to linger in the neighborhood of betraying lilac bushes and apple trees. But even deep into the woods along the old cart roads, other plant immigrants have wandered.

The yellow rocket and wild mustard that gleam in May; most of the clovers—the red, the pink alsike, the yellow hop, and the tall sweet white and sweet yellow clover—are immigrants. So are the feathery white wild carrot ("Queen Anne's lace") and the familiar yellow wild parsnip, the daisies and the starry yarrow, the sky-blue chicory and the coarse blueweed that looks so lovely at a distance (I brought some of it into my garden once and had a time getting rid of it). So too are a golden army: the roadside buttercups, dandelions, butter-and-eggs, St.-John's-wort, the delicate celandine poppy, tansy, the velvety-leaved mulleins, and the great coarse elecampane that some call "wild sun flower."

Ezra [1] probably never saw a black-eyed Susan; it came from our own West, years later, with clover seed. Our common thistles are from Europe, even that which we miscall Canada thistle. So is teasel. The handsome orange hawkweed, often called "devil's paintbrush," and the brilliant spiked loosestrife that paints the marshes purple in August, both invaded this countryside within the memory of living man; the pestiferous shrubby cinquefoil (which

---

[1] This refers to the Reverend Ezra Stiles, Lewis Gannett's great-great-grandfather, and to the period of two hundred years ago.

our farmers call "hardhack," the name I give to steeplebush) is another European invader. Our "wild" roadsides are not native American at all.

Weeding in our gardens today, we are mostly rescuing European flowers and vegetables from European weeds. Not merely the useful timothy and redtop but the pernicious crab, quack, bent, foxtail, and wire grasses are importations; so is that pesky tiny daisy-like weed that my neighbors dub "German-weed" and the more poetic call "gallant soldiers." So are the wiry-rooted sheep sorrel and the tough-rooted big docks, including the clinging burdock, most of our stinging nettles, the woolly catnip and the smoother peppermint, the ugly common plaintain and the pretty little thyme-leaved speedwell that nestles in the lawn, shepherd's purse, purple self-heal and the creeping gill-over-the-ground, the nightshade that is not really so deadly as its name indicates and the little cheese mallow whose fruits the children munch, almost all the various pigweeds, both the common chickweed that blooms, in a year of thaws, during every month of the calendar, and the coarser mouse-ear chickweed.

I have only to add that the bees which are busily humming over and around these escapes and adventive varieties belong to the same category. The honeybee is not native to the Western Hemisphere but was introduced by English sailors in 1638 in the northeast. A second introduction took place in Florida in 1763 (and another six years later in Cuba) but by that time the descendants of the first hives had already spread like dandelions.

Just before the Second World War the Smithsonian Institution made a census of plants which had established a roothold in the Western Hemisphere since Columbus's first voyage. The list, compromising both conscious imports and adventive flora, consists of more than a thousand names and may have grown a little longer since. The Smithsonian scientists added to their list the sad comment that only about 10 per cent of these plants could be labeled "welcome."

In that respect Europe has been better off. The plants the Europeans got from America are virtually without exception on a high-priority welcome list. The four names at the top of the list are: potato, tomato, maize, and tobacco. If you know the food habits of Europeans of today you can't help wondering what they did eat in the north before they had the potato and how they got along in the countries bordering the Mediterranean before they had maize and tomatoes—and how anybody got along without tobacco.

In addition to the plants mentioned they could also have got the sweet potato, the pineapple, and the cocoa bean from the New World, except that the European climate will not allow the latter two to grow and European food tastes will not tolerate the first. Quite a number of American flowers found their way to Europe and some of them have meantime returned to our shores after considerable breeding on the other side. Needless to say, there were some escapes over there too. American goldenrod grows where nobody ever planted it and American asters are as much taken for granted as "natives" as European buttercups and daisies are in New England.

Europeans, in short, did not have many reasons for complaints about adventive plants from America—fortunately Sicilian and Greek fishermen who sit down on a cactus by mistake are not aware of the fact that it is adventive flora. There was only one case which proved annoying. It was a plant which in America is usually just called water weed. The variety in question was the one botanists know as *Helodea canadensis*. You can see it in almost any home aquarium, but the owner of that aquarium is likely to call it anacharis. In Europe it was called—expressively enough—water pest.

Helodea made its first European appearance in Ireland in 1836. Even in its native habitat the plant can and will choke a small pond or creek on occasion. In Europe it went wild. Irish lakes and slow-flowing rivers were filled up solid with it. Twenty years later the plant somehow crossed over to the European mainland. In 1859 it filled the lakes near Berlin. In 1860 it was found in Holland, in several tributaries of the Rhine, in the Elbe River near Leipzig; in 1869 it reached Stuttgart. In 1880 it fringed the waters of Lake Constance (or Bodensee), had invaded the Danube system, spread through Austria in the east and to Switzerland in the west. For hundreds of miles all ponds and small lakes were so crowded with the plant that in many cases it was almost impossible to use a rowboat on them. The same was true for small rivers. The river fishermen complained not only that they could not work on these waters, but that the fish had left for less congested areas. In 1885 the plant even impeded the movements of lake steamers in some places; in that year the harbor of Constance had to be cleared at great expense.

In Zürich the City Council deliberated on what measures should be taken to clear the large Zürich Lake. That some measures had to be taken did not need discussion. In the following year there was no need for any measures; the plant had disappeared. In 1888 it had almost disappeared everywhere! Of course one could find specimens without trying too hard. But the period of choking the rivers was over. In a few years the plant had become a normal and well-behaved water weed which did not do any harm.

Since then there have been sporadic outbreaks of mass growth again, but only in small, limited areas and only for a year or two at a time. As for the reason, one might say that the obvious reason is known but the reason for that reason is not. The obvious reason is that in Europe the water weed does not produce seeds. Like the much more respectable ginkgo, the water weed *Helodea* produces male flowers on one plant and female flowers on another. The uncounted billions of water weeds which ruined the lake and river fisheries and even interfered with lake traffic were all female plants. The incredible spread had been accomplished asexually, by way of continued growth of any portion of the plant that was torn off.

Even with the case of the water pest in mind, one can still say that adventive flora never progressed beyond the point of being annoying, for different reasons and to varying degrees. Adventive fauna, especially insect fauna, are a different story. Again and again whole branches of agriculture have been almost ruined by insect pests, as a rule adventive insect pests.

The tale about the endless battle between man and insects is, well, endless. Even when restricted to adventive forms it would still fill a book larger than this one. Only the highlights can be mentioned, which means, most of the time, the cases of maximum damage.

Probably the worst of all was caused by an insect not only small in size but of life habits which rendered it invisible most of the time. You know the so-called plant lice, which you can find especially on nasturtiums. Aphid is a more dignified term for the same thing. In addition to leaf aphids, which are the ones you usually see, there are also root aphids. It was a root aphid originally native to America which cost the French Republic the round sum of two billion dollars, gold.

The small insect was described for the first time in 1853 by the first man to hold the job (if not the official designation) of state entomologist. The state in question was New York and the man was Asa Fitch, M.D. The name chosen by Dr. Fitch was *Pemphigus vitifolii,* and according to all the rules of priority the insect should be known by that name. But it misbehaves even in that respect; it is known by the name given to it fifteen years later in France. And that was its fourth scientific name. In the meantime the German Professor Schimer had said that Fitch's classification had been wrong and the name should be *Dactylosphaera,* and a little later the Englishman Professor John Obadiah Westwood, thinking that it was a new variety, had called it *Peritymbia,* precisely ten years after Fitch had first named it. Westwood's mistake is understandable; the root aphid had been found in hothouses in England and had not been suspected of having come from America. Hence nobody had bothered to check American records.

In 1868 the insect appeared in the vineyards of France, at first in the area of Avignon. The vines began to fail inexplicably and the infestation, when discovered, may have been a few years old. The nature of the insect was determined by Professor Jules Emile Planchon (he always looked like a worried parson) who also believed he was confronted with a new variety and who coined the resounding name of *Phylloxera vastatrix.* It has been known as the "vine phylloxera" since that time and any attempt to stick to the rules and revive Dr. Fitch's name for it would have as much chance of success as a possible proposal (also according to the rules) to abolish the name of "America" and to substitute Leif Erikson's "Vinland."

The vine phylloxera spread at the rate of 12 to 15 miles per year, usually following the valleys of rivers in both directions. But it appeared at about the same time (1869) near Geneva in Switzerland, in the vicinity of Bonn, and at Klosterneuburg near Vienna. At the height of the catastrophe—no lesser word will serve—the vine phylloxera had destroyed 2,500,000 acres of vineyards. The French vineyards not only lost virtually their whole harvest, but also had to import grapes and even raisins to be able to fulfill their obligations for deliveries. By 1900, when the worst was over, the French government estimated the total damage as above 10 billion gold francs. Together with the lost war of 1870–1871 this was serious enough to strain the financial resources of France.

Since the insect had come from America, French science turned to America for help, knowing that the state entomologist of Missouri, Charles Valentine Riley, had made a special study of the vine phylloxera in its native habitat. In the course of these studies Riley had found a predatory mite feeding upon phylloxera and he suggested introducing this mite into France too, the first known case of attempted "biological control." Of greatest practical importance were Riley's observation that a number of American vines were rather resistant to the ravages of phylloxera and his suggestion of replanting the devastated vineyards with American vines.

This was what actually saved the situation, although a number of additional measures proved moderately successful. One was to grow the vines—those strains which could stand it—in almost pure sand. Another was to flood the vineyards once a year, drowning the root form of phylloxera. And still another one was to add poisonous substances to the soil.

During the same period that the vintners of Europe and especially of France fought a desperate battle with the American phylloxera, the foresters of America and especially of New England fought an equally desperate battle with the caterpillars of a European moth. Earlier in the nineteenth century, caterpillars by the trillion had devastated European forests, especially in East Prussia where they had appeared in such numbers that private owners of forests, in desperation, set the forests afire. This measure would have worked, except for the fact that these forests were neighbors of state-owned forests and the officials in charge of those did not have either the authority or the courage (or both) to do the same. And since the caterpillars had already attacked state property, without caring in the slightest about the legal difference, the situation got most thoroughly out of hand. Square miles of forest were denuded. As a countermeasure the bark (where the moths had laid their eggs) had been removed and burned in huge bonfires. In the following year the bare trunks of the trees were literally covered with eggs. Nothing speaks so clearly for their incredible numbers as the statement that the local population offered to collect moth eggs for a payment of four copper coins "per measure" of eggs.

The moth which caused that destruction was the type which Englishmen call the "black arches moth"; on the continent it is known as the "nun"; the scientific name is *Ocneria monacha*. It is a European species which then and also later suddenly increased enormously in numbers. The damage in America in the 1870s and later was not caused by that moth, but by a related species: the gypsy moth, originally called *Ocneria dispar,* a name which since then has been changed to *Porthetria dispar.*

While the vine phylloxera had been brought to Europe inadvertently (nobody is sure just how and when), the gypsy moth was brought to America for purposes of research. In fact it was imported with the best of intentions. At that time the French silk industries were suffering too, although not quite as badly as the vineyards. The silk "worms," which are actually the caterpillars of a moth, were dying of something called "pebrine disease." And while one group of scientists tried to find a way of fighting the disease, another group began looking around for types of silk moths which did not catch it in the first place. A French astronomer named Leopold Trouvelot, who worked at Harvard Observatory, was one of those who hoped to replace the original silk moth with a more resistant species. More specifically, he hoped to produce a silk-producing moth by the cross-breeding of some thread-spinning European moths. One of the subjects of his work was egg masses of the gypsy moth. It was known to be occasionally destructive to forests in Europe but to a far lesser extent than the black arches moth.

One day in 1869 the caterpillars escaped from Trouvelot's laboratory and settled on waste land near his house in Medford, Mass.

For subsequent developments I quote:

[Trouvelot] notified the scientific public, but nothing was seen of the gipsy moth which remained, however, gradually increasing, on this wasteland until 1889 when a tremendous plague of caterpillars almost overwhelmed the little town. The numbers were so enormous that the trees were completely stripped of their leaves, the crawling caterpillars covered the sidewalks, the trunks of the shade trees, the fences and the sides of the houses, entering the houses and getting into the food and into the beds. They were killed in countless numbers by the inhabitants, who swept them into piles, poured kerosene over them and set them on fire. Thousands upon thousands were crushed under the feet of pedestrians, and a pungent and filthy stench arose from their decaying bodies. The numbers were so great that in the still summer nights the sound of their feeding could plainly be heard, while the pattering of their excremental pellets on the ground sounded like rain. Valuable fruit and shade trees were killed in numbers by their work, and the value of real estate was very considerably reduced. So great was the nuisance that it was impossible, for example, to hang clothes upon the garden clothesline, as they would become covered with caterpillars and stained with their excrement. Persons walking along the streets would become covered with caterpillars spinning down from the trees. To read the testimony of the older inhabitants of the town, which was collected and published by a committee, reminds one vividly of one of the plagues of Egypt as described in the Bible.

During all this the Medford people had been under the impression that the insect which they were fighting in their gardens was a native species, and they knew it simply as "the caterpillar" or "the army worm"; but in June, 1889, when the plague was at its height, specimens were sent to the Agricultural Experiment Station at Amherst, and were identified by Mrs. C. H. Fernald as the famous gipsy moth of Europe.[2]

For the following ten years the State of Massachusetts made a regular annual appropriation for fighting the caterpillars and although by 1900 the total infested area had grown to about 400 square miles, the caterpillar fighters were well satisfied. In many places they had succeeded in exterminating the caterpillar and they could hope that their job would be finished in a few more years. In 1901 the appropriation suddenly stopped and nobody thought of asking the federal government to supply the money the state could not or would not furnish. During the following four years the gypsy moth extended its domain from 400 to 4000 square miles!

In 1905, after the moths had spread through several states, somebody drew the conclusion that this might, after all, be a matter worthy of the attention of the federal government. Since then sums of federal money have been spent every year for combating the gypsy moth, with the result that it has been confined to an area which might be described as "east of the Hudson valley." While it is probably too late to exterminate the moth completely, the case is no longer one of prime importance but has turned into a routine engagement in the routine insect war.

It is an interesting fact that the last third of the nineteenth century was the period of the big insect invasions. Prior to that time there had also been an intermittent war between man and insects, but the insects

[2] L. O. Howard, *A History of Applied Entomology* (Smithsonian Institution, 1930).

had usually been just one kind: namely, locusts. And there had never been much of a struggle—the locusts always won. By 1860 the picture began to change, in that man helped the insects to spread, chiefly by inventing the steamship. The steamship was fast enough so that insect stowaways did not die off en route. Nor did the plants which carried them. The invasion of the vine phylloxera in Europe, the invasion of the gypsy moth (and of the allied brown-tailed moth), of the cotton boll weevil, and of the so-called San José scale in the United States all occurred between 1860 and 1900.

The story of the San José scale is one of exceptional carelessness which fortunately did not end as badly as it might have. The insect, as was later established, came from China and was brought in with trees. It gained its first foothold in the Santa Clara Valley in California where it was found by Professor Comstock in the summer of 1880 and called *Aspidiotus perniciosus.* For quite some time it was restricted to California, the Rocky Mountains forming an effective natural barrier in the east. In 1893 it was suddenly reported from Virginia, Maryland, Florida, and places in between. As it turned out, two nursery firms in New Jersey had imported heavily infested stock from California and had sold it everywhere in the United States, without either knowing or caring that the plants were full of scale insects. The Department of Agriculture sent out a warning leaflet, and a copy of that leaflet made its way to Germany, resulting in an imperial decree forbidding the import of fruit or live plants from the United States into Germany. The decree, in turn, brought on a press campaign and that press campaign promptly caused other countries to look into the matter with the result that Austria-Hungary and Canada passed similar laws.

Actually this marked the beginning of the measures which had been needed to counteract the invention of the steamship. After the means of involuntary import came into existence, measures to prevent such imports had to be developed. There is now a long list of laws, both federal and state, which are designed to accomplish just that, and most of the time do.

As for the misnamed San José scale, it failed to become as destructive as had been feared at first. The fight against it is a steady one, and not inexpensive, but on the whole it can be won.

The case of the cotton boll weevil is somewhat different and the final outcome is such that in retrospect it has even been called "a blessing in a terrible disguise." The terrible weevil was discovered in 1843 by a Swedish entomologist who worked at home with specimens collected near Veracruz in Mexico. To the Swedish scientist—his name was C. H. Boheman—it was just a small beetle which he named *Anthonomous grandis*. Quite some time later, in 1871, a German entomologist, E. Suffrian, recorded that it could also be found in Cuba. Nine years later an English botanist, Dr. Edward Palmer, who traveled in North America, reported to the United States Department of Agriculture that this weevil had stopped cotton planting in a certain part of Mexico. By virtue of a kind of musical comedy situation, consisting of transfers and vacations, nobody in the Department knew anything about the small beetle of which Dr. Palmer had sent specimens. Nor had such a beetle ever been seen by a Washington beetle expert not connected with the government. Nor by Dr. George H. Horn of Philadelphia, who was considered the foremost beetle expert in the United States. The specimens had to be shipped to Paris to Monsieur A. Sallé for identification. I am happy to be able to report that Monsieur Sallé could tell the Department of Agriculture what beetle ruined the cotton fields south of the Rio Grande.

But that people with well-established and also well-deserved reputations failed to recognize the cotton boll weevil mainly proves how rare it was then. What was needed for identification was not merely a beetle specialist, but a beetle specialist who happened to have studied a particular family of beetles.

In 1880 the virtually unknown cotton boll weevil had just set out on its march of conquest. In October 1894 it was reported to Washington from Corpus Christi, Texas; the report said that "a peculiar weevil or bug" had destroyed a cotton crop. The Department of Agriculture was sufficiently alarmed to send an expert to Texas and Mexico, one C. H. Townsend. He traveled around in the infested area for some two months and returned with a report that painted the future of cotton in black on a dark background. Where the weevil had crossed the Rio Grande and found cotton fields—it did not always find them—the crops had dropped to 20 or even 10 per cent of their former average. But Townsend did have a good suggestion. If, he wrote, all cotton planting were abandoned permanently in a 50-mile wide belt around the infested area, the weevil could probably be stopped. During the following year the governor of Texas, having heard the experts, requested a law to that effect. But his state legislature did not pass it, thereby opening the way for the infestation of some 600,000 square miles of land in the so-called cotton belt. Moreover, the legislature passed a bill establishing a state entomologist of Texas, hinting strongly by that action that it did not wish the federal government to interfere in "local affairs."

The legislators who had so bravely upheld state's rights may have realized later on that there is no such thing as a local affair. In fact nobody said anything when the federal government took over again five years later. But it was then too late. In 1903 the weevil was in Louisiana, in 1907 in Mississippi. As things became progressively worse some collaboration developed. The State of Louisiana can be said to have grasped the seriousness of the situation. Delegations from the Carolinas and from Georgia went to Washington for advice. But the entomologists (both federal and state) did not find the going easy. Their instruction was rejected as "alarmist." The planters felt, and said in no uncertain terms, that the bookish fellows who had never planted cotton themselves couldn't tell them anything. After they had been ruined they were indignant—to use a mild term—when they were told that the cotton crop, once infested, could not be saved and that they should grow other crops.

This pattern repeated itself with deadly monotony all through the South, bringing poverty, migrations, suicides. But in spite of everything some cotton growers won out, since it proved possible to bring in an early crop ahead of the development cycle of the weevil. And the "blessing" of the final outcome is that the weevil forced a general improvement in agriculture.

And now we come to the "potato beetle."
One of the early "applied entomologists," Professor Thomas Say, who for a while taught at the University of Pennsylvania, described it first from specimens he had received from Texas. The name he gave was *Doryphora decemlineata,* the latter part of the name meaning "ten lines" and self-explanatory if you have seen the beetle. Later the name was

changed to *Leptinotarsa decemlineata*. Nobody thought of calling it
"potato beetle" in those days—Say died in 1834—and nobody thought
that it was even important. The beetle then lived quietly along the eastern
slopes of the Rocky Mountains, eating the leaves of a local weed, the
nightshade *Solanum rostratum*. Nor did that beetle make any attempt
known to man to enlarge its habitat.

The potato beetle did not come to man. Man came to the potato beetle.
As the United States spread westward the potato fields spread too. And
the potato, as you may remember from an earlier reference, is also a nightshade in the eyes of the botanist. The beetle agreed with the botanists.
And as the beetles went on and multiplied they found acres and acres of
tasty nightshade plants. In about 1860 the beetle reached Omaha, Nebraska. In 1865 it crossed the Mississippi and invaded Illinois. In 1870 it
was well known, in fact hard to overlook, in Ohio, Pennsylvania, New
York State, and Massachusetts. In 1871 it crossed Lake Erie, and also
reached the shore of the Atlantic Ocean.

Up to that point man had not contributed anything but the potato fields
themselves. A few years later man furnished transportation across the
Atlantic: in 1877 the potato beetle suddenly appeared in Germany. Distressed peasants brought specimens to the nearest offices of the Forestry
Service or to nearby universities. The beetle was recognized quickly and
somebody whose handbook listed Colorado as one of the places where it
had originally occurred provided the name "Colorado beetle," under
which it has been unpopular in Europe ever since. The men of science
and the officials of the Forestry Service were equally distressed, not to
say panicky. The story of what the vine phylloxera had done in France
was only too well known and while the gentlemen in question had not
cared too much about French economics they had felt strongly about the
scarcity of French wines. But this Colorado beetle was even worse. One
could do without French wines, if necessary. One could do without any
wine, if it could not be helped. But one could not do without potatoes.

Their warnings must have been potent and urgent. The government
took notice. On the one hand the Reichstag passed a law prohibiting the
import of potatoes and potato plants from America. (The French government followed suit half a year later, although not a single potato beetle
had then displayed its black stripes on French soil.) On the other hand

the army was mobilized. Several regiments of infantry and engineers spent months digging deep trenches around the potato fields of the danger area, by hand, of course, since tractors and bulldozers were still in the future. The fields were searched for beetles. Some were sprayed experimentally with various chemicals, an arsenic-copper compound proving effective. The fields that were too badly infested were mowed by hand, and the plants and beetles dumped into deep pits and soaked with crude oil.

During the following year the fields were left untilled except for a few rows of potato plants intended to attract any beetles of another generation that might have escaped. The plants were searched daily and when no potato beetle appeared in 1879 the battle was considered won.

In 1887 the beetles were back. It could not have been a case of quiet survival of a few individuals, because they infested a different section of the country. Another battle like the first was fought, again successfully. And another one in 1914. Both these invasions, while comparatively minor, are quite mystifying. The law prohibiting the import of American potatoes was not only on the books, it was strictly enforced. Although other European countries—except France—did not then have such laws and beetles might have conceivably been brought into Germany by import of originally American potatoes, the "Colorado beetle" failed to show up in any other country.

When it was found in Europe again it was in France, in the vicinity of Bordeaux, in 1922. It was then suspected of having arrived with American troop or supply transports during the First World War. While the place where the beetle appeared seems to favor this hypothesis, it is somewhat strange that it should have escaped detection for over four years. Potato beetles appear in mass formations, if at all. Because of that time lag, it seems more likely that the beetles traveled to Europe after the war, with well-meant relief shipments. When they were discovered, they had already infested an area of more than 100 square miles: all of the Département Gironde, and spilling over into the neighboring Départements Dordogne, Charente, and Charente-Maritime.

The methods which had been successful in Germany fifty years earlier were tried in a modernized form. The French army went to work with flame throwers and poison gas. Machinery which had been developed during the First World War to blow smoke screens across battlefields was used to disperse powdered poisonous chemicals. But what had worked in a much cruder fashion in Germany for an area of a square mile or two proved fruitless because 100 square miles were invaded. And with the aid of the prevailing winds, which blow in the general direction of Orléans, the beetles progressed some 20 miles per year toward the northeast in an ever-widening front.

By the end of 1930 the beetle could be found in eighteen of the eighty-three Départements of the French Republic. The French press reproached the French Ministry of Agriculture in most severe terms and with countless repetitions, but even if it had been possible to pin the whole blame on one individual or one office, that would not have changed the situation. Nor could anybody be held responsible for the fact that in 1931, just during the months of May and June, when the beetles are most in evidence above ground in their adult form, a number of severe storms came in from the Atlantic and extended the infested area by some 150 miles. By the end of 1931 the beetles infested thirty-two Départements.

In 1933 the French Ministry of Agriculture officially informed the corresponding Ministries of Belgium, Germany, and Switzerland that confinement of the beetle within the borders of France was considered impossible and that the infested area was 60 kilometers (about 38 miles) from the Swiss border, less than 40 kilometers from the Belgian border, and 250 kilometers (156 miles) from the German. Of course, trains, and especially freight trains, were carefully searched. But everybody concerned knew that the main vehicle of the beetle was the wind. The best that could be done was to distribute leaflets among the rural population, describing the beetles in detail and requesting immediate notification of the authorities. The authorities, on their part, got spraying equipment ready and began to amass stores of arsenate of lead, which had been found to be more effective than the arsenic-copper compounds first used. In 1933 and 1934 the three governments which had been notified were still waiting. Instead the beetles had "jumped" to England, where they were found in the fall of 1933 near Tilbury in the County of Essex.

By the end of 1935 almost all of France was infested (seventy-eight of the eighty-three Départements) and the beetles had established themselves in a few areas of Belgium. In 1936 they appeared in Holland, in

Switzerland, and in two places in West Germany, the Saar Territory and the District of Trier.

During the last ten years, as newspaper readers may remember, the blame for the prevailing winds from the west was laid squarely on the shoulders of the United States. When the potato beetle showed up in a few places inside Germany during the Second World War, the government of Hitler *et al.* blamed American bombardment squadrons for having dropped beetles along with high-explosive bombs and incendiaries. That claim was mostly for home consumption. But after the war it almost became an international issue. The East German Communists considered the cooperation of the beetle and the prevailing winds a part of the ever-useful Capitalist Conspiracy. Radio Moscow announced that a formal protest had been launched to the United States. But after this overture there was no performance. The accusations stopped . . . but the potato beetle probably marches on.

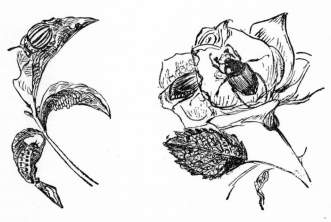

"Adventive insects": (left) potato beetle; (right) Japanese beetle

Let me write down a short list of plants, with the remark that in a case of a name like "apple" I mean the tree as well as the fruit. The list runs: grape, raspberry, apple, cherry, corn, soybean, rose, Virginia creeper, dahlia, hollyhock, zinnia, elm, horse chestnut, linden, poplar, willow, evening primrose, sassafras, wild grape. Those of my readers who live along the Atlantic seaboard north of the Carolinas will have guessed by now what pest I have in mind. The list just given is the list of "preferred feeding plants" of *Popillia japonica,* the Japanese beetle.

It was first discovered in the United States in 1916 near Riverton, New Jersey. The men who saw the beetles first probably thought them very pretty. Later this particular aspect of the visitors from the Far East came to be discounted.

It is now fairly certain that the beetle was introduced in its larval stage, probably with soil around the roots of plants. For several years it was, at most, a local nuisance in some places in New Jersey. It spread rather slowly and did not become numerous until about five years after its first discovery. Then we suddenly found that we had another pest to cope with.

As of 1940 the infestation was continuous in New Jersey, Maryland, and Delaware. Local colonies were found in all New England states, New York, Pennsylvania, Ohio, Indiana, Virginia, West Virginia, and North Carolina; and isolated spots of infestation in a few other states bordering those mentioned.

For a while one could hope that some of our native insect-eaters and some of those insects that are parasitic on other insects might curb the spread of the Japanese beetle. That hope did not materialize. Of course the insect-eating birds will snap up a Japanese beetle on occasion, but they don't seem to like them. Even the voracious fat toads are not too eager. I kept a few big specimens of *Bufo americanus,* the toad of the northeastern section, for a while. They lived up to their reputation for an appetite that never falters, except when it came to Japanese beetles. When hungry they would take one or two and then ignore the others.

Ducks do eat them. I have fed the beetles to a flock of ducks literally by the pailful and the ducks enjoyed the meal so much that they followed me around for days afterward. But that is not much help, since the majority of the beetles were out of reach for the ducks without my assistance. However, when the grubs of the Japanese beetle have killed a lawn and you pull the dead turf off, exposing the grubs, ducks and chickens get every last one of them. But that does not help the lawn any more.

The Department of Agriculture's entomologists realized early that they would have to introduce a beetle parasite from Japan. Five insects which are parasitic on the Japanese beetle were introduced in this country; unfortunately three of them failed to acclimatize. The two that did were a tiphiid wasp from Japan and one from Korea.

Anybody who has had his roses eaten up by Japanese beetles or his corn destroyed or even the foliage of his grapes skeletonized will enjoy the description of what *Tiphia popilliavora* ("the Popillia-eating Tiphia") does to a Japanese beetle grub. The slight little wasp will find the beetle grub—don't ask how, it does. The first thing that happens is that the wasp stings the grub so that it cannot wiggle. Then the wasp finds a crease between two segments of the grub, rakes it with her mouth parts until the skin is worn away, and places a single egg there. That egg will later hatch and devour the grub. But the adult wasp is hungry too, so she is likely to clip off the tip of one of the grub's legs and get a nourishing drink of blood.

Then the wasp leaves; she has many more eggs to deposit. If she gets thirsty between finding beetle grubs she'll drink nectar from flowers. That wasp from Korea and Japan has developed a preference for the nectar from American goldenrod. When all the eggs are cared for the wasp will die. In the following year there will be as many more wasps as there will be fewer Japanese beetles.

Just about the time when the Japanese beetle began to spread through the northeastern United States, another invasion from the Far East was going on in Europe. But this invader was not a beetle, not even an insect. It was a crab—*Eriocheir sinensis,* to give it its proper scientific name. The English name is "Chinese mitten crab," which refers to very typical and very conspicuous brownish muffs of long and silky hairs on the nippers of the crabs, especially of the males. The crabs live essentially in the China Sea, but near the shores and there near the mouths of rivers. They need brackish water to propagate but can live with ease in fresh water; in China mitten crabs have been found a thousand miles upstream in the Yang-tse-kiang.

It was barely put on record when the first Chinese mitten crab was caught in the Aller River, a tributary of the Weser River in northwestern Germany. The date was September 29, 1912. Two years later one was caught outside the mouth of the Elbe River and for the next ten years they were sporadically found in fishermen's nets off the German coast of the North Sea. By 1927 they were plentiful in the Elbe River. A year later a single specimen was caught in Prague in the Moldau River. Two years after that the Weser was heavily infested, and by 1935 the European range extended from Flanders to Finland. In that year the only British specimen so far was caught, near the Power Station of Chelsea.

While the vine phylloxera and the potato beetle had been mostly French problems, the mitten crab became mostly a German problem.

Chinese mitten crab

The crab did penetrate into the Baltic, but remained more or less a curiosity. The same can be said of the river systems west of the German border. But the German rivers which empty into the North Sea were literally crawling with them. From January to May 1935 not less than three and a half million specimens were caught in the Weser River near Bremen.

The crab also occurred in large numbers in the Elbe River but for unknown reasons it preferred not so much the classical "Eridanus" itself as one of its tributaries, the Havel River which at one point skirts the suburbs of Berlin. During 1935 the daily "yield" in the Havel was often 30,000 pounds of crabs in all stages of development. Although German newspapers and magazines were full of thunder against the "intruder," it actually did no harm. Its worst crime was to fill up the nets of river fishermen who hoped for fish and got inedible crabs instead. The mitten crab is said to be used for food in some sections of China. White men who had tried it once were always emphatic in asserting that they had tried it "once." The fishermen believed that the crabs ate their fish, but that was a mistake. The mitten crab cannot catch a live fish of any size, as was demonstrated in aquariums, and the investigation of the stomachs of thousands of mitten crabs revealed fish in them in just three cases, most likely fish that had been dead before the crabs began feeding upon them.

What the Germans actually got for their work was some 10 tons of fertilizer per day—of course a chemical plant will produce the same amount with much less work and much less expense.

How the crab got to the North Sea is a mystery. Best guess is that a freighter failed to get cargo in China and returned to Europe with ballast tanks filled with water from the China Sea.

Snails, the story book says, travel slowly.

That may be so when individual snails are under consideration. As a species, and especially as an adventive species, they do at least as well as beetles. As of 1950 there are about forty-five different varieties of adventive snails in America and strict watch is kept for one specific variety which has been repeatedly caught at attempts of unauthorized immigration and which, so far, has been kept out successfully.

One adventive snail whose case received considerable publicity in its time was a common European type known to experts as *Bulimus tentaculatus*. Nobody knows how and when it reached the Western Hemisphere; suspicion centers on the St. Lawrence River. In June 1879 an enthusiast named Beauchamp found a strange snail near Oswego, in New York State, which he thought was a new species. But it turned out to be a European variety.

Within 10 years it had mastered the barge canal from Albany to Buffalo. a distance of 300 miles. By 1888, nine years after its American landing, it had broken out into Lake Erie and established itself at Ashtabula, Ohio. From its lake beachhead it moved inland a year later to Sandusky, Ohio, and into the marshes of Toledo, Ohio, by 1911. About 1891, it had extended its range westward into Lake Michigan, striking Black Lake, Holland, Michigan, in 1891 where it was reported as "spreading rapidly." It had reached the Lake View waterworks at Chicago in full force by August 1898. In the meantime, consolidation was being accomplished in Erie, Pennsylvania, where older residents may still remember the episode of the "faucet snails." A pincer movement was initiated against New England in 1890 with the invasion of Burlington, Vermont. The snails were in the Thousand Islands by 1911, in Cornwall and Toronto, Ontario, in 1913 and in Washington, D.C., by 1927.[3]

While this fresh-water snail, which does not do any specific harm except occasionally by sheer volume of numbers, is an adventive type, a few others have to be classed as "escapes." The so-called "French edible snail" (*Helix aspersa*) was brought by French emigrants as an article of food, escaped, and can now be found in California and Oregon, near the mouth of the Mississippi and in a few widely separated spots on the Atlantic Coast. Similarly, the "Spanish edible snail" (*Otala lactea*) occurs mostly in Louisiana and Florida. The white garden snail (*Theba pisana*) which nobody wanted, not even in its original home in the Mediterranean countries of Europe, was first noticed in southern California in June 1914, and is still restricted to southern California where it does a great deal of damage. Several shelless European garden slugs must have become adventive in early times, because they can now be found almost anywhere in the United States, except in the Middle West and the extreme South.

The main danger of snail imports, especially from the Far East, is that some snails are carriers of diseases fatal to human beings, but so far we have had the good luck that those which have established a foothold in America did not happen to be disease carriers.

The specific variety on which an especial watch is being kept presents the problem, not of actual or potential carrying of a disease, but of plain voracity. The snail in question is second in size among the land snails in existence on our planet at this moment, a monster of the general appearance of smaller garden snails, but with a shell 5 inches long and a body length of 9 inches. Its scientific name is *Achatina fulica,* and as of

---

[3] R. Tucker Abbott (of the United States National Museum), *Natural History Magazine,* February 1950.

1950 it has succeeded in traveling more than halfway around the globe, partly with the aid of man, partly under its own power.

It is believed that this snail originally lived along the east coast of Africa, from the southern portion of Somaliland down to the latitude of Zanzibar. By the time naturalists began to take stock of the fauna of Africa it had already spread to Madagascar. The manner in which it did so is unknown but the trip was considerable, because Madagascar is separated from the African mainland by salty ocean water, some 200 miles at the very narrowest part. In 1803 a French naturalist recorded this snail from the Mascarene Islands, especially Mauritius, some 700 miles east of Madagascar. Apparently it was not too common, because the French governor of the island of Réunion imported the snail at that time from Madagascar, for a romantic reason. It seems that the governor's *maîtresse en titre* either suffered from tuberculosis or suspected herself of suffering from this disease, for which snail soup was thought to be an effective remedy. The governor obliged by importing snails of remarkable size.

A generation later a snail expert, W. H. Benson, saw the big snails on Mauritius, became interested, and took a number of specimens with him to Calcutta, India. That was in 1847. The snails escaped, reached Ceylon in 1900, and traveled, presumably unaided, all the way from Calcutta to Perak (Straits Settlements) where they arrived in 1927. One year later they destroyed thousands of young rubber plants in Malaya. In 1930 they ate up the gardens of Singapore. In 1931 they were in southern China; the East Indies were invaded in 1933, Java reached in 1935, and Sumatra in 1936.

Then came the war and the Japanese conceived the idea of using the big edible snails for provisioning their island garrisons. Let the snails eat the vegetation and the men eat the snails. The snails did not need encouragement; the men were ordered to catch snails to supplement their rations. They were also, one suspects, ordered to like the snails.

When the Americans took Saipan Island in the Marianas, the giant African snail was not merely well established, it had overrun the island. And then pandanus leaves were shipped from Saipan to Guam (in 1946) and the snails promptly appeared in the new habitat. And because they were not fought at once with any means possible, they overran the island

within one year. They did the same with other Pacific islands. The snail
is not only voracious, it is also prolific. About three hundred eggs are
laid at one sitting and this production seems to be repeated at intervals
of a few weeks all through the rainy season.

Two years after the Guam episode living Achatina snails were discovered in gardens in San Pedro, California. Since then they have been
found (and destroyed) on various vessels returning from Pacific islands.
Fortunately the climatic conditions in the United States are not ideal
for the invader; not even California is quite "tropical" enough. But
Hawaii is another story. So far, however, the owners of plantations and
the National Research Council have won.

And that is the story of the march of the Achatina snail so far.

I still have to tell you about what may be regarded as the climax of
the adventures of adventive fauna. You remember that it required considerable scientific effort to identify the *Impatiens* plant in the Rhine
forests, and that it took trans-Atlantic correspondence to establish the
identity of the cotton boll weevil. These stories might lead one to try
to imagine a case where an arrival cannot be identified at all; a case in
which there can be no doubt that we deal with adventive fauna but there
is no answer to the question: adventive from where?

You don't need to imagine such a case; there are several of them on
record.

In England they have a wormlike animal, one of the *Turbellariae*. Its
scientific name is significant: *Placocephalus kewensis*. The second part
of the name is taken from its geographical locality in England, the
Botanical Garden of Kew near London. Zoologists are sure that its
original home must be the tropics but the worms that live in the Botanical Garden of Kew are the only specimens known to science. Nobody
can tell when this worm arrived, how, or from where.

And in the Botanical Garden of Dahlem near Berlin there existed a
greenhouse called the Palmenhaus, of enormous size, accommodating
a small forest of tropical trees. It was kept at a constant, day-and-night,
year-round temperature of 76 degrees Fahrenheit with a relative humidity of 80 per cent, until it was accidentally hit by an air attack in 1944 and
partially destroyed. The Palmenhaus enjoyed a special fame, not only

as the largest of its kind but also because of all the things living in it which had never been knowingly imported. There were tropical ants and other insects, such as beetles; there were small spiders and on occasion a small centipede, all of which normally live in Madagascar, West Africa, Brazil, or Sumatra. Budding entomologists could do "field work" without needing more expensive transportation than the trolley car.

Among the unintentionally imported insects there was—the name is again the clue—*Phlugiola dahlemica,* thus named by Dr. Wolfdietrich

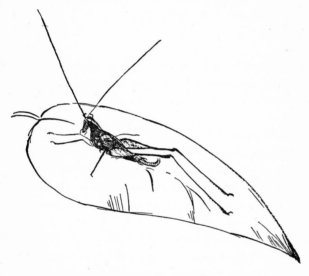

The Palmenhaus cricket

Eichler who produced the first scientific description and wrote several later papers about the insect. It was a pretty and most fragile-looking cricketlike creature, slightly more than ½-inch in length, with folded-under legs, but with antennae that grew to a length of 2 inches. The color was a uniform light green, the antennae and terminal sections of the legs black, the mandibles and the ovipositor brown, and the eyes a bright reddish gold. The wings were completely atrophied, and no male was ever found. The females produced fertile eggs in small numbers, but regularly. If *Phlugiola dahlemica* multiplied rapidly it would be a boon to any plantation; its food consists of aphids, scale insects, ants, and small insects generally.

German scientists watched *Phlugiola* for many years with the greatest of interest. They wrote a total of fourteen "Contributions" to the knowledge about it. Its biology and habits are exceptionally well known. But the date of its arrival is uncertain, and the original home is a mere guess. Once a related form was caught, but only a single specimen of that one, in tropical South America. The guess is, logically, that *Phlugiola* was a South American.

I have to write "was" because *Phlugiola* must have perished, along with nearly everything else in the Palmenhaus, when the north-European cold entered through the smashed frames. A number of the plants could be transferred to other buildings in time to save them. But *Phlugiola* was not found afterward. It is known to science only as a past case of adventive fauna.

15: The Islands
of Adventive Fauna

AS A DATE in a school history book, 1883 is probably absent. As far as I know, no war or revolution started in that year, no peace was concluded for lack of a war, no ruler abdicated. Naturally a few things had to happen even during a peaceful year. Richard Wagner died. So did the Russian novelist Turgenev, and Karl Marx. Mussolini was born. Still, the year doesn't get special notice or heavy type in a history book for any of those reasons.

But you are likely to find it in a natural history book. Because in 1883 the island of Krakatoa in the Strait of Sunda blew up, and a whole generation of naturalists grew up in the shadow of the volcanic cloud that had been thrown into the stratosphere. In many respects it was the most important, and certainly it was the most impressive, natural phenomenon of the whole century. Scientists watched the event and its aftermath with deep appreciation and if they had any complaint it was that the strait separating Sumatra and Java is so far away from the centers of civilization and research.

The pleasure of observing something entirely novel in scientific experience was also faintly marred by the fact that nobody had seen it coming. Prior to 1883 Krakatoa and its two neighbors, Lang Island and Verlaten Island, had been just like many thousands of other such small tropical islands which rose from the equatorial sea between Sumatra and New Guinea. Nobody had ever taken the trouble of exploring that small group. Nobody had a list of the plants which grew there naturally in, say, 1880. Nobody knew with certainty what animals had lived there. And when the scientists of the Royal Society in London compiled all available material for the magnificent *Report of the Krakatoa Committee* (published in 1888) they found to their dismay that there was not even a perfect map available. Of course the islands could be found on the British Admiralty Chart. But the Admiralty Chart did not agree with other maps, for example, those used by the Dutch in whose colonial empire the islands were situated. The channels around the islands had been carefully sounded; the islands themselves had been put down as they appeared from shipboard.

Geologists, from what they saw later, could reconstruct the past of the islands in general outline. Some time ago, say ten thousand years for the sake of naming a figure, a volcanic island must have formed in the center of the channel now called the Sunda Strait. It was just one large volcano which grew by means of steady slow eruptions until it acquired the typical shape of a large volcano, like Mount Etna on Sicily and Fuji-san in Japan. A number of centuries after the volcano was finished, a paroxysmal eruption blew the cone of the mountain away, leaving only what Charles Darwin called the "basal wreck," a broken ring of three islands. Subsequently smaller volcanic cones formed again, but the accumulation of volcanic material was not quite enough to fill in all the space separating the three islands and unify them again into one large island. The development of the new cones must have been completed by the time of Christ at the very latest, probably two or three thousand years earlier.

So much for the geological evidence, reliable in itself, but providing no definite dates.

The history of the islands, in terms of their relationship to human beings, is also quite fragmentary. Nobody "discovered" Krakatoa. The general area has been known since early historical times, to the Chinese as well as to peoples from the West, including Arabs. But apparently there was no reason for singling out Krakatoa; it was never mentioned specifically. The name itself is a native name, which the Dutch learned much later when they founded their colonies in the vicinity. After Krakatoa had become famous through committing suicide, a Dutchman, N. P. van den Berg, spent much time looking for early references. Probably the earliest one appeared in a book called *Ost-Indianische Reise-Beschreibung,* by a German traveler, J. W. Vogel, who passed the Krakatoa group in midsummer 1679 on his way to Batavia and saw it again in the early days of February 1681. He was astonished that the island of "Cracketow" which had been pleasantly green with trees, looked "burned and desolate, and in four places ejected large incandescent blocks." When Vogel asked the captain when the island had "burst," he was told that it had been in May 1680.[1]

But that cannot have been a serious eruption, for the very next witness, the Dutchman Wouter Schouten, asserted in October 1685 that "Cracatouw" and the other islands in the Sunda Strait are covered with tall trees and jungle.[2]

The next visitors were the homeward-bound crews of Captain James Cook's ships, which arrived in February 1780—Cook himself had been murdered a year earlier. The men probably landed in search of fresh water and did find a small brook. They also found a warm spring in which the few native inhabitants of the island used to bathe. The natives had cleared a few spots where they grew rice; otherwise the island was densely wooded. Near that brook a small settlement came into existence; in about 1810 ships called there for firewood, poultry, fresh water, and fresh fruit. Afterward criminals from Sumatra were banished to Krakatoa for a while. When that colony was disbanded, the islands were uninhabited. Only native fishermen occasionally stopped there for the night.

From those sketches of the islands which were drawn from shipboard, the last by R. D. M. Verbeek in 1880, we know that Krakatoa was roughly rectangular in shape, measuring about 5 miles from north to south and about 3 miles across at its widest part. It showed three volcanic cones, the tallest, Mount Rakata, 2620 feet high, being farthest south. The next cone, going north, was Mount Danan, 1500 feet high and located almost in the center of the island. Near the northern end was a still

---

[1] For those who know German and would like to thread their way through a quaint and old-fashioned example, I quote the two pertinent sentences: *"Dass die Insul Cracketow so bei meiner Hinreise gantz grün und lustig mit Bäumen sich präsentirte nunmehr als gantz verbrannt und wüst vor unseren Augen lag, und an vier Orthen grosse Feuerblöcke aus wurffe. Und als ich den Schiff-Capitain befragte, zur welcher Zeit ermeldete Insul gesprungen, so berichtete er mich, das solches in May des 1680 Jahres geschehen."*
[2] *"Dat Cracatouw en de andere eilanden, welke allen midden in Straat van Sunda leggen, voorsien syn met hoge bomen en wildernissen."*

smaller cone, Mount Perboewatan, only 400 feet high. Verlaten and
Lang Islands, portions of the old "basal wreck," did not rise much above
sea level. In addition there were a number of single volcanic rocks, the
two largest of them called White Rock and Polish Hat.

In about 1880 earthquakes began to be felt occasionally over much of
the area of the Dutch East Indies, but there was no definite volcanic activity. On the morning of Sunday, May 20, 1883, sounds like artillery fire
were heard in the towns of Batavia and Buitenzorg on Java and doors
and windows rattled for hours. A mail steamer which had passed
through the strait reported that the compass needles had been violently
agitated at that time. The next morning a light fall of volcanic ashes was
noticed at Buitenzorg, a hundred miles east of Krakatoa. Simultaneously
falls of ashes were reported from Teloekbetoeng, a harbor in Lampong
Bay at the south end of Sumatra. In the evening of the same day a column of steam was seen to rise from the island of Krakatoa, the first
indication of the origin of the volcanic phenomena which had made
everybody apprehensive.

A passing vessel reported that this column did not issue from the tall
peak of Mount Rakata but from the low parts of the island, probably
Mount Perboewatan. The volcanic activity was considerable: the officers
of the German corvette *Elisabeth* which happened to be in the vicinity
measured the height of the steam column and found it to be 7 miles.

During the next few days the activity lessened and a party of curious
people in Batavia decided to visit the scene. They chartered a small
steamer and arrived at Krakatoa in the morning hours of Sunday, May
27, just one week after the first explosions. They saw that it was actually
Mount Perboewatan which was erupting, with a steam column that
was now only about 2 miles high. Every five to ten minutes there was a
loud explosion which shot pumice into the air and uncovered lava in the
crater, because after each explosion the steam cloud lightened up and
glowed for a number of seconds. The general noise was loud enough so
that the discharge of a rifle among the spectators failed to attract much
attention.

The party saw that all the islands were covered with a fine white dust
looking like snow and that most of the trees on Krakatoa and on Verlaten Island had been stripped of their foliage and branches by falling

pumice. With more courage than good sense they landed on Krakatoa and waded through loose pumice to the top of Mount Perboewatan. They saw a crater about 3000 feet across from rim to rim, with sloping sides so that the crater floor had only about half that diameter. The floor was covered with a black crust, and in the center there was a hole about 150 feet in diameter from which the steam escaped with tremendous noise.

During the following week the intensity of the eruption lessened still more, but on June 19 it increased suddenly. One June 24 the steam column rising from Mount Perboewatan was joined by another one emanating from Mount Danan. This continued all through July 1883. On August 11 the chief of the topographical staff of the colonial government, Captain Ferzenaar, went to Krakatoa in a native boat. He sailed along the northeast side of the island and made sketches. The other side was inaccessible, because the wind came from the northeast, driving heavy masses of vapor, steam, and dust southwestward. Captain Ferzenaar felt certain that all vegetation on Krakatoa had been destroyed. Only dead tree trunks stuck out through the thick cover of pumice debris and dust. Near the shore the dust layer was 20 inches thick.

There were then three columns of steam, one from Mount Perboewatan which had been virtually worn away, one from the summit of Mount Danan, and a third somewhat to the north of the crater of Mount Danan, probably issuing from a fissure in the foot of the same volcano. But in addition to the three main columns, Captain Ferzenaar counted a total of eleven small new fissures ejecting pumice and steam. On the other side of island which could not be observed there may have been as many or more others.

The ships which passed through the strait during the following two weeks reported incessant activity and a heavy rain of pumice and dust; considerable falls of dust extended as far as Teloekbetoeng in the north, a distance of 50 miles. During the three days preceding Sunday, August 26, all the ships passing through the strait unanimously reported a marked if gradual increase in volcanic activity.

At 1 P.M. on that Sunday there were loud explosions, very clearly audible in hundred-mile distant Buitenzorg. At 2 P.M. Captain Thomson of the ship *Medea,* which at that time was 76 miles east-northeast of

Krakatoa, noticed an enormous black mass of clouds "rising like smoke." He estimated the height as well as he could—it must have been 17 miles. The detonations were then occurring at intervals of about ten minutes and had increased in loudness so that they could be heard at points 150 miles distant from the islands. A large number of Dutch officials and other Europeans, all with technical training of some sort, began to be attentive and took notes, which were later carefully collected by Verbeek.

At 5 P.M. the noise could be heard all over Java and for similar distances in all other directions. Just at that time a British ship, the *Charles Bal,* commanded by Captain Watson, was only 10 miles from Krakatoa. The islands were covered with a dense dark cloud, explosions occurred at intervals of seconds, and there was a crackling noise in the air. Captain Watson did not dare to go on and ordered sails shortened, which was done under a steady rain of dust. From 5 to 6 P.M. the ship was bombarded with pieces of pumice, rather large and quite warm to the touch. Captain W. T. Wooldridge of the ship *Sir Robert Sale* watched the eruption at the same time from a distance of about 40 miles. The sky, he reported later, had "a most terrible appearance, the dense mass of clouds being covered with a murky tinge, with fierce flashes of lightning." At 7 P.M. the whole strait was in intense darkness, illuminated only from time to time by discharges of atmospheric electricity.

During the night nobody could sleep, either in Batavia or in Buitenzorg or in Teloekbetoeng. But nobody reported any earthquakes; it was all noise and darkness. Captain Watson with the *Charles Bal* could not move and was "beating about" a dozen miles to the east of Krakatoa. He reported "hot and choking air, sulphurous, with a smell as of burning cinders." There was a steady rain of "cinders," as he called them. Trying to see whether he had enough water under his keel, he ordered a lead dropped in the intense darkness, sometimes relieved by lightning. The lead showed 30 fathoms of water but came up hot. Captain Watson also told that he saw "chains of fire" ascend from the island to the sky while on the south end of the island there was a "continuous roll of balls of white fire"—lava which slid or rolled down the sides of Mount Rakata.

The ship *Gouverneur-Generaal Loudon,* commanded by T. H. Lindeman, had reached Teloekbetoeng at about 7:30 P.M. with passengers, but finding it impossible to land, had anchored in the bay some distance from the piers which she had wanted to reach and at which the Dutch man-of-war *Berouw* was tied up. During the night a rain of mud covered the masts, rigging, and deck. It appeared to be phosphorescent and St. Elmo's fire appeared on masts and rigging, frightening the natives no end. "Lightning struck the mainmast-conductor five or six times."

At about the time Captain Watson ordered his crew to shorten sail, harbor officials in many places along the coasts of Java and Sumatra began to notice the arrival of small waves, only a few feet in height. They kept coming all through the night at irregular intervals, probably caused by steam explosions when sea water found access to hot lava.

Though nobody could sleep that night over an area 300 miles in diameter, all this was still only "preliminary stage." The first of the major explosions occurred on Monday morning at 5:30 A.M. local time. It was so incredibly loud that its sound penetrated the din of ceaseless explosions and steam ejections as if everything had been quiet. A similar explosion followed at 6:44. Then, at 10:02, there was another one, overshadowing everything that had gone before. And another very loud major explosion occurred at 10:52. These four explosions, and especially the third, marked the disappearance of the island of Krakatoa. More than two-thirds of its whole area was obliterated; Mount Perboewatan and Mount Danan disappeared completely; Mount Rakata burst in the center, leaving half of its former cone as a steep cliff.

An estimated 4½ cubic miles of lava and pumice were thrown into the air—and the only criticism that has ever been leveled against this estimate is that it is probably too low.

First the sound waves reached the nearby portions of Sumatra and Java. The sound beat upon Teloekbetoeng 25 minutes after it had been originated by the explosion of the island. It took 55 minutes to reach Batavia. Some 3 hours after the sound came darkness; the cloud had spread so that the inhabitants of Teloekbetoeng, of Batavia, and of Buitenzorg needed lamps to see. With the cloud came a rain of mud. The crews of the ships *Charles Bal* and *Sir Robert Sale* were kept busy shoveling the mud overboard as fast as it fell. On board the *Gouverneur-Generaal Loudon,* riding at anchor, they measured the rate of fall when it was at its densest. Six inches of mud accumulated on deck in 10 minutes. In addition to the mud the *Sir Robert Sale* was pelted by pumice, some of the pieces as large as pumpkins. On Java, falling blocks of pumice killed a number of natives.

Of course the cloud did not spread as fast as the sound. And the sea waves which followed were still slower. The main wave, estimated to have been 80 feet high near Krakatoa, raced across both Lang and Verlaten Islands, wiped out the small island of Polish Hat, and razed the island of Sebesi to the north. It hit the shores of the neighboring large islands in the later afternoon hours, being still over 50 feet high after 50 miles of travel. At Teloekbetoeng the *Loudon,* being anchored some distance off shore, rode out the wave, as did another smaller ship. But two schooners and the man-of-war *Berouw,* being at the piers, were lifted bodily and carried inland up the valley. The *Berouw* was later found 30 feet above sea level and almost 2 miles from the shoreline. A hill near the harbor provided an especially good measurement: it stands 78 feet above sea level and the water rose to within 6 feet of the summit.

The enormous wave, crashing against the shores of Java and Sumatra, carried native craft inland by the thousands. It swept away native villages and even more solid structures like two lighthouses. A census, completed months afterward, established that a total of 163 native villages had been razed and 36,380 people drowned.

Meanwhile the sound waves had raced on. All of Java, all of Sumatra, and all of Borneo heard the end of Krakatoa. Of course not everybody knew what it was. In Macassar (Celebes) they believed that the explosions were distress signals of a ship off shore. Two ships were sent out to find the distressed vessel. Naturally they returned without any result, since the source of the noise was 969 miles away. In Lucia Bay, Borneo, a number of natives, guilty of murder but not convicted, left their village and fled inland, believing that evil spirits were coming after them. They did not even know of the existence of the island of Krakatoa, 1116 miles from the scene of their crime.

Skipping from surface to lower stratosphere as massive sound waves do, the noise of the catastrophe fell on the island of Timor, 1351 miles from the erupted volcanoes. It descended on Victoria Plains in West Australia, where people wonderingly asked one another when troops had arrived in the neighborhood and why they were engaged in artillery practice. It roused the people of Daly Waters, Australia, from their sleep.

They thought that somebody was blasting rock—not in itself a wrong guess, except that the rock that had been blasted was 2023 miles from the aroused sleepers. In Diego Garcia, 2267 miles from the source, they believed in distress signals again. And the chief of police of the island of Rodriguez, James Wallis, made a notation about "distant roar of heavy guns, coming from the eastward." He learned much later that it had been Krakatoa, 2968 miles away on a great circle route and that the sounds he had heard had been traveling for four hours.

The sea wave, greatly attenuated, followed the sound wave days later. At Table Bay in South Africa, 5100 miles from Krakatoa, it still measured 18 inches. Farther away, instruments were needed to detect the wave; with these it was detected on the French coast and in California.

In Europe people knew that something had happened somewhere, long before the first considerably garbled reports had come in. Ten hours after the explosion the recording barographs of Russian, German, French, and British observatories traced sudden jumps on their smoked cylinders or rolls of paper. They traced them in the order mentioned; it was the pressure wave arriving via India and Asia. Meanwhile Washington had obtained a similar trace, from the pressure wave that had traveled across the Pacific Ocean and the North American continent. That wave continued on to Europe, arriving there 16 hours after the first. The two wave fronts must have met at Krakatoa's antipodal point, which is in Colombia; unfortunately there were no modern instruments near that point. In Europe there were again jump traces 34 and 36 hours after the first; the waves had circled the globe and were back. Slowly they grew weaker and gradually became unnoticeable; the last recording which one can be certain was caused by Krakatoa was obtained on September 4, 1883.

One of the most amazing aspects of the whole complex of events is how the people in the immediate vicinity of the catastrophe carried on. The island exploded with a noise that could be heard over four times the area of the United States, creating sea waves and pressure waves that could be detected all around the planet. But Captain Watson of the *Charles Bal,* having zigzagged all through the night only 12 miles or so from the center of the explosion, brought his ship through falling pumice and mud rain, through lightning and 80-foot waves, and then calmly proceeded into the Java Sea, without trying to make port as soon as he could. The two ships *Sir Robert Sale* and *Norham Castle,* which had been trying to enter the strait from the Java Sea, just kept on trying until it could be done. They fell in with each other and proceeded together, working their way through a sea carpeted with floating pumice which ground along the sides of the vessels. They passed within 10 miles of Krakatoa on Thursday, August 30. Both captains asserted that there was no volcanic activity on Krakatoa then. Neither of them noticed any major changes—a dust cloud was probably still hovering over the islands, and the captains indubitably had their hands full with other matters.

Meanwhile the *Gouverneur-Generaal Loudon* had made a preliminary survey. Her master, after the great waves had passed and the darkness caused by the volcanic cloud had become daylight again, decided that he should complete the run which had been interrupted, his destination having been a Javanese port. He forced his ship through the floating pumice out of the bay and sailed round the Krakatoa group in order to reach Java. He reported that most of Krakatoa had disappeared and that no steam or smoke rose from it anymore. But he reported a new reef between Krakatoa and Sebesi, a reef with several small craters emitting smoke.

The changes that had taken place in one night were not only of interest to scientists; they created an immediate practical problem. The Sunda Strait is the western exit from the Java Sea, and quite a number of vessels had to pass through it. The charts on board these vessels were now absolutely unreliable. That one still could sail through the strait had been demonstrated by the masters of the *Norham Castle* and the *Sir Robert Sale;* the problem was which route should be suggested to captains. A ship, the *Konigin Emma,* was stationed in the strait to warn approaching vessels. Soundings were made quickly. It was found that for 10 miles from the original center of the Krakatoa group, but only outside the old "basal wreck," the depth of the strait had been decreased by varying amounts, as much as 60 feet in some areas, as little as 10 feet elsewhere.

Both Lang and Verlaten Islands had been covered with dust, pumice, cinders, and lava to a depth varying between 60 and more than 100 feet. Lang Island had grown a little in the north because of this additional material; Verlaten Island was four times as large as it had been before.

In the old channel between the Krakatoa group and Sebesi accumulations of volcanic material reached the surface in various places. Two new islands, called Steers Island and Calmeyer Island, had formed. But they did not last long; being loose heaps of rather light material, they were washed away by the waves and their substance was distributed over the sea bottom. One could still sail through the strait by avoiding what had once been a channel between the Krakatoa group and Sebesi.

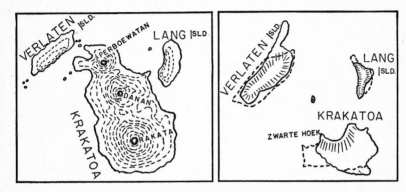

The Krakatoa group

(Left) Before the catastrophe. (Right) As it appears now; the tiny volcano in the center is Anak Krakatoa. Dotted lines show appearance immediately after the catastrophe.

One of the officers aboard the ship *Konigin Emma,* G. F. Tydeman, described how Krakatoa and Sebesi looked at that time: "No more trace of green, nothing but a reddish-gray layer of pumice and ash, in places many dozens of meters thick, still hot internally but already furrowed by rain; and along the edges full of ravines hollowed by the tidal waves and streaming rainwater, which still steamed from these furrows, as though the volcano were still active."

And a Dr. Vorderman who sailed through the strait about a week after the explosion reported that the vessel ground its way through floating pumice and that thousands of dead sea turtles drifted past the ship. Being an ornithologist in addition to his profession as a doctor, Dr. Vorderman watched especially for bird life. Except for terns and frigate birds there was none, but after a while four large hornbills appeared, flying south, apparently looking for food. One of them gradually sank lower and lower in flight and finally fell among the pumice in the sea, making fruitless attempts to rise again.

The pumice floated out into the Indian Ocean. Ship after ship encountered it. The entries made in their logs were later collected and incorporated into the Royal Society's Krakatoa Report. "Passed large quantities of pumice-stone"; ship *Invercauld,* Capt. Leslie, Dec. 15, 1883, at 7° 56′ S; 89° 32′ E (somewhat east and south of Ceylon). "Passed through a great quantity of pumice today"; schooner *Lord Tredegar,* Capt. Clarke, Jan. 5, 1884, at 14° 56′ S; 65° 18′ E (say halfway between the coast of Africa and Ceylon). *"Une infinité de débris volcaniques";* barque *May Queen,* Capt. Hugon, Jan. 12, 1884, at 11° 23′ S; 75° 46′ E (somewhat to the southeast of Diego Garcia island).

Some entries are especially interesting. Captain F. Gray of the *Parthenope* reported on March 10, 1884 from 5° 52′ S, 88° 16′ E (south of the Bay of Bengal): "Sea strewed with pumice stones covered with barnacles." As the time elapsed since the explosion was too short for a fresh growth of barnacles, this must have been material which, when still part of Krakatoa, was under water. That this conclusion is justified has been proved by other pieces, fished up by other vessels and saved. The barnacles were examined by experts and found to be species which occur on Krakatoa rock below the water line. Under March 11, the *Parthenope's* log has an entry reading: "Sea covered with lava and pumice 2 feet thick." On May 24, 1884, the barque *Iris,* also being near the equator south of the Bay of Bengal, still logged: "A great quantity of floating pumice." On May 31, the log of the barque *Louise Collet,* in the same area, said the same thing in French: *"On rencontre toujours des pierres-ponce."* On the same day another French log, that of the brig *Flora,* contributed an unexpected touch of humor: *"Le capitaine tombe à la mer en pêchant des pierres-ponce."*

Charts assembled from all these entries show that the pumice by December 1883 had floated to the longitude of Ceylon, staying generally a little south of the equator. By November 1884 it had passed Rodriguez, Mauritius, and Réunion and had drifted ashore on the east coast of Madagascar. All that time the world enjoyed spectacular sunsets such as had never been seen within the recent memory of man. During the first weeks after the explosion and near the Sunda Strait, the sun sometimes appeared green or blue. Later and elsewhere the sky was just unusually vivid, glowing for a long time after the sun had set. One special phenomenon was the so-called "noctilucent" night clouds which hung in the sky for decades and which were still illuminated by the sun when the ground below was in compelete darkness. Measurements indicated an altitude of about 50 miles for these clouds. That was then received with mild doubts, but since the clouds persisted for a long time it could be established as a fact.

As for the Krakatoa group itself, the most interesting thing was still to happen: the reconquest of the dead islands by life. Here was an area where everything had been killed off, scalded by steam, poisoned by sulphur-dioxide, mashed by falling stones, and torn apart by explosions, buried under yards and yards of glowing lava and hot ashes. If ever islands were dead, these were.[3]

Nobody doubted that the abundant life of the tropical zone would come back. The point was to watch life come back as adventive forms, to observe the sequence of their arrival and their means of transportation.

The first man to visit Krakatoa, eight weeks after the catastrophe, was the geologist R. D. M. Verbeek. He saw a picture of volcanic desolation. "The masses of pumice were still very hot, everywhere steam escaped from small crevices; the bare-footed natives tripped when coming near or on such a crevice." This was no longer volcanic activity, but the gradual process of cooling of the large masses of lava and pumice. About half a year after Verbeek came the French Bréon-Korthals Expedition, sent specifically to study the results of the eruption on the spot. The naturalist of that expedition was a Belgian, Professor Edouard Cotteau. Cotteau landed on May 24, 1884, on Krakatoa itself, after having seen Verlaten Island which, with its 100-foot cover of ashes, deeply furrowed by rain, reminded him of a glacier landscape.

---

[3] In 1929 the former government botanist for the island of Java, Dr. A. C. Backer, wrote *The Problem of Krakatoa as Seen by a Botanist,* a book devoted to the proposition that the plant life of the island of Krakatoa was *not* completely destroyed by the catastrophe, although that of Verlaten and Lang Islands was. The book is full of interesting information but as regards the main proposition it contains the most annoying variety of quibbling: There were areas on the slopes of the volcano only thinly covered by pumice; it has not been proved that roots burned there. Trees were mostly burned, but one man by making a test boring found unburned wood under six yards of lava. One botanist collected a plant but failed to note whether that plant was abundant; hence, according to Backer, the whole expedition was a failure. Needless to say, nobody took that book seriously.

Being a naturalist, Cotteau looked for life: "Notwithstanding all my searches, I was not able to observe any symptoms of animal life. I only discovered one microscopic spider;—only one: this strange pioneer of the renovation was busy spinning its web." The only way in which this tiny spider could have traveled to Krakatoa was through the air, as small spiders often do, hanging on to threads of their own making.

During the following years Melchior Treub, the director of *'s Lands Plantentuin* (Botanical Institute) at Buitenzorg, made it a habit to question ship's masters and sailors who had passed close to the islands about vegetation. The answers he got were generally unsatisfactory. Some asserted that everything was bare and dead; others claimed that they had seen plants either near the water line or on the slope of the southern half of Rakata which was still standing. Treub realized that the matter could be settled only by means of an expedition made especially for this purpose. He contacted Verbeek and late in June 1886 the steamer *Soerabaja* sailed for Krakatoa, with Verbeek, Treub, and eight other scientists aboard. One of the problems was where to land. Verbeek, who already had experience in landing on Krakatoa, suggested to skipper Mahne that he should approach the place called Zwarte Hoek. This is a peninsula extending some 2000 feet from the northwestern corner of the island's ruin. It was, as geologists and especially Verbeek already knew, not a result of the explosion of 1883 but much older, in all probability a part of the old "basal wreck." For several years loose ashes and lava had filled up the sea near Zwarte Hoek so that the water was quite shallow.

The party could see that Krakatoa had vegetation again before they actually landed. After landing, when they climbed the bare rock of Zwarte Hoek and looked around, they saw that the rock was not completely bare even where it looked to be at first glance. Everywhere on the lava there were little flat clumps, bluish-green in color, in all sizes from a small speck up to about the size of a silver dollar. The scientist knew what that was: colonies of "blue-greens," as botanists often call them. The full name is blue-green algae, or *Cyanophyceae*. They are the most primitive of chlorophyll-bearing plants. In addition to the green chlorophyll they also have a blue pigment, called phycocyanin, which often hides the chlorophyll's green. Some of these algae occur as single cells, often in absolutely incredible numbers which can discolor whole lakes.

Many of them, like *Chroöcoccus,* form colonies, and one very common form, *Nostoc,* produces gelatinous sheaths for its filaments, presumably to keep them from drying out. The name *Nostoc,* incidentally, is a made-up one, with no special meaning.

There could be no doubt as to how these "blue-greens" had made their way to Krakatoa. Their dry spores are carried everywhere by the wind and are undamaged by heat or cold or dryness. All they need to become active is a little moisture and a reasonable amount of warmth. Fossil blue-greens are the earliest known fossils of *any* kind of living thing. In the far distant past of our planet these algae may have been the first living things to go on land. They probably were the first to appear on Krakatoa and their presence heralded higher plants to come, because these primitive algae prepare the soil for other plants which have somewhat more exacting requirements.

To the Dutch scientists who knew German, the presence of nostoc must also have been mildly ironic, because in German folklore these very nostoc colonies have a special name, which may be translated as "shooting-star jelly." The peasant population, seeing them appear suddenly, apparently overnight, without any previous signs, took them to be the remains of shooting stars, believing that they had literally fallen from the sky. The lava ridges and pumice mounds of Krakatoa looked as if something would have to fall from the sky in order to get there. Or they would have, if nostoc and the other blue-greens had still been alone. But at the time of that visit there were already other plants which most certainly had not fallen from the stars.

In all there were six species of blue-greens. There were two species of tough grasses. There were two kinds of mosses. No lichens.

There were, growing at or near the beach, nine species of shrubs and trees, all of which are very common in the Dutch East Indies. There were also the seeds of six additional species which had not yet sprouted and some of which had drifted ashore in spots where they were not likely to sprout. Among them were the inevitable coconut and the seeds of the so-called screw pine (*Pandanus*), which has nothing to do with pines at all, but is a common tropical tree that looks rather like a heavy palm tree with palmettolike leaves and is equipped, typically for the genus, with numerous "prop roots."

There were, farther inland, eleven species of ferns. The most numerous of them was the kind which is named *Ceropteris calomelanos* and which is, ironically, not a native of that region at all but of American origin. It was introduced in the East Indies sometime during the eighteenth century and has been especially successful on Java.

And there were four flowers of the kind which botanists call *Compositae*. Daisies, sunflowers, and dandelions are examples of such flowers. Very often their seeds are equipped with small "parachutes"—think of dandelion seeds. The seeds of the four species on Krakatoa were so equipped.

Treub did not hesitate to assign air transport to all four *Compositae* with their winged seeds, to all eleven ferns with their tiny spores, and, of course, to the spores of the six blue-greens and the two mosses. The others had probably arrived via waves and currents in the strait. It is true that the seeds of some of them would be killed by salt water in time, but Krakatoa is close enough to other land that the seeds could be assumed to have withstood the sea for the comparatively short time required to reach there.

Treub returned in 1888 for a very short visit to the Zwarte Hoek area with C. Ph. Sluiter, who had been on Krakatoa before the eruption, in 1880, investigating several small coral reefs which had existed then. These reefs had all been destroyed by the explosion. But there was a new one, some 3 to 5 feet wide and about 6 inches thick, off Zwarte Hoek. Sluiter noted that the small reef had been built up mostly by the species *Madrepora nobilis* but that two other species of corals were in evidence too. Then he departed. He returned for another short visit, to verify his findings, during the year 1889.

During the latter year the island was also visited by another specialist, Strubell, who was looking for mollusks. It is of interest that he found only marine forms. The same year a German naturalist and anatomist, Selenka, also paid a brief curiosity visit. He was mostly interested in monkeys and apes, fossil monkeys and apes somewhat preferred. He related later that the island presented the "peaceful picture" of small tropical islands, but that it was not without movement because of the numerous beetles, bugs, butterflies, flies, and spiders. He also saw "gigantic lizards," meaning in all probability the large monitor *Varanus salvator* of southeastern Asia and the East Indies. The large monitor can swim well, as is known to every naturalist. Whether it swam the 30-odd miles from the nearest point of the Java coast or traveled part way by means of driftwood and then swam from island to island is not very important. The driftwood method has been assumed by many because it is thought that the monitor would not swim out to sea unless it could see its goal.

Some years later, in 1896, Lang Island was visited for a peculiar reason. The Topographical Survey needed a triangulation point in the middle of the strait, and the burst volcano of Rakata, being the highest point available, had been chosen. But when Dr. Boerlage, the head of the survey party, arrived on Krakatoa he found that the summit of Rakata was not accessible, at least not to his party. Attempts to climb the mountain were not only unsuccessful, they were even dangerous because of the loose lava and pumice. Finally Dr. Boerlage settled for Lang Island, where he found life most disagreeable. The average daytime temperature was around 94 degrees Fahrenheit, the nights dropped to a cool 88, and the temperature of the ground was 140. There was no water; a steamer had to come from Batavia every second week to bring some. The weather was also unsatisfactory for the work, so that the party had to stay for four and a half months. Doctor Boerlage reported that he had seen large monitors, a number of marine birds, and some insects.

In March 1897 followed what is sometimes called "Treub's Second Expedition," though actually he had been on Krakatoa in the meantime, and sometimes the "Penzig Expedition," because the German botanist Professor O. Penzig was a member of the party and published some of the results. Other members were Boerlage, the botanists Raciborski and Clautriau (the latter died soon after; Penzig used his notes and photographs), and, last but not least, a native named Pa Idan, whom even Dr. Backer admits to have been "a most excellent collector with phenomenal knowledge of the flora." The party again landed near Zwarte Hoek.

They found themselves greeted by pandanus and euphorbia, both characteristic of tropical islands. There were now more grasses. There grew the sweet-smelling but poisonous *Canavalia rosea,* which is both conspicuous and common and reproduces both by creeping stems and by seeds which float well. There was hibiscus (Indian mallow) with its velvety leaves and yellow flowers. And there was the strange and beautiful casuarina. The name is derived from the flightless large bird cassowary, because the branches of casuarina droop like the bird's large feathers. The cassowary tree is Australian but had spread through the East Indies. On its native continent it is most inelegantly called beefwood tree because of its red wood. At first glance a cassowary tree looks like a long-needled pine tree about to wilt; the long and soft "needles," however, are not leaves, but very numerous small and thin twigs which are green and do not bear any true leaves.[4]

The main difference, as compared to Treub's first visit, would not show clearly on a mere list of the plant species represented. It was the number of individuals. From Treub's description one gets the impression that on his first visit he found a number of plants growing on otherwise bare soil. Penzig stressed that the plants formed a dense vegetation. When the scientists broke through the coastal zone they found a grassy plain, with grass as tall as the visitors themselves. Morning glory and other vines grew among the grasses, matting them together so that it was almost impossible to penetrate. Still farther inland the mountain still proved unclimbable, because of either hard glassy lava or loose blocks which gave way when one tried to step on them. But it was obvious, from what the men could see, that the now luxuriant growth near the coastline had pushed the ferns inland and up the slopes. There they still dominated the picture, the one which had originally come from America holding its own very well. In and beyond the fern belt there were still colonies of blue-greens on the rocks.

On their way back to Batavia the party stopped briefly at Verlaten Island. There, too, it was impossible to penetrate far into the interior. Tropical rains had gouged deep ravines into the thick layers of ashes and pumice, but these ravines could not be climbed because they would not support the weight of a man. What struck the visitors most forcibly in the accessible area were whole copses of cassowary trees.

After they had returned they assembled the specimens they had taken. Professor Penzig carefully pointed out that the absence of a plant from the collection did not necessarily prove that it did not yet grow on Krakatoa. The difficulties of the terrain and the limited time could easily have

---

[4] Cassowary trees have been successfully introduced in California and especially in Florida. There are fine specimens at Indian River.

caused them to miss something. In addition to twenty-two different kinds of seeds and fruits not yet sprouted, which they did not count in their tabulation, they had twenty-two species of algae, mosses, and lower plants; twelve ferns; and fifty higher (flowering) plants. The corresponding figures of Treub's first visit had been eight, eleven, and fifteen.

As Treub had done earlier, Penzig assigned air transportation to all the lower plants and all the ferns. Of the fifty higher plants, thirty-two had in all probability arrived with the aid of the currents of the strait. For seventeen of them direct air transport was a probability. But for all those cases where one could harbor doubts there still was air transport of another sort—by birds. Seeds could have clung to the feet and feathers of birds. Or they could have been transported internally; most seeds are digestion-proof, provided that their skin has not been cracked.

While this fact is generally known, it was later proved specifically for one of the euphorbias growing on Krakatoa by Professor W. M. Docters van Leeuwen. He shot a bird on Krakatoa and in its intestines found seeds which he planted in the Botanical Garden at Buitenzorg. They grew up into euphorbias of a kind common on Java and already recorded from Krakatoa.

The next visitor to Krakatoa was a Russian scientist named Golenkin. He was not interested in the adventive flora of the island but in marine algae. But a Dutch botanist, one Dr. Th. Valeton who was the author of a very thorough work on the trees native to Java, went along. He said later that he went with Golenkin "merely as a tourist," but that did not prevent him from collecting a few specimens and taking notes. This particular trip is of special interest because, besides visiting the Zwarte Hoek area, they also landed on the east coast of the island. There, to his intense surprise, Dr. Valeton found a specimen of *Cycas rumphii,* a species often confused with the much better known *Cycas circinalis.* The tree was about 5 feet tall, which indicates high age for the slow-growing cycads. Its seed must have arrived very soon after the catastrophe to make a tree that size in 1905, when Valeton found it. He also found three species of wild fig trees. In all he reported twenty plants new to Krakatoa, which is a respectable number for a trip not planned as a collecting trip.

A more systematic collecting trip was made a year later by Dr. A. Ernst, accompanied by Doctors Pulle, Campbell, and Backer. Doctor Ernst's account of his impressions while his vessel approached the island was published by the Natural History Society of Zürich (Switzerland) in 1907. He wrote (in translation):

> With growing surprise we noticed, while approaching the east coast of Krakatoa, the astonishing progress made by the vegetation. Most of the southeastern portion, from the water line to the summit, is covered with verdure. On the southeast coast, where we intend to land first, a forest belt parallels the beach, even from the distance the many gray-green casuarinas are clearly discernible. Farther to the south there are slender leafy trees (*Terminalia*) and next to them the darker fronds of several coconut palms. On the plain which gradually slopes upward to the foot of the volcano we can make out single trees and shrubbery. In some ravines halfway up the mountain they unite again to form copses and some more isolated trees and shrubs can be seen even on the uppermost slopes and on the summit itself.

The total list of plants collected by Dr. Ernst comprises some 140 species. Twenty-three years after the explosion the reconquest of Krakatoa by plants adventive from Java and Sumatra (abetted by the fairly fast currents of the strait and the often violent winds) had reached a stage where only the eye of the expert could still notice differences. In fact, if the island had just been discovered and there had been no information about its previous history, a botanist might not even have been suspicious. Some forms which he might have expected because they can be found on similar islands in the same area might have been missing or surprisingly rare, but the distribution of plants is always subjected to some factors of chance.

A zoologist would have become suspicious very quickly.

The first zoological collecting trip to Krakatoa was made a quarter-century after the catastrophe, in 1908, by the Dutch zoologist Dr. Edward R. Jacobson. He reported a total of 202 species, of such a nature as to make it evident at once that something must have been radically wrong in the past history of the island. He did not find mammals of any kind; there were not even bats. He did not find any snakes or tortoises; the only two reptiles which he could put on record were the large monitors first mentioned by Selenka and the so-called house gecko (*Hemidactylus*). He was surprised by the large number of ants, which were a nuisance, and by the numerous centipedes, which were almost a danger. He did search very industriously and carefully for something that is never missing: earthworms. But he did not find any. There were only two species of land snails. But there were large numbers of winged insects.

The reason why the adventive fauna lagged so far behind the adventive flora is not difficult to understand. Plants, as individuals, are immobile. They travel in the seed stage. And the mechanisms which have evolved to distribute plant seeds functioned as usual over the 30 miles of sea water separating Krakatoa from Java and the 40-odd miles separating it from Sumatra. But animals are mobile and travel as individuals, usually when fully grown. To them the 30 miles of sea water were a barrier. This naturally does not apply to birds. Nor does it apply to winged insects, although the latter probably made the trip as passively as winged or tufted plant seeds. The ants most likely had arrived in the winged stage.

The centipedes and spiders probably traveled as eggs, attached to plant material which was transported by the currents of the strait. The snails must have made the trip in the same manner. It is a fortunate fact that somebody who was especially interested in land snails had visited Krakatoa in 1867. He described six species, but the two found by Jacobson in 1908 were not among these six. The monitors can swim; Jacobson actually saw one swimming around in the sea near Krakatoa. That does not mean that it arrived from one of the larger islands just at that time; more likely it had been disturbed by Jacobson and fled into the water. With regard to the house gecko, critics have pointed out that in these parts it is virtually impossible *not* to transport a gecko with luggage or equipment and that Jacobson probably brought it himself. Maybe. But twenty years later, in 1928, a tree trunk was found at Zwarte Hoek with a number of eggs of just this species of gecko under the bark. The eggs were hatched out to show that sea water had not injured them. It is well-known to zoologists that this lizard and a number of closely related species have a preference for depositing their eggs in the loose bark of dead trees at the seashore; often enough a high tide will pick up the trees again, eggs and all.

Subsequent full-scale investigations were carried out in 1919–20 and in 1933, the latter marking a half-century since the catastrophe. It took some six years after the second investigation to classify the material, and when the finished manuscript arrived in Holland the German invasion came too, so that the printing was delayed until 1948. Nothing demonstrates the increase in animal life as do the over-all figures for these years. Jacobson had reported a total of 202 species in 1908. Professor K. W. Dammerman identified 621 in 1921 and 1100 in 1933.

Between Jacobson's investigation and Dammerman's first one, there was an interesting interlude. In 1917 one Mr. Händl received permission to settle on Krakatoa because he wanted to "mine" pumice for conversion into termite-proof building materials. When he arrived there were no rats on the islands, but the common house rat of the area appeared soon afterward. It had probably been brought in with his equipment or with one of the food shipments which were brought over at regular intervals. The rats multiplied enormously. But a few years earlier, in about 1911, the giant python had arrived on Krakatoa. It was rare, presumably because there was not much food for it. When the rats became numerous, so did the pythons. The rats had all but disappeared in 1924 and there were many pythons on the island. But then their numbers diminished. By 1933 the rats were again numerous. We don't know what has happened since.

Mr. Händl abandoned the island in 1921. Professor Dammerman's party knew about his former presence, but "when we arrived in 1929 nothing remained of his house and grounds. So completely had it vanished that it was difficult to find the place where it had been amongst the luxuriant vegetation that had sprung up." It may be remarked that Mr. Händl also planted mangoes while he was there. They disappeared later, unable to hold their own without the aid of Man. One of the things which Mr. Händl had done was to dig a cistern for catching rain water. As long as it existed Kratakoa had insects which pass their larval stage in fresh water, like dragonflies. Later the cistern disappeared and the insects which require fresh water for breeding became rare.

Of course every chance visitor must not be expected to establish himself permanently. Doctor Jacobson had mentioned a few birds, well-known species otherwise, which were not seen again on Krakatoa; apparently they did not find the conditions they needed. And in 1924 a crocodile was seen by Dammerman and his party on Verlaten Island near the brackish lake which existed there. It was the kind common in the area, *Crocodilus porosus,* which not only grows to remarkable size but is also known to swim well and is often encountered far from shore. This particular specimen was 9 feet 3 inches long. "It was very lazy and apathetic and we could easily get hold of it by tying a noose around its snout, after which it was killed by a shot in the head. The stomach of this male specimen proved to be nearly empty, only some sand and pumice was found, no remains of food except a rather large number of nails, apparently those of *Varanus.*" (Dammerman.)

Since then no crocodiles have been encountered on the islands.

One extremely interesting episode of the reconquest of Krakatoa was recently related by Professor F. W. Wents.[5] All over the area of the Dutch Indies there occur so-called ant-plants. They are epiphytic, which means that they grow on the branches of trees, but just for lodging purposes, without being parasitic to the tree. The ant-plants form bulbous growths with numerous hollows and tunnels which are always inhabited by ants. The important point is that each ant-plant harbors a specific ant. One of the most common ant-plants of Java, for example, is the epiphytic fern *Polypodium sinuosum.* In its rhizome there are always nests of the ant *Iridomyrmex myrmecodiae,* never any other species. Whether this epiphytic fern and the ants which go with it grew on Krakatoa prior to 1883 is not known, but it very likely did. In any event, after the explosion the ant *Iridomyrmex* somehow got to Krakatoa. But its nesting plant was not there. The ants, it is reported, ran around nervously, helpless, looking for their customary nesting plant. Somehow they managed to survive and sometime prior to 1930 spores of the fern were finally blown across the strait by the wind. As soon as the fern had taken hold, the ants moved in, resuming the old association.

Professor Dammerman did not neglect the island of Sebesi. Situated only some 9 miles from Verlaten Island, Sebesi suffered from the explosion of Krakatoa almost as badly as did Verlaten Island. The great waves swept across it, drowning its 2000 inhabitants, sweeping all but very deep-rooted vegetation into the sea. After that it was covered by the mud rain. Cotteau reported a cover of dried mud about 20 feet thick. But Cotteau also reported that shoots of wild banana were breaking through the ash where it was thin enough and that coconuts from the

---

[5] "The Plants of Krakatoa," *Scientific American,* September 1949.

trees that had originally grown there germinated at the time of his visit. Sebesi had only been scraped clean mechanically; it had not been sterilized by heat like the islands of the Krakatoa group proper.

The differences in vegetation are quite noticeable to the expert. Professor W. M. Docters van Leeuwen stated in 1922 that the large forms of vegetation had a comparatively easy way of "returning" on Sebesi; they merely had to grow again from their roots. And the restoration of the other forms also proceeded faster, possibly because the island is closer to Sumatra. In addition to this, there have been artificial changes. Government officials informed Professor Dammerman that the island remained uninhabited until 1890 but that in that year one Hadji Djamaludin went to the island with a large number of coolies to clear the land. They planted numerous coconut palms, a number of other fruit trees, and laid out a number of rice fields. In addition to these cultivated plants, Hadji Djamaludin introduced domesticated animals, fifteen head of cattle, twenty goats, and five horses. A number of them escaped in 1910 and have run wild since then. They also have increased in numbers to an incredible extent. Only the horses seem to be rare. The goats are often seen but have never been counted because they stay high on the mountain of Sebesi. The cattle have increased to an estimated thousand head. At present, it may be added, nobody lives on Sebesi permanently. Natives live there for a few days at a time for legitimate purposes, like collecting coconuts, and for less legitimate purposes, like shooting cattle.

But while the vegetation on Sebesi is not completely adventive as is that of the Krakatoa group, the fauna obviously is. It is highly unlikely that any animal could stay on the island when the waves washed it clean. And interestingly enough, if you don't count those horses, goats, and cattle, the fauna of Sebesi is practically the same as that of Krakatoa. There are some very minute differences (for example, in beetle population) which can well be ascribed to accident of distribution. The table on p. 319, derived from Professor Dammerman's tabulations, shows not only how the fauna of Krakatoa grew, but also how it compares to that of Sebesi.

All in all, one may say that the flora of Krakatoa was about restored in the space of half a century. But its fauna is far from complete.

And now scientists are watching something new.

THE ADVENTIVE FAUNA
OF KRAKATOA AND NEIGHBORING ISLANDS

Condensed from *The Fauna of Krakatau, 1883–1933*, by K. W. Dammerman (*Verhandelingen der Koninklijke Nederlandsche Akademie van Wetenschappen, Afd. Natuurkunde*, Tweede Sectie, Deel XLIV), Amsterdam, 1948.

	KRAKATOA			VERLATEN ISLAND			SEBESI
	1908	1921	1933	1908	1921	1933	1920–22.
Mammals							
bats	0	2	3	0	1	2	2
others	0	1	1	0	0	0	2
Birds							
resident	13	27	30	1	25	29	31
migrants	1	6	8	0	5	12	7
Reptiles							
snakes	0	1	1	0	1	1	3
others	2	3	5	0	4	4	4
Amphibians	—	—	—	—	—	—	—
Fishes (fresh water)	—	—	—	—	—	—	—
Insects							
beetles	25	117	175	2	66	97	95
butterflies and moths	14	115	183	0	58	100	139
others	115	262	362	24	128	181	220
Spiders							
and related forms	36	131	?	0	68	?	113
Centipedes	6	7	7	0	1	2	9
Crustaceans							
terrestrial	3	4	4	0	3	4	4
fresh water	0	0	0	0	0	0	1
Mollusks							
terrestrial	2	5	9	0	4	5	13
fresh water	0	0	0	0	0	0	2
Oligochaeta	1	3	4	0	0	1	5

Late in 1927 there were submarine eruptions in about the center of the original island of Krakatoa, the one that existed before the later Krakatoa and Verlaten and Lang Islands were formed. In January 1928 a new volcano began to appear above the surface of the sea. It grew into an island not quite 600 feet long and 10 feet high. The natives quickly

named it Anak Krakatoa (Krakatoa's child) and the Dutch adopted the
name as the official designation. But a few months later the waves had
washed Anak Krakatoa away. By the end of January 1929 it appeared
again and rapidly increased in size. A month later a new sickle-shaped
island had formed, 900 feet long and 125 feet high. It was called Anak
Krakatoa II. It disappeared in July 1929. In June 1930 it came back—
Anak Krakatoa III—but destroyed itself almost immediately by a fairly
severe eruption which killed off some of the plant life on Lang and Verlaten Islands. On August 11, 1930, Anak Krakatoa IV arose, taking the
shape of a small atoll about two-thirds of a mile across, with a large crater
lake somewhat off center. It was then only 30 feet high but continued to
eject material in a nonviolent fashion so that by May 1933 it had attained
a maximum height of 320 feet.

Some insect life was collected from Anak Krakatoa IV immediately,
but all the early arrivals were charred to death by the heat of the island.
Scientists now hope that Anak Krakatoa will persist and that it will cool
and be conquered by life like the others. And they are ready for a very
close watch.

Krakatoa after the catastrophe
The large lizard on the drifting tree is *Varanus salvator.*

Index

(Figures in italics refer to illustrations)